COMMUNITY

Community

THE AWAKENING

Nicole Meredith

Golden Star Publishing

This book is a work of fiction. References to real people, events, establishments, organizations, or locales are intended only to provide a sense of authenticity and are used fictitiously. All other characters, and all incidents and dialogue, are drawn from the author's imagination and are not to be constructed as real.

COMMUNITY: THE AWAKENING
Copyright © 2023 by Nicole Meredith

All rights reserved. No part of this book may be reproduced in any manner whatsoever without written permission except in the case of brief quotations embodied in critical articles and reviews.

ISBN 979-8-9879767-1-5 (print)
ISBN 979-8-9879767-3-9 (ebook)

First Printing, 2023

1

SEREN

Every night, Seren Quinn dreamed of Earth, and every morning, she woke up with an ache in her chest, knowing she'd never get to see it. Still, she could feel its presence, the life pulsating just beyond the concrete walls of Community.

This idea of Earth—a place where life was an adventure and people were free to roam wherever they pleased—was utterly intoxicating. Out there, things had been different. But here in Community, every day was the same. At 7:00 a.m., the lights in Seren's room flickered on, fueled by power from a sun Seren would never see. A moment later, the Community anthem began, its catchy melodic tune surrounding her, reverberating off every surface. And then, at precisely 7:30 a.m., the Awakening began.

Nothing ever changed. Even the anthem was the same as it had been the day Seren was born sixteen years before. It remained the same trite melody on a loop, a microcosm of life in Community: cyclical and infinite. Every morning, Seren ate the same bland vitamin-fortified oats and drank the same mint tea. She and her parents made the same trifling small talk until she left to go to class—

with the same people she'd taken every class with since she was old enough to speak. And with each additional day, Seren came closer to the conclusion that this Earth she'd been told about—always in such contradictory ways—did not actually exist. Earth was about as concrete as the God people used to praise; she could believe in it as much as she wanted, but there would never be any proof that it was out there.

But despite the monotony, Seren remained optomistic. From the day she was old enough to understand, she had set her sights on a thing she could control: Trade Day. For most of her life, it had seemed so distant. Now that it was only a week away, she could scarcely contain her excitement – or her anxiety.

At breakfast, she was bouncing in her chair so hard that she rocked the table, splashing Pa's tea onto his uniform. He looked at her with narrowed but understanding eyes.

"Sorry," she mumbled, stilling her knee.

Ma passed Pa an old dish rag. "Big week," she said with a kind smile.

"Sure is," Pa agreed, blotting at the stain. "Are you nervous?"

As if the bouncing didn't give it away… Seren feared how her voice would sound if she tried to speak, so she merely shook her head.

"Really?" Pa looked at her with an expression tinged with disbelief. "I was nervous as all hell during my trade week! I didn't eat a thing. They had a Nutritionist force-feed me. Took a feeding tube, stuck it right up my—"

"Richard!" Ma scolded. Her face wrinkled like the skin of an overripe peach as her brows converted into a deep V. Seren made the same face whenever she was upset; in fact, she was probably making the same face right now. It was the only time she ever resembled her mother. While Ma had black curls and wide brown eyes, Seren's skin was pale, her eyes as blue as Earth's sky. She'd always wondered how Ma's genes had disappeared so completely in herself.

Ma hit Pa over the head with the towel in his lap. Pa laughed and pulled her in with it, planting a kiss on her cheek.

"We're going to embarrass her," Ma said, pulling away and taking the towel with her.

Involuntarily, Seren smiled. Yes, there had been a time when her parents' affection embarrassed her, but now she appreciated it. She was lucky to have parents who were truly in love. Love was all too rare in Community, where strict family trees were maintained and the pickings for life partners were slim.

Ma went back to stirring the oats, and Pa continued to work at the stain, shaking his uniform to dry it out. "You're braver than I am, chickpea," he said. "Always have been. I know you'll make the right choice."

This time, Seren didn't smile. She looked down at her hands, avoiding Pa's gaze. If she met his eyes, she knew he would see just how terrified she was.

Pa and Ma had their own ideas of what she should do for a career. Ma wanted Seren to be a nurse, while Pa tried to push infrastructure on her. Seren hated that idea. The thought of spending her days maintaining the bunker's structures was completely unappealing. She didn't want to keep Community's walls up; she wanted to tear them down.

"I might become Governor," Seren offered.

Pa laughed. "Not without the last name Warren, you won't."

"Watch yourself," Ma said, in a small voice. Her eyes darted up to the camera mounted in the corner of their kitchen. Pa's gaze followed, and his cheeks went gray. They looked at each other with an understanding nod, then swiftly changed the subject.

"Work has been interesting lately," Ma said, and she delved into a detailed description of her newest case in the healing center—

some odd disease that Eugenics should have long since eliminated. Seren had already heard it, and she decided she did not want or need to hear it again.

"I'm going for a run at the track with Lucas," she said, pushing away from the table.

"Hold on, you haven't even eaten yet!" Ma said.

A wave of nausea washed over Seren at the thought of eating the bland, chalky oats for yet another tasteless breakfast. Maybe she could dump them out again without Ma noticing.

Seren nodded. "I will. Later. I promised to meet him right after the Awakening." She paused. "He needs me today."

Ma's expression softened. "I know. Send Lucas our love, okay? And tell him that if he needs anything at all, we're here."

"I will."

Ma shook her wooden spoon at Seren. "And eat your breakfast when you get home. I don't want a Nutritionist coming by, asking why the trash monitors sensed an uneaten serving of oats again, understood?"

Seren blushed. *Busted.* "Understood," she said, giving Ma and Pa kisses on the cheek before bounding out into the poorly lit halls of Community.

A familiar antiseptic smell hit her as soon as she left their apartment. It lingered from the nightly custodial cleaning, an ever-present hazy chemical scent. No matter how long it had been since the last cleaning, the scent remained. As usual, the halls were crammed with morning commuters. Seren skirted the edge of the crowd, exchanging "Good morning" and "Happy Creation Day!" with her neighbors. She could feel a different energy pulsing through the air as everyone buzzed about the upcoming Trade Day. Like Seren and her classmates, they all had something to look for-ward to—a little excitement in their otherwise monotonous lives.

Trade Day meant new coworkers, new people to meet, new people to talk to—and to talk about. There was no shortage of gossip in Community; it was perhaps the only thing preventing them all from dying of boredom.

Then the Awakening's low-pitched tone rang through the halls, and all greetings ceased. The walls flanking Seren buzzed to life, the beige replaced by a blue projection. A brief moment of silence passed before Marcie McIntosh's image manifested on every wall, surrounding Seren like a fun house mirror. Today, Marcie wore a sheer lilac gown that fell over her shoulders, accentuating her sharp collarbone and dark, strong arms. Seren always envied the colors that Marcie and the other Tier Twos were permitted to wear. They added so much personality—personality that Seren could never achieve in her dull gray uniform. Marcie was at least as old as Ma, but she looked much younger, with not a visible wrinkle in sight. Seren had said as much to Lucas once, but he'd just frowned at her.

"She had surgery to look like that," he said.

Seren didn't understand. "You can't get surgery to have smooth skin."

"You can if you're a Tier Two."

Somehow, Lucas always seemed to know more about Community and the other Tiers than she did. It wasn't something they covered in school, but Lucas regularly revealed this kind of information as if it were general knowledge. If Seren hadn't found it so fascinating, she might have been annoyed.

"Good morning, all, and happy Creation Day!" Marcie said brightly, bringing Seren back to the present. "Today, we celebrate the two hundred and twentieth annual Creation Day, marking the day Community first came together."

Flashes of video images replaced Marcie in the projection: scientists injecting steroids into fruit in the labs of Tier Three; Tier Fives planting vegetation in the greenhouses below; an intense council meeting in Tier One, with Governor Warren standing in front, a serious expression on his face.

He looks handsome when he's angry, Seren thought, and a slight blush formed on her cheeks. Governor Warren was Pa's age, but like Marcie, he had aged more gracefully.

The videos disappeared, and Marcie's image returned. "And here to celebrate Creation Day with us this morning is your Governor, Pluto Warren."

Seren joined in her neighbors' applause as Governor Warren stepped into view. He smiled brightly at Marcie and then into the camera, giving a brief, modest wave. He looked regal in his well-fitted suit and blood-red tie. Whoever dressed him did it well. The black of his suit felt like a callout to the lower tiers. It seemed to say, *"I see you, and I appreciate you,"* while the red reminded them of his status.

Governor Warren took a seat beside Marcie and smiled directly into the camera, his confidence radiating through the screen. "Good morning, Marcie," he said, taking her hand in his. "It's great to see you."

Marcie blushed. "It is always a pleasure to see you, Governor Warren. And may I say, you look dashing, as always."

Governor Warren waved her off. "It's an honor to be back here with you on this momentous day."

"Momentous, indeed," Marcie said. "Governor, would you remind the great members of Community why we celebrate Creation Day?"

"Certainly, Marcie," he said.

Seren smiled. She knew that somewhere out there, Lucas was rolling his eyes, but she liked the campy banter between Governor Warren and Marcie. She *liked* the Awakening. Seren might not know much about the upper Tiers and their lifestyles, but she knew she enjoyed every minute of being privy to it. So, she was grateful that Lucas was not here to watch as she leaned in towards the screen, genuinely interested in Governor Warren's annual Creation Day speech.

"Creation Day is a day of remembrance for my great-great-grandfather, Jeffery Warren," he began. "He was an incredible mind and a generous spirit. He stepped up when no one else would. By creating Community, he allowed our ancestors to thrive during a time of terror and uncertainty, and he is the reason we are all alive today."

There was another round of applause, and though Governor Warren couldn't actually see or hear them, he smiled, paused, and waited for the applause to end.

Seren looked overhead to where the small camera flickered. *Maybe he could see them.*

"As you all know, our ancestors lived in a time of extraordinary change. They witnessed the great fall of Earth—a planet they'd grown to love dearly."

A video replaced Governor Warren's face. In it, children with big, swollen bellies, hollow faces, and brittle legs milled about listlessly. In the distance, a child, not more than two years old, lay crying in her mother's arms. A ripple of sadness stroked Seren's spine as the woman looked into the camera with her hand held out, begging for something to eat.

Governor Warren's voice continued over the video. "Our ancestors saw the irreversible destruction of Planet Earth. Forests were consumed by wildfires. Their land was destroyed by surges of hurricanes and tropical storms. They faced diseases, malnutrition, and so much worse."

Images of men, women, and children dying on homemade cots were projected on the walls, their skin clinging to their frail, emaciated bodies. One of her neighbors gasped, drawing her hand up to her chest.

The camera returned to Marcie and Governor Warren. Marcie was crying. "I've seen those images so many times, but they're still so painful," she said bravely through her sniffles. Governor Warren and Seren's neighbors nodded together, bobbleheads of agreement. The images *were* awful.

"It's hard to see," Governor Warren agreed. "But it's an important reminder of the mistakes our ancestors made, and the Earth we left behind." He motioned to a projected image behind him of the starving child in her mother's arms. "This is what Jeffery Warren battled. To prevent total extinction of mankind, he built this Community—the only one of its kind. He hired thousands of men and women—construction workers, farmers, plumbers—to build this magnificent two-hundred-acre, ten-floor bunker we call home."

An animation of Community's creation replaced the gruesome image behind him, showing Community being built from the ground up in ultra fast-forward, with little animated men and women working cranes, installing beams, and wielding hammers.

Governor Warren looked directly into the camera as he motioned once again to the wall behind him. "Those were *your* ancestors, and they proved there are no unsolvable problems if we face them courageously together."

The video ended, and Marcie applauded, her tears miraculously gone. "Incredible," she said.

"I couldn't agree more, Marcie," Governor Warren said. "This Community is resilient, and it will continue to be so. As we celebrate Creation Day, we must remember where we came from. We cannot return. We must continue to act as individuals in a quest for excellence. We must *continue our Community spirit.*" He paused and smiled through the applause. "Thank you, and bless you all."

The camera zoomed back in on Marcie. She dabbed her eyes with a lilac handkerchief that was the exact shade of her dress. "The story of our creation still touches my heart, even after all these years. Enjoy your Creation Day, and we'll see you all tonight!"

Then the outro music played, and the screens dutifully flickered off.

There was a brief round of applause before the traffic in the hallway returned to its regular pace. Seren fell back into step with the crowd. The images of the starving children played on a loop in her mind as she waited in a bottleneck that had formed between the residential hallways and Tier Four's wider commercial space. As it tapered off, Seren allowed herself to be swept back into the human current.

She was grateful for Community. Every Creation Day was a good reminder that, despite life's monotony, things could be a lot worse. She could be starving, or choking on poisoned air, or dead in a ditch... And they all had Governor Warren to thank.

Seren soon came upon the track, the only dedicated place for physical activity in Tier Four. Lucas was already in the corner, mid-stretch, his back to her. He had one arm bent above his head and was pulling at his elbow. Seren could make out the characteristic birthmark that covered his arm in round, dark blotches. *"Spots,"* she affectionately called them—like the spots on giraffes in Lucas's father's books.

"Hey, Lu!" she called, crossing the track towards him. An older gentleman nearly ran her over, cussing her out as she skipped past. "Sorry!"

Lucas turned. "You're intolerable," he said with a hint of a grin. "If you call me 'Lu' one more time, I'll tell your mother you've been skipping class."

Seren narrowed her eyes. "You *wouldn't*."

"Try me."

They faced off, eyes narrowed in an unspoken staring contest. There was silence. Then Lucas blew in her eyes, and Seren was the first to blink. "Cheater," she grumbled.

"There are no rules to staring contests," Lucas said. He appraised her. "Happy Creation Day, by the way." Behind him, the walls glowed with the message Happy Creation Day typed out in big, bold letters. Beside the phrase was a photo of a Governor Warren and his son, Zaiden Warren, both smiling their big, charming smiles. "As always, they're unassuming in their décor."

"If they didn't remind us every few seconds, we might forget to celebrate," Seren joked, then quickly clamped her lips shut. *Risky...* She and Lucas sometimes got too close to the line. They had to be more careful.

"How're you doing today?" she asked in an attempt to redirect the conversation.

"I'm great," Lucas said. "I saw you nearly get plowed down by an old guy. There's no better start to my day."

As if on cue, the aforementioned "old guy" lapped them with a huff—a gesture seemingly directed right at Seren.

"I'm serious," she said.

"So am I," Lucas replied. He bent down to tie his shoe, shifting his face away from hers in a purposeful way.

Seren looked down at him. Lucas was all too proficient in the art of using humor to push away his emotions. She didn't want to upset him, but it felt wrong to ignore the topic altogether.

"Ma and Pa send their love," she said.

His smile faltered as he stood. "Thank them for me, will you?"

"Thank them yourself. You haven't been around in a while. They miss you."

"I've been busy."

He hadn't been busy; he'd been avoiding, just like he always did. Seren wished Lucas felt comfortable enough in their friendship to talk to her, to *confide* in her, but he wasn't like that. He'd never been like that, even before his father died.

"When you're less busy, then," Seren said finally.

"Deal." Lucas's lips turned up into a mischievous smile, and he eyed the track. "What do you think? Should we start with a hundred laps?"

"Absolutely not," Seren said.

Lucas took this as a challenge, and he sprinted away in a burst of movement, leaving Seren no choice but to follow. She caught up only after he lapped her, and he slowed his pace to match hers. They fell into a synchronized rhythm, their feet pounding on the track in unison.

"I will do no more than thirty laps," Seren huffed through strained breaths. Each lap was a tenth of a mile, and three miles seemed more than reasonable.

"We'll see," Lucas said, a twinkle in his bright blue eyes.

Seren ran sideways, nearly knocking him off-balance. He caught himself just before he fell into the man running beside him—the old guy. The man looked at her and Lucas with immense hatred before running ahead of them. This time, Seren couldn't help but laugh.

"He's going to kill you," Lucas said.

Seren clutched her side as she laughed some more. They hit lap three.

"Have you considered your trade yet?" she asked through bated breath.

"It's hard," he said. "There are so many to choose from." Sarcasm laced his words.

"If it's that easy, then why haven't you chosen yet?"

He frowned in her direction. "You haven't, either."

Seren said nothing. Her chest heaved as she ran to maintain their pace. Dear Warren, no matter how many times she ran with Lucas, she still felt out of shape. Lucas wasn't out of breath at all.

"You're not still considering applying to be a Thinker, are you?"

Lucas' question surprised her. Seren hadn't thought he remembered their conversation about that; it was so long ago.

"No," she said quickly. It had been a mistake to mention it to him, even in passing.

"Good. Because no Tier Four—"

"Has been chosen for a higher position in over twenty years. I know, I know."

"Especially not a Tier Two position," Lucas said pointedly.

Seren ignored him. She wasn't interested in Lucas's cynicism. She had already turned in her application to become a Thinker in Tier Two, and she preferred to keep her dream alive—at least until she got her results. Becoming a Thinker wasn't *that* lofty of a goal. She was the best in her class, after all. Who better to take a role for the betterment of Community than her?

"So, what're you thinking, then?" Lucas asked.

Seren's heart pounded as she considered her answer. In the corner, a young child yanked on his mother's arm. Seren said the first thing that came to mind. "I've been considering becoming an Edu for Year Ones or Twos," she said.

Lucas turned and blinked at her. "You hate children."

The child let out a scream, and Seren cringed.

"'Hate' is a strong word," she said. "I just prefer not to be around them."

"Then why become an Edu?"

"Because I like to learn."

"Learning and teaching aren't the same thing."

"Aren't they?"

Lucas said nothing as they finished their sixth lap.

"I wish I'd been born a Tier Five," he said finally. "I wouldn't have to think about a trade. I could just be a farmer and get on with it."

"That isn't the only Tier Five job."

"No, but it's the only one that wouldn't make me miserable."

Seren glanced at him out of the corner of her eye. "You could become a Tier Five, if you wanted to."

And he *could* ... hypothetically. It wasn't against any Community rules to drop down a Tier voluntarily, but no one in their right mind would want to. There was no way Tier Fives had it better than they did.

For a painstaking moment, Lucas said nothing, and Seren wondered if she'd made a mistake in bringing up the topic at all. Today was the last day she should be pressing Lucas on his future. She'd been trying to distract him, but it seemed like she'd only made things worse.

Finally, Lucas shook his head. "I couldn't do that to my mother."

"Or to me."

"Or you." Lucas shoved Seren's shoulder playfully, and she grinned.

And just like that, they were back to normal, the remnants of the bizarre conversation stripped from her mind. They continued running for twenty more unbearable laps until Lucas declared that they'd finished.

"Thank Warren," Seren breathed, collapsing to the floor with an exasperated sigh. The coolness of the ground refreshed her, and she sprawled out in a star shape and waited for her heart rate to return to normal.

Lucas dropped down beside her and began doing push-ups.

"You're a machine," Seren breathed, her chest heaving. Lucas laughed and continued the push-ups: up, down, up, down... It was painful to watch. "I don't get why you always work so hard. You act like you're training for something."

Lucas did another push-up, and a small grunt escaped his lips. "Maybe I am."

Seren rolled over to watch as he continued.

"You could do a few push-ups too, you know," he said. "A stronger upper body wouldn't hurt."

"No, but the push-ups would."

Lucas pushed out a laugh as he went down. He finished his daily bout of torture with one last grunt and rolled onto his side to face Seren. Beads of sweat dripped from his hairline and down his sharp cheekbones.

Ignoring her protesting legs, Seren stood and stretched her arms above her head. Lucas didn't follow.

"I'm not ignoring my trade," he said finally, his eyebrows furrowed in deep thought. "I just think there are more important things to worry about than our placements."

Seren frowned at him. "What could be more important than the job we're going to be doing for the rest of our lives?"

"I don't know." Lucas looked like he wanted to say something else, but he just shrugged. "I should get going. My mom expects me to come home for breakfast."

Seren nodded and helped him up from the floor. She squeezed his hand before letting go. "Tell Jean I'm thinking about her and that I love her, okay?"

"Okay."

Seren felt an overwhelming desire to wrap her arms around him, the way she had eight years ago today when his father had passed. But Lucas didn't like her to talk about Henry's death, and she didn't want to push him. She also didn't want him to smell her right now.

"I'll see you later?" Lucas didn't meet her eyes.

"Yeah. I'll see you then."

They said goodbye before heading their separate ways, back through the drab halls of Community.

2

ZAIDEN

Zaiden Warren woke up feeling like shit. His entire body ached. The moonshine he'd knocked back the night before still lingered in his system, leaving him with a dry mouth and a pounding headache.

The Community anthem only served to make the pain worse. Its agitating melody brought to mind a knife on glass, providing an effectual punishment for the previous night's idiotic behavior.

Why the hell do I drink? Zaiden asked himself, as he did every morning after he overindulged. As usual, he was unable to provide a satisfactory answer.

At 7:30, Marcie's peppy "Goooood morning!" resounded through his apartment, and Zaiden buried his head in his pillow. Her sharp voice cut through with ease. He moaned and rolled over, tossing the comforter over his head for good measure. He'd nearly found sleep again when another familiar voice came over the speakers. Zaiden sat up so fast that dots spun in front of his eyes.

"Shit," he muttered. "Shit, shit, *shit!*"

There on his wall was the smiling projection of his father giving the annual Creation Day speech. Next to him was an empty space—where Zaiden should have been.

Zaiden swore again.

He was supposed to be sitting beside his father, smiling, dressed in the dapper suit that had been provided for him. Instead, he was still lying in bed, hungover as all hell, once again proving that he was nothing but an irresponsible disappointment.

Shit. He's going to kill me...

How had he slept through all the alarms he'd set? He'd set four of them. He was *prepared for this.* Zaiden lifted the clock from his bedside table and shook it. "Piece of crap!" he yelled, throwing it against the wall. It hit his father's image with a crack and broke into pieces, littering the floor with wires and bits of black plastic. He buried his head in his hand. "I'm a dead man."

If Zaiden had thought his father was mad when he'd come home drunk at 3:00 a.m. two weeks prior, imagine how angry he'd be now that Zaiden had missed the most important day of the year. *Why can't I do anything right?*

A knock sounded through the room. Zaiden lifted his throbbing head and cracked open an eye.

One of his maids, a Tier Five by birth, stood hovering in the doorway. She held a steaming hot coffee in one hand and a vitamin packet in the other.

"Come in," Zaiden said, trying to keep his voice steady. He attempted a smile, but it felt more like a grimace.

Unfazed, the maid stepped over the shattered alarm clock and set the coffee and vitamins down beside him. Zaiden eyed them wearily. He wasn't sure whether he could stomach either in his state. "Thanks," he said anyway.

She nodded and clasped her hands behind her back. "Governor Warren would like a word with you when he returns. In the sparring room."

Zaiden leaned his head against his headboard and sighed. He should have expected as much. "Very well," he said, and with a nod, he excused her.

The news, though unsurprising, sent a rush of anxious energy through him. Zaiden couldn't deal with his father's wrath this morning—not in his current state. Hell, he could hardly deal with it sober.

Pushing the anxiety aside, Zaiden stood, his body unusually stiff. He had a vague memory of taking a tumble down the stairs towards the end of the night. If memory served, he'd spilled his drink on the woman in front of him. At the time, he and his friends had found it hilarious, but now he felt a pang of regret.

Oh, well. There was nothing he could do about it now.

Zaiden sipped his coffee as he dressed, allowing the bitter warmth to wash over his taste buds. The caffeine resurrected him, and he finally felt well enough to turn on his bedroom lights without wincing. As the stark fluorescent light brightened his room, Zaiden caught a glimpse of himself in the mirror. He looked horrendous. Dark circles rested heavily under his eyes, and his hair stood up in every direction, like the top of a pineapple. Cringing, he turned his lights back off. He didn't want to deal with his own shameful reflection this morning. He pulled on a T-shirt and shorts and attempted to smooth out his hair before making his way through the penthouse he shared with his father.

Their penthouse was magnificent, especially by Community standards. It spanned four thousand square feet—nearly ten times the size of the living spaces that the lower Tiers shared. The walls were predominantly simulated windows, portraying an overview of a city from old Earth that Zaiden's father was obsessed with. Such "windows" were a rare luxury in Community, reserved only for those in Tier One. His father had the ability to change the images projected, but they'd been the same for as long as Zaiden could remember.

The penthouse's slick mahogany floors and white brick walls were another rarity in Community. Along with the golden chandeliers and twirling glass staircase, they were cleaned by maids daily and always seemed to sparkle in the simulated sunlight.

When Zaiden passed the kitchen, sweet wafts of raisin bread toast hit his nose. The usually pleasant smell made his stomach heave. He leaned against the wall and closed his eyes until the nausea subsided.

Did his father really expect him to spar in this condition?

I shouldn't have gotten so drunk, he thought bitterly. Maybe then he wouldn't have missed the most important day of the year.

Zaiden soon arrived at the sparring room. His father was already waiting in the center. He stood up straight. His eyes narrowed as Zaiden entered.

"Zaiden," he said, barely keeping the disgust from his voice.

"Father."

Governor Warren wore a suit that mirrored the one still lying across the chair in Zaiden's bedroom—the suit he should have been wearing this morning. Though Zaiden stood taller than his father, he still felt dwarfed by him, especially on days like today, when his expression was so condescending.

His father removed his suit jacket and placed it on a coatrack in the corner, taking great care to smooth out the creases before rolling up his shirt sleeves. He motioned for his son to meet him in the center of the room. Reluctantly, Zaiden did.

The sparring room was the plainest room in their penthouse, frequented only by Zaiden and his father. Apart from the large, heavy mat in the center, the room was empty, leaving nowhere to look but your opponent's eyes. Though it was the least impressive room, it was perhaps the place Zaiden had spent the most time growing up, except for his bedroom or the Simulator. His father had expressed to Zaiden since he was very young that every man should learn to fight. Zaiden didn't really understand why, but he never argued. Apart from fearing what would result from a debate, he didn't mind this use of his time; fighting was the only time he and his father spent together. When Zaiden was growing up, his father was aloof at best, but things had only gotten worse after Zaiden's mother passed. His father engulfed himself in his work, emerging from his study only to sleep. Zaiden was lucky if he saw him once a week, so he was grateful for any time they spent together, sparring or not.

"You look unwell," his father said, stretching his well-chiseled arms across his chest.

"I'm fine," Zaiden said. His reduced ability to fight today wouldn't change his father's view on whether they should. Admitting weakness was futile.

When Zaiden was young, the sparring was far from fair. His father was of superior size, speed, and experience. He used to take him down in a single swipe, knocking Zaiden's tiny legs out from under him. But things had changed as Zaiden grew. He began to match his father's height and strength, and the fights became more equal. Zaiden still rarely won, but now he could at least defend himself. He no longer walked away from the fights with the welts and bruises he'd endured as a child. Rather, he walked away stronger, faster, more resilient. Today would be no different, despite the pounding in his head telling him otherwise.

"Ready?"

"Ready." Zaiden got into position: feet spread slightly wider than his hips with equal weight distribution, fists up to protect his jaw. His father did the same.

"You disappointed me this morning," his father said without even meeting his glance. The words cut through Zaiden; his father's disapproval hurt every time. "The members of Community would have liked to see their future leader today."

He threw a punch, and Zaiden ducked, just missing the impact of his fist. They circled around each other, maintaining eye contact.

"I know. I'm sorry."

His father skimmed over the apology. "You are going to be inaugurated into the council in a week. You cannot continue gallivanting about. You're a man now, not some idiotic boy, no matter how hard you try to prove otherwise."

Zaiden flinched and advanced towards his father with more force. He kicked, and to his surprise, his foot made contact with his father's side. Governor Warren stumbled backwards, regaining his balance just in time.

"Sorry," Zaiden said automatically. The word tasted dishonest in his mouth.

His father took a step forward, his eyes darkening. "Do not say 'sorry.' Only weak people apologize. Are you weak?"

Zaiden recoiled. "No."

They continued to stalk around each other, maintaining a safe distance between them. Zaiden waited for an opportune moment to attack, but his father was quick. Pluto moved blindingly fast, and before Zaiden could register the movement, his father punched him hard in the jaw. The impact knocked Zaiden sideways, and he fell to the ground. Pain spread from his jaw to his eye as he looked up at his father in surprise. Pluto Warren was a man who fought hard and dirty; Zaiden knew this about him, but today's fight went beyond that. He was angry—more so than usual. Reluctantly, Zaiden got back to his feet and lifted his chin.

"Be better," his father growled. He kicked, striking his son in the side. Zaiden stumbled, his stomach heaving for a moment before he regained his footing and returned to an upright position. The alcohol shifted sickeningly in his stomach, threatening to come to the surface. He and his father stared at each other, neither blinking.

Zaiden's reflexes were weak, impaired by the hangover. He was in no position to be fighting; his father knew that. Zaiden suspected this early morning spar had been planned purposefully. His father was using it just as he had when Zaiden was young: as a way to punish his son. Zaiden had been just a kid when his father used to leave him crying on the sparring room floor.

He straightened up, a new resolve setting in. He would not allow his father to prey on him just because he was weak. He'd done that for too many years.

They circled each other, and Zaiden's breaths quickened. He ignored his pounding head and focused on his opponent's quick and meticulous movements. His father regarded Zaiden like an animal stalking its prey, ready to attack at any moment. Zaiden tried to predict his next move, watching for any twitch or flex in his muscles, but his father betrayed nothing. Governor Warren was too experienced.

Grunting, his father hooked a foot around Zaiden's legs and yanked him back, knocking him to the ground again. A moan escaped Zaiden's lips as pain shot through his body. He stayed on the floor; he didn't want to move. He didn't want to do anything. He closed his eyes and allowed himself to drift back in time, imagining lying in bed with his mother, reading a book over her shoulder. The memory momentarily comforted him. If Ivory were here, she wouldn't let this happen.

Then his father's voice cut through his reverie, jerking Zaiden back to the present. "Get up," he hissed. "Get up and fight."

Painfully, Zaiden hauled himself back into a fighting position. The memory of his mother and her voice steadied him as he planted his feet on the ground and lifted his fists. *"Come on, Zaiden,"* he imagined her saying. *"You can do this."*

Zaiden threw a punch, but the movement was clumsy. His father saw the strike coming and blocked it with his forearm. Zaiden's fist collided with the sharpness of his father's elbow, and pain lanced through his hand. Ignoring it, Zaiden threw another punch, but his father blocked it as easily as he had the first.

With a grunt, Zaiden threw himself forward, knocking both of them to the ground. He rolled on top of his father and raised a fist, but the man was too fast. He struck Zaiden square in the nose, and a sickening crack sounded through the room as the young man fell back. Blood gushed from his nostrils in a sea of red, and pain pulsed all the way up to his forehead. He winced, placing his shirt sleeve against his nose to stop the flow of blood. The fight was over.

A laugh echoed through the room as his father carefully unrolled his shirt sleeves and smoothed out the wrinkles. His heels clicked on the floor as he approached and knelt down to examine Zaiden's gushing nose.

"Looks painful," Governor Warren said, a smile forming on his thin lips. He stood and stepped over Zaiden's limp body to remove his jacket from the coatrack. The air in the room stilled as Zaiden's father paused in the doorway. "Maybe next time, you won't be so slow."

3

SEREN

After her run, Seren made her way back home through a notably quieter Community. The Tier Four halls had cleared out, and she passed few neighbors.

She took a different path than usual, opting to walk past her Year Eleven classroom on the way home. Her conversation with Lucas had left her feeling nostalgic. Only one week left of classes before she'd work for the rest of her life.

The door to her classroom was slightly ajar. Surprised, Seren peeked in and saw Edu Marcus seated at his desk in the front of the room, his eyes dancing over his tablet. Edu Marcus was a gentle looking man, with mousy brown hair, pale skin, and a strong, pointed nose.

"Hi, Edu Marcus," Seren called.

The man startled, spotted Seren, and grinned. "Hi, Seren."

"I thought you had the day off."

"No days off for educators," he said, putting the tablet down and pushing a pair of glasses up his nose. "Happy Creation Day! How are you?"

"Oh, I'm good."

Seren shifted from one foot to the other and cleared her throat.

"When did you know you wanted to be an Edu?" she asked suddenly.

Edu Marcus smiled, like this was a question he was prepared for and loved to be asked. "I think I always knew," he said. "I have a younger brother—this ages me, but I was born before the one child policy—and I used to sit him down after school and teach him everything I'd learned that day. He *hated* it, because I wasn't a very good teacher at the time." He grinned. "I like to think I've gotten better."

"I didn't know you have a brother," Seren said. It was rare these days to hear about people with siblings.

Edu Marcus's smile wavered. "He passed a few years back. Heart attack."

"Oh," Seren said. "I'm so sorry."

"Thank you. It was a long time ago." Edu Marcus cleared his throat. "What brings you by the classroom today?"

"I'm just coming back from a run. But, uh…" Seren bit her lip. "Speaking of trades … have you heard anything about … any applications or anything?"

Edu Marcus gave her a knowing smile. Seren hadn't told him about her Thinker application, but she knew he'd seen her working on it in class. The results of the application would likely be run past her Edu first, if things worked the same as they had when the last Tier Four was accepted, over twenty years ago.

"Nothing yet. If something comes in, you'll be the first to know."

"Okay, thank you. I'll see you tomorrow." Seren turned to leave.

"Seren?"

"Yes?"

Edu Marcus stood and approached her. He wore a green lanyard around his neck with his identity card in full view, its lime color signifying the expanded access granted to Edus.

"Have you given any thought to what you will do if your application isn't accepted?" he asked. "Trade rankings are coming up in two days. I just don't want you to be ill-prepared."

"I understand."

He placed a kind hand on her shoulder. "If you want to discuss your options, you know where to find me."

Seren nodded, feeling a pit form in her stomach. Even Edu Marcus didn't believe in her. She cleared her throat gently. "Well, I should go."

"See you in class tomorrow," Edu Marcus said with a soft smile. "Enjoy your day off."

4

SEREN

Seren went to shower when she returned home. Her heartbeat had finally slowed, and her body almost felt back to normal, apart from her aching legs.

She tried not to think about Edu Marcus's warning. She wanted to believe that at least *someone* believed in her. Who cared if no Tier Fours had been chosen as a Thinker in decades? Seren was at the top of her class. She was smart, hardworking. Surely they'd see that. They *had* to see that. She couldn't think of a single thing she'd rather do.

The apartment was quiet, as expected, and she made a beeline for the bathroom, thrilled at the idea of rinsing off. But the bathroom door was locked when she tried it. *Weird...* Ma and Pa should have been gone by now. Seren tried the door handle again, but it still didn't budge.

"Hello?" she called.

"Just a second," Ma's voice replied.

"Ma? What're you doing here?"

"I'll be right out."

Seren frowned. Ma sounded tense.

There was a banging sound, and the toilet flushed.

"Is everything alright in there?" Seren asked.

"Everything's fine!"

Ma had never been good at hiding things. She made that clear every time she accidentally ruined a surprise for Seren's birthday. And today, it was unmistakable; something was wrong. Seren pressed her ear to the door.

"Are you sure?"

Ma opened the door a crack and gave Seren a quick smile. "Yes, chickpea. All is well."

"Shouldn't you be at work?" Seren asked.

"I don't have to go in until later. Happy Creation Day to me!"

Seren's frown deepened. Ma's tone may have been bright, but her eyes were emotionless.

"What's going on?" Seren asked.

Ma opened her mouth to answer, but then a look of alarm crossed her face. She ran back to the toilet, gripped the sides, and threw up violently. Seren's own guts heaved as the scent of bile filled the room, but she followed Ma anyway and knelt beside her, pulling back the woman's curls as she continued vomiting.

"I'm really okay," Ma said from within the toilet bowl.

She threw up again, and Seren looked away. Keeping her eyes glued to the wall, she rubbed a hand up and down Ma's back. *She'd do the same for you,* Seren reminded herself. She had before. Back when Seren was younger and Community's food restrictions were less stringent, she had eaten an entire bowl of chickpeas—so many that she got sick only moments later, all over the table. Ma had held her hair as she threw up, then cleaned up the table and put Seren to bed with a cup of peppermint tea and a cool cloth, all without blinking an eye. That's where the nickname "chickpea" had come from. At first, Seren had hated it. Now she wouldn't have it any other way.

Finally, Ma sighed and leaned against the bathroom wall, her face glistening with a thin layer of sweat. "Must be a bug," she mumbled.

"Ma," Seren said, her heart clenching. "We both know that's not true."

Illness was rare in Community. Occasionally, someone would get sick, but whenever that happened, it was a frenzy. Outbreaks of any illness spread like wildfire within these walls. Community had to shut down for days to contain the spread, and people were confined to their apartments while groups of workers in hazmat suits took on the infected halls, sanitizing every square inch until the illness disappeared. If Seren's mother were truly sick, there would have been an announcement on the Awakening, and Tier Four would be under strict quarantine.

"What's really going on?" Seren asked. She pushed Ma's sweat-soaked hair from her forehead and stroked her cheek. It was a motherly gesture—one Ma had used on Seren many times before. It felt strange to be on the other side of it.

"Seren..."

"Ma, please," Seren said. "Tell me what's going on."

Ma looked at Seren, her eyes welling with tears. Carefully, she lifted her baggy khaki shirt to reveal a small swollen belly. Ma placed her finger on her lips.

Seren's brows furrowed. "I don't..."

Suddenly, it hit her. The swollen belly. The sickness.

Dismay, confusion, and concern ripped through Seren in a matter of seconds. It couldn't be. Her mother *couldn't* be...

Seren collapsed backwards and laid her head against their tub, her heart pounding.

"No," she whispered, shaking her head. "No, no, no, *no!*"

"Seren—"

"It's not possible."

"Chickpea…"

Seren sat up. "But you got the shot!"

"I must have forgotten," Ma murmured.

"You can't just forget, Ma! It's mandatory." Seren's voice had a rough edge to it now. She couldn't keep the distress out of her tone. "When were you going to tell me?"

"I don't know."

"Have you told Pa?"

"No."

Dear Warren, how long had Ma been keeping this secret?

"When are you going to tell *them?*" Seren asked. Once the government found out about Ma's pregnancy… Seren couldn't bear to think about it. The one-child policy was clear: if a woman bore a second child, that child would take her place. They referred to it as "one in, one out"—as if they were talking about an organizational tool, not taking a woman's life.

Ma shook her head. "I don't know."

A wave of nausea rolled through Seren. "How could this happen?" They gave birth control shots at Ma's office. Seren had seen her with a bandage. Ma didn't forget. She *never* forgot. How could she, when her life was on the line?

"Nothing is definite, chickpea."

Seren placed her elbows on her thighs and braced her head between her hands. "I thought this was," she choked out. Tier Three scientists boasted about the 99.99 percent efficacy rate. How could Ma be pregnant with those odds? Was she just that unlucky?

Ma wrapped her arms around Seren as the tears started to flow.

I shouldn't be crying, Seren thought. Her shoulders quaked with each sob. *I should be strong for Ma.* She tried to stop the flow of tears, but her sobs only got louder.

"They're going to kill you!" she whimpered.

"I know."

Ma rubbed Seren's arm. The gesture, calming and familiar, only served to make Seren more upset. What would she do without Ma here to comfort her when she was inconsolable? What would she and Pa do, all alone?

They wouldn't survive. This would destroy them.

Seren looked up, her pale cheeks flushed from crying. "You can't have it."

That was the only option: they had to stop the baby from being born.

Ma let out a small, sad sigh. "I don't have a choice, chickpea."

"There's *always* a choice," Seren said firmly. That's what Ma and Pa always said. There was always a way out. Nothing was permanent; this wasn't, either.

It couldn't be.

Ma lifted Seren's chin with her warm, soft hands and looked deep into her eyes. "You can't tell anyone about this, okay? Not even Pa. Not until I figure things out."

Seren looked at Ma's stomach. In a few weeks, it wouldn't matter who Seren told. Ma wouldn't be able to hide the baby anymore. People in Tier Four didn't just gain weight; their food supply was too regulated for that. Someone was bound to notice if Ma kept getting bigger.

"I think Pa's going to figure it out soon."

"Your father wouldn't notice if I painted my face blue," Ma joked.

Seren tried to smile, but her face felt tight and immobile. "Do you still have to go to work?" she asked. She didn't want to talk about this anymore—not now. Ma nodded. "Go get ready. I'll clean up."

. . . .

Seren spent the next few hours of Creation Day in a state of disarray. She finished cleaning Ma's sickness from the rim of the toilet before stripping off her clothes and climbing into the shower. She turned the temperature up so high that the water seared her skin and turned it a bright strawberry red. For a few glorious minutes, she closed her eyes and allowed the water to scorch her and drown out her thoughts. The shower turned off automatically after five minutes, but Seren stayed there for a while longer, just staring blankly at the tile and watching the steam dissipate. Her mind kept flickering back to Ma kneeling on the bathroom floor, the smell of her sickness permeating the room.

Seren couldn't believe she was pregnant.

They would find out soon. They always did. Population control was important. Community had a fixed amount of resources—an amount that seemed to be getting smaller by the day. Getting pregnant with a second child was not a crime that could go unpunished. Once they found out, they would monitor Ma's pregnancy. She would get in trouble for not reporting it, but her treachery wouldn't matter in the long run. In the end, they'd kill her anyway.

Seren looked down at her own stomach, imagining what it would be like to have a child in there. Ma must be so scared, so confused. She didn't want this for herself any more than Seren wanted it for her.

The tears came flooding back.

There *had* to be a way to fix this.

In higher Tiers, there were options for women who got pregnant. No one talked about it, but Seren knew that there was medication for such predicaments. If it was taken early enough, the pregnancy could be terminated before anyone found out.

But they weren't in a higher tier. They were Tier Four. And here, if you got pregnant, you had the baby.

Seren wrung out her hair and splashed her face with cold water. From the hall, she could hear the her neighbors celebrating Creation Day. How could anyone be celebrating when women were dying—when Ma was going to die?

The excited energy and loud chatter suffocated her. She needed to get out. *Now.*

5

ZAIDEN

Zaiden looked in the mirror and touched his broken nose gingerly. He could feel his heartbeat pulsing through the bridge where a bruise had begun to form, dotting his face in blues and purples. He'd done his best to cover it with concealer, but it penetrated the makeup easily. The bruise would stay.

"Please keep still, Mr. Warren," Geoff said. This was the third time that Zaiden's tailor had had to ask him to stop fidgeting, and Geoff was not good at hiding his annoyance.

"Sorry."

"That's quite alright," Geoff said, though the edge in his tone said otherwise. He kneeled and began working on hemming Zaiden's suit pants, his nimble fingers moving quickly to sew the material. "Navy is a very nice color on you. It complements your complexion nicely. How does the fabric feel?"

"Smooth," Zaiden replied, running his thumb along the slick cuff of his jacket.

"It's silk. Your father wore the same when he was inaugurated."

"Hmm." Zaiden wasn't in the mood to hear about his father—especially not after the beating he'd taken this morning. His body still ached, and the humiliation of it all turned his cheeks a perpetual red.

"His inauguration was magnificent, though I'm sure yours will dwarf it. You will certainly be better dressed." Geoff stood and took a step back to examine the suit. He frowned and knelt back down to fix the right pant leg, and Zaiden sighed, imagining what it would feel like to wear this suit in front of all his peers.

The gala was only a week away. After that, Zaiden would become a council member alongside his father. Meanwhile, his classmates would choose their careers. They'd become Harmonizers, Surgeons, Information Security Analysts... They had a choice. Sometimes he wished he had the same.

Geoff stepped around Zaiden and worked on the right sleeve. "Will you be bringing a date to the gala? The girl who gave you that bruised nose, perhaps?" He winked at Zaiden in the mirror, a sparkle in his dull brown eyes.

Zaiden's eyes narrowed. Geoff's nosiness rubbed him the wrong way. Maybe it wouldn't have on any other day, but he was sensitive today. "You should mind your own business," he said coolly. "Unless, of course, you want to end up with a broken nose, too."

Geoff flinched. Smugly, Zaiden returned his attention to the wall.

Gossip was not new to Zaiden, nor was being at the center of scandals. He'd worked up quite the reputation for himself in the last few years. People said he was a party animal and a playboy. Zaiden didn't mind. The gossip came with the job, and anyway, it was better than the words people used to describe his father. Though the Governor was adored by most, a select group spoke poorly of him when they thought they would not be overheard. They called him a tyrant, a dictator, and other words that should not have been in their vocabulary. The good thing was that it wasn't difficult to find these people and weed them out. After all, slander and libel were illegal. Either could impact the fragile system of Community's government, and therefore, anyone participating had to be extinguished. That was why the lower Tiers only had access to a select few books; the knowledge found in old books could lead to anarchist ideation. Books could tell lies. As his father once put it, "Ideas are more powerful than guns. We would not let our enemies have guns; why should we let them have ideas?"

Zaiden knew, along with most of Community, that his father was not a tyrant. He was just a man trying to maintain the fragile homeostasis of Community and keep their world afloat. After all, if Community ceased to exist, so would the remainder of the human population.

Geoff studied the suit and stroked his chin. "One final touch," he said. He procured a tie from his back room and wrapped it around Zaiden's neck. "Your father requested this tie specifically."

Of course he had. The tie was a deep blood red—the color of power, his father said.

Geoff tied the tie around Zaiden's neck in a clean knot. "What do you think?" he asked. He took a step back, allowing the young man to see himself in the mirror. Zaiden examined his appearance. The suit fit better than it had when he'd first tried it on. He no longer looked like a young boy playing dress-up in his father's clothing; he looked like a true leader.

"It's perfect."

Geoff beamed. "I'm glad you think so. The suit will be ready by the morning of your gala. I'll have it sent up to you when it's finished."

"Good."

"Please forgive me for my nosiness earlier. Occupational hazard." Geoff stepped back off the platform and clasped his hands together. "And please tell your father what a wonderful job you think I did."

Yeah, right, Zaiden thought. But he nodded anyway.

Geoff lingered.

"Is that all?" Zaiden asked somewhat sharply.

"Oh, yes! My apologies. I will allow you to get dressed."

Geoff scampered from the room, his short legs bounding beneath him, and Zaiden removed his suit, reviewing his script for the Evening Broadcast as he changed.

"Members of Community," he began, "good evening…"

He watched himself in the mirror as he spoke, practicing his facial expressions and tone of voice. Zaiden did not like appearing in front of Community. Even with just the camera and crew in the room, he could never forget that every member of Community was watching—all 22,384 of them. As hard as he tried, he could not seem to look as serious or diplomatic as his father. He would be their leader one day; he needed to gain their respect now. But a part of him feared he never would.

Zaiden finished dressing just as he was coming to the end of the speech. Taking one final look at himself, he smiled as he said the last line.

"Thank you, and may Warren bless you all."

6

SEREN

Seren lay in bed, her eyes glued to the stars on her ceiling, her mind running circles around itself. Though usually comforting, the stars did little today to ease her mind. Her eyes traced over each of them with their jagged edges and odd colors, trying to find solace in them.

She still remembered the day she'd put them up. She and Lucas had created them from cut-out pieces of scraps that Lucas's father, Henry, had brought home one day, just weeks before his death. Seren remembered that Lucas's mother, Jean, had been upset when Henry helped stick them on his bedroom ceiling.

"You need to stop," Jean had muttered.

"I just want my son to have some magic in his life. Is that so wrong?"

Seren hadn't thought so. She snuck a few of her own out of Lucas's trash after Jean had thrown them all away, and she stuck them on her own bedroom ceiling with Lucas's help.

Now she wanted to rip them down and toss them in the incinerator.

Seren's body felt numb from the tips of her fingers down to her toes. She felt separated from her physical being, her soul unattached, floating somewhere far away.

There was a way to keep a baby from being born; that much Seren knew to be true. There were whispers throughout Community that other women had done it. In fact, she'd heard a rumor just last year that her classmate Maive was pregnant. Seren had waited all year for Maive's belly to grow, but it never did. People whispered that Maive lost her baby on purpose, but they never said how.

Seren wished she could ask Maive how to lose a baby.

If Henry were still alive, he might know what to do. But Henry had died years ago, taking his knowledge along with him.

Henry had been like Lucas in that way, always knowing more than any Tier Four should, always having answers to everything. Throughout his life, Henry had kept a collection of illegal books hidden deep beneath their floorboards. It was a major point of contention between him and Jean. Many of his books were about old Earth, from its oceans to its skies to all the creatures that lived there. Unbeknownst to Lucas's mother, he used to allow Lucas and Seren to peruse them, giving answers to any questions they might have. That had been before the era of the cameras, before each home in Tier Four had them installed in an upper corner.

Seren remembered a peculiar conversation she'd had with Henry when she was very young.

"Why do you need these when you have plenty of books at school?" she'd asked him, one of his many books in her tiny hands.

Henry had looked down at her and smiled. "The greatest enemy of knowledge is not ignorance, Seren. It is the illusion of knowledge."

She still wasn't sure what that meant, but she did like the pictures in his books. Of course, the Earth they depicted was long gone, replaced with the deadly, poisonous world sitting just outside Community's airtight walls.

Seren hadn't recognized the danger of books until she got older, around the time Henry died of a heart attack. After he passed, Lucas moved the books under his own floorboards, where they remained to this day, yellowing and collecting dust. Seren's memories of their contents had all but faded. Sometimes she wished she could look at them one more time, just to see what she was missing.

Seren suddenly sat up, her heart racing. *The books!* It was a stretch, but maybe, just maybe there was an answer hidden somewhere deep in those books.

Seren left her apartment and ran to Lucas's faster than she ever had, causing more than one of her passing neighbors to look at her oddly as she breezed by. When she arrived, she rapped her knuckles against his door until he opened it, half dressed. A look of surprise crossed his face.

"Seren! What are you doing here?"

"I need your help," she said. Anxiously, she looked over her shoulder at the bustling hallway. "Inside."

Seren pushed past Lucas into his apartment. Hesitantly, he closed the door behind her. "What's going on?"

Her eyes darted around the listless apartment. There was a small camera in one corner of the kitchen, another by the projector, and a final one in his family room. There wouldn't be one in his bedroom, but there could be a recording device. Safe places to speak were limited.

"Bathroom," she said.

"First door on the left," Lucas said, as if she hadn't been to his place countless times before. As if her own apartment didn't have the exact same layout. Seren rolled her eyes.

"Can you *show me?*" she asked, staring at him pointedly.

"Uh, sure. I guess."

He led her the ten steps to the bathroom and opened the door. Seren stepped inside, and her eyes scanned the upper and lower corners, keeping a lookout for any recording device. She couldn't be certain, but when she was pretty sure it was bug-free, she turned to look at Lucas expectantly. He raised an eyebrow.

"You want me to…"

Seren nodded. Lucas looked at her like she was crazy—maybe she was—but he followed her into the bathroom anyway and shut the door behind them.

Without another word, Seren turned on the shower and stripped off the top layers of her gray uniform. She could feel Lucas's confused eyes boring into her back, but she ignored them.

"What are you—"

"Shhhhh!"

She motioned for him to follow as she climbed into the shower. The steaming hot water hit her skin, and her hair turned a darker shade of auburn as it cascaded down her back. Seren motioned for Lucas again, more frantically this time. They only had five minutes until the water turned off, and she couldn't risk talking about this without the background noise covering their words.

Lucas averted his eyes and removed his clothes so that he stood in his boxers with his arms crossed tightly against his chest. Seren let out an exasperated sigh and yanked him into the shower beside her.

"What is going on?" Lucas asked again as Seren pulled the shower curtain shut.

"Ma is *pregnant*," she said in a hushed voice. The pitter-patter of the water hitting the bottom of the tub nearly drowned out her words.

"What?!"

"Shhh!"

Lucas leaned in closer so that they were only inches apart. Water sprayed his face and entered his mouth as he spoke. "What do you mean, she's pregnant?!"

"I saw her getting sick this morning."

His brows creased. "Maybe she ate something bad…?"

"No, Lucas. She's pregnant. She showed me her stomach." Seren's eyes welled up again. She moved closer to the showerhead, hoping the running water would mask her tears if they started to flow.

The severity of the situation fell upon them, like a darkness they couldn't shake. Lucas didn't seem to know *what* to say, but his despair was apparent; he loved Ma like a second mother. "Oh," he managed to choke out.

"I need you to go into your dad's old things and see if he has a book on terminating pregnancies," Seren whispered.

Lucas shook his head. "I don't think my dad had those kinds of book, Ren."

"Lucas, please." Seren looked up at him with wide eyes. "If anyone finds out, Ma will be on their list. Then it'll be too late. I can't lose her. You understand that more than anyone."

She was referring, of course, to his father's passing. Maybe that was unfair of her; maybe she should've kept Henry out of it. But Seren wasn't thinking straight. She needed those books; she needed answers.

Lucas sighed and rubbed his hand up and down his arm. He always did that when he got anxious, ever since they were young. Seren waited for him to say something, but he just stood there, his lips pressed together. She held her breath. Maybe she'd made the wrong decision in asking him for something like this.

After a moment of intense concentration, Lucas spoke. "I might have a solution."

Seren's breath caught. "Really?"

"Yes—but this is important, Seren." He grabbed her shoulders and stared at her more intensely than she'd ever been stared at in her life. She held her breath again. "You cannot say anything about this. To *anyone*. You have to be careful. If you aren't, you could get us both killed. Understand?"

Seren nodded.

The shower shut off.

Lucas, suddenly filled with a determination Seren rarely saw in him, grabbed a towel from the rack and handed it to her. She wrapped it tightly around herself like a protective shield and wrung out her hair before stepping out of the tub.

Lucas exited the bathroom, leaving drops of water on the floor behind him like a trail of breadcrumbs. Seren followed, then hesitated in his doorway. She'd been in Lucas's bedroom plenty of times when they were younger, but now, dressed only in a towel, it felt strangely intimate, like she *shouldn't* go in.

Lucas seemed undeterred. He went to his bed and reached into his pillowcase. Seren glanced at the cameras in the kitchen, then back at Lucas, her heart pounding. What could he have hidden that could help Ma *and* get them both killed?

Lucas motioned for her to meet him at his bed. Her legs shook as he pulled her close. He guided her hand, bringing it into the pillowcase with his. Seren wasn't sure what he was doing until she felt something small within the case. Nervous shivers spread through her body.

What the...?

Lucas nodded at her, indicating that she should take it. As quickly as she could manage, Seren pulled it out and slipped it beneath her towel, but not before catching a glimpse of it.

A bright sapphire identity card. She stifled a gasp.

It can't be.

Every member of Community was given an IC at birth. It kept track of their food pickups, their whereabouts, and their location authorization. Seren carried her own yellow IC with her everywhere. The sapphire color of this one indicated that it belonged to a Tier Two.

How had Lucas gotten this? Having someone else's IC was illegal—and identity theft was not taken lightly in Community. The penalty was death.

She stumbled back. The card felt suddenly heavy. Seren imagined it melting into her skin, burning the words Tier Two Identity Card into her chest, permanently marking her as a thief. Her throat tightened.

"I don't understand," Seren whispered. The illegal nature of the card was one thing, but what was the purpose of it? "How is it supposed to help?"

Lucas mimed placing a pill in his mouth. Seren shook her head, still not understanding.

And then it hit her.

Of course.

The pill. This identity card provided Seren access to Tier Two. She could get to the special medication kept there. This was the solution she'd been hoping for.

In that moment, the gravity of the crime and its potential consequences slipped from her mind. All that mattered was that she had a chance. *Ma has a chance.*

Seren pulled Lucas into a lung-crushing hug. Her eyes brimmed with tears. "Thank you," she mumbled.

Lucas wrapped his arms around her and squeezed her tightly.

"I don't deserve you," she whispered.

Lucas rested his chin on her head. "You deserve better than me."

They stayed there for a long moment, their bodies intertwined, breathing slow, before Seren pulled away.

"I should get going," she said.

"I know."

They returned to the bathroom and put their uniforms on over their wet undergarments. Seren checked the mirror to ensure that the card was completely hidden before she left the bathroom. Lucas trailed behind.

"You should come by tomorrow," he said, his gaze focused intently on the camera above her head.

Seren nodded. She didn't know where the card came from or what Lucas used it for, but she didn't care. If she got the medication tonight and brought the card back by tomorrow, there would be no questions asked.

"I'll be by in the morning."

7

SEREN

Seren hid the card in her own pillowcase when she got home, then changed from her wet clothes into something dry.

Dinner that night was quiet. Ma had little to say, and Seren had even less. Pa prepared dinner, boiling potatoes over their electric stove and roasting mushrooms. He hummed to himself as he cooked, glancing periodically at Ma and Seren.

"You two are quiet tonight," he said, removing the mushrooms and bread from the oven. "Am I missing something?"

"I just have a lot on my mind," Seren said. Her voice sounded strained, but Pa didn't seem to notice. He nodded and patted her reassuringly on the back.

The three of them ate in silence. Seren forced herself to take bites, trying to appear normal, but the fork kept slipping from her sweaty hand.

"The bread is delicious," Ma said.

Seren thought it tasted like cardboard, though that was no reflection on Pa's cooking; her anxiety was too high for her to taste anything. Her plans felt more foolhardy now that she was away from Lucas. Before, it had been the two of them. Now she was alone.

"Thank you," Pa said.

More silence ensued.

Seren felt Ma looking at her, but she ignored it, focusing instead on the food on her plate. She wasn't supposed to leave any food; the Nutritionists rationed it out for optimal health, but Seren really didn't think she could eat any more.

"May I be excused?" she asked.

"You haven't finished your dinner," Pa said.

"I'm not hungry."

"Seren." Pa's tone was cautionary. *Don't mess with the rations.*

"Let her go," Ma said quietly into her own plate.

Pa sighed. If he sensed that something else was going on, he didn't say anything. "Fine. You may be excused."

Ma stopped Seren before she could clear her plate. "I'll finish yours," she said with a small smile.

Seren's stomach twisted as she was reminded of the extra life growing in Ma's belly.

Leaving the table, Seren closed the door behind her and leaned her head against the wall. She had only a few hours until the 10:30 p.m. curfew. At that time, all the lights in Tier Four would turn off without fail, just like they came on every morning at 7:00 a.m. She thought of curfew as a way to preserve energy, but Lucas always suspected it was truly a way to preserve order. Maybe it was a bit of both.

She'd have to wait until then, or she'd risk being seen by a Tier Four out for a walk—or more likely, she'd be captured on camera, and the Harmonizers would be notified. When 10:30 came, she'd have to act. All she could do until then was wait.

When the Evening Broadcast came on at 7:30, Seren sat on the edge of her bed to watch. This time, it was not Governor Warren who made an appearance, but his son, Zaiden. Marcie introduced the young man brightly, and he began his speech.

"Good evening, members of Community," Zaiden said with a firm smile on his sharp features. "I hope you all had a wonderful Creation Day."

Seren frowned. *Hardly...*

"Today, we celebrated our origins and similarities," Zaiden said. He spoke a lot like this father, his eyes seeming to reach Seren through the screen. It was simultaneously admirable and unnerving. "With shades of difference, we all have the same beginning, the same strength and resilience. You have, in a common cause, survived the end of the world as we knew it—the dangers and suffering that other people endured."

It feels like we're still suffering, Seren thought.

"As you all well know, Jeffery Warren, my great-great-great-grandfather, built this Community from the ground up to prevent the total extinction of humanity. We are all ancestors of the construction workers, farmers, plumbers, and many others who built this magnificent bunker we call home. We should be so proud of what they accomplished."

Seren's eyes traveled from the projection back up to the stars on her ceiling. Zaiden continued to speak, but her thoughts drowned out his voice. Nothing he said tonight would be any different from what she'd heard every Creation Day for the last sixteen years. And she couldn't keep her mind on him. Not with the task at hand.

The risks of what she was about to do were great. She could be executed for identity theft, stealing, or entering a Tier to which she was not permitted access. Or she could be successful and make it all the way to the pharmacy, simply to find out the magical pill did not really exist. There were so many things that could go wrong, and Seren hadn't had proper time to think it all through. There just wasn't time.

Were the risks worth it?

Seren's thoughts flashed to Ma lying on the floor of the bathroom, her mouth outlined in her own sick, her stomach protruding over the waist of her pants.

Of course it was worth it. For Ma.

Seren tore her eyes from the ceiling, resting them instead on her reflection in the mirror. She was more powerful than she believed. She could do this.

She had to. Tonight.

8

SEREN

After a lifetime of waiting, the speakers dinged.

"Beginning curfew," a robotic voice said. Immediately, the lights in Seren's bedroom shut off.

Seren stayed lying down, feeling the rise and fall of her chest. She stared into the all-encompassing darkness as she listened for Pa's inevitable snores. They came quickly, shaking the walls with their might. Her parents were asleep; there was no point in waiting any longer.

Seren swung her legs out of bed and stepped blindly into her sneakers, the sapphire identity card tucked away in her shirt. Dragging her hand against the walls, she made her way from her bedroom to the front door, careful to tread lightly. The door creaked as she opened it.

Seren waited with bated breath.

Pa's snores continued without pause.

Seren's lips tugged up into a smile as she stepped into the dark hallway. For once, she was grateful for Pa's snoring.

Seren left the door slightly ajar so she wouldn't need her IC to open it when she returned. That was the kind of thing they could track, and she needed to leave as few digital footprints as she could tonight.

As expected, the hallway was deserted. Quietly, Seren started down the hall, keeping her hand on the wall to get her bearings. She remained tucked tightly out of the way in case someone else happened to be out on a night stroll. The odds were slim, but not impossible.

Seren moved faster as her vision began to adjust to the darkness. She watched for live cameras, indicated by floating red dots, but the hallways were all black. It appeared that the cameras, too, turned off at 10:30.

Seren was truly alone.

She continued past the cafeteria, past her Year Eight classroom, past Lucas's apartment, to the entranceway to Zone Six. Luckily, Seren had a semblance of an idea of where she was going, as she'd been to the Tier Two pharmacy once before. A nurse had taken her when she had a nasty cold. He'd been concerned that her illness might require a Community-wide quarantine, but the Pharmacist determined that Seren's bizarre symptoms resulted from an allergic reaction to a medication, not a new disease. Seren left Tier Two shortly after with a steroid—and an eternal memory of the magnificent world above her.

She made it to one of the few stairways to the upper tiers. She paused at the door and stared. If she got caught now, she might still be able to come up with an excuse as to why she was out past curfew. She could say something about sleepwalking or getting lost. But once she climbed these stairs, there would be no more excuses. If she got caught, she'd face the death penalty.

Seren shuddered and considered turning back, but once again, Ma's image popped into her head.

You can't stop now.

She took one more breath, opened the door, and stepped inside.

By the time she climbed the six flights up, Seren was out of breath and once again reconsidering her decision. She wondered if Lucas was awake, questioning his decision to lend her the card.

You can still turn around, she thought as she stared at the final door standing between her and Tier Two. That Seren could not visit other Tiers was a fact she never questioned, but now, as she stared down shakily at the dark padlock handle, she felt the rules dissipate. She removed the identity card from her shirt.

Here goes nothing...

The click of the opening lock was music to Seren's ears. *I did it!* She held back a cry of joy as she opened the door.

9

SEREN

Light blinded her.

Seren jumped back and slammed the door. *Shit! Does Tier Two not have a curfew?*

This threw a wrench in everything.

The dark backdrop of Tier Four had made it easy to hide, but if she stepped through these doors, she'd be completely exposed. She couldn't go on; she had to turn back.

"No," Seren said to the empty stairwell. "I will *not* turn back."

Seren had lived in the shadows for a long time. She'd learned to go unnoticed. She could still do this.

Once more, Seren stepped into the world of Tier Two. This time, she stayed put, blinking as her eyes adjusted to the light. Her breath caught in her throat. It was, as she remembered, absolutely breathtaking.

In the dancing lights of the chandeliers, the hallways sparkled. While the Tier Four halls were dull and monotonous, Tier Two was a floor of color. Dark and light mingled in the tiled floor, creating swirls of beauty, like art built right into the ground. The smell was different, too. It was as if someone had melted sugar and infused the caramelized crystals into the air.

The hallways were empty, but they wouldn't be that way forever. If Tier Twos were anything like Tier Fours, they would know their neighbors, and Seren would immediately be pegged an outsider.

Seren could hardly keep her eyes to herself as she followed her vague memory of the path to the Pharmacy. She ran her hands over the smooth marble walls. *How could any place in Community be this beautiful?*

Recentering herself, Seren made quick time down the hall, keeping alert to the movements around her. It was a wide hall—wider than any Tier Four spaces. What did the Tier Twos need with all this space? Their population was only a quarter of that of Tier Four.

Pushing her concern with the disparities down, Seren sharply rounded a corner—and nearly collided with a man dressed from head to toe in a red uniform.

A Harmonizer. The law keeping body in Community.

Seren's heart stopped. In the man's dark, almost black eyes, she saw a lack of recognition.

"Sorry," she mumbled, moving past. Her heart raced. *Don't look back. Don't look back...*

Seren counted to twenty before allowing herself to glance over her shoulder. To her relief, the Harmonizer was gone. She allowed herself a moment to regroup before continuing.

You're fine. Keep going.

Seren passed through a narrower residential hallway into the area where she believed the medical center to be. She turned a corner, expecting to find the familiar blue doors and waiting room, but instead she found a hallway with dimmer lights and signs reading, Laboratories. She did not remember this part from her time here. Squirming, she searched her mind. She thought she'd memorized this route, but now she doubted her memory. If she kept going without tracking her path, she'd never find her way home, and she already couldn't remember which direction she'd come from.

Just keep going. Stay calm.

With a deep breath, Seren crept along until she reached another corner. She ducked down another hall. A couple wandered towards her, and Seren's body went rigid, but they paid her no attention. They were too busy laughing and drinking. The couple passed close enough that the sweetness from their bottles filled Seren's nose. They stumbled down the hallway, the man's arm wrapped tightly around the woman's waist, their cheeks flushed red. The woman giggled and planted a kiss on her partner's mouth, and Seren turned away, blushing. Their love reminded her of Ma and Pa. Her heart swelled.

After a few more minutes of uncertainty, Seren stumbled upon the entrance to the medical center. Its baby-blue doors were open, leaving the waiting room on display. It looked just as she remembered, with large, olive-green chairs positioned around glass tables and intricate fake shrubbery potted around the corners of the room. Tonight, though, the center was nearly empty, apart from two young women sitting in the far corner. One had her head in a trash can and was getting sick. The other was sitting beside her, holding her hair back and looking mildly disgusted.

Mounted around the room were large screens playing back the Evening Broadcast, their volume set to low. Zaiden's face stared at Seren from all angles, his voice like a whisper.

Seren lowered her gaze. She kept her eyes diverted as she walked past the check in, attempting to appear as if she belonged here. The young man at the front desk did not so much as look at her. Quickly, she walked past the inpatient rooms and towards the back of the medical center.

Then she saw it: the door at the end of the hallway—a big metal door. It was the same door the Pharmacist had gone through all those years ago to precure the steroids Seren needed to quell her allergic reaction. Seren ducked into an empty examination room, rested her head against the door, and tried to slow her breathing.

If memory served her right, that metal door required facial recognition to enter. All she had to do now was figure out how to get past the security measures and make herself as inconspicuous as possible. The sapphire card wouldn't unlock it; she'd have to think of another way.

Seren opened the door a crack. The hallway was no longer empty. A Pharmacist stood by the metal door, his face illuminated in a sea of precise green squares. The facial recognition software scanned him and blinked green, and the door clicked open. The Pharmacist stepped through.

Seren closed the door again and breathed. If she waited long enough, someone else would have to go into the Pharmacy. Maybe then she could catch the door before it fully shut.

Again, Seren opened the door just slightly and peaked through the crack. For over twenty minutes she waited, terrified someone would come into the examination room. The original Pharmasist exited after five and came back once more fifteen minutes later. Seren held her breath as the software scanned his face and the door opened.

This time Seren didn't hesitate. She sprang from her hiding place and raced towards the door, catching it a moment before it closed. Her heart raced, and she looked around, praying no one had seen her.

No one had.

Seren took a breath and counted to ten before following the Pharmacist.

10

SEREN

Shelves of medications towered above Seren's head. The neat rows reminded her of the cushion mazes Henry used to build for her and Lucas. She ducked behind a far row and listened.

On the one hand, the room's size was a relief. She could stay hidden well enough if she just kept quiet. Unfortunately, the daunting size also meant that it would be more difficult to find the pill than she'd anticipated, and Seren had no idea where to start.

Not a problem. She could do this.

Seren peeked around the shelf. She could just make out the Pharmacist's bright white shoes beneath one of the rows of medication. His feet were unmoving, and the light sound of bottles popping open sounded through the room. She breathed deep and stayed in place, hidden behind the back row, until she heard the door open and close. Breathlessly, she peeked around the shelves again. He was gone.

Seren's hands shook as she began her search, quietly moving the bottles on the shelves to get a better look. Each bottle was labeled with names she'd never heard of: Charcoal Poultice, Elderberry

Capsules, Willow Bark Pain Reliever. None said anything about pregnancy.

As swiftly as she could, Seren searched the entire Pharmacy, examining each bottle's contents, trying to make sense of the medications in front of her. There were fever reducers, sleep aids, vitamins, but still nothing about terminating a pregnancy.

Doubt crept into her mind. She was back at square one, and each moment she spent in the Pharmacy was a moment too long. It was only a matter of time before another Pharmacist entered, and then what?

Seren's hope had all but vanished when her eyes landed on a beige cabinet in the far corner of the room. The cabinet was large enough for her to climb in to. She stepped inside to get a better look at the bottles on the shelf in the back. There was an assortment of medications ranging from orange pain relievers to round blue fever reducers to oblong white pills with illegible writing, and—

Seren's eyes landed on a tiny translucent bottle in the very back of the cabinet. It held a singular trapezoidal green pill, and on it, the words Pregnancy Termination shined back at her.

Her heart lurched. *This has to be right!* Joy cascaded down her spine. She grabbed the bottle and shoved it into her pocket. Time to go. Seren was moving to climb out of the cabinet when the door to the pharmacy burst open.

Shit!

In one swift motion, Seren yanked the medicine cabinet doors closed, shutting herself inside. She pressed herself back against the shelves, held her breath, and listened.

The Pharmacist hummed a gentle tune as he walked between the rows of medications. Seren watched through the crack in the cabinet doors as he lifted bottles at random before placing them back on their shelves. His motions were slow and relaxed. She dug her nails into her palms. Her heart had never beat so loud. She feared the Pharmacist would be able to hear it from across the room. The shelves dug into her lower back. She shifted, and her elbow knocked against something. A bottle of medication tumbled to the ground and spilled open. Seren swore involuntarily.

The Pharmacist's humming stopped. He looked up from the shelf and over at the cabinet. Seren held in a gasp. They both stood there, frozen.

Drop it, Seren thought. *Please. You're hearing things. Please think you're hearing things...* And for one blissful moment, it seemed as though Seren's prayers had been answered.

Until the Pharmacist suddenly changed course and started right towards her.

Dread filled Seren's lungs.

No.

No, no, no...

Just like that, all hope was gone. Hope of saving Ma, of keeping her family safe and alive. Seren clamped her eyes shut as the Pharmacist reached towards the cabinet.

I'm sorry, Ma. Please forgive me.

"Parker?" a voice called. "You're needed in room seven."

Seren cracked open an eye. The Pharmacist, Parker, had stopped not even a foot away and now stood there, arm still outstretched towards her. His eyes were narrowed in annoyance.

Seren pressed back further against the shelves, her stomach contracting in terror.

"Is it Nadia again?" Parker asked, barely keeping the frustration from his voice.

"Yup."

With an exasperated sigh, Parker turned away from the cabinet. Seren remained completely still, hesitant to even blink an eye. She stayed frozen for at least a minute after the sound of the door closing again before she got up the nerve to peer out through the cabinet doors.

The room was empty.

Seren's quaking legs gave way, and she collapsed to the ground. That was too close. She didn't bother cleaning up the spilled bottle; there wasn't time. She needed to get out of here—*now.*

Heart pumping, Seren raced to the door, the medicine bottle clutched tightly in one hand, but when she tried the door, she found it was locked. She tried again, but still, the door did not budge.

"No," Seren said, trying it again. "No, no, no!"

Who locked a door from the outside *and* from the inside?

Tears formed. She was so close, *so close,* to getting her mom the pill. This could not be where things went wrong. She could still figure this out. *Okay, Seren, think!*

Seren reasoned that she could wait for a pharmacist to come in, but not without being seen. She couldn't hide in the cabinet; there wouldn't be enough time for her to get out before the door shut, and she'd surely be seen then.

An option floated into her mind. Stupid, she knew ... but it just might work.

Silently, Seren pushed some of the bottles off a nearby shelf within the cabinet. She yanked the shelf free from the rest of the structure (thank Warren it was the kind of cabinet that could be taken apart), then she poised herself behind the door.

This is for Ma, she reminded herself. And then she waited.

Just when Seren feared another Pharmacist would not come, she heard the sound of approaching footsteps. She pushed herself back further against the cabinet, poised to strike.

The door opened with a click, and Seren lifted the shelf up high and brought it down forcefully onto the Pharmacist's head. He let out an "oof!" of surprise before collapsing to the floor in a heap, out cold. Seren caught the door with her foot, and the shelf clattered from her hand.

"I am so, so, so sorry," she whispered to the unconscious Pharmacist (not Parker). She checked his pulse (alive, Thank Warren) and gently pushed him out of the way of the door before exiting and closing it carefully behind her.

With an entirely new sense of purpose, Seren left the medical center. The young man at the front desk still paid her no attention. Once she was out of sight, she broke into a run, startling a Tier Two stumbling home from the bar. She did not stop running until she made it back to the staircase. She checked behind her once more to ensure she was not followed before throwing open the door and sprinting down the stairs.

When she hit the bottom, she finally allowed herself to breathe. Seren clutched the medication to her chest, and to her surprise, burst into tears. She stayed there on the floor at the bottom of the steps for a moment, sobbing, until she managed to calm herself down. Then she shoved the pill bottle under her shirt and went home.

11

SEREN

Seren got home late.

Adrenaline still pulsed through her veins as she pushed open the unlocked door to her apartment, careful to avoid its squeak. Though it was past midnight, Seren was not tired. She'd done it. Dear Warren, she had *done it!* Without thinking, she let out a small whoop of glee, then clamped her hands over her mouth.

Ma was fast asleep on the couch, her mouth hanging open. Ma slept on the couch sometimes to avoid Pa's snores. Seren couldn't blame her; Pa's snoring made the entire apartment quake. Seren tiptoed over to her, knelt, and stroked Ma's hair. Despite the circumstances, Seren smiled. Touching Ma's hair made her think back to Haircut Sundays, a monthly tradition from Seren's youth. She recalled how excited she would get when Ma would announce that it was, once again, time for a Haircut Sunday. She'd sit Seren up on the counter, and Pa would sit on a tall chair, so that her hands were level with their heads. Seren would nibble on cacao beans as Ma snipped, repeatedly reminding her to sit still. Pa would plant himself in front of Seren and make funny faces. Her favorite was when he would stick his tongue so far out of his mouth that it almost reached her nose. Seren would giggle and giggle while her mother scolded them both, warning them that if they didn't sit still, their hair would end up looking like the head of a celery stick. That only made Seren giggle louder.

When it was Pa's turn, Ma would let Seren watch. She even let Seren cut Pa's hair sometimes, though Pa's hair was difficult to cut because it was short and fine and not at all like Seren's. Afterwards, Seren got to sweep up the fallen hair. That was her favorite part. She would sweep until her reddish locks mixed in with Pa's thin salt-and-pepper strands, creating what Ma referred to as "Quinn Hair Soup." Seren would squeal with laughter as her mom vacuumed it all up, and the three of them would sit together on the couch with their fresh haircuts and watch the Evening Broadcast, cuddled up as a happy family.

They still were a happy family, but things felt different now. Maybe that was just collateral damage from growing up: suddenly, life no longer held the happy glow of youth. Community had become ever less exciting as Seren aged. No more looking through books with Lucas, no true choice in her future, no variety in her day-to-day. Slowly, she began to realize that her life would not change until the day she died.

Seren missed her early days, sometimes as fiercely as she missed Henry—especially on days like today, when it seemed as though the whole world might collapse around her. She wished she still had Sundays to look forward to, when she could sit cuddled between Ma and Pa with her fresh haircut.

But that was just a dream. Seren cut her own hair now.

Ma stirred, pulling Seren from her thoughts.

"Chickpea," she murmured, smiling softly. "What're you doing up?"

Seren stroked Ma's curls, brushing the baby hairs from her forehead with her thumb. "I brought you something," she whispered. Pa's snores continued steadily as Seren pulled the pill bottle from beneath her shirt and pressed it into Ma's palm.

Ma cracked open her eyes. She looked at the bottle, and her expression turned grave.

"Is this what I think it is?" she whispered, holding the bottle away from her body as if it were poison. In truth, it was just as dangerous.

"Yes."

Ma shook her head. "Where did you get this?"

"It doesn't matter."

"Seren…" Ma tried to hand the bottle back, but Seren wouldn't take it.

"Ma, this is the answer you've been looking for. This could save you. We can cover for you at work if you still feel sick by morning. I could go in and tell them—"

"Seren!" Ma snapped. Then upon seeing Seren's surprise, her expression softened. "I'm sorry," she whispered, cupping her daughter's cheek in her dainty hands. Pa always made fun of how small Ma's hands were. He called them "doll hands." They were cool on Seren's flushed skin.

"I already told them, Chickpea," she whispered, rubbing her thumb up and down Seren's cheeks. "I told them this morning—but it didn't matter. They already knew."

Her eyes were reassuring, but Seren could feel her entire world crashing down around her. *They know. I'm too late.* A wave of nausea washed over her, as if her heart had dropped all the way into her stomach, and now each cadenced heartbeat kicked at the inside of her organs.

"Chickpea? Are you okay?" Ma asked quietly.

Seren thought she might be sick.

"But you can still take it," she said. "People lose these things all the time." *"These things..."* She kept her voice low. Discretion was important in case someone was listening.

"No. They don't."

The worst part of it all was that Ma was right. People in Community didn't just lose their babies. Not anymore.

Seren backed away from the couch, her head spinning in great big circles. "You can't do this," she whispered.

"I don't have a choice."

Seren shut her eyes. "What about me and Pa?" she whispered.

"Everything will be okay," Ma said quietly.

Seren shook her head. She would hate this child. She would hate this child with her entire being—and she would never forgive Ma for having it. Seren's fist closed around the pill bottle. All that work, all that risk, for nothing.

"Even if they didn't know … if someone ever found out about..." Ma's eyes darted towards the bottle in Seren's hand. Seren clutched it tighter. "… *that*… we'd all be dead. Understand?"

Hot tears sprung into Seren's eyes. She blinked, and they cascaded down her cheeks in streaks. "Don't pretend like you're doing this to protect me."

Ma's forehead became a wrinkled peach as her brows furrowed. "I'm just trying to do what's best for our family."

"No," Seren spat. "You're doing what's best for *you*."

"Seren…" Ma reached for her hand, but Seren pulled away.

"Don't touch me. I hate you!" The words sprung out of her before Seren could stop them.

Ma flinched. "You don't mean that."

Seren opened her mouth to speak, but Pa's voice interrupted.

"What's going on?" he asked from the bedroom doorway. He rubbed his tired eyes and looked between his wife and daughter. Seren couldn't bring herself to look back at him.

No one said a word.

Ma gave the slightest shake of her head, and Seren realized that she still had not told Pa.

Seren took a step back, heart pounding. How had Ma not even told her husband yet? Suddenly, the apartment walls began to move towards her, trapping Seren within the narrow confines of the apartment. She felt suffocated.

"What's going on?" Pa asked again.

Seren couldn't take it. She couldn't take Pa's concerned glances or Ma's hurt expression. She had to get out. *Now.*

Without a second thought, Seren ran back into the hallway, leaving her parents in her wake. She heard Ma and Pa calling after her, but their voices faded as she tore around the corners, choking on the antiseptic aroma. The darkness didn't feel as much like a barrier anymore. She could make out the familiar landmarks: the old Playroom, her Year Three classroom, and the local bakery. She had been in each place so routinely that they had become extensions of her apartment and extensions of her mother's words. It all felt too familiar. Seren didn't want to be in Community anymore. She longed to escape, to go outside, to see something new.

But that was impossible.

So, Seren did the next best thing: she ran until the familiar became unfamiliar. Her pounding pulse filled her ears as she rounded corner after corner, longing to find some place, *any place*, she had not yet been. She eventually found her way back to the staircase that led to the other Tiers. She didn't question herself as she burst through the door and bounded back up the stairway, past Tier Two, to a place she'd never been.

Tier One.

Home of the Governor, of his son, of the council, and of so many unknowns. The only true unfamiliarity left.

Seren stared at the door, the sapphire identity card burning in her palm. The IC might not work—or worse yet, it might alert the Harmonizers. If it did, they'd find her with the stolen card in minutes, and she'd be as good as dead.

But did she care?

She couldn't live without Ma, she couldn't help raise the child that would kill her mother, and she certainly couldn't go back to Tier Four.

Knowing that she might deeply regret it, Seren raised the sapphire identity card to the keypad and waited.

It flashed green.

The door opened.

Seren stepped through into the quiet hallways of Tier One.

The layout of Tier One was different than anything Seren had ever seen. She'd thought Tier Two was breathtaking, but she didn't have a word in her vocabulary to describe Tier One. The amount of space alone was almost incomprehensible. The hallways were three times as wide as in Tier Four, the ceilings twice as high. She peeked into the windows of various rooms and saw that they, too, were massive. Wealth and prosperity dripped from every inch of the place. Golden lights, cream-colored walls, wooden floors… She was still in Community, but it felt as though she'd stepped into another world. She had never stopped to contemplate the stark disparities in the ways the Tiers lived. Lucas was right: a little knowledge was a dangerous thing.

Seren knew she should go home; every moment she stayed here was a moment that she could get caught. But something kept her going. It was as if an invisible force were compelling her forward, further into the depths of Tier One. She was tempted to open every door, explore every crevice, soak in every new bit of this world that she could. She'd lived in Community her whole life and had never had any idea that this existed.

Henry's words echoed in her mind as she rounded a corner: *"The greatest enemy of knowledge is not ignorance, Seren. It is the illusion of knowledge."*

Seren's exploration led her through the empty halls and down one hall that seemed to glisten brighter than all the others. Her heart pounded as her feet led her, as if they had a mind of their own, to the end of the mysterious hallway. But there was nothing there but a dead end.

Seren moved to turn back the way she came, but something stopped her. On the far wall, well blended with its surroundings, was a small script. As she moved closer, she found that the hallway was not a dead end at all. The door hadn't been apparent at first. It blended into the dark marble wall, but it was a door, alright. It stood at least six feet wide and towered three feet above her head. Above it in dark letters were two words: The Simulator.

Seren blinked twice, convinced that her tired eyes were betraying her.

It can't be.

The words triggered a memory buried deep in Seren's mind. It was from years ago—she couldn't have been more than seven at the time—but she remembered it vividly. She, Lucas, and Henry were on the floor of Lucas's family room, sitting with their legs crossed and their elbows resting on their knees. They were playing a game, something silly, while Ma and Pa sat at the kitchen table with Jean, chatting and sipping tea.

"Sandwich!" Seren had yelled, hitting the ground. This earned her another point, and she won the game.

Lucas pouted and crossed his arms. "Cheater," he said.

Seren gasped, appalled at the accusation. "Am not!" she yelled.

"Are too!"

Henry placed a hand between the two of them. "Hey, now," he said strictly, giving Lucas the kind of look a father gives when he doesn't want to scold his child in front of others—the kind of look that makes a child clamp their lips shut and behave.

Lucas seemed unbothered. "This game is boring. I want to go outside."

"We can go for a walk through the hall, if you want," Henry said, not unkindly.

"No! I want to go *outside*. To Earth."

Henry shot a look at the other adults in the room to see if they'd heard. They hadn't.

"You know we can't do that," he said, his voice low.

"I just want to see it," Lucas said. "Just once."

"Me too," Seren said. And she *had* wanted to see Earth, ever since she'd learned of its existence. She'd always dreamed of seeing what it was really like outside Community's stifling walls.

Henry glanced again to the table of adults. They remained deep in conversation. "Do you want to know a secret?" he asked, leaning in close.

Seren and Lucas nodded enthusiastically, their eyes wide.

"I've seen it," Henry whispered.

"No way," Seren breathed.

"How?" Lucas demanded.

Henry motioned for Seren and Lucas to move in even closer. They did.

"There's this big room in Community," Henry said. "Floors above where we are right now. The room is a magic room—one where you can wish to see anything from Earth, and it'll appear right there in front of you."

"What's it called?" Seren asked.

"The Simulator."

Seren and Lucas were aghast. Seren imagined Henry standing in a big room, wishing for all sorts of amazing things. She wondered what Henry would wish for. She wondered what *she* might wish for.

"Could we ask for chocolate?" Lucas asked.

His father laughed and threw Lucas down on the couch. "Chocolate? You think you need more treats?" He tickled Lucas's belly while the boy squealed and begged Seren to come save him.

After Henry died, Seren didn't think about the Simulator. She thought Henry had made it up, the way adults often did to make children's lives more magical.

But maybe he hadn't made it up at all. As Seren stood in front of it, it looked as real as anything.

"No way," she whispered.

To the right of the door, a list was engraved into the marble in black letters.

Simulation Policy

1. No violence. No simulating violence or acting out violence.
2. Sexual acts of any kind PROHIBITED
3. No simulations involving specific members of Community.
4. Please note: for the safety of our users, all simulations will be recorded.

Outside the door was the same keypad as the one in the stairwell. Seren looked at it, then back to the card in her hand. Curiosity prickled her skin, and excitement coursed down her spine. She knew she should turn around, but she couldn't leave now. Not with the Simulator *right here!*

This is by far the most idiotic thing I have ever done, she thought as she brought the card up to the door of the Simulator.

The green light flickered.

The door opened.

Seren stepped in.

12

SEREN

Black, all around.

It wasn't what she expected. Grass, maybe, or a bright blue sky—not matte black walls and flooring with no lights in sight.

Had Henry been lying after all?

The door closed behind her, and the room became engulfed in darkness. Everything was still.

"Hello?" Seren called into the dauntingly blank space.

A spotlight suddenly flickered on above her, illuminating Seren in brightness. She blinked and squinted, blocking the light from her eyes.

"Hello, Mr. Holland," a voice boomed from above. It took Seren a startled moment to realize that the female voice belonged to a machine, echoing off the walls and sending vibrations through her body. "What would you like to see?"

Mr. Holland…? Seren looked at the card in her hand. She had not noticed it before, but in the top right corner, the card's owner was identified as one Alaster Holland. The Simulator knew her identity from her using the card.

Magnificent.

Excitement buzzed through her. "What are my choices?" she asked.

For a moment, there was silence, then: "Choice unidentifiable. Please repeat or change command."

Seren paused. Could she really choose *anything?*

There was so much she wanted to see. The books she'd studied with Lucas were full of photographs, each capturing beauty beyond belief. Mountains, oceans, animals, cities... There were so many things to choose from; how could she just pick one?

Seren bit her lip and racked her brain. What did she want to see? A sunset? A tornado? Rain...?

Oh, I know! She thought. One Earthly pleasure stood out above all others, a light amongst the confusion. Seren wanted to see the celestial anomalies she'd been named after: the lights of the old world.

"I'd like to see the stars," she called out to the machine. Her pulse quickened as the words left her lips.

"Generating star simulation," the mechanical voice boomed.

For a moment, nothing happened.

Then the light above her shut off, and the room returned to black. The darkness intensified for a moment, and then suddenly, thousands of tiny white lights lit up the ceiling. They sparkled and shifted to form groups of stars.

Seren let out an involuntary gasp. *Constellations!*

Some burned brighter than others, shining luminously amongst the duller lights. Some twinkled playfully, reminding Seren that stars were just balls of gas, mere jumbles of the leftovers from the formation of the universe. It was beyond anything she could have hoped for. Her eyes scanned the constellations, picking out those she knew from the books: Orion with his bow, Ursa Major and its handle, the scales of Libra. They were magnificent, more astonishing than anything she had ever seen.

Still, something was missing. Seren had stared at photos of stars for years. This simulation felt like just another photograph.

"Is this satisfactory?" asked the Simulator, perhaps sensing her discontent.

Seren paused and considered how to vocalize her desires.

"Can you make it more ... real?" she asked finally, a slight quiver in her voice. "I want to feel the elements."

"Simulating elements. Please hold on."

Hold on...?

Abruptly, the floor beneath her feet rose into the air. Seren stumbled. She had barely caught her balance before she was ten feet above the ground. Water spurted from the walls, filling up the Simulator at an alarming rate. Not ten seconds later, air started to push at her from all directions, whipping her hair across her face. The water continued to flow until the room was completely full. It moved in bizarre ways, shifting into mountains that crashed against each other. The platform quaked. She squealed as water splashed at her from every direction, soaking her clothes and bringing goose bumps to the surface of her skin. It was a new, glorious sensation for Seren, who had never felt true cold before; she'd never felt *anything* like this!

From there, the simulation only intensified. The wind howled, and water soaked the platform, making it slippery and unstable. She nearly lost her balance a few times. Steadfast, she held tight, whooping gleefully as the water shook her. The stars reflected off the black waves, and Seren cried into them. How odd to be soaked by something other than a shower. How odd to feel *cold*!

In her excitement, Seren totally forgot about her mother's pregnancy and Trade Day. She forgot about her application to be a

Thinker, she forgot about Lucas's stolen identity card. Each of her stressors melted blissfully away, like metal in a fire. As she breathed in the salty air, it felt like it could be her last breath. She'd finally seen Earth.

If she'd died at that moment, she would have died happy.

The stars remained calm while chaos reigned. *People used to get to look up at these every night,* Seren thought over the deafening roar of the wind. Had her ancestors truly appreciated them, or had they treated them like they treated the rest of the Earth: something to use and ruin?

All at once, while gazing upon the stars, Seren was struck by a monstrous mountain of water. It knocked her from the platform into the sputtering waves below. She hit the frigid surface with a smack, and her body went rigid. Before she could attempt to take a breath, the rough water yanked her down beneath the surface. Panic consumed her; she couldn't swim!

Seren tried to fight against the water, but it continued to pull her covetously into its depths, engulfing her with ease, like a sugar cube being stirred into a cup of tea until it lost all shape and form.

Fighting against the water was nothing like she had imagined swimming would be. No matter how hard she tried to resist it, it tossed her around with no regard for her comfort or safety. She struggled to stay above the surface, but each time it pulled her down, she became increasingly disoriented. Salty water entered her eyes, nose, and mouth, each a new sensation of its own. It burned her throat, her lungs. She coughed and sputtered, fighting a losing battle for her life.

"STOP!" she screamed into the Simulator as she pulled her body back above the water. It didn't seem to hear her over the roar of the wind. "PLEASE, STOP!"

Once again, she was pulled under mercilessly. Her lungs cried out for air, but she couldn't remember how to breathe. As exhaustion overcame her, Seren wondered if this was how she was destined to die. She'd spent her whole life following the rules, and now here she was, taking the first real risk of her life—and she was going to die for it.

In a roundabout way, Seren realized that she'd solved Ma's problem. If she drowned today, Ma could keep the baby and her own life. She wouldn't have to worry anymore.

Seren gasped for air once more. The stars above seemed to smile obliviously down at her. Through her struggle to stay afloat, she was able to make out the constellation of Pyxis, the compass. Pyxis seemed to point down, as if to say, "Give in to the ocean, Seren. Your mother will forgive you".

Fighting the roaring water finally became too much. Seren felt too weak to carry on. She gave into the sea, allowing it to toss her around like a child tossing a toy. As the water consumed her, she prayed to a god that she did not believe in.

Please watch over Ma and Pa and Lucas. Keep them safe. And please help Ma forgive me. Don't let her suffer over my loss.

With no energy left to fight, Seren relaxed her body and waited for death to come.

And then everything stopped.

The water drained away as quickly as it had entered, and Seren found herself lying on her back on the sodden floor of the Simulator. She coughed and sputtered, spitting out mouthfuls of salty water.

What happened?

She was there; she had knocked at death's door. How could she be alive? Why had the simulation stopped? Seren tried to make sense of it all, but her mind was no longer working. She was so exhausted, and the lack of oxygen left her feeling dizzy. She allowed her eyes to drift shut.

"What the hell do you think you're doing?"

Seren's eyes shot open.

Against her screaming body's wishes, she sat up and turned slowly to see a boy standing in the doorway, his arms crossed over his broad chest.

Zaiden. Zaiden Warren.

No. Please, no... God, please don't fail me now!

Seren clenched her eyes shut, hoping that when she opened them, this nightmare would be over. But Zaiden was still there.

He looked at her with an eyebrow raised. "Well?"

Seren didn't know what to say. Is this how her adventure was destined to end—soaking wet on the floor, her life in the hands of the Governor's son?

"I ... I wanted to see what it was like," she said quietly.

"Drowning?"

She didn't answer.

"What's your name?" he asked, stepping closer. She could make out the details of his face now. Zaiden's features were not as harsh as his father's, but his jawline was sharp enough to cut glass, and his eyes were a piercing blue—so blue that Seren wondered if they were real.

Zaiden's lips tightened. "Your name," he repeated.

It was not a question. Seren held her tongue. As soon as she told him, her life would be over. Forget whatever would happen to Lucas for giving her the card, forget whatever would happen to Ma. She would be killed, and Ma might be killed—even Pa, if they deemed her crime significant enough.

Seren considered a lie, but what would be the point? She had nowhere to hide. Community was not designed to harbor a lifelong fugitive.

"Seren," she said finally.

"Seren what?"

"Seren Quinn." They were the same age, but dropping her eyes, Seren felt like a child being scolded.

"I haven't seen you around before. Are you a Tier One?"

"Tier Four." Seren almost didn't recognize the sound of her own voice.

Zaiden's eyebrows shot up. "How the hell did you get in here, Seren Quinn?"

If there was a time to lie, it would be now. She couldn't let Lucas suffer for her actions. Seren pulled Alaster Holland's identity card from her pocket, held it out, and looked Zaiden directly in the eyes as she said, "I stole it."

Zaiden took it from her and examined it. Recognition crossed his face before he looked back up at her, frowning. "You *stole* it?"

He doesn't believe me.

"Yes."

A small chuckle escaped Zaiden's lips.

What's funny? Seren wanted to ask, but she was not that brave.

Zaiden looked at the card once more before pocketing it. "You're either very brave, or extremely stupid," he said.

Seren tried to keep her expression blank, but fear pulsed through her stronger than the blood in her veins. Zaiden Warren. She'd gotten caught by *Zaiden Warren.* There was no surer way for her to get the death sentence than this.

The two stared at each other in silence.

"I think you should go now," Zaiden said.

Seren nodded and stood, her body still quaking from the cold. Her clothes clung to her as she wrapped her arms tightly around her body.

"Here," Zaiden said. He tossed her his jacket.

Seren caught it, surprised, and stared at it for a moment before throwing it on over her shoulders. Zaiden's lingering warmth seeped into her skin, and after a moment, she stopped shaking.

With a solitary nod, she thanked him.

Seren could feel his eyes on her as she walked towards the exit. *This is not real,* she thought. *This is just a bad dream.*

"Seren?" he called after her. She turned. "You know that the punishment for identity theft is death, right? It would be in your best interest to avoid committing such crimes again."

There it was, the dreaded word: *death.* Was it a warning, or a threat? Seren examined Zaiden, looking for any trace of what he was thinking, but his body language revealed nothing. With nothing further to say, she exited the Simulator.

13

ZAIDEN

Zaiden watched Seren close the door with an odd sensation in his chest. He couldn't shake the feeling that she looked familiar, though their paths should never have crossed if she really was a Tier Four like she claimed. Curiously, he turned the identity card over in his hand. Alaster Holland. His father would be interested to learn that Alaster's card had been stolen. Alaster's carelessness might make Zaiden's father take his attention off Zaiden long enough for him to breathe.

Then again, maybe Zaiden shouldn't throw Alaster under scrutiny. He was, after all, innocent in this whole situation. It was Seren who'd broken the law.

Seren Quinn. The name played on repeat in Zaiden's mind. What had a Tier Four been doing in the Simulator? How had she even known of its existence? And what was so important that she'd risk her life to see it?

Unable to suppress his curiosity, Zaiden checked the most recent simulation run. The Simulator maintained a diligent memory of all past simulations, so long as they were not deleted. Few people knew how to delete simulations, so nearly every simulation run was saved somewhere in the backlog; you just had to know where to find it.

Luckily, Zaiden did.

He played around with the buttons for a moment until the projector buzzed to life. Seren's image appeared, depicting her in the center of the Simulator, her auburn hair glowing beneath the stars. Zaiden zoomed in. She had such wonder in her eyes. It was as if she had never seen the stars before.

Maybe she hadn't, Zaiden realized. He was one of the select few with access to the Simulator. What an odd concept, to live without it. The Simulator was where he'd spent his days growing up and his nights in adulthood; it's where he went to escape. He'd explored so many different places and seen so many different things within the Simulator's four black walls that he felt as if he'd lived on Earth.

"Can you make it feel more ... real?" the video playback of Seren asked.

Zaiden chuckled. That had been her error: not specifying what she meant. The Simulator was a beautiful creation, a technological masterpiece, but it had a mind of its own. A request like that would only lead to disaster. Seren had learned that the hard way.

Zaiden watched her demeanor change from amazed to terrified as the curling waters crashed harder against the platform. She fell into the roaring waves and struggled to stay afloat, until he came in and the simulation ended. That's where the memory stopped.

"Well, well, well, Seren. You certainly went through a lot of trouble just to see some stars," he murmured.

The screen flickered off, and Zaiden stepped away from the controller.

Stars wouldn't have been his first choice. Pictures could almost do them justice. But the experience of being in the ocean during a storm—that was something he'd never tried. He would have to give it a go. Carefully, of course, lest he almost drown like Seren.

Come to think of it, he had saved her life. Well, not *saved* her life so much… He'd only bought her some time. Once Alaster found out what she had done, he would demand her head on a plate, and his father wouldn't be opposed.

He could tell his father that he'd found Alaster's card somewhere, but that would ultimately lead to questions he couldn't answer. And what would be the purpose of that lie, anyhow? Why should he help Seren when she'd broken the law?

He would not lie, Zaiden decided. It was his father's job to administer justice, not his. Zaiden would turn Seren Quinn in and allow his father to make the decision. With that settled, Zaiden stepped into the center of the Simulator. The floor was dry now, all signs of Seren's simulation gone. That was the magic of the Simulator: it erased all secrets.

The lights turned off automatically, and Zaiden stood, consumed by the darkness.

"Hello, Mr. Warren." The voice that came over the speaker was smooth and familiar, like the smell of morning coffee. "Would you like your usual simulation?"

"Yes."

The ground beneath Zaiden's feet grew warm and coarse. His toes sank into the floor as sand formed. It grew warmer as the sun appeared in the sky and shined down on his olive skin. A light breeze blew through as the ocean formed to his left.

Finally, the simulation was fully formed. Zaiden stood on the beach near the Santa Monica Pier at sunrise. As always, the boardwalk was eerily empty. It lacked its usual hustle, and Zaiden preferred it that way. He would rather be alone than be surrounded by hundreds of simulated people.

This was a simulation that Zaiden had returned to hundreds of times before, but today, like always, it felt new. That was also the magic of the Simulator: it could create the same simulation in a multitude of ways. Each time Zaiden returned, the weather was a little different. Each time, the sky was a slightly different hue, the water a different temperament, and even the people themselves changed.

Zaiden kicked off his shoes and let his feet sink into the cool sand as the sun rose higher in the sky. People often forgot how magical the beginning of a day could be. He imagined that many people would come into the Simulator to watch sunsets if they had the opportunity, observing the day turning to night. Zaiden much preferred watching the birth of a new day. It held so much more excitement, so many promises. And besides, his mother had always preferred sunrises. This simulation had been her favorite. His father would mock her for choosing the same one time and time again, but she would just smile and say, "When you know, you know". Now Zaiden adopted the same habits. He refused to change the simulation he ran; it reminded him of her. It was the only thing he had that connected him with her memory. When he walked along the Santa Monica Pier as night turned to day, he could pretend that she was there, walking beside him, singing quietly to herself.

They used to go on the Ferris wheel when they would come here together. At sunrise, when the sky was a mixture of red and orange and the moon was still the brightest source of light in the sky, they would sit together in those tiny little cars and rise into the air. Zaiden could see the entire beach and beyond from up there. The simulation blurred in the distance (the Simulator had a difficult time with areas that were not commonly photographed during Earth's prime), but still, the view was glorious.

Zaiden had not been on the Ferris wheel since his mother's death. He didn't think he was ready for that. Today, as he had every day before, he stayed on the beach, walking along the lapping water and thinking of the happier times when he was not alone.

14

SEREN

Ma and Pa's door was closed when Seren got home, but she knew they were awake, waiting anxiously for her return. She could hear their whispering voices, but they did not come out of their room, and she was grateful; she couldn't face them tonight. Still, she made a little extra noise so they'd know she was home.

That night, Seren lay awake in bed for a long time. Her hair became stiff when it dried, and it felt crispy between her fingers. Her skin prickled from a thin layer of dried salt. She wished she could take a shower, but she would have to wait for the running water to turn back on in the morning.

Assuming she made it until morning.

As the excitement wore off, Seren realized just how stupid the whole thing had been. She'd taken an unnecessary risk. Not even a risk; she'd practically walked herself into a death trap. And of course, of all the people who could have caught her, it had to be Zaiden Warren. He'd turn her in tonight, and the Harmonizers would be at her door before the morning Awakening even began. She could picture Ma's horrified expression as they ripped her from the apartment. Ma's final memory of Seren would be their fight earlier and the last three words her daughter had spoken to her: "I hate you."

At least Seren wouldn't have to live with that guilt.

Hours later, the Harmonizers had not come, and Seren was finally tired enough to close her weary eyes and fall asleep.

. . .

Seven o'clock came too quickly. Seren woke in a cold sweat, her body weak from the nearly sleepless night. Her sleep had been tormented by nightmares. Seren dreamed of her mother, dead, with a crying baby in her arms. She dreamed of water pulling her down into its icy depths until her breathing stopped. She dreamed of her own execution. *"Will lethal injection suffice?"* Zaiden laughed as Seren struggled against the straps that held her down.

When she woke, the nightmare continued. Memories from the night before came flying back as the anthem played. Seren thought about the smug look on Zaiden's face as he'd taken the identity card from her. *"You know that the punishment for identity theft is death, right?"* His eyes had sparkled as he spoke, like he got joy from the idea of her body lying limp on the execution table.

Surely, Zaiden would have told his father immediately. What would that mean for Seren? How much time did she have before the Harmonizers came? The thought consumed her.

Seren brushed past Ma and Pa that morning as they watched the Awakening, not even able to offer up a hello. She felt utterly detached. She could feel Ma's gaze on her as Marcie spoke, but Seren couldn't bring herself to look her mother in the eyes. Not after what she'd done.

Without so much as a good morning or a goodbye, she left the apartment.

"When are we going to ask about last night?" Seren heard Pa say as she shut the door behind her. She didn't catch Ma's response.

Seren followed the familiar path to Lucas's apartment. Her heart slammed against her chest as she considered what she might say.

"Hey, guess what I did last night! I lost the identity card you gave me and put both of our lives in danger. No, I didn't lose it trying to save my mother's life. That part went swimmingly. I lost it after the fact, because I was upset. I'm going to get the death penalty—but you'll probably be fine."

Yeah, right.

She had been careless and impulsive, two things that she never thought she'd be. And what had it all been for? To fulfill some selfish desire to see the stars?

Was it worth it, Seren?

Marcie's image followed Seren as she walked through Community's halls, her shrill voice reverberating off every wall. No matter where she turned, the Governor's messaging followed her, reminding her what exactly she was up against. Seren couldn't find silence. Her anxiety heightened.

Seren finally made it to Lucas's apartment and stood petrified, staring at the door. Her hands felt clammy. *Turn around!* A voice in her head screamed. She didn't have to tell Lucas anything. She could just go about her day as if nothing had happened. Maybe she'd be arrested before she had to explain anything to him.

Seren wanted nothing more than to run away, but she couldn't bring herself to do it. Lucas was her best friend. The least she owed him was an honest explanation—especially after he had entrusted her with such a dangerous secret. And given the uncertainty of her future, the explanation couldn't wait.

Seren knocked twice. The door flew open before she could knock again. Lucas looked anxious; his eyes were ringed from lack of sleep. Seren's stomach clenched as he looked at her.

"Hey," she mumbled.

"Who is it?" Lucas's mother called from the kitchen.

"It's Seren, Mom," Lucas said. He ushered Seren in and shut the door behind them.

"Good morning, Seren!" Jean said with a wide smile. She was standing over a hot plate making something that smelled mildly unpleasant. Chalky oats. Seren's nose crinkled.

"Good morning, Edu Snyder," Seren said. She tried not to let on how anxious she felt.

Jean worked as a teacher and had taught Seren and Lucas together when they were Year Eights. Seren recalled that she'd thought Jean was strict as a teacher, but she'd always loved her as Lucas's mom. Jean was compassionate, brave, and polished, all of which she'd passed on to her son, who bore her resemblance so clearly.

When Henry died, it had only taken Jean a week to get back to work. *"The children need me,"* she'd said to anyone who asked about her swift return. Seren always thought that Jean and Henry were perfect together—curious, educated, resourceful.

"Would you like anything to eat?" Jean asked. A formality, not a genuine offer; she only had enough to feed herself and Lucas.

"No, thank you," Seren said. "It smells good, though."

They all knew she was lying.

"Wanna go talk?" Lucas asked.

Seren nodded and followed him into his bedroom. Yesterday, it had been spotless, but now his room was in a state of disarray.

He's worried about the card, Seren realized. Guilt ate away at her.

Lucas closed the door behind them, and Seren heard Jean let out a *"humph"* of disapproval, but she didn't say anything to stop them.

Seren wished she would.

"How'd it go?" Lucas asked.

Seren's heart beat violently in her chest. "I stole the pill," she said.

Lucas's eyes widened. "Well, that's great, isn't it? Why don't you look happy?"

Seren shook her head. The words caught in her throat. She thought about Ma, the absolute disapproval in her eyes as Seren handed her the pill. She thought about the risks she'd taken and the people she'd hurt along the way—people like Lucas. She couldn't look him in the eye.

"I was too late," she managed to say.

Lucas took a seat on his bed, pulling Seren down with him. He grabbed her chin and forced their eyes to meet. "What happened?" he asked.

He cared about her *so much*; she could see it in his eyes. He cared so much that he'd risk his life.

And all she cared about was herself.

Seren's chest felt tight, like she'd swallowed water the wrong way, and now it crept through her torso, slowly suffocating her. She shrunk deeper into herself, feeling small and powerless. Finally, she met Lucas's gaze. "There's something I need to tell you," she whispered.

Lucas's eyebrows furrowed in concern. "What is it? Seren, anything that's wrong, you can tell me."

God, why was he being *so kind?* She couldn't take it.

"Please don't be mad," she whispered. Tears formed in her eyes. Lucas said nothing, just stared at her, waiting. Seren took a deep breath. "I lost it."

Lucas looked confused. "Lost what?"

"I ... I can't..." She couldn't say the words out loud. If *they* were listening, anything she said could get Lucas or Ma in trouble, too. Seren looked at him, urging him to be calm, urging him to forgive her.

An uncomfortable silence fell between them. The words sat for a moment, hanging in the air. For a second, it seemed like Lucas would forgive her—but then the realization dawned on his face, and his expression turned sour. Seren felt as though the temperature in the room had dropped thirty degrees. She shuddered.

After a few long seconds, he spoke, his voice a low growl. "You have no idea what you've done."

"Lucas..." She reached for him, but he stood, backing away from her.

"You need to go, Seren," he said.

"Lucas, please," Seren pleaded. "Please understand, I—"

"Leave!" he bellowed.

She shrunk back, tears springing to her eyes. She couldn't speak.

"What if something happens to me? What if..." ... *this is the last time we ever see each other,* Seren wanted to say, but she choked on the words.

"You'll be fine," Lucas responded coolly, and he stormed out of his own room, slamming the door in her face.

15

ZAIDEN

Zaiden allowed the moonshine to cloud his mind. It burned on the way down and sat like a rock in his stomach. His glass, which at the beginning of the night had been full, had now dwindled down to its final drops.

"You, my friend, need a refill," Zaiden's classmate and lifelong friend Rocco pronounced, throwing his arm around Zaiden's neck. Zaiden didn't argue. He allowed Rocco to pour more of the clear, potent liquid into his cup.

"Hey, comrade, why the long face?" asked Atlas, another of Zaiden's friends. "This is a *celebration*! We finished our education, and we finally have our freedom!"

Zaiden thought "freedom" was the wrong word. He'd had his entire life planned out for him since birth. Where was the freedom in that?

Atlas grabbed Zaiden's shoulder and shook. "Whatever self-pity ride you're on tonight, it's time to hop off. I'm sick of the negativity."

Rocco nodded. "You may be the future leader of our free world, but tonight, your job is to drink until your mind goes black."

Neither Rocco nor Atlas seemed to have trouble with this notion of forgetting. They certainly didn't seem worried about the prospect of choosing their futures. Both had ranked highly in their class—not that it mattered. As sons of powerful government officials, they could get any job they wanted.

For once, though, it wasn't Zaiden's future that was on his mind. He couldn't stop thinking about the girl from the Simulator. He'd never experienced this level of guilt before, as if he carried the burden of her inevitable death.

His father hadn't been surprised by her crime. A warning signal had gone off when Seren, acting as Alaster, had entered Tier Two before sneaking into Tier One. He'd been alerted immediately. However, Governor Warren had been interested to learn that she'd gone all the way to Tier One and used the Simulator. He insisted that Zaiden show him the footage, which Zaiden had—though part of him had wanted to keep that piece of her to himself.

"What will happen to her?" Zaiden asked after the recording ended.

Zaiden's father shrugged. "The law is the law."

Zaiden knew that. So, why did it seem so hard to swallow?

He knew what his father would say: *"Reject the notion that you are to blame for her actions. You are not responsible for the lawbreakers; you are simply in charge of ensuring that they see the proper repercussions for their errors."*

His father was right. Zaiden had played no part in Seren's actions. She had known the consequences, and she had to pay for her mistakes. Otherwise, how could other members of Community be expected to do the same?

Zaiden continued to tell himself this as he pulled himself back into the moment with his friends.

"Kaiya is staring at you, comrade," Atlas said with a suggestive grin.

Zaiden looked over his shoulder to find that Atlas was right: his classmate Kaiya and her friends Haven and Faye were looking at him. When he met her eyes, she turned to her friends and giggled.

Zaiden shrugged. "Been there, done that."

"I think we all have," Atlas chimed in. Rocco slapped him upside the head.

"I don't know about you two, but I think this party could use a little revival," Rocco said with a mischievous grin.

"I already don't like where this is going." Atlas laughed as Rocco stepped up onto the bar.

"What're you doing? Get down from there!" Zaiden said.

Rocco grinned and pretended not to have heard. "May I have everyone's attention please? Quiet down, everyone."

The sound diminished as Zaiden's classmates turned to face Rocco, their curiosity piqued.

"Friends, acquaintances, and nemeses, congratulations! After eleven grueling years, we have managed to complete our education without killing ourselves or anyone else."

There were a few scattered laughs. Rocco took that in stride.

"We are in the midst of the future of Community—a future that will be bright and prosperous for all, thanks to my personal friend Zaiden Warren, our next Governor," he said, his voice becoming more boisterous by the second.

There were a few whoops. Zaiden caught Kaiya's eyes. She blushed.

"Tonight, we celebrate our success and the future, no matter how bleak some of our futures may be. Cheers!"

Once again, laughter filled the room, followed by a thunderous round of applause. There were a few cheers of "Hear, hear!" and Rocco jumped down from the table.

"You're an idiot." Zaiden laughed. He'd finally begun to feel lighter. The moonshine was doing its job after all.

"I share your sentiment," Rocco said with a wink. "Now, if you'll excuse me, I'm going to go try my luck with your fan club."

He gave Zaiden one last slap on the back and sauntered over to Kaiya, his arms outstretched. Zaiden and Atlas watched as he pulled Haven and Faye into his arms.

"We're friends with an idiot," Atlas said.

"Yes, but he's *our* idiot." Zaiden took a swig of his drink. It burned.

The law is the law, he reminded himself.

He took swig after swig, and slowly his guilt subsided, until finally the moonshine took over.

His mind went black.

16

SEREN

They stopped her on the way home. Seren had barely made it halfway back to her apartment before a strong hand was on her arm, tugging at her. She didn't have to look to know it was a Harmonizer.

"Let's do this quietly," a voice murmured in her ear.

The halls were empty. Everyone had already gone to work for the day. Seren should have been on her way to school. Today was the day she was supposed to rank her trade choices. At least now she wouldn't have to.

"Governor Warren would like a word."

Seren snuck a glance at her captor. He was a burly fellow, with broad shoulders and an unkempt beard. He was not dressed in uniform. Rather, he wore gray, blending in with the Tier Fours. For the briefest moment, Seren considered running. But there was nowhere to go, and she did not have the energy.

The man gently pulled her along the way she'd gone the night before, bringing her to the stairwell that led to other Tiers. He looked both ways before swiping his card. The door beeped and lit up green, and he opened it, pulling her along with him.

As they climbed the stairs, Seren's mind went to Ma. When would they tell her? Before or after Seren's execution? Would she be made to watch?

Tier One looked like an entirely different world than it had the night before. It had lost its magic; the golden lights and magnificent sculptures seemed suddenly dull. It was as if overnight, the whole Tier had been covered in a gloomy gray haze. Even the beautiful fragrant smell, which had once been intoxicating, was now sickening.

After what felt like an eternity, they arrived. Seren had not come this way the night before, but it quickly became apparent that this was where Governor Warren worked. His full title, Governor Pluto Warren, was engraved on a shimmering golden plate mounted on the door. It should've been the most beautiful door Seren had ever seen, with its deep mahogany wood and intricate golden handles. But the door wasn't beautiful; it was utterly terrifying.

"We're here," the Harmonizer said, stating the obvious. "You can go on in."

"Alone?" Seren didn't know why, but that made her even more afraid—as if having a Harmonizer there with her would keep her safe.

"Yes." His expression was unreadable, but Seren thought she might've seen a hint of pity in his hardened eyes.

When the Harmonizers start to pity you, that's when you know you're screwed.

Seren stared at the double doors, the only barrier between her and her fate. She shifted, biding her time. This could be her last living moment, and she didn't want to rush it.

After a moment, the Harmonizer cleared his throat, and Seren knew she could not stall any longer. She took a deep breath and pushed.

The doors were heavy, as if meant to be a barrier to weed out the weak. The Harmonizer merely watched as Seren shoved her full body weight against them until they opened reluctantly with a soft moan. She stepped into the Governor's office, and the doors closed behind her.

Governor Warren's office was eerily orderly. Everything was stacked neatly in ninety-degree angles, from the books to the papers, all the way to the diagonally sliced sandwich sitting on his mahogany desk. On the far wall hung a Community flag with the Warren family crest proudly displayed: a gold-and-blue shield flanked by a ferocious-looking tiger and dragon. Behind the desk was a large simulated window displaying a series of skyscrapers, each taller than the last. In the back right corner was a statue of a large animal that Seren did not recognize, its wings outstretched.

This could be the last room I'm in before I die, Seren thought. With that thought, the orderly office turned sinister. She shivered.

Governor Warren stood behind his desk, looking out across his simulated city. "It's beautiful, isn't it? And yet, so tragic." He paused. "Just like you."

A painful silence ensued, and Seren struggled to remain standing as her trembling legs threatened to collapse. Finally, Governor Warren turned to face her.

"Miss Quinn," he said, his intense eyes meeting hers. "Welcome."

Governor Warren was more intimidating in person than he appeared in the Awakenings. He stood over six feet tall, towering above Seren, and his eyes were so dark that his pupils disappeared. Seren could see the resemblance between him and his son. Both were striking, but frightening.

"Please, have a seat." Governor Warren motioned to the chair in front of his desk. His lips pulled up into a tight smile as she sat. "You had yourself quite an adventure last night."

Seren watched in trepidation as Governor Warren lifted a remote from his desk and pointed it. The simulated city morphed, slowly becoming another image entirely. It took Seren a moment to recognize the Tier Two medical center, captured by what must have been a camera above. The image was sharp and clear. Just when she thought it must be a live feed, a perfect image of herself came on screen. She watched herself run past the front desk, unbeknownst to the young man working there. Panic flowed through her as the image on his screen morphed into the interior of the Pharmacy.

How had she not realized there were cameras? Seren's cheeks grew warm. She watched in horror as last night's events unfolded: her search for the medication, her climbing into the medicine cabinet, the moment she hid when the Pharmacist entered.

Seren averted her eyes, knowing all too well what would come next.

"Oh, no. Please, keep watching," Governor Warren said, beaming. "This is my favorite part."

Seren looked up just as the recording showed her bringing down the shelf on the Pharmacist's head. The man crumpled to the floor. Seren left the room—but the man did not get up.

Governor Warren clicked off the recording, and the simulated city returned.

"All of this to help your mother have an illegal abortion," Governor Warren said.

Seren's heart turned to ice. He knew everything.

Governor Warren set the remote down, and Seren sunk backwards into her chair, hugging herself tight. Why was he showing her all of this? *What's the point?*

"He's fine, by the way," Governor Warren said. Relief flooded through Seren, but it didn't last long. His eyes found her again. "I assume that you understand the consequences for your actions?"

"Yes," Seren said. Her voice came out as barely a whisper.

Governor Warren smiled—an expression that failed to reach his eyes. "The thing about laws," he said, "is that they rely on certain things to maintain order. They keep our Community running. They keep our people happy and healthy." He paused. "Have you ever heard of the deterrence theory?"

Seren shook her head.

"The deterrence theory says that people tend not to act in unfavorable ways, based on the perceived risks and the fear of punishment. In layman's terms, people are less likely to commit crimes if they think there will be a punishment. The greater the severity and certainty of that punishment, the less crime." Governor Warren tilted his head ever so slightly. "Do you understand?"

She nodded wordlessly.

"The deterrence theory relies on three things. Can you guess what those three things are?" Seren shook her head, and the Governor appeared mildly annoyed. "Please, Seren, I thought you were smart. Give it a go."

"I … I don't know," she said.

Governor Warren clicked his tongue in disapproval. "It's quite simple. The deterrence theory relies on the rationality of individuals." He held up a pencil and pointed it at his head. "It also relies on these individuals fearing the negative consequences of their actions. Finally, it depends on the enforcement of the laws."

The Governor walked around the desk slowly and deliberately. With each step he took closer to Seren, she felt smaller and smaller, until she was barely an ant beneath his feet. Governor Warren leaned in close—close enough that Seren could feel his breath—

and whispered, "Do you understand why I'm telling you this, Miss Quinn?"

Seren shook her head.

"People in Community know that if they commit a crime, they will be caught. They fear the consequences of their actions. Community *relies* on this theory for its very livelihood. The deterrence theory, Miss Quinn, *matters.*" He leaned away and examined her carefully, his eyes tracing the outlines of her face.

Seren held her breath.

"With that in mind, we must make some assumptions. Either you are irrational, which I don't believe you to be, or you do not fear death, which I also do not think is true, or..." He leaned down and put his mouth close to her ear. "You didn't think you'd get caught."

He pulled away, and Seren shuddered.

The Governor walked back around to the other side of his desk. "But you *were* caught—and now you sit here across from me, your life in my hands." He sighed, almost gleefully. "It's a terrifying feeling, the uncertainty of what's to come. You must be wondering what I'm thinking now. Is that correct, Miss Quinn?"

Bile made its way up into her throat. Every bone in her body screamed at her to run.

But there was nowhere to go.

"I'm thinking," Governor Warren continued unprompted, "that you do not want your life to culminate in this way. After all, there was no harm done. Your mother did not take the pill. You didn't break any Simulator laws. The Pharmacist you maimed is in good enough health, barring a slight concussion, but he'll be perfectly fine."

Seren felt a wave of guilt.

"I'm also thinking that if I began allowing criminals to walk away, punishment-free, then the deterrence theory would no longer benefit Community, as people would no longer fear punishment. Do you know what that could do to such a delicate ecosystem? For the safety of my people and the integrity of what my ancestors have built, I cannot have that."

Seren watched as Governor Warren picked up a pen and twisted it in his hands, the same way he was twisting her life around in his calloused fingers.

"With all of that in mind, I have a proposition for you."

"What kind of proposition?" Seren asked, her voice trembling.

Governor Warren smiled. "I believe it to be an equitable one. We both have something the other wants, Miss Quinn. You want your mother to stay alive … and I want a friend."

Seren wasn't sure she'd heard him correctly. "A *friend?*"

"I have your school records right here," Governor Warren said, lifting a report from the top of one of his meticulous piles. "And last night, I read your Thinker application. You're smart. At the top of your class in almost all groups, apart from physical fitness." He looked up briefly. "Which anyone could see. I had no intention of bringing on a new Thinker, especially not a Tier Four … but I could certainly find a space for you in Tier Two."

He paused.

Seren didn't know what to say. She'd come in expecting him to kill her on the spot, and now he wanted to bring her on as a Thinker? Her head spun.

Governor Warren must have taken her silence as an invitation for him to continue. "There is, of course, a bit more to it. I have reason to believe that there are people that run in my circles who are helping to plan a rebellion." He stared at Seren for a long moment, as if searching her face for a sign of recognition.

She didn't know what to say. Seren didn't know anyone who wanted to see the Warrens fall—not even Lucas, who found them insufferable.

"These rebels want to see an end to Community. They want us all dead."

Seren let out an involuntary gasp, and Governor Warren nodded in solidarity.

"I want this rebellion squashed. I believe you're just the person to help me do that."

"But why would anyone tell *me* anything?"

Governor Warren chuckled, but there was little humor behind the sound. "I do not *expect* them to tell you anything, Miss Quinn. I expect you to employ the cunning and deceitful nature that you displayed last night to gather information for me. You're in a unique position, being a Tier Four. Rebels are more likely to trust you, and to try to bring you in."

He looked at her meaningfully, a tight-lipped smile on his otherwise stiff face. "If you do a good job, I will allow you to keep your life. I will also spare your mother's life when her child is born. If you do not, then things return to the way they were before we had this conversation. So, do we have a deal?"

Seren bit her nails—a nervous habit she thought she'd gotten rid of years ago. She didn't know *why* she could possibly be hesitating. It would solve all her problems. And saving Community from bloodthirsty rebels was a noble cause, right?

Governor Warren watched her, unsmiling. "I will extend this offer to you only once. You leave this office tonight as a spy, or you leave in handcuffs, with your execution date set. The choice is yours."

For how long? Seren wondered. How long would she be a pawn, living a deceitful life to help Governor Warren weed out his enemies? A few weeks? A few months? Years? The rest of her life? Was her future to be decided now, this early on?

She took a deep breath. There was really only one thing she could say.

"I'll do it."

Governor Warren clapped his hands together and stood from his desk. "Oh, good. I expect you'll be convincing tomorrow when you're offered the role of Thinker. From there, it is in your hands. I will see you very, very soon."

Seren stood, ready to be the hell out of this room, but Governor Warren stopped her. "Miss Quinn?"

"Yes?"

"Best not to tell anyone about this little agreement of ours, or their head will be on the chopping block, too."

17

SEREN

The next morning, a note appeared on Seren's front door:

Dear Mr. and Mrs. Quinn,

On behalf of Governor Pluto Warren, I am pleased to inform you that your daughter, Seren Quinn, has been selected as a Thinker in Think Tank Six located in Tier Two. Seren was selected from an extraordinarily accomplished and academically talented group of individuals.

As a Thinker, Seren will have unparalleled opportunities to shape the future of Community. This acceptance comes with the stipulation that Seren be moved to Tier Two within the next twenty-four hours. Harmonizers will be arriving to escort her there later this afternoon. Enclosed, please find her new identity card.

Again, congratulations to you both, and to your daughter.

Kind Regards,
Alaster Holland

Ma and Pa cried with joy when they read it. Seren, too, found her eyes wet with tears—but for an entirely different reason.

"We were so worried," Ma said, pulling Seren into a tight lung-crushing hug. When she finally released her, Seren pulled the sapphire identity card from the envelope and flipped it over a few times. It had a photo of her smiling on it, her auburn hair pulled neatly back in a ponytail. The photo was an old one; Seren couldn't even remember when it was taken. She looked young in the picture.

"I didn't even know you applied!" Pa said. "Why didn't you say anything?"

"I didn't think I would be accepted," Seren mumbled. At least that wasn't a lie.

"We are so proud of you, chickpea," Ma said, pulling Seren tightly into her chest. "I'm going to bring out the Creation Day cake. It may be a bit stale, but I think a celebration is in order, don't you?"

Seren nodded vaguely, trying to appear excited. It had always been her dream to be a Thinker—but not like this.

Ma clapped her hands. "I think I'll invite Lucas and Jean over for the cake. They'll want to celebrate, too. Jean will be thrilled, being your Edu and all."

Lucas. Seren's heart clenched. She hadn't even thought about him. If Governor Warren knew everything ... did he know the role Lucas had played? Would Lucas's sentencing be next? She couldn't live with herself if she got Lucas killed.

No, Governor Warren would have mentioned it. He would have loved an opportunity to exploit her further. He must not have known.

Still, Seren didn't want to face Lucas just yet. He was still mad at her, and rightfully so, and he would know something was up as soon as he heard the news. A Tier Four hadn't been chosen as a Thinker in thirty years; he'd told her so himself. Ma and Pa might not have been suspicious, but Lucas would be.

"I don't know, Ma," Seren said. "I'm sure they have things to do."

But Seren's protests fell on deaf ears. Ma had already made up her mind. "Nonsense. I haven't seen either of them in months. I'll go to their place after the Awakening."

And she did.

"Jean couldn't come," Ma said brightly when she returned. "She had to go to class early. But look who I brought!"

Seren was shocked to see Lucas had agreed to come.

"Hi, Mr. Quinn," he said with his lips drawn into a tight smile. He avoided Seren's gaze as he sat down across from her and silently rested his hands on the table.

"Hi, Lucas," Pa said. "So wonderful to see you! It's been too long."

"Yeah, I've been busy. Trade Day and all," Lucas said.

"Lots of choices to make," Pa said.

Seren bit her tongue.

Ma, oblivious to the palpable tension, hummed as she placed thick pieces of cake in front of the three of them, along with forks. Seren picked up her fork and poked the cake once, feeling nausea rise in her stomach. Pa dug in immediately.

"Cake?" Lucas asked. "Are we celebrating?"

"I didn't tell him yet," Ma said, an excited glimmer in her eyes. "I thought maybe you'd want to."

"Oh," Seren said uncomfortably. "I, uh… I got my trade placement."

Lucas's eyes finally met hers, and his brows furrowed. "What? How? We haven't gotten our ranks yet."

Pa and Ma smiled at each other, practically beaming. Seren's throat grew tighter. She turned her acceptance letter towards Lucas, unable to say the words. If she spoke, she might cry—and she really did not want to cry.

Lucas skimmed the document quickly. As he read, his face tightened, and when he finished reading, he slammed the paper down on the table with such force that Seren's fork clattered to the floor. Ma jumped back in surprise, but Lucas either didn't notice or didn't care. For the first time in days, his focus was entirely on Seren.

"You can't work for them," Lucas growled, his voice low. "I won't let you."

Seren looked down at her plate. "It's not your choice," she said quietly.

"Do you seriously expect me to believe that you want to be a Tier Two? That you want to leave your family?"

"I can visit."

"Really?" Lucas asked incredulously. His voice amplified. "Because I don't think I've ever seen a Tier Two walking the Tier Four halls—unless it's a Harmonizer coming to kill somebody."

Ma gasped. Lucas's face turned beet red, and he looked at Ma apologetically before lowering his voice to a whisper so quiet that not even Ma or Pa could hear. "Seren, if you're in trouble—"

"So what if I am? You didn't seem to care that much yesterday," Seren snapped.

That shut him up momentarily. The room went silent. Seren could feel her parents looking at her, but she avoided their gaze. Lucas scoffed and pushed away from the table. "Fine. You do whatever makes you happy. Best of luck to you," he said. "I'm absolutely *thrilled* for you. Tier Two is lucky to have you."

There was an unfamiliar fire in his eyes, and it scared Seren. She'd never seen this side of him.

Lucas stood. He didn't look at her as he passed her on his way out. "Thank you for the cake, Mrs. Quinn," he said, though he hadn't even taken a bite. He slammed the door behind him.

After a moment of painful silence, Ma spoke. "You want to tell me what that was about?"

Seren's eyes filled with tears, which she blinked away. "No."

Seren could see the innumerable questions hanging on the corner of her parents' lips, but neither of them pushed.

"I'm going to go pack," Seren mumbled, and she left her parents sitting in their kitchen, looking just as lost and confused as she felt.

. . .

They came for her a few hours later.

Her goodbye with Ma was tearful. Seren could see Pa trying to keep his face blank, but tears formed at the corners of his eyes as Seren hugged him goodbye.

Seren felt odd, being ripped from the place she'd grown up. She knew what Governor Pluto was trying to do; he wanted her to be uncomfortable, to have nothing familiar to depend on. He wanted her to rely solely on him.

Seren wouldn't let that happen.

Her new home was situated amidst the rest of the Tier Two apartments, just one door amongst hundreds of others. The Harmonizers led her to the middle, room 115, and indicated that Seren should use her new identity card to unlock the door. She did.

"Thanks," she mumbled as they turned to go. They gave her one final nod before leaving her alone.

With a sigh, Seren pushed open the door to her new apartment. She was immediately struck by its beauty. The lights in the high ceilings glittered like gems, and the room smelled rich and buttery, like warm vanilla. The place was homey—but to Seren, it felt nothing like home.

Exhausted, Seren lay down on the luxurious plush carpets and ran her skin across them. In Tier Four, the apartment floors were made of painted cement. Compared to that, this floor felt like a bed. She closed her eyes and tried to breathe, in for three, out for three, until her body felt lighter. Once she'd calmed down enough, she explored the rest of the apartment.

There was a bedroom, a bathroom with a large tub (Seren had never seen a bathtub before), a small kitchen, and a living room with a love seat and a cushioned chair.

Is this all for me? She wondered, tracing the chair's big round buttons.

Though she was still anxious, her exploration continued with increased vigor. She tore open cabinets, looked beneath the couch and chair, and peeked into her closet. As she closed the doors, her eyes landed on a large black box sitting atop her bed. Next to the box was a white envelope sealed with wax and stamped with the Warren family crest. Seren looked at it cautiously before tearing it open.

Miss Quinn,
You are cordially invited to
Zaiden Warren's inauguration gala,
An evening of cocktails, music, dinner, and dancing,
Hosted by
The Warren Family
Friday, October 13th
From 8:00 p.m. until midnight
The Governor's Hall

At the bottom of the invitation was a handwritten note from Governor Warren. *This will be your perfect coming-out party*, it said. *P.S. I hope you like the dress.*

Seren opened the box on her bed and let out a small gasp. Inside, perfectly folded, was an awe-inspiring golden dress. She lifted it from the box and held it up to the light. It shimmered seductively.

He can't seriously think I'll accept this, Seren thought, staring at it.

Seren had never worn anything this luxurious in her life. Hell, she'd never even worn a *color* before, just neutral tones: cream, gray, white. The idea of putting something like this on was enticing, sure —but not if Governor Warren had chosen it.

Seren placed the dress back into the box and stared at herself in the mirror. She tried picturing herself draped in gold, but she couldn't get past her appearance. The last few days had taken their toll. Dark purple bags rested under her eyes, her forehead was oily, and her hair was a ratty mess (come to think of it, she hadn't run a comb through it in days). She desperately needed to wash off.

With a sigh, Seren stripped off her clothes and went into the bathroom. It took her a moment to figure out how the bath worked, but once she got it, she watched as the tub filled with steaming hot water. The spout continued to spurt out water long after the usual five-minute limit was up. Once it was filled, she climbed in. The water surrounded her like a warm blanket as she submerged herself beneath the surface. It was only her second time being fully submerged in water, and this time was far more pleasurable than the last, to say the least. Seren shut her eyes and allowed her body to relax.

Once the allure of being submerged had worn off, she took her time rubbing the bar of soap over her skin, watching the little suds form and dissolve. Next, she went to work on her hair, untangling it strand by strand.

Eventually, the water became cold, and Seren stepped out of the tub and wrapped a towel around herself. She returned to the dress and stared at it a moment longer, weighing her options.

When it came to attending the ball, she didn't have much of a choice in the matter; Governor Warren had made that clear. But if putting on a beautiful dress and parading through a ballroom was what she had to do to save Ma's life, maybe things wouldn't be so bad.

Seren looked back down at the dress, running the silky golden fabric through her fingers.

Well, she thought, *here goes nothing.*

18

SEREN

The Governor's Hall was breathtaking, a spectacle beyond belief. Massive crystal chandeliers hung from the ceiling, throwing dazzling lights around like streams of water. Every time their crystal teardrops moved, a multicolored beam was cast upon the golden walls. Seren found herself unable to move as she took it all in.

The women in the room were just as beautiful as the room itself, all of them dressed lavishly in brightly colored gowns that flowed gracefully to the tiled floor. Some wore dresses exposing their collarbones, while others wore more modest pieces. The women here were better fed than Seren was used to, and it showed in their sturdy midsections and round faces. Every inch of them was stunning.

The men were dressed less uniquely, in nearly identical suits with colorful ties or bow ties around their necks. They spoke to each other in booming voices, glasses of dark liquid in their meaty hands. The reverberating buzz of small talk filled the entire space like a chorus of voices humming an unfamiliar melody. It was extraordinary, regal, and extravagant—and Seren hated every moment of it.

Her stomach churned as she walked through the ballroom. She tried to appear inconspicuous, but this proved nearly impossible. Whispers followed her everywhere she went. Everyone here knew that she did not belong.

"Seren Quinn."

Seren turned to find a man in an emerald suit approaching her with a wide smile. His bright white hair stood out against his darkened skin, though he looked too young for his hair to have turned that color naturally. She realized that that was yet another thing the upper Tiers had that the lower Tiers did not: a way to alter their appearance. It seemed the women did, at least, for many of them had their lips painted an unusual color. Seren saw deep red, purple, and bright pink.

"You look absolutely stunning tonight, my dear," the man said, running his eyes over Seren's dress. He took her hand and spun her around, and the golden dress expanded. She stumbled out of the spin and barely caught herself from falling into a nearby couple.

"I'm sorry, who are you?" Seren asked as politely as she could manage.

The man clutched his chest. "I've forgotten my manners. Geoff Dickson. I am the man who designed your glorious dress."

Seren smiled, unsure of what an appropriate response would be. "Oh. Uh, it's nice to meet you. The dress is lovely."

"The pleasure is all mine. When Governor Warren came to me with this last-minute request, I must admit I was a touch anxious, but you look ravishing." Geoff leaned in, his eyes twinkling. "You're a Tier Four by birth, right? I must ask, how did you end up here?"

"I was moved here to become a Thinker," Seren said.

"Spare me the lies, darling," Geoff said with a grin. He lowered his voice. "I heard you were having an affair with a council member."

Seren nearly choked. *"What?!"*

Geoff laughed. "Kidding! You are precious. I adore you already. I look forward to seeing who you *do* have an affair with, once you're old enough."

"That's not ... I'm not..." Seren stammered.

Geoff gave her a knowing look and winked. "I'm sure I'll be seeing you again soon, Miss Quinn."

And in the same whirlwind in which he had arrived, Geoff left.

Seren rubbed her temples. *Dear Warren...* If everyone here gossiped like that, getting information out of them should be no problem. She went to put as much space between her and the designer as possible when she nearly toppled over a short metal machine.

"Drink, miss?" an automated voice from within it asked.

Seren's mouth fell open as she took in the strange contraption. Built like a plate of drinks on wheels, it sat just above her waist and held thick, short glasses with filled with a dark golden liquid. It was made of a dark metal, and it seemed to buzz continuously, making the glasses quiver along with it.

"Drink, miss?" it repeated.

"Uh, yeah. Thanks." Seren reached down tentatively to grab one and placed it to her lips. Before she could take a sip, a whiff of the liquid hit her nose like a boxing glove. It had a pungent, nauseating smell that resembled the Tier Four hallways after they'd been sanitized. She gagged and reflexively placed the glass back on the machine, and it buzzed away to offer the revolting liquid to someone else.

"Remarkable, isn't it?" a voice asked from behind her.

She spun to find the unfamiliar voice accompanied by an all too familiar face. The man looked older than he did in his photo; his face had rounded out, and his hair had grayed, but he had the same dark brown, crescent-shaped eyes.

"Mr. Holland," Seren breathed.

"Alaster," he said, offering her a hand. Seren stared at it, then at him, and took it in her own. His hands were soft and warm to the touch. She felt suddenly self-conscious about the roughness of her own.

Alaster turned his gaze to the machine, which was now positioned in the middle of a large group of women, spinning around in circles. The women all laughed maniacally as they each picked up another drink and placed their empties on the machine.

"They've always creeped me out," Alaster said.

"The women, or the wheels?" Seren asked.

He chuckled, which surprised Seren; she hadn't meant it as a joke. "Both, I suppose," he said with a grin. "You didn't like your drink?"

Seren blushed. He must have seen her put the glass back down. "No. I … I didn't try it. It smelled like cleaning solution."

Alaster smiled knowingly. "Ah, yes, you're right there. And it tastes just as bad. But it does plenty to ease the mind." As if to prove his point, he took a sip from his own glass. He grimaced as the liquid made its way down his throat.

"Did you enjoy your trip to the Simulator at my expense?" he asked. His expression was unreadable. Seren flinched.

"I'm so sorry—"

Alaster held up a hand to stop her. "Don't apologize. Everyone in Community should get a chance to explore the wonders of Earth. There are marvels to be seen—marvels beyond belief. There's no harm in a little curiosity." He tilted his head ever so slightly. "Governor Warren and I tend to disagree on that."

There was no judgement in his tone, but his eyes seemed to glow at this statement. Was this a test? Was she meant to press him on this, or tell Governor Warren that Alaster disagreed with him? How minute of details did Governor Warren want?

"And how could you not take advantage of the opportunity you'd been presented?" Alaster went on before Seren had a chance to contemplate this further. "It's not every day you get to explore Tier One privileges—though they aren't always as glamorous as they seem."

"They seem pretty glamorous to me," Seren said.

As if on cue, someone rolled a table full of colorful fruits, vegetables, breads, and potatoes through the doors from the kitchen. There was more variety on that one table than Seren had eaten in the last year.

Alaster smiled. "Beauty and extravagance mask reality," he said in a voice barely above a whisper. He leaned in closer and lowered himself further. Seren had to strain to hear him. "Ignorance is dangerous, Seren. I'd advise you to fight against it."

Seren wasn't sure how to reply.

Before she could think on it further, though, Alaster pulled away and finished his drink in one long, impressive sip. Seren stared. *It does plenty to ease the mind,* "he had said. What was it Alaster Holland wanted to ease?

He handed her the empty glass with a smile. "Now it'll look as though you're at least *trying* to have fun," he said. Seren held the glass awkwardly as Alaster straightened his tie. "If you'll excuse me, I'd better go find the Governor. It was wonderful to meet you, Seren."

Alaster walked away with a bit of a sway in his step. As he disappeared amongst the bustling crowd, Seren's mind raced. *"Ignorance is dangerous. I'd advise you to fight against it."*

What in the hell did that mean?

Hoping it would provide her some solace, Seren searched the crowd for familiar faces. In the far right corner, she saw Marcie McIntosh, the face of the Awakening and the Evening Broadcast, surrounded by a group of men. When Marcie spoke, her dark, full lips stretched wide into a smile. Seren stared at her. She was just as beautiful, if not more so, than she was on screen. She was taller than Seren had envisioned; she towered over almost all of the men in her circle.

Just a few feet away from Marcie stood the lanky Harmonizer who had accompanied Seren to the Governor's office. He stared into his drink, nodding as a woman spoke to him. The Harmonizer appeared less frightening now, dressed in a suit meant for someone a few inches taller than him. The pants draped all the way onto the floor, covering his shoes, and he'd had to roll up the sleeves of his black jacket. He looked like a child playing dress-up in the ensemble. It humanized him.

Seren continued to scan the crowd. She didn't want to admit it to herself, but she was looking for Zaiden. Why? She wasn't sure. It wasn't as if she'd planned on confronting him at his inaugural gala. What would she say? *"Surprise! Not dead, try as you might to ensure I would be"?* Unlikely.

The weird thing was, he'd saved her from drowning. She wasn't sure why he'd bothered when he had just turned her in anyway. Maybe it saved his conscience in some screwed-up way. Or maybe he hadn't meant to save her at all. Though Seren supposed it didn't matter that he'd turned her in; Governor Warren would have found out about her crimes anyway. He seemed to know every little move she'd made that night. *They* weren't just listening; *they* were watching, too. She had been naive to believe that the cameras were off just because they weren't lit up.

A voice from behind her pulled her from her thoughts.

"Miss Quinn."

Oh, no.

Seren turned slowly, plastering a tight smile onto her face. Governor Warren opened his arms wide in a diplomatic gesture, like the one he'd used on the Awakening, and placed one around Seren's shoulder. "There's someone I'd like you to meet," he said with a charming smile. Beside him stood Alaster Holland, a new drink in his hand. "Alaster Holland, this is Seren Quinn."

"So, you're the young lady who stole my card," Alaster said.

Seren tried to keep the confusion from her face. Was Alaster's mind so "eased" that he'd already forgotten their interaction just moments before?

"Guilty," she said. She meant it to sound humorous; it came out more like a croak.

Governor Pluto moved his hand from Seren's shoulder to midway down her back. She quailed. "Gotta keep our eyes on this one," he joked. "She's got a mind of her own."

There was an unspoken threat behind his words. Seren shrunk further.

"I'm sure she does," Alaster said politely. Then, with more seriousness, "Governor, I believe the Cottos want to speak with you. Would you mind if we—"

"Ah, the Cottos. Of course." The Governor removed his hand from Seren's back, but not before giving her a quick pat on the shoulder. "Keep mingling, yes? And you look lovely in the dress."

The two walked away, and Seren let out a breath she hadn't realized she'd been holding. There was something about the Governor's presence that sucked the confidence right out of her. She hated every moment of their interactions, and it pained her to know that there would be plenty more to come.

I've seen Governor Warren, Seren thought bitterly. *Can I leave now?*

She stood for a moment longer before navigating her way to the food table. If she was going to suffer through this event, she should at least try the food. Seren's eyes scanned the produce, much of it unfamiliar to her, and settled on a piece of sliced green fruit.

Raising it to her lips uncertainly, she took a bite. The texture threw her off; it was mushy, and the seeds were sturdier than she thought they'd be based on their size. She didn't like it much. Next, she tried a piece of bread with dried fruit baked into it. It was still warm. The bread seemed to dissolve in her mouth. Seren savored its sweetness. She had another piece.

The ballroom buzzed on. Seren enjoyed the food, standing at the table and gorging herself until she felt nauseous. It was a new feeling for her; she'd never in her life had enough food to feel truly full. As she stood in discomfort, she decided that she didn't enjoy the feeling. It brought a wave of exhaustion over her. She craved her bed. Not the new bed—her old bed, with all its lumps and rough sheets and awkwardly shaped pillows. She wished that she was home now, not at some ridiculous gala with a group of people she'd never had a desire to meet in the first place.

Seren stood at the table for a moment longer before she decided she'd stayed long enough.

Maybe she should have been eavesdropping or spying or whatever it was Governor Warren wanted her to do, but she'd had a long day, and it was nearly 11:00 p.m. She could begin her deceitful behavior tomorrow. Tonight, she wanted to cozy up in the warmth of her covers and sleep. Maybe in a dream state, she could forget how dreadful the last forty-eight hours had been.

Seren walked to the entrance of the ballroom, dress in tow. People parted as she stepped through them. Once again, their eyes followed her. She sighed. How could Governor Warren expect her to get any information from these people if they viewed her as a complete outsider?

Seren was nearly to the door when her exit was interrupted by a familiar face.

"Zaiden," she breathed.

He looked shocked to see her.

"Seren Quinn," he said, blinking. He looked at her as though he were looking at a ghost. He bounced back quickly, though, shaking his head once before saying, "You look nice."

"You do, too."

Zaiden's suit was deep black with a red tie—practically a replica of what his father had been wearing on the Awakening a few days prior. His wild hair was tamer tonight, pressed down into a neat style that suited him. Standing beneath the bright white light of the chandeliers, he looked like a spitting image of his father. It made Seren shiver.

"I'm surprised to see you," Zaiden said.

Seren knew what he really meant: *I'm surprised to see you alive.*

"I'm sure you didn't think you'd be seeing me ever again," she replied.

Zaiden raised an eyebrow, doubtless surprised by her directness. He probably wasn't used to being spoken to that way. "Well, I suppose I should apologize for telling my father about your little incident."

Seren smiled stiffly. "I'm still alive, so, no harm done."

"I admit that comes as a surprise as well." Zaiden placed his hands in the pockets of his dress pants. "My father isn't known for being merciful."

"I'm sorry to disappoint," Seren said flatly.

"You haven't," Zaiden said quickly. "If I'm being honest, I haven't stopped thinking about you."

"Guilty conscience?" Seren asked, her tone sharp.

Zaiden didn't answer.

She knew she shouldn't be so harsh; just because she was working for the Governor now didn't make her invincible. But she couldn't stop herself. She was angry. And she wanted to keep being angry, no matter how apologetic Zaiden's stupid face was right now.

A bout of laughter pierced the dance hall. Seren searched for the source, and her eyes landed on Marcie McIntosh, who was laughing at what some tall, dark, handsome man had said, her hand resting flirtatiously on his arm.

"What're your thoughts on all this?" Zaiden asked, breaking her concentration.

Seren looked around the massive dance hall. What *did* she think about it all?

"It's overwhelming," she said finally.

"It is," Zaiden agreed. "But you get used to it."

I'm not sure I want to. Seren watched a woman throw her head so far back when she laughed that she feared it might snap right off.

Zaiden studied her quietly, and Seren felt self-conscious.

"You weren't planning on leaving, were you?" he asked, motioning to the door behind him.

"It's been a long day."

Zaiden shook his head. "Seren Quinn, I insist that you stay. It is, after all, my inauguration gala. I'd hate to see a guest leave so quickly; it reflects poorly on me. People may think I'm..." He leaned in and whispered, *"Lame."*

Seren resisted the urge to roll her eyes. "Fine, I'll stay a bit longer," she said. But she had no real intention of staying more than a moment. After Zaiden melted back into the crowd to shake hands and kiss babies, she'd leave.

Zaiden grinned. "Wonderful. Shall we?" He held out his hand to Seren.

She just stared at it. "What?"

He laughed. "Dance with me."

"I don't dance," Seren said quickly.

"It's not a request." Zaiden gave her his most charming smile.

Something about his total lack of self-awareness made her want to scream, and yet, his honesty was refreshing. Maybe it was the way he was unapologetically interacting with her now, after nearly having her killed, that made Seren feel respect for him. Okay, maybe not respect, but something close to it.

"Well?" Zaiden pressed.

Begrudgingly, Seren took his hand and allowed him to lead her into the center of the ballroom. Several pairs of curious eyes followed them, Geoff's included. She did her best to ignore them, though she could feel the blush spreading over her cheeks.

Zaiden placed her hands around his neck and rested his own on her lower back. The gesture felt new and bizarre to Seren, who had never danced in her life. She allowed Zaiden to lead her as they swayed, rather uncomfortably, to the low music.

"I don't mean to be rude," Zaiden said, "but how *is* it you're alive and at my inauguration ball?"

Seren couldn't help but laugh. "You don't have much of a filter, do you?"

"I've been told that I don't." Zaiden spun her around once, as Geoff had, and Seren managed to maintain her balance as she found her way back into his grasp.

"Your father saw my Thinker application," she said, thinking fast. "He decided to accept it after the incident. He said he admired the way I..." She hesitated, searching for the appropriate word. "... *bent* his rules."

Now it was Zaiden's turn to laugh. "My father never fails to surprise me."

The look in his eyes was her undoing. No one had ever looked at her like that. Seren felt her anger melting away.

"I guess I'm just relieved that you came out of this all unscathed," he said.

They swayed to the music for a bit longer, and Seren made a point of avoiding Zaiden's gaze. Already he'd softened her, and she couldn't afford to be softened any further. She didn't want any of this. She didn't want to be here amongst the higher Tiers, or dancing with the son of the Governor. It was all wrong. What would Lucas say if he could see her now?

"I shouldn't have told my father," Zaiden said finally, breaking the uncomfortable silence.

Seren wasn't sure what to say to that.

When the song ended, Seren awkwardly cleared her throat and removed her hands from around Zaiden's neck. They stood uncomfortably as the next song began.

Zaiden looked at her for a long moment. "You're not having a good time," he said.

Seren considered lying, but couldn't bring herself to. "No, I'm not."

"Me neither," he said. "Want to get out of here?"

He saw her hesitation.

"Oh, come on, Seren Quinn. I saved you from drowning. The least you can do is accompany me on a little field trip."

Seren bit her lip to keep from pointing out that he had only "saved" her until his father had the chance to kill her. She glanced around the room, considering this.

Despite her best efforts, Seren found herself intrigued by Zaiden Warren. From what she'd seen of him, he was adventurous, daring, and suave—three things she had never been. And besides, anything would be better than this stuffy gala.

"Fine. I'm in."

19

SEREN

"Am I allowed to be here?" Seren asked.

At first, she hadn't known where Zaiden was taking her. But as soon as they came upon the Simulator door, Seren was unenthused. Her last nearly fatal experience was still at the forefront of her mind, and she didn't feel ready to relive it.

"Not technically, no," Zaiden said. "But that didn't stop you before."

Seren opened her mouth to protest, but Zaiden stepped through the door before she could say anything. The light caught his movements, making him appear like an angel gliding through the dark space. Against her better judgement, she followed.

Seren looked around for remnants of her last time in the Simulator, but there was nothing—just the ever-expanding blank canvas waiting to be filled.

Seren flinched as the door shut behind her and the room went black. Panic crept in. What if this had all just been one big plot to get her alone? One big mind game that ended in her death.

"Zaiden?" she called uncertainly into the darkness.

"I'm right here."

A warm hand clasped her arm, and Seren jumped.

She didn't like the darkness; it frightened her. And Zaiden's touch didn't seem to soothe her fears. If anything, it put her more on edge, sending shivers down her arm.

The spotlight flickered on over their heads, and Zaiden let go of her as the Simulator spoke.

"Hello, Mr. Warren," the voice said. "Would you like your regular simulation?"

It was slight, but Seren thought she saw Zaiden stiffen. *What simulation is that?* She wondered. She watched him for a further response, but his stiffness was as gone as swiftly as it had come, replaced once again by his usual confident demeanor.

"I think you made a mistake in here the other day," he said to Seren, his voice soft. "Stars are beautiful, but they're nothing compared to everything else Earth has to offer."

A chill ran up Seren's spine. "What else does Earth have to offer?"

Zaiden grinned, like that was the exact question he was hoping for. "You'll see."

When he spoke again, his voice was strong. "Show me the Rainbow Mountains of Zhangye Danxia."

Seren did not recognize a single thing he'd said, and she waited in anticipation as the Simulator purred for a moment. Then, it burst into life. The floor ahead of her and Zaiden shifted, forming peaks and troughs and everything in between until the landscape dwarfed the two of them. Seren craned her neck as she looked up at the formations.

Mountains!

A rush of excitement burst through her. They were taller than she'd imagined they'd be. Seren watched, dumbfounded, as colors began to form on the peaks. They created perfect stripes, as if a giant had bent down and painted them with careful strokes. Shades of red, blue, and yellow formed, blending to create orange and green. The colors were accentuated by a magnificent waterfall that cascaded down the mountainside. Lastly, the Simulator formed a sun, which illuminated the mountains in a sea of fire. It was breathtaking.

Beauty…

Before this moment, Seren had not truly understood the meaning of the word. To her, beauty was Ma's laugh, Lucas's giraffe marks, the photos in the books she'd flipped through as a child. Those things were all still beautiful, but now her definition of beauty shifted as she took in the marvel before her.

"Wow," she breathed, unable to stop herself.

There was no breeze, but the sun beamed down through the scarce clouds and warmed Seren's skin.

"I know," Zaiden said.

Seren shook her head wordlessly. She couldn't believe people had let such a beautiful world die. *No,* she corrected herself. *They didn't just let it die; they killed it themselves—every one of them.*

I would've taken care of you, Seren thought as her eyes traced the peaks of the mountain. *I would have given you everything I had.*

Seren could have stood there amongst the rainbow mountains for days, but Zaiden seemed to have other ideas.

"Ready?" he challenged, a smile dangling on the corner of his lips.

"For what?" she asked. She didn't want to leave yet.

Luckily, Zaiden didn't want to, either. Refocusing his attention ahead, he said, "Simulator, show us Bagan, Myanmar."

Seren waited once again in anticipation as the colorful mountains in the distance turned to black before collapsing back to the floor as swiftly as they'd risen.

For a second, the air was still. Then the ground rose again, slowly creating curious shapes that pointed into the sky. Green forest formed as the shapes merged into chestnut-colored ruins fashioned like upside-down bells. Unlike the previous simulation, this one took place at dusk. A layer of fog blanketed the horizon, shielding the trees in a dreamy haze. As the simulation grew and shifted, large, colorful objects formed in midair, floating just beyond the clouds. They hung there, weightless. Seren had never seen something suspended in the air that way. They were *flying,* the way she sometimes did in her dreams.

"Those are hot air balloons," Zaiden explained. "An open flame pushes heated air into the balloon, causing it to fly."

"And those?" Seren asked, pointing to the strange buildings.

"Buddhist temples. They're thousands of years old."

Seren shook her head—amazed, impressed, all the above. "How do you know all this?"

Zaiden shrugged. "I spend a lot of time here."

Seren suspected there was more to it than that, but she didn't push.

"One last one," he said. "I saved the best for last. Simulator, show us the northern lights."

The Simulator buzzed back to life, and the scene ahead of them shimmered. The temples shifted downward, and the sun disappeared completely. Seren waited as the room became dark once more. As the moments passed, the floor beneath her feet became slippery. The temperature dropped, and Seren's senses became overwhelmed by a smell: smoky, like leather and driftwood.

Suddenly, a forest grew from nothingness, standing amidst the darkness like nothing more than shadows. In the black night, the cold seemed even more intense. She shivered.

"Take my coat," Zaiden said, removing the black jacket from around his broad shoulders and draping it over Seren. She froze, momentarily stunned by the gesture. *This is the second time Zaiden*

Warren has given me his coat, she realized with an uncomfortable twist in her stomach. She considered objecting, but the warmth from his jacket enveloped her, and her shivering slowed. Now more comfortable, Seren looked out into the vast expanse of snow-covered ice.

"This is beautiful," she breathed. Her breath hit the air in a puff of white smoke.

"Just wait."

She did. White snowflakes drifted from the sky, a sea of dark illuminated only by the stars, but nothing else happened. Seren tugged at the sleeves of the jacket and waited.

And then, without warning, the sky burst to life in a flurry of greens, pinks, and blues. The colors blurred upwards towards the stars before manifesting into shimmering lights that mystically swayed across the sky.

"Oh my Warren!" Seren whispered.

"They're called auroras," Zaiden nearly whispered, as if raising his voice would startle the lights away. "Some legends say that the lights are the visible spirits of unborn children, playing ball in the heavens."

Unborn children… Seren's mind flashed to Ma, lying in bed with a child in her arms.

Zaiden touched Seren's arm gently. "Well? Did I nail it?"

Seren could do nothing but nod.

Zaiden curled his arm around her waist and tugged her close. Her body seized up before she realized he was just trying to pull her to where she could get a better view. He pointed into the distance. "And look—we can still see your stars."

They could, indeed. The stars sparkled as a cool breeze blew by. Seren pulled Zaiden's jacket more tightly around her.

"Do you ever wish you could see this for real?" Seren asked, looking up at Zaiden. She felt heat rise to her cheeks as she realized how close they were.

Zaiden looked back at her quizzically. "Is this not real?"

His eyes held hers for an eternity. She could feel his warm breath on her skin, could smell the drinks on his breath. He dropped his hand from her waist. Her skin tingled where his hands had touched her.

Clouds rolled across the moon, and the air grew colder still. Seren fumbled to remove Zaiden's jacket from her shoulders and handed it back to him, allowing the cold to consume her once more. He took it from her slowly. She felt the wind drying her lips as Zaiden looked at her. His eyes were arresting.

"Why did you bring me here, Zaiden?"

His eyebrows furrowed. "You were bored."

Seren shook her head. "Why did you *really* bring me?" *Is it to gain my trust, Zaiden?* She wanted to ask. *Did your father tell you to keep an eye on me?*

Zaiden paused, and for a moment, it seemed like he might give her a serious answer—but then a goofy smile grew on his face. "I guess I just can't say no to a thrill."

His answer was unsatisfactory.

Seren looked back at the night sky. She'd always known that Earth would be beautiful, but she had no idea it would be like this! And she was grateful for Zaiden showing it all to her. But Seren couldn't risk being manipulated by two Warrens—not with what was at stake.

"I should get going," she mumbled. If Zaiden was surprised by the sudden shift in her demeanor, he did not show it. She stared down at the ground. "Goodnight, Zaiden. Congratulations on your inauguration."

Zaiden said nothing as she shut the door behind her.

20

ZAIDEN

Zaiden walked to his first council meeting feeling hungover and ill-prepared. It seemed that drinking too much had become a bad habit. Zaiden made a mental note to work on this bad behavior.

He had vague memories from the night before, but he couldn't determine what was real and what was a dream. Seren Quinn being alive, for instance. Real, or falsely remembered? Why would she have been at his Gala instead of in an incinerator? What purpose would his father have for saving her life?

Zaiden supposed he shouldn't care. The important thing was that his father had saved her life, and in doing so, he had lifted a huge weight from Zaiden's chest. Zaiden had not realized how suffocating guilt could be.

On top of his hangover, he was experiencing an overwhelming imposter syndrome. He was by far the youngest member on the council, and he had the least amount of experience. Zaiden's father had handpicked his council, just as Zaiden would when the time came, and every person on it had either worked as a Thinker, a Scientist, a Harmonizer, or a Judge prior to their selection. Meanwhile,

Zaiden had completed his education a mere forty-eight hours ago and had no real experience in decision making. Doing well today would be important. These people would work for him one day, would look up to *him*. If he lost their respect now, he'd never get it back. As his father always said, "*Respect is earned. You have one chance to earn it. Don't screw it up.*"

No pressure or anything.

Zaiden had been in the Council Room once before, years earlier, the day after his mother died. The room had felt so large then. It seemed so much smaller now. The back wall was lined with paintings of past Governors. Zaiden's Grandfather, Arch; his great-grandfather, Mosaic; and his great-great-grandfather, Jeffery, hung next to his father's portrait. All four men were posed in their studies, their stances strong. The rest of the walls were simulations. When Zaiden's mother passed, they'd been covered in simulations of her. Now they displayed an expansive city, just like the ones in Zaiden's penthouse.

When Zaiden entered the Council Room, he was given a standing ovation by the council members. He gave a small wave before taking a seat at the right hand of his father.

Alaster Holland sat at his father's left. Slightly graying with soft brown eyes and a warm smile, Alaster was the closest thing to a friend that Zaiden's father had. He was a loyal servant to the Governor, providing him with advice, guidance, and a quiet ear. Zaiden liked Alaster, though they weren't close. Then again, no one was close to Alaster. The man was guarded and closed off, rarely showing emotion or engaging in conversation. He was a mystery—and he seemed to like it that way. Zaiden avoided eye contact with him, fearing Alaster might have negative feelings about Zaiden turning his stolen IC in to his father rather than going straight to him.

The rest of the council members (there were eleven: eight men and three women) sat poised around the table. Among them was Atlas' father, Sawyer; a woman named Penelope Cotto, whom Zaiden was convinced was having an affair with Sawyer; and Rocco's father, Eli. Rocco and Atlas would take their father's places someday if Zaiden chose to appoint them, which he would. It was an unspoken deal amongst the three of them. Council positions usually remained within families, anyway.

Zaiden's father stood, and the room went silent. The Governor had complete control of his people; that much was clear. Zaiden only hoped to possess that level of control one day.

"Today, we welcome my son to his first of many meetings," Governor Warren said. He turned to Zaiden. "I'm looking forward to having his youthful energy on the council."

Zaiden's father gave him a firm pat on the back. There was once again applause, and Zaiden grinned. The approval felt good. It always did, coming from his father.

"Welcome, Zaiden. We're thrilled to have you," Penelope Cotto cooed.

"Zaiden, did you want to say anything before we begin?" his father asked.

Zaiden froze. He hadn't anticipated speaking. He cleared his throat and stood.

"I, uh ... just that I'm excited to be here today, and I'm looking forward to supporting my father and all of you in the wonderful work you're doing for Community."

"Hear, hear!" Sawyer exclaimed, and the council applauded politely as Zaiden returned to his seat. Alaster gave Zaiden a reassuring smile, and Governor Warren began the meeting.

"Okay, what do we have on the agenda today?"

Childa, a middle-aged woman who had been a member of the council for longer than Zaiden had been alive, stood. "The census numbers came back this morning," she said grimly. "The findings are not good. The number of people over the age of sixty is continuing to grow, but the one child policy we issued twenty years ago has significantly decreased the number of people entering our workforce. If we don't alter the policy, it may be catastrophic for our economy."

Atlas's father, Sawyer, stood. "Community can only safely support a population of twenty-five thousand. We are already dangerously close to hitting that figure in the next three years if we remove this policy," he said. A few people nodded.

"I'm not saying that the solution is to *end* the one child policy, but we do need to come up with a solution—and fast," Childa said.

Zaiden racked his brain for something to add. It would be ballsy of him to speak now, in his first meeting, but it would give him the opportunity to gain the council members' respect.

Nothing came to mind.

Apparently, everyone else felt the same. The quiet stretched on. Zaiden had begun to wonder if it would ever end, when Penelope spoke.

"We could … get rid of some of the older men and women in the lower tiers."

Zaiden looked around. *"Get rid of"?* What the hell did that mean?

No one else seemed disoriented by Penelope's words.

Childa shook her head. "The members of Tiers Four and Five will notice an uptick in suspicious deaths and will be more likely to revolt."

Penelope opened her mouth to say something else, but Governor Warren held up a hand to silence her.

"Alaster and I have generated a plan to take care of it. I no longer wish to discuss this issue. What else do you have?"

Zaiden eyed his father. No one else questioned the "solution" they had come up with, but Zaiden couldn't help but wonder. Both Alaster and Governor Warren kept their gazes straight ahead, and the topic was dropped.

From there, the meeting dragged on. They discussed food generation, a new scientific invention being worked on for power conservation, and an odd number of camera malfunctions in Tier Five. By the end, Zaiden's eyelids were heavy. How his father did this every day was beyond him. Problem after problem was brought up, until finally the meeting ended, and the council members stood to leave. Each of them shook Zaiden's hand on their way out.

Sawyer was the last to go. "We're glad to have you, kid," he said, grabbing and squeezing Zaiden's shoulders. "I'm looking forward to having some more youth on this council."

"Thanks, Sawyer," Zaiden said. "Send your wife my love."

Sawyer winked. "Will do."

That wasn't too bad, Zaiden thought as Sawyer left. He might not have gained the council's trust yet, but he certainly hadn't lost it, either.

Zaiden was feeling pretty pleased with himself, when he noticed his father and Alaster deep in conversation in the corner. Their voices became steadily louder as Sawyer shut the door behind him.

"You can't send out another round of placebos," Alaster said. "People talk. They'll notice."

"I think you're overestimating the intelligence of the lower Tiers. They're not nearly as smart as you give them credit for," his father replied coolly.

Alaster rubbed a hand over his eyes. He looked exhausted as he said, "Pluto, with all due respect, you already have one rebellion on your hands. You don't want to start another."

Zaiden froze. *A rebellion?*

Governor Warren looked poised to respond, when he realized Zaiden was still present. His mouth clamped shut. Zaiden felt his face turn a bright red. He felt like a child about to be scolded, but Pluto merely gave him a tight smile.

"You may go," he said, nodding at the exit. "We've finished here"

Then he shut the door in Zaiden's face.

21

SEREN

Two days after the ball, Seren had her first day as a Thinker. At precisely eight o'clock, right as the Awakening finished, a woman named Daria came to collect her. Daria was an older woman, at least thirty years Seren's senior, but she had the energy and social awareness of one of the boys in Seren's class. Daria stood out to Seren as skeletally thin, with a collarbone that popped out from beneath her extravagant green shirt. Her thin lips pulled into a tight smile when she greeted Seren. Daria explained that she, too, was a Thinker, and was in charge of showing Seren around Tier Two, as well as taking her to her first day of work.

Seren had not been prepared for this. She'd been lying in bed since the ball, unable to get her mind off the things that Zaiden had shown her. No matter how hard she tried, she could not take her mind off Earth. When she closed her eyes, she dreamed of it, and when she woke, she saw it in everything she looked at. Her orange chair was the burning sun. The high ceilings were mountains. The golden dress, now hanging in her closet, was the stars.

"Oh, I'm sorry, I wasn't... I didn't realize... Give me a minute," Seren said sheepishly. She left Daria in the hallway as she threw on some clothes and brushed her teeth.

Daria made a face when Seren came out, dressed in a Tier Four gray uniform, but said nothing, instead beginning their tour in stride.

Daria was not a Tier Two by birth, which she made known immediately. She had been born a Tier Three. "You and I have a lot in common that way," she said. But that was about the only thing they had in common. As Daria led Seren through the sparkling halls of Tier Two, that became more and more clear.

"That is my gym," Daria said, pointing a colored nail at a glass door to their right. "They have a great masseuse there. He gets out *all* my knots. Rubs all the right places. I can refer you, if you want. He's cute, too." She winked. "And over here is where I typically grab my morning coffee and a low-carb bagel." She pointed at an automated machine to their left, where a line of Tier Twos waited for a boiling cup of dark liquid. Seren stared.

"The Nutritionists don't deliver your food?"

Daria looked at her strangely and then laughed, like Seren was joking. "You're precious. Oh, and here, we have the Thinker Dome." She stepped over to the right, nearly plowing over two children on their way to school.

Seren followed hastily, staring up at the wide door. Inside was a line of five long wooden tables surrounded by shelves of books. About thirty men and women sat at the tables, chatting animatedly with half-eaten pastries sprawled in front of them. A few looked up at Seren as she entered, but most stayed entrenched in their conversations.

"And here we are!" Daria said. "Help yourself to the food, and the books, and happy first day!"

Seren looked around the room sheepishly. "What do I do?"

Daria blinked at her, then laughed. "Just think!"

Just think.

"How do I..." Seren began, but Daria had already bounded away. Seren stood at the door for a moment, absolutely petrified. Shouldn't there be some sort of training for Thinkers—some problem given to them to solve?

She felt the attention of the other Thinkers on her, so, desperate to appear like she knew what she was doing, she walked over to one of the bookshelves. It was magnificent, really. Seren had never seen so many books in her life! They were in good condition, too. Each binding looked new and well kept. She examined the titles. Community's History, one read. Creation of Community, said another. The Warren Family Legacy.

Down a bit were more technical books—books about farming through adverse conditions, about electricity and human behavior. Seren pulled one of the books off the shelf and flipped through its pages. It was a book that defined words, but various pages were missing, and some words were crossed out in deep black ink. She flipped some more.

She spent the whole morning exploring the shelves. She found quickly that these books were different than the ones Henry used to keep. Most of these had been written *after* the formation of Community, by people who'd spent most of their lives here.

Seren grabbed a pile of the books and brought them to the table. As she flipped through their thin, coarse pages, she recognized the irony of these books. Even the ones written about a time before Community had been written less than a hundred years earlier, by people who had never set foot on Earth. These were not like Henry's books at all.

Around her, people talked and laughed and sporadically discussed policies and food opportunities. All the while, Seren read, stopping only to eat one of the odd sweet pastries on the table (delicious). She hardly noticed as the end of the day came and people began to leave.

Daria put a hand on her shoulder. "Time to go," she said.

Seren bit her lip and looked at all the books laid out in front of her. She'd barely made a dent. "Am I allowed to take these with me?" she asked.

Daria eyed the stack. "I don't know," she said, appearing more than a little appalled by the question. "No one else does… I don't see why not—but you know they'll be here tomorrow, don't you?"

Daria waited for Seren to collect the books before walking her out and locking the door to the Thinker Dome behind them. "Do you think you can get home okay?" she asked.

"Yes, thanks," Seren said, and Daria gave her a not so warm smile before heading towards her gym.

Seren watched her go and wondered what kind of secrets a woman like Daria was holding onto. Maybe she could befriend her and get some information on the other Thinkers. Of all the people in Tier Two, the Thinkers were most likely to revolt, right? They had more information than anyone else. Once again, she thought of Henry and his warning: *"The greatest enemy of knowledge is not ignorance. It is the illusion of knowledge."*

Seren walked home slowly, taking in the vastness of space in Tier Two. It was still beautiful to her, but Tier Two's beauty was soured by what she'd been brought here to do.

Her mind and attention wandered, and Seren realized that she did not in fact remember where she lived. She found herself in the middle of a completely different residential space. An overwhelming feeling swept over her. She had lived her whole life taking five-minute showers, being in bed by 10:30 for lights out, eating the same mushy foods. She had never realized that just a few floors up, life was vastly different. She could imagine what Lucas would say if he were here. He'd make some bold comment about the disparities between the upper and lower Tiers, calling it a travesty or a crime against humanity. She missed Lucas. She couldn't believe they were still in a fight. She feared for his life, and she feared for her own ... and for Ma's.

Anxiety began to crush her as Seren slipped into an empty room, closed the door behind her, and burst into tears.

22

ZAIDEN

"Zaiden, could you come in here for a moment?"

Zaiden's father sat at his desk, his palms driven into his forehead. He looked stressed—more so than usual, if that was possible. Alaster stood beside him, his expression unreadable. They looked like they had just broken out of an intense conversation when Zaiden entered.

"Yes?" Zaiden asked, uncertainty creeping into his voice. He feared this conversation might be related to his eavesdropping at the council meeting the morning before.

His father removed his hands from his forehead and lifted a flimsy white paper from his desk. "Alaster has made some changes to the speech you will give tonight," he said, holding out the new page.

"I was under the impression it would be less of a speech and more of a conversation," Zaiden said, taking the paper from his father.

He was meant to appear on the Evening Broadcast tonight. It would be his first appearance as a member of the council, and the idea was to give him more exposure to public speaking and to garner public respect. He had been preparing talking points all day; the idea of changing them now sent waves of anxiety through him.

Zaiden skimmed the new speech. It spoke of loyalty, strength, and resilience. "'Loyalty is paramount, and Community will continue to terminate any and all forms of rebellious behavior,'" he read aloud. His brows furrowed. There was rarely a mention of insurgent behavior in speeches given by the Warrens or their council. Zaiden's father liked to portray Community as a perfect society, no matter what demons were lurking beneath the surface. "What does this mean?"

He expected Alaster and his father to sidestep the question, as they usually did with every question he asked. But to his surprise, Alaster said, "It may be time to fill him in."

"He's still a child," Zaiden's father snapped.

Alaster was undeterred. "He's a member of the council now, and he's going to be part of the decision-making process soon. He can't be an informed leader if we continue to withhold information from him."

Zaiden felt a surge of gratitude towards Alaster. It was nice having someone who believed in him, who recognized that he was no longer a child. Zaiden looked to his father.

Though clearly uncertain, Governor Warren nodded. "Very well."

The simulated window behind his desk displayed a threatening gray sky—the perfect ambiance for the room's mood. Zaiden felt like he could almost smell fear in the air. For a moment, the room was silent apart from the gentle pitter-patter of simulated rain.

"We fear there may be a rebellion stirring in Tier Five," his father said finally.

This was the last thing Zaiden expected. "A rebellion?" He took a moment to formulate his thoughts. "I don't understand. Why would there be a rebellion?"

He looked to his father, but it was Alaster who answered.

"Jealousy, discontentment, exhaustion… It could be for any number of reasons."

A rebellion. Zaiden couldn't believe it. After all the Warren family had done for the members of Community, they wanted to rebel? It didn't make sense. People were *happy* in Community. They were alive and cared for. "What do they want?"

"Freedom from my suffocating rule," Governor Warren said, sarcasm dripping heavily from his words. He looked exhausted—more so than Zaiden had seen him in a long time—and Zaiden found himself at a loss for words. How could the members of Community even consider such a thing, when Zaiden's family had given them the opportunity to live while ten billion others died? How could they be so *selfish*? Their family members had not done nearly as much for the creation and continuation of Community as the Warrens had, or any other members of the upper Tiers, for that matter. Why would they want to see Governor Warren deposed, after all he'd done for them?

Zaiden supposed it didn't matter. When he served as Governor in the future, the question wouldn't be why people did the idiotic things they did; it would be how to squash it before it became a real issue.

"What are you doing to stop it?" Zaiden asked.

"We're starting with an increase in Community-positive rhetoric," Alaster said, stepping in as Zaiden's father retreated further from the conversation. "Your speech will be the first of many. If that proves futile, we will begin public executions of known rebels."

"We haven't had a public execution in years," Zaiden said. "Didn't our analysis show that it just lowered morale and Community loyalty?"

Alaster shrugged. "It did, but fear may be our only option. We are completely in the dark about the timing and magnitude of the rebellion."

"What about the cameras? Or the bugs?" Zaiden asked.

"The Tier Fives have figured out a way to render those useless."

"How?"

Alaster paced back and forth, and Zaiden's eyes followed. "We aren't sure. Our Technologists think that the rebels have created an interference device that disables the transmission of the bugs. We don't know where they would have gotten the knowledge or materials to create such devices. Governor Warren and I suspect that there are people amongst us working for the rebellion."

Dread sat heavily in Zaiden's chest as that news sunk in. Why would anyone betray his family?

"How bad is it?" Zaiden asked.

Alaster exhaled a long breath. "Bad," he said. "Tier Fives have already begun to slow their food production. We fear they may try to starve us out."

A rush of fear ran through Zaiden. Tier Fives were the only source of food, apart from a few bakeries in Tier Four, but even those relied on the wheat grown in the greenhouses. Without their efforts... Zaiden couldn't even imagine.

"Can't we send Harmonizers down there to force them to co-operate?" he asked, fear painfully evident in his voice. He hoped his father wouldn't notice.

"That would be a short-term option," Alaster said with a nod. "But Tier Fives outnumber the rest of Community four to one. If even a quarter of their population is in on the rebellion, we may be in deep trouble."

Shit.

"A long-term option would be to kill anyone who is part of the rebellion," Alaster continued thoughtfully, "but that would cull the population too much. We wouldn't have enough people to farm or generate power."

Zaiden looked to his father. "What do you think about all this?"

"What good fortune for governments where the people do not think," Governor Warren said. His eyes were void of emotion. Zaiden looked to Alaster for clarification.

"We believe this is the same group that was responsible for the death of your mother," Alaster said quietly.

His father's bizarre behavior suddenly made sense. He had loved Ivory Warren more than he loved anything in Community. It must have come as a terrible shock to hear that the rebels who'd killed his wife were still plotting to bring him down.

Zaiden felt a sudden surge of hatred for the rebels—every one of them. They deserved to die, and he resolved to do everything in his power to ensure that their rebellion never happened.

"Tell me what I can do."

23

SEREN

Seren quickly realized that life in Tier Two would be more isolating than she'd thought. Though she always had access to light, she felt totally in the dark. Though she was always within a few yards of another person, she'd never felt more alone.

On her third day in Tier Two, Geoff brought her a pile of clothes in colors like pink and green and purple. "Governor Warren said this may help you fit in better," he said. Then, much to Seren's dismay, he invited himself in for tea, which ended up being four hours of him talking to her about nothing. Undeterred, Seren was excited to try the clothes on. But even with the new clothes, everyone still seemed to know that she was an outsider.

Maybe she was being dramatic. She now enjoyed things she'd never had before: unlimited showers, access to delicious foods she'd never tried, more books than she knew existed. But even in her brief moments of joy, Ma's situation weighed on her. She still had not gotten any closer to finding out information for Governor Warren, and she feared what would happen if she had nothing of substance to say at their first meeting.

She did, however, find solace in her new role as a Thinker. It might not have been everything she'd dreamed it would be, but she almost looked forward to her time in the Thinker Dome. There, at least, she felt a little more at home. In the Thinker Dome, Seren studied each book with surgical precision until it was time to go. Every other Thinker seemed to spend the day drinking, laughing, and talking. They largely ignored her. Even Daria, who had been so enthusiastic to show her around on her first day, didn't pay her any attention. Still, Seren read.

Seren knew she should put her focus on finding out information for Governor Warren, but no matter what she did, she could not focus. All she could think about was the baby growing in Ma's stomach, and the magical world inside the Simulator.

Every night after the lights dimmed, Seren went for a walk. She hoped that the darkness would provide a sense of security for those who had something to hide, encouraging them to speak more openly. But each night, all she heard was Community gossip—no different than in Tier Four. She soon became discouraged. If Governor Warren, who had eyes and ears all over Community, had not yet heard something about the rebellion, how was she expected to?

On her sixth night in Tier Two, Seren went for her usual walk. She carried a book with her, which she read as she walked, hugging the walls to avoid bumping into any drunkards on their way home. It was a book on the creation of the Community Tiers. She'd already read through it twice and was trying once again to understand it. The language was odd.

The Tiers were created for job selection purposes, the book read. *The most skilled workers were chosen to be in higher Tiers. Those with a higher IQ and an advanced capacity for learning were given the opportunity to be higher up.*

Seren struggled with this idea. She'd never questioned that the higher Tiers were smarter—until she'd gotten here. But the other Thinkers didn't seem particularly smart or hard-working. In fact, it seemed like nearly every member of her Tier Four class was smarter than the Thinkers she spent her days with. She read it over again: *Those with higher Iqs and an advanced capacity for learning were given the opportunity to be higher up.*

Seren was barely paying attention as she turned a corner. Her nose was deep in the book when she collided with something hard. She looked up, surprised.

Scratch that; *someone.*

"Seren Quinn!" Zaiden slurred. "What a surprise!"

Zaiden's eyes were clouded over, and his smile was wide and goofy. On either side of him were two guys Seren's age. One had dark skin, bright green eyes, and matted curls. The other was even paler than she was, with blond hair so light that it was almost white. They both stared at her with curious gazes, their eyes going from her clothes to the book to her shoes. Seren wanted to disappear.

"You're out late," Zaiden observed.

Seren tucked the book under her arm. "I couldn't sleep," she said quietly.

"Comrade, who's this?" the pale friend asked, his lips pulling up into a sly smile.

"Oh! Gents, this is Seren, Community's newest Thinker. Seren, this is Rocco." He motioned towards the blond. "And Atlas."

"Hi," Seren muttered.

"You were at the ball, weren't you?" Atlas asked. Seren nodded.

The four of them stood there for a long moment—quite uncomfortably, Seren thought, though Zaiden appeared oblivious.

"Shall we?" Rocco finally asked.

Zaiden snapped to attention and grinned. His eyes were empty.

He's freeing his mind, Seren thought—though what Zaiden would need to free himself from, she wasn't sure.

"We're going to a party tonight, Seren Quinn," Zaiden said. Seren couldn't help but smile at the way her full name sounded coming from his relaxed lips. "Would you like to join us?"

Atlas and Rocco gave their friend the side eye, and Seren could feel, despite the sincerity of Zaiden's question, that she would not be welcome wherever they were going.

"No, I should really be off to bed. I—"

"Don't have to work tomorrow," Zaiden finished with a flourish. He grinned. "Take some time off from thinking and join us, yeah? I insist."

Seren bit her lip. It *would* be a good opportunity to get information for Governor Warren... Being around a bunch of drunk teenagers would surely give her *something* to tell him, right?

She nodded. "Sure. Why not?"

24

SEREN

Seren soon learned that "party" meant a large group of people her age all crammed into an apartment, drinking heavily. She should have assumed this based on her experience at the ball, but she still felt unprepared.

It was hot in the stranger's apartment, and overwhelmingly loud. Bodies rubbed up against each other, both accidentally and on purpose. In the corner, two girls laughed at a guy doing a handstand, drinking something from a hose while upside down. It was unlike anything Seren had ever experienced, and her body itched with discomfort.

This feeling of being wildly out of place had plagued Seren as she followed Zaiden and his friends into the apartment, which apparently belonged to the beautiful girl who greeted the four of them at the door. She eyed Seren distastefully, but forced a smile as Zaiden introduced them, placing a firm hand on his bare forearm. She then dragged him away, and Atlas and Rocco disappeared, leaving Seren standing in the doorway, feeling like an idiot. In Tier Four, she had never felt out of place, but here, she hadn't been able to *stop* feeling out of place. Her cheeks were warm, and though no one was actually looking at her, she felt as though the whole room's attention were on her. She considered bolting, but stopped herself. *Ma is counting on you,* she thought.

Right—because drunk teenagers are going to have information about a rebellion, she retorted to herself.

You never know...

Huffing, Seren took a step deeper into the apartment. It was lavish, larger and more spacious than hers, with a similar clean and calming feel, despite being crowded with loud and boisterous drunk kids. She clung to the walls, her book still tucked beneath her arm. Her mind raced, and she had to keep bringing it back to the goal at hand: information.

Seren felt invisible as she walked the outskirts of the party, picking up little tidbits of nothingness. She was a fly on the wall, and she was sure someone would swat her away at any moment.

Despite her best efforts, her attention kept returning to Zaiden. No matter where he was in the room, her eyes seemed to find him. First, he was laughing with that beautiful girl. Then he was drinking with Atlas and Rocco. No matter where he went, others followed. He was clearly a natural born leader. Seren could tell that the others felt the same pull towards him that she did; they swarmed him everywhere he went. She had to actively pull her gaze away more times than she could count.

Nearly an hour into the party, Seren still had heard nothing of value. And beyond that, she was certain that people actually *were* looking at her. More than once, she heard laughter follow as she walked by, and she was certain that it was directed at her.

I need to get out of here.

Seren pushed through the crowd, feeling eyes turning to her as she went. When she was just feet away from the door, she heard her name.

"Seren Quinn?"

Zaiden stood against the wall, leaning his head back against a painting of Governor Warren. He grinned at her with that same mischievous grin he'd had when he took her in the Simulator.

"I was just leaving," Seren said.

Zaiden pushed himself off the wall with his upper back and stumbled forward so that he was only a few inches from Seren. He smiled down at her, and she felt suddenly aware of his towering height.

"No! Don't go! We're going to play a game."

"I should really be—"

"What're you reading?" he interrupted, motioning towards the book. Seren paused before handing it to him. Zaiden examined the cover. "'The Creation of the Tiers.' I don't think I've read this one. Is it any good?"

Seren shrugged.

Zaiden began to flip clumsily through the pages, pausing for a second or two to look at an image more closely. He flipped to the page Seren had bookmarked and began to read. "'Tiers were assigned based on intelligence and ability. The lowest of Tiers, Tier Five, is comprised of people with little intelligence or creativity'. Damn. They don't hold back, huh?" He laughed and flipped to the next page. "Oh, hey, look! There's a picture of my great-grandfather." He held the book open for her and pointed to a drawing of a man that resembled Governor Warren.

Seren nodded absentmindedly. Her brain was stuck on the words he'd read and the amusement on his face. *People with little intelligence or creativity.* Her heart felt cold. When reading it before, she hadn't given the words much thought, but now hearing them come from Zaiden's mouth, she felt her cheeks becoming warm.

Zaiden closed the book, set it down on a table, and smiled at her again. She quailed under his gaze, like she had under his father's, and took a shuddering breath.

"Do you think that's true?" Seren asked quietly.

His smile remained. "Do I think what's true?"

"That the lower Tiers are less … intelligent."

Zaiden took a swig from his glass and gulped it down, considering. "I don't know. Hadn't really thought about it. Yeah, I guess. Why else would they say that?"

"So, you think I'm dumb?" Seren asked.

Zaiden looked surprised. "I didn't say that."

"You didn't have to."

Zaiden opened his mouth to speak, but she cut him off. "Everyone I know in Tier Four is smart. Smarter than the Thinkers I work with—who, by the way, do anything all day *but* think."

Zaiden put his hands up, a smirk growing on his face. "My mistake," he said. "It doesn't really matter, though, who's smarter."

"It matters to me," Seren said, fully aware of how hurt she sounded. She lifted the book from the table and held it up in front of his face. "This book makes it seem like the Tiers exist based on intelligence, but they seem like they exist more to keep us down and keep you up. Have you even been to Tier Four? Do you have any idea what it's like down there?"

These were stupid things to say to the Governor's son, but they came out anyway. Lucas would be proud of her; she sounded just like him.

Zaiden frowned. "You're taking this too seriously. I didn't mean it, okay?"

"You're not taking this seriously enough!" she snapped. "You're going to be the leader of Community someday. You have the opportunity to make real, lasting change. And you're throwing all of that away."

She shoved the book into his chest, causing him to stumble against the wall. His drink clattered to the ground and spilled on the carpet. Nearby, she heard someone say, "Damn, girl. Calm down." Seren opened her mouth, then closed it. An apology danced on her lips, but she couldn't bring herself to say it. Instead, she stormed out, feeling the eyes of Zaiden's peers on her as she left.

25

SEREN

Seren stayed in bed for most of the next day, replaying her conversation with Zaiden in her mind. It wasn't so much the danger of it that upset her; it was more how mortifying it was to realize his opinion of her, her friends, and her family. Maybe the higher Tiers *were* more intelligent—but how did that justify the differences in their way of life? She tossed and turned in her bed, feeling guilty for the luxuries she'd been abusing the last few weeks, while those below still suffered strict curfews and ate chalky oats.

Finally, staying in bed felt like its own kind of crime. She hopped up just a few hours past noon, threw on a colorful shirt courtesy of Geoff, and stepped into the halls for a walk.

Tier Two was busier than usual, swarming with people on their day off. Seren frowned. Was there nowhere in this forsaken place that she could be *alone*?!

She skirted the edges of the hall, keeping her head down and her eyes on the ground, regretting leaving her room. She tried to turn off her senses, to imagine that she *was* alone, but her imagination was not that powerful. She considered returning to her room, but feared that would feel even more suffocating than this, so she kept walking along, tuning out the silly gossip and complaints of the higher Tier. Almost desperately, Seren searched for the nearest entrance to Tier One. There, perhaps, she could find a space to be alone.

She found it easily and made her way up to the halls of Tier One. There, Seren allowed her feet to guide her way, until subconsciously, as if tugged by an invisible string, she found herself in front of the Simulator. *You could be alone in there,* her brain said. If only she had access. On her first walk, she'd tried to open it, but her new identity card hadn't worked. Only members of the council had access. Most people didn't even know it existed—or didn't care.

Seren was moving to leave when she noticed that the door was ajar by an inch. Her heart raced. She was not allowed to be in there; she knew that. But she hadn't felt this trapped since Ma told her she had to keep the baby. Seren *needed* to experience Earth. She ached for it in a way she'd never ached for anything before.

Seren glanced over her shoulder. She was alone. Taking a deep breath, she pulled the door open and shut it behind her.

The breeze in the Simulator was warm and salty. Seren blinked up at the bright sky—*the sun*—and realized that the Simulator was already in use. She was by a body of water—an *ocean*, maybe— with sand beneath her feet. In the center of it all was Zaiden. He turned to look at her, surprised, as the voice came from above. "Simulation paused," it said, and the world around them collapsed into blackness.

"I'm sorry," Seren said, stumbling over her words. "I didn't mean to... I'll just..."

Swiftly, she backed out of the Simulator, shut the door behind her, and closed her eyes. *Why does Zaiden have to be everywhere?* He was like a plague. No, that was mean; it was Seren's fault she ran into him. She wasn't supposed to be in the Simulator. Seren sighed and leaned her head back against the wall. There was a rush of air as the door opened beside her.

"You aren't supposed to come here alone," said Zaiden's voice.

Seren breathed deeply. "I know. I'm sorry. I just needed some space."

She could feel Zaiden's gaze on her, even with her eyes closed.

"I know the feeling," Zaiden said finally.

There was a long pause. She felt his body near hers—the warmth, the uncertainty. He took an audible breath, and the rush of air came again.

"Just come in," he said. Seren opened her eyes. Zaiden was holding the door open for them both.

She looked at him. "What?"

"Come in." He did not wait for a response. Seren bit her lip, took a deep breath, and followed him.

The door swung shut behind her, and the Simulator voice came over the speaker: "Simulation resumed." In a rush, the noises began again: the ocean crashing, birds chirping, screams of joy. Seren stayed a few steps behind Zaiden, just along the edge of the simulation. It felt as though she were intruding on something private, and she questioned whether she should be here at all.

Zaiden turned to her. "Are you coming?"

"I ... yeah."

Tentatively, Seren took a few steps forward until they stood on the same plane, a few feet apart. His presence weighed on her. She tried to focus on the beach and the water, but her mind replayed their conversation from the night before. Did he remember? He'd had a lot to drink, that had to have affected his memory. But maybe her words remained. Seren offended him—she *had* to have offended him—but so far, he'd acted like nothing was different—aside, maybe, from seeming a bit standoffish.

"This is Santa Monica Pier," Zaiden said suddenly. "It was in California."

Seren didn't know what to say. It was uncomfortable, standing here with Zaiden. There was a swell of tension. Did he feel it, too?

"I've never been," she finally managed.

I've never been? What a stupid thing to say. But Zaiden grinned, actually *chuckled,* and picked up a stone from the sand. He threw it, hard, and it skipped across the water—once, twice, three times before disappearing beneath the surface. Seren looked out at the wood jutting into the water, and up to the giant illuminated spinning wheel at the end. Zaiden followed her gaze.

"That's a Ferris wheel," he said. "The wheel turns, and the cars go with it. You can see the whole city from up there."

"Oh. Wow."

"Do you want to try it?"

"I..."

"I know you're scared from your last experience in here, but I promise it's safe."

Seren bit her lip and stared at the wheel. At its highest point, it stood above the surrounding buildings. It seemed to be the tallest thing around. Imagining herself all the way up in the air sent a nervous pulse through her body. "I don't know."

"You only live once, Seren Quinn."

Zaiden didn't wait for an answer. He walked away slowly, as if daring her to follow. It worked; she did.

They made their way down the wooden Pier, and Seren strolled from stand to stand, reading the signs. One stand in particular caught her eye. It had a large red sign that read, Japadog. Her eyes skimmed over the photos and menu items listed, and her lips moved with the more unfamiliar words—words like *okonami.*

"That's Japanese," Zaiden said.

Seren blinked at him, feeling stupid. She'd never heard that word before: *Japanese.*

Zaiden must've seen the confusion on her face. "It's a different language. Not everyone on Earth spoke the same language we do. They had different words with the same meanings. Like, uh, 'hello' is a greeting to us, but in Japanese, it would be different."

"What is 'hello' in Japanese?"

"I don't know."

Seren looked at the photos of the menu items. There were various depictions of food with different toppings, and only a few that Seren recognized: avocado, cabbage.

"What's a Japadog?" she asked.

"I think it's a play on words. A Japanese hot dog."

Her cheeks grew warm. Maybe the book was right; maybe she *was* an idiot. "What's a hot dog?"

"A hot dog? It's a type of meat. I think it's different parts of an animal mushed together." Seeing Seren's confusion, he continued, "Uh, they used to have these animals that were like people, I guess, but different. I don't really know."

Seren's mouth dropped open. "And they would *eat* them?"

"Yes."

Despite herself, Seren made a disgusted face.

Zaiden laughed. "I think they were actually pretty tasty."

They made it to the base of the Ferris wheel, and Seren stared up at the massive contraption. Now that she was standing at the base of it, it somehow felt even bigger. She considered backing out, making some excuse about needing to get home—but when she turned,

Zaiden was right behind her. There was something in his eyes that comforted her, made her feel safe. She took a grounding breath.

"Ready?" Zaiden asked.

No.

"Yes," she said.

The car shook as she stepped in, causing her to fall backwards. Zaiden grabbed her waist to keep her from tumbling over, and the two of them both froze, his hands planted on her waist. Her breath hitched in her throat as he hastily removed them and took a seat beside her.

The Ferris wheel started. Her body was as stiff as the boards of the pier as the car lifted into the air. Seren gripped the sides so hard that her knuckles turned white, and she clamped her eyes shut.

"We won't fall," Zaiden assured her.

Seren could only nod. The cart swayed as they went higher and higher, until finally, everything stopped moving. They'd reached the top.

"Open your eyes," Zaiden whispered.

Seren did. The city was in full view. "Wow," she breathed.

The sun had begun to set, filling the sky with an array of reds, oranges, and purples. The lights in the city looked like little stars, sparkling and shimmering below. Seren's fear slowly away. Her body relaxed.

"My mother loved heights," Zaiden said quietly.

Seren looked at him. This was the first time Zaiden had mentioned his mother.

"She said the thrill of being high up was something that she never thought she'd get to experience. She said, 'Enjoy the fear, Zaiden. Not many people in Community will ever feel fear. It is a privilege to experience it.'"

"That's a beautiful way to look at something difficult," Seren said.

"She had a beautiful way of looking at life."

They looked out towards the ocean, glistening in the light of the falling sun. The waves seemed to move in tandem, expanding as far as the eye could see. Seren knew there was a place far out there where the Simulator ended, but her eyes couldn't perceive it, and she didn't want to. She wanted to stay in this moment with Zaiden, as if they were just two normal people living on Earth.

If only…

"I haven't been up here since she died," Zaiden said.

Seren's eyes danced over his. She could feel herself looking at him the same way she looked at the stars: with curiosity and wonder. Every time she thought she understood him, he surprised her.

"That must be hard," she said. "I'm sorry."

"Thank you."

Seren watched Zaiden look over the darkening sky. She knew enough about the Simulator to know that he could have altered the simulation so that it was light again—all it would take was a single command—but she was happy he didn't. Letting the darkness take over felt organic. It felt like they were really at the mercy of time, unable to see the sun's brightness again until morning. And she hoped that the darkness would come with stars. She held her breath, and her eyes drifted up to the sky.

Zaiden cleared his throat. "I'm sorry for my behavior the other day," he said. "I don't remember much from that night, but I remember talking about that book, and I know I upset you, and … I'm sorry."

His apology felt sincere, and in the chill of the night, it wrapped around her like a warm blanket. An odd feeling of heat spread through her chest, different from the feeling she had with Ma or Pa or Lucas. This went beyond that.

"I've been thinking about what you said—about making a change when I come into power." He stared ahead at the setting sun. "I think I forget that I have a chance to make a difference when I take over the role of the Governor. I forget I'm going to *be* Governor. But I don't want to just follow the status quo. I want things to be different. Maybe not *that* different, but different all the same."

He turned to look at her, and his eyes searched hers. Seren's breath caught in her throat. It was a different feeling now than it had been before when he'd looked at her. Something had changed.

"When that day comes, I want people like you on my council. People who think differently. Thinkers who actually *think*." He paused. "Anyway, I got you something." He fished around in his pocket, pulled out a sapphire IC, and handed it to her. "This will allow you to access to all the Tiers. So you can visit your family."

Seren's breath caught. "Oh," she whispered.

Tears rose to her eyes. *Ma, Pa, Lucas...* She hadn't allowed herself to think about how much she missed them, because she knew she couldn't see them. With this, she could. "Is it allowed?" she managed to ask, thinking of how Governor Warren would take this new access.

"My father has enough to worry about without caring if a Tier Four Thinker goes to see her family," Zaiden said.

She forgot how little Zaiden knew about her relationship with his father. He probably *would* care. Guilt built up in her chest. She pushed it down. "Thank you, Zaiden. You have no idea how much this means to me."

"Thank you for being honest with me. People don't do that often."

Seren smiled. "Any time."

"Do you think ... maybe I could stop by your place sometime? Bring you some better books? My dad has a whole library."

Seren felt her heart swell. "I'd like that."

Zaiden helped her out of the car after it found its way back to the ground. She thanked him again, and together, they walked back down the pier.

26

SEREN

Seren's meeting with Governor Warren came too quickly. For two weeks, she went about her daily routine: reading at work, reading at home. She kept her ears open for any information she could gather, but none came readily, and she did little beyond going to the party to find it. Governor Warren's deal remained in the back of her mind, but as a distant thought. That is, until the day came for her to update him.

She had nothing.

When Seren arrived at Governor Warren's office, she felt overwhelming anxiety. His office's mahogany double doors stared down at her, just as imposing as they'd been before. Fear tugged at her. She took a deep breath. *It's a privilege to feel fear,* she reminded herself, and she pushed the doors open.

Governor Warren looked up when she entered. He looked more tired now than he had in the past. His face seemed older, and the few grays in his hair had multiplied, but his eyes remained just as cold and black as they had during their first meeting.

"Miss Quinn," Governor Warren said with a chilling smile. "How nice to see you. Please come in. Sit."

Seren did as she was told, perching herself on the edge of the chair. Her heart pounded. *I shouldn't have come here*, she thought. She should have said that she'd gotten lost, or that she was sick. Better yet, she should have said she was dying of some rare disease and then hidden away deep in the depths of her room, beneath her bed, or in her closet.

"What do you have for me?" Governor Warren asked asked.

"I ... I haven't been able to find anything out yet."

Governor Warren raised an eyebrow. "Is that right? I must admit, Miss Quinn, I expected more from you." He frowned. "I really thought you wanted to save your mother."

This was harsher than the response she'd expected. It gripped her chest.

"I do," she said. Tears swarmed her eyes, but she refused to cry.

"Then perhaps," Governor Warren said, his voice becoming suddenly harsh, "you should stop gallivanting in the Simulator with my son and start doing what I asked you to do."

He knew. *Of course he does!* The man knew everything. He probably knew exactly what Zaiden had shown her. Seren's teeth dug so hard into her lower lip that she tasted blood.

"I'd like to show you something," Governor Warren said, his expression softening, "if I may."

Without waiting for her consent, he turned off his office lights until only one remained. The lingering light cast a shadow over his eyes, so they looked like black holes. He stood and moved around Seren, focusing on her so intently that she felt like he was trying to read her mind.

For one horrifying moment, she was sure he could.

"It's my understanding that you're curious about Earth," Governor Warren said as he circled, his hands clasped together at his chin. "I will not stand here and pretend that I don't understand your preoccupation, but I feel you have been misled, and as your friend—"

Seren cringed.

"—I feel that it is my duty to show you the truth."

Governor Warren lifted a remote from his desk and pressed a button, and the simulated city on the screen behind his desk was replaced by darkness.

"The Simulator exists, Miss Quinn, not to make people long for Earth, but as an escape from their daily lives, a distraction. Distracted people are happy people. When they go into the Simulator, they forget. Maybe they travel to Paris. They go to the Eiffel Tower, the Louvre. They watch those people in their silly hats bike along the Seine."

Governor Warren clicked the remote again, and his window buzzed back to life.

"Those people are ignorant, Miss Quinn. Earth is not all giant glamorous towers and silly little hats. It is not safe. It is horrifying."

He turned to look at her. The smile on his face replaced by something new—a determination of sorts.

"The images you have seen, which my son has so carelessly shown you, do not paint a truthful picture of your beloved planet. You may think that stars and mountains and rainbow lights in the sky are what's out there, but it's not. There is much more to be seen."

His face hardened. "Community is a special place. Some people have more than others, yes, but that is the way that life has *always* been, long before our own little world existed. There have always been rich and poor, fortunate and wretched. These are not new ideas. We did not create them. Do you understand?"

"Community offers a sanctuary where food and warmth are always available. People are safe here—given, of course, that they follow the law. Following a few laws and abiding by a code hardly seems a high price to pay, given the gifts that we have been given." Governor Warren turned to face her. "Things were not always that simple, Miss Quinn."

His eyes bored into her. They were angry now—sinister, even— and still cast in a shadow that made them appear all the more frightening.

"You know nothing of hunger or fear or pain. People living on Earth were not so lucky. People on Earth faced horrors beyond belief. Until you witness such horrors, you cannot fully appreciate the gift that you've been given. I've spared the people of Community from these images, and in doing so, I've given them the gift of ignorance. But ignorance is dangerous, Miss Quinn, and it is time that you learned the truth."

Slowly, images began to formulate on the screen.

"Earth was filled with many terrible things—things you and I cannot imagine or understand. People were cruel. There was mass starvation."

The blurred images became suddenly clear as two children with big, swollen bellies, hollow faces, and brittle legs appeared. Another child not more than two years old lay crying in its mother's arms, its ribs protruding from its skin. Seren felt sick. The image moved, and the woman looked into the camera and held out her hand, as if asking for something to eat.

"War."

A loud crack vibrated through the room, and screams surrounded Seren, chilling her to the bone. The images changed, and men and women dressed to blend in with the trees laid in bloody heaps, their foreheads glistening beneath a dark sky. At the front of the screen, a man was struck down, and blood pooled in his mouth from the knife that sliced his throat.

Governor Warren clicked the remote over and over. "Homicide, genocide, torture, abuse..."

Images flashed: first a man killing a woman, then a man with water being poured over a rag on his face, a father hitting his child.

"This is Earth. This is humanity at its finest!" Governor Warren bellowed.

The images continued to flash in an endless cycle of terror. Seren clamped her eyes shut. She couldn't watch anymore; she couldn't bear it. She clenched her fists, willing the images away, but she knew that they would be there, etched in her mind, for as long as she lived.

"Open your eyes, Seren."

Governor Warren placed a finger under her chin and lifted it so that they looked at each other. His eyes twinkled upon seeing her tears.

"Earth is not the magical place you believe it to be. I am only trying to protect you."

Seren shook her head. The governor held on tight, his nose just inches from hers. He smelled harsh and raw, like wood and smoke. She choked.

Governor Warren stroked her face with his calloused fingers and brushed away a tear that had fallen. Seren flinched.

"I have shown you these images not to frighten you, but to remind you of the gifts that you've been blessed with by living here. I just don't want to see you do anything you'll regret."

At that moment, Seren felt hatred like never before. Governor Warren was a monster, a manipulative sadist. She nodded, if only to get him to remove his disgusting fingers from her face. He held steadfast, and her skin ached beneath his touch.

"Remember that if you see anything unusual, you should keep me informed," he whispered, running one finger across her cheek. "Even if it is regarding my son."

27

SEREN

Seren took a long shower that night, taking full advantage of her unlimited access to hot water. She scrubbed her body until the bar of soap was as thin as a sheet of paper, though no amount of scrubbing could fully remove the feeling of the Governor's hands on her or the images he had shown her. Every time Seren closed her eyes, she was haunted by starving children, by men and women bloody on the ground, by violence.

Had Henry been wrong this whole time? Had he told her of a false version of Earth? Was Earth truly as bad as Governor Warren made it out to be? The simulations Seren had seen up to that point—the stars, the northern lights, the Rainbow Mountains, the gorgeous hot air balloons, the Ferris wheel—all of it had existed without humans. Had Zaiden done that on purpose? Was he trying to hide humanity's cruelty from Seren?

And if he was ... *why?*

Seren climbed out of the tub, still feeling just as filthy as when she'd stepped in. She wasn't sure of the time, but she knew it was well into the night. After what she'd seen, there was no chance that she would be able to sleep. She couldn't be alone, either. It felt suffocating to be by herself. So, without much thought, she grabbed a flashlight and went to the one place she might find solstice.

. . .

Lucas was in his pajamas when he came to the door. His eyes were tired and swollen, as if he, too, had tried to sleep, but had spent the last few nights restlessly.

As soon as she saw him, Seren sprung forward and wrapped her arms around him, knocking him backwards into his apartment. Lucas let out an *"umph,"* but Seren held on tight until he wrapped his arms around her, too. When his hands touched the small of her back, she knew that she'd been forgiven.

"What're you doing here?" Lucas asked, pulling away.

"I couldn't sleep," she said. Lucas looked down at the flashlight in her hands, and a goofy smile crept onto his face.

"Cool gadget," he said, eyeing the flashlight. "I could have used one a few minutes ago, when I stubbed my toe trying to get to the door."

Seren handed it to him and followed him to his couch. "Is your mom asleep?" she asked.

"Yeah, she's asleep. She can sleep through anything, though, so we don't have to be quiet." He placed the flashlight on the ground, angling it so that it lit up their faces. His was thinner and sharper than when Seren had last seen him. She wondered if he'd been eating. "What's going on with you? How is Tier Two life?"

There were so many unasked questions behind his words. Seren bit her lip. She wanted to tell him *everything.* Lucas was wiser than her, a problem-solver. He'd know what to do about Governor Warren, about Earth and its horrors. But Governor Warren had made himself clear: one small slip, and Lucas's life could be in danger, too. Seren couldn't do that.

So, she said, "Tier Two is different."

"Good different?"

She shrugged. "Could we talk about you instead?"

Lucas's eyes searched hers. Seren could tell he didn't want to drop it, but he nodded.

"I've taken a position as a nurse," he said.

Seren clamped her hand over her mouth. She'd been so wrapped up in her own stuff, she had completely forgotten that Year Elevens had chosen their trades a few weeks ago.

She should have been among them.

"Lucas! That's incredible!"

He smiled sheepishly. "Your Ma thought so, too. I chose her as my trainer—mostly to keep an eye on her."

Seren's heart clenched. "Lucas, that's so kind of you... How is she doing?"

Lucas shrugged. "She doesn't have much time, Ren. She's doing all she can, but..." He trailed off. "She won't be working much longer. The baby bump is starting to show. They'll want her on bed rest soon, I'd imagine."

That's why I have to be in Tier Two, Seren wanted to say. *I have to save her.* She wished Lucas could know, could *understand,* why she'd done everything she had.

"Does she... Is she eating enough?"

"They've upped her food allowances," Lucas said, nodding. "She misses you, though."

Seren's eyes welled up with tears, and Lucas placed an arm around her.

"I'm sorry, I didn't mean to upset you," he said.

"No, you didn't, I..." Seren sniffed. "I'm really glad you're there for her."

She sunk into him, allowing Lucas's body to engulf her. Seren felt at peace. His arms were the home she had been stripped from. His warmth was the first of its kind that she had felt in a long time. He reminded her of her childhood and that bright, happy bubble that surrounded those earlier memories, when all there was to worry about was cacao nibs and sugar tea.

"I've missed you," Lucas whispered into her hair.

"I've missed you, too," she choked out.

He allowed her to cry, holding her through the body-quaking sobs, until she couldn't cry any longer. The images that Governor Warren had shown her dulled as she lay in Lucas's arms, as if he were slowly erasing them from her memory with just his embrace.

You really are a healer, Lucas, Seren thought, wiping tears from her eyes.

"I'm so sorry," Seren whispered. "For everything."

Lucas held her tighter. "Everything is forgotten," he said. And it really felt like he meant it.

It was those words that gave Seren the push she needed to finally let go.

Just as sleep was about to come, Lucas lifted her and carried her to his bed. He laid her down and pulled the blankets up so that they covered her up to her neck. The coarseness of the sheets reminded her of her own Tier Four bed and put her further at ease.

"Goodnight, Ren," he whispered.

Seren cracked open an eye. "Where are you going?"

"To sleep on the couch."

"Don't go," she whispered. She feared that if he left her alone, the memories would come back in full force.

Lucas hesitated.

"Please."

"Okay."

Seren felt her body move as Lucas's weight altered the slant of the mattress. There was barely enough room for the two of them, but it felt right that way.

Sleep found Lucas quickly. Within minutes, his breathing slowed. Seren watched his chest rise and fall. She tried to remember what he used to be like, before his father died and everything changed. Somehow, she couldn't remember him like that. To her, he'd always been the strong, self-sustaining young man that he was now—hard on the outside, but with a wonderfully soft interior.

She thought then of Zaiden. Zaiden, who'd also lost a parent, and had learned to hide his softness. The two boys could not be more different, and yet, they were so much alike.

Seren closed her eyes and remembered the Ferris wheel.

Eventually, sleep found her too.

28

ZAIDEN

Zaiden was in high spirits the next day. Whether it was his time with Seren or waking up without a hangover, he wasn't sure, but it was a nice change. Did he mean the things he'd said to her on the Ferris wheel? Maybe. He couldn't see why not. When he was Governor, he could make changes for the betterment of Community. And as for the lower Tiers, Zaiden supposed he had always seen them as lesser than himself—but Seren was changing that. Maybe they weren't as different from him as he liked to believe.

Zaiden's maid came to his door after the Awakening. She knocked timidly.

"Good morning," Zaiden said brightly as she placed a vitamin packet and a coffee beside him. She looked taken aback by his positivity.

"Good morning," she stammered. After a moment, she rallied, saying, "Governor Warren wanted me to tell you about a hearing this morning. He asked that you be in the Council Room in fifteen minutes."

"Great," Zaiden said. "Thanks."

She looked at him oddly before exiting, and Zaiden smiled, emptying the vitamins into his coffee.

All the council members were present when Zaiden arrived at the Council Room. They looked up as he entered, his steaming cup of coffee still in hand.

"You're late," Zaiden's father said coolly.

"Oh. Sorry," Zaiden said. He looked up at the clock, which, as he'd thought, indicated he was five minutes earlier than told. He suspected his father had given him the wrong time to undermine him in front of the council. Most days, that would have made Zaiden angry, but today, nothing could seem to bring him down. He took a seat in the empty chair to the right of his father, and Governor Warren returned his attention to the woman who had been speaking.

"Penelope, please resume."

"Thank you, Governor. Owing allegiance to Community and all those within it, Marcus Milligan has been charged with high treason. The accused is suspected of conspiring against you and attempting to overthrow the government. The punishment for these crimes is death by execution. Is there any opposition to this damnation?"

Zaiden blinked, a sudden nausea rising in his gut. He blamed it on drinking coffee on an empty stomach, but perhaps it was the idea of deciding whether to sentence someone to death before 10:00 a.m. He glanced around the Council Room, waiting for at least one person to object, but no one did.

"Very well," Penelope said. "All those in favor of a guilty verdict?"

Every member apart for Zaiden raised their hand. Zaiden cleared his throat uncomfortably, taken aback by the speed with which the council had just decided to take a man's life.

"Shouldn't we be hearing from the accused?" Zaiden asked before he could stop himself.

Every head in the room snapped to look at him. Out of the corner of his eye, he saw his father's jaw tighten.

Zaiden sunk back into his chair. Was he wrong to say something? He didn't think so. In his law class, his teacher had talked about the right to a fair trial. The accused should have the right to be heard by a competent, independent, impartial tribunal, the right to a public hearing, and the right to counsel. He and his classmates had been taught that these rights existed in Community. Zaiden put his faith in the law because he believed that there was always a right to a fair trial, but the council was deciding Marcus's fate without his presence and without any concrete evidence to suggest his guilt. Wasn't that illegal—or at the very least, unethical?

"There is no need," Zaiden's father said, his expression threatening. "His crimes have been investigated, and he has been found guilty of all charges. His execution will be set for this afternoon. Council is dismissed."

The members of the council stood to leave. They chatted as they left, seemingly unbothered by the fact that they had just sentenced someone to death. Zaiden stood to follow, but his father grabbed his arm and pulled him close.

"Do not undermine me like that again," he snarled.

Zaiden pulled his arm away.

"Sorry," he said, for once not feeling sorry at all. He left the room in a huff, his good mood sufficiently squashed.

29

ZAIDEN

Knock, knock.

Alaster Holland did not wait for Zaiden's response before he opened the door. Zaiden was lying on the floor, in the middle of his fifth set of sit-ups, trying to get his frustration at his father out in a healthy way. His forehead was dripping with sweat.

Alaster leaned against his doorframe and looked down at him. "Your father would like for you to witness the execution."

Zaiden's stomach twisted. "Do I have to?"

Knowing his father, this was just another way to demonstrate his dominance and scare him into submission, and Zaiden didn't have the energy to deal with that today.

Alaster nodded. "I'm afraid so. I'm heading there now, if you'd like to join me."

Zaiden sighed and hauled himself up from the floor. A cruel chill hit him as he stood, and he grabbed a sweatshirt to throw on.

Annoyed, Zaiden followed Alaster through the halls of Tier One. Neither of them spoke as Alaster led them to a room that Zaiden had never been to before. A sign above it read, No Entrance. Zaiden looked at it warily as Alaster scanned his identity card and opened the door.

When they entered, Zaiden's father was standing inside the dark room with two Harmonizers and a man in a lab coat. Strapped to the metal table in the center was a fair-skinned man with sunken brown eyes, a well-trimmed beard, and a hooked nose. He looked thin and frail and seemed to be awake, but he did not struggle against his restraints or look up when Zaiden and Alaster entered.

"I think another round of shock treatment may do Mr. Milligan some good," Governor Warren said without acknowledging Zaiden's entrance. Alaster guided Zaiden to a corner of the room, where they stood with their backs against the wall.

Zaiden stared at the man strapped to the table. He looked broken, more dead than alive. His pale forehead shone with sweat, and his chest rose and fell as if he'd just completed a grueling workout.

"I usually look away for this," Alaster mumbled.

But Zaiden couldn't bring himself to look away. The man in the lab coat pressed a button, and Marcus began to convulse and scream. His cries were low and guttural and nothing like Zaiden had ever heard before. Alaster diverted his gaze, but Zaiden stood frozen in horror. Marcus's body spasmed for what felt like an eternity, until Governor Warren said, "That's enough"—and the screaming ceased.

Zaiden felt the remnants of his lunch coming up his throat. He forced it down and took a breath.

"I'll ask again," Governor Warren said, bringing his face just inches from the man on the table. "Who else is working with you?"

When Marcus spoke, his voice was weak and raspy. Each word sounded like a struggle. "Screw..." He gasped for breath. "... you."

Zaiden's father shook his head. "Very well. Angelo, please administer the serum."

The man in the lab coat, Angelo, poised himself above Marcus. Zaiden dug his nails into the palms of his hands. Marcus shouldn't have to be awake during this. Why didn't they put him to sleep?

Just as Angelo was about to plunge the poison into Marcus's veins, Governor Warren stopped him. "Why don't we let my son do the honors?"

Zaiden felt the color draining from his face. He thought he might pass out. Alaster placed a strong hand on his shoulder.

"Governor Warren, this is the boy's first execution," he interjected. "I hardly think—"

"He is going to be Governor someday," Zaiden's father snarled. "He needs to understand the consequences of Community's laws. Come here, son."

Zaiden looked to Alaster desperately, but Alaster said nothing. Instead, he gave Zaiden a firm push in Marcus's direction. Slowly, Zaiden walked over and took the needle into his shaky hands.

"Just put it into his skin here..." Angelo pointed to a small black dot that had been drawn on Marcus's arm. "... and push."

Marcus looked up at Zaiden, ailing and spent. There was so much hopelessness and exhaustion in the man's eyes.

With a deep breath, Zaiden put the tip of the needle on the dot. His pulse raced.

This man had committed a crime. He had conspired against Zaiden's father, against Community as a whole, knowing full well the consequences of such actions. This man had been part of the resistance that killed Zaiden's mother. He probably wanted Zaiden himself dead. He did not deserve mercy.

So, then, why is this so hard?

Zaiden trembled.

With the crimes she had committed, it could have been Seren strapped to this table, Zaiden thought. Seren facing the death penalty for identity theft. It could have been her thin, pale arm with the black dot guiding the needle. It could have been *her* screams filling the room.

Zaiden pulled away. "I can't."

His father scowled. "I should have known you'd be too weak."

The words felt like a slap to the face. Anger overcame him. Without a second thought, Zaiden plunged the needle into Marcus's skin and injected the cloudy blue tainted liquid into his veins. Zaiden's chest heaved.

The room fell silent and stayed that way for a long, dragging moment.

Until Marcus started to scream.

Zaiden startled, and the needle clambered from his hand onto the floor, its glass cartridge shattering. He took four steps back and tripped over his own feet. "What's happening?" he gasped. "Is he okay? Did I do it wrong?"

His father smiled a cold, malicious smile. "You did it perfectly."

Zaiden's skin turned hot. Bile rose to his throat as Marcus continued to scream. It seemed to go on for eternity. Somewhere in the thick of it all, Alaster placed his hand on Zaiden's shoulder and pulled him back into the corner, but Zaiden hardly noticed. He was oblivious to everything but Marcus. The blue veins in Marcus's neck bulged and twisted as he thrashed against his restraints.

Finally, the screaming stopped, and Marcus stilled.

No one said anything as Angelo placed two fingers to Marcus's neck, just below his chin, and nodded.

"I thought that the serum was painless," Zaiden choked out.

Angelo nodded. "It is."

Then why did Marcus scream?

"Are we done here?" Alaster asked firmly.

Governor Warren's strange trance broke, and he tore his gaze from Marcus's dead body.

"Yes. You may go."

Numbly, Zaiden allowed Alaster to guide him back into the hallway. The sudden change in lighting blinded him. He was grateful for the momentary distraction, but as his eyes adjusted, the thoughts returned.

Marcus's screams… His bulging veins… The way he thrashed… And above all, the horrible feeling of ending a man's life.

"Who was he?" Zaiden asked finally, Marcus's dead body still etched into his mind. He wanted to know. He wanted to understand who the man he had just killed was.

"He was an Educator in Tier Four."

Zaiden nodded wordlessly. An Educator. Tier Four. Had Seren known him? Had that man taught her? He thought he might pass out.

Alaster looked at Zaiden. "I think we should get you some tea," he said kindly.

"I don't want tea."

"No, but I do. Come."

30

ZAIDEN

Zaiden and Alaster sat silently in Alaster's apartment, both with steaming cups in front of them. Alaster's maid brought them a small bowl of sugar and a plate of warm blueberry-and-lemon scones. The buttery sweet scent made Zaiden feel ill; he shoved the plate away.

Alaster's apartment was modest in comparison to the Warrens'. He'd had his choice of apartments when he was elected to the council, and for some inexplicable reason, he had picked the smallest one. Zaiden wasn't sure whether that was a reflection on Alaster's lack of a social life or his modesty.

"How are you feeling?" Alaster asked, taking a sip from his cup.

Zaiden stared down at his. "I'm fine."

Alaster looked over his cup at Zaiden. "It's okay not to be fine."

"I'm fine," Zaiden repeated, his tone sharp.

"Okay. You're fine." Alaster paused. "The important thing to remember is that men like Marcus threaten the order of Community. We know enough about history to recognize that our system is too fragile to deal with people who wish for disorder. You did the right thing today."

Zaiden wished he could believe that. His father believed it. The Council believed it. Alaster believed it. Why was it so hard for him?

"Your father is hard on you because he cares," Alaster said.

Zaiden scoffed. "You don't know anything about my relationship with my father."

"I didn't mean to overstep," Alaster said.

"Then don't."

Alaster didn't seem upset by Zaiden's coarseness; quite the opposite. He remained composed. His gentle nature and compassion reminded Zaiden of his mother. Zaiden's heart clenched at the thought of her.

"You look just like her, you know," Alaster said softly, as if reading Zaiden's mind.

Zaiden looked up from his steaming cup. "Really?"

"She would be proud of the man you've become."

Would she? Zaiden didn't remember enough about her to know if he would have made her proud.

"What were you and my father talking about the other day in the Council Room?" he asked, remembering their hushed conversation.

Alaster raised an eyebrow. "We talk about a lot of things."

"This was about placebos," Zaiden said. Alaster didn't answer, and Zaiden felt his blood pressure rise. "I just executed a rebel, yet you still treat me like a child."

Alaster looked at Zaiden, his face devoid of all feeling. The tension in the air was strong. Finally, he spoke. "You're right. Of course you're right—but your father would not be pleased if I told you."

"I won't say anything," Zaiden said.

Another pause. Alaster sighed and set down his mug. "Are you familiar with the monthly shots that women of who've already born one child receive?"

The birth control shots. Zaiden had heard of them, but never gave them much thought. He didn't have to; they didn't apply to him.

"Yes."

"A few years ago, we began giving out placebo shots to 0.05 percent of the populations in Tiers Four and Five."

Zaiden's eyebrows furrowed. "Placebo shots?"

Alaster nodded and leaned in closer. "The shots seem to be a real medical treatment, but in actuality are just a saline solution."

Zaiden frowned. "I know what placebo shots are. But why give them out?"

"You heard the census data," Alaster said. "The one child policy has caused our population to become an aging one. The placebo shot ensures that a small number of women who've already conceived continue to get pregnant to at least slow the problem."

Zaiden didn't understand. "Wouldn't the woman be executed after having the child?"

Alaster nodded. "The child lives; the woman dies. Our population remains the same size, and the aging problem fixes itself."

Zaiden could barely believe what he was hearing. Placebo shots, given out randomly to the lower Tiers? These weren't just forced pregnancies; they were death sentences.

"Isn't that wrong?" Zaiden asked tentatively.

"Maybe, but it is a necessary evil to keep Community afloat."

Zaiden didn't know what to say. Today had turned his very perception of Community on its head. Everything he thought he knew about the way Community was run was wrong. There were no fair trials, the executions were inhumane, and now his father was slaughtering women for something he was forcing on them?

What would his mother have said about all this?

Alaster seemed to sense his discomfort. "Zaiden, I understand this news may be upsetting, but you must understand that your father does all of this for the greater good. Community cannot continue as it has. This is the only way."

"Right," Zaiden said. His tongue felt like sandpaper. He pushed away from the table. "Thank you for the tea."

Alaster looked like there were so many more things he wanted to say, but he just pressed his lips together and nodded. "You're welcome," he said.

He had the maid show Zaiden out.

31

SEREN

When Seren woke up, Lucas was gone. She rolled over, smelling the place where his head had been. There was a moment of ignorant bliss before the memories from the day before came crashing back down. She wrapped her head in the pillow and tried to make the thoughts disappear.

A small, gentle lump beneath the pillowcase caught her attention. Her hands fluttered over the object, curious. Hard, rectangular, flat... just like... *No. He wouldn't do it again, would he?*

Seren crawled beneath the covers, bringing the pillow with her. She removed the object from his pillowcase and lifted the blanket slightly to allow in some light.

Just as she thought, it was another identity card. This one was the same turquoise color as her new one, granting all access. Seren didn't understand. What could Lucas possibly need another IC for? Had he not learned his lesson from the first?

A bubble of dread rose in Seren's chest as a realization dawned on her. Was Lucas a part of...? No. He *couldn't* be.

"Seren? What're you doing under there?"

Seren snapped up from beneath the sheets. Lucas stood in his doorway, a towel wrapped around his waist, water dripping from his skin.

Her breath caught. "I was just..."

Seren shoved the card back into the pillowcase as swiftly as she could manage, but it was too late. He'd already seen. Understanding dawned on his face. Seren feared he'd be mad at her for snooping, but instead, he looked apologetic.

"I can explain," he said.

She shook her head. *Not here. Not now.*

He'd showered; the five minutes were up. They wouldn't be able to drown out their words.

"I have work," Lucas said.

"I know."

"Will you come back here later? Around dinner? We could..."

"Okay."

. . .

Seren left in a hurry, her brain a mush of confusion. She clung to her own IC, the one Zaiden had gifted her. She considered visiting Ma and Pa, but she couldn't bring herself to do it. What was Lucas *thinking?*

Work in the Thinker Dome moved slow. Seren found herself reading the same passages over and over, trying to glean meaning from the words, but unable to focus her mind. Dinnertime could not come quickly enough.

Finally, the day ended, and Seren followed her fellow Thinkers back out into the halls. It was the first day of her job that she did not take a book to bring home with her. She walked impatiently towards Lucas's apartment, so entwined in her own thoughts that she did not see Zaiden. He, apparently, was having the same experience. The two of them collided, and Seren toppled backwards.

"Oh! I'm so sorry, I—Seren!" Zaiden said. "I'm sorry, I didn't see you there."

"Me, either," Seren said, a blush creeping across her face.

"Are you alright?"

"I'm fine."

"Sorry I haven't been by with those books yet. Life has been—"

"That's okay," Seren said, too quickly. Her face warmed. "I mean, I've been busy, too."

Zaiden nodded absentmindedly. "Okay, well, great. Sometime soon, though."

Seren thought about Governor Warren's warning: *"Perhaps you should stop gallivanting in the Simulator with my son and start doing what I asked you to do."*

"Yeah," she said vaguely. "Sometime soon."

She made it to Lucas's just as he was finishing his dinner.

"My mom is working tonight," he said, leading her into the apartment and closing the door behind her. "So, we've got the place to ourselves."

They went instinctively into the bathroom, both aware that this was not a conversation for out in the open.

"Mom's going to be pissed that I used up her shower time," he said.

Seren nodded distractedly. She found herself almost angry at Lucas for getting another IC and putting himself in danger. She knew firsthand the consequences of actions like that; hell, she was living with them.

If Lucas sensed her anger, he didn't show it. He turned on the shower and settled down on the edge of the tub.

"We probably don't need to get undressed this time," he said, smiling sheepishly at her.

Seren crossed her arms. "Why do you have that card, Lucas?"

Lucas sighed and patted the spot beside him, and Seren perched on the bathtub's edge. Water splashed the shower curtain, creating a dull pitter-patter effect like falling rain. Some droplets escaped and landed on Seren's skin and the floor beside her. She shifted away from the splatter and closer to Lucas.

"Well?" she asked. Five minutes was not a lot of time.

"I'm a member of an organization," Lucas said quietly. He spoke in such a soft tone that Seren had to lean in close to hear him. "A group called Defectio."

I knew it, Seren thought. Her stomach dropped. "Why?" she whispered. "How?"

The pitter-patter took over as Lucas formulated his words.

"When I was just fourteen years old, a girl approached me on my way home from school," he said. "Noa. She was our age, but I'd never seen her before. I knew immediately that she couldn't be a Tier Four."

Noa told Lucas that their fathers had been good friends before both of them died mysteriously of the same ailment. At first, Lucas hadn't believed her. He'd thought it was a prank, maybe, or a trap. But when Noa told him to meet up with her later that night, he couldn't help himself. He agreed to meet her after curfew.

That night, Noa took him to a deserted part of Tier Four, a place he'd never been before, and pulled him into the ruins of an old bathroom. From there, she led him down a deep tunnel—a tunnel to Tier Five.

In Tier Five, she introduced Lucas to a group of men and women who called themselves Defectio. They told Lucas that his father's death had not been an accident, but an execution for his treason against Governor Warren. Henry had been one of their leaders.

Lucas told her this part gently, laying his hand on top of hers. "They killed him, Seren," Lucas said. "They killed my father."

The news shouldn't have surprised her; she'd seen what Governor Warren could do, and she knew the punishment for treason, but it sent her into a spiral. It didn't make sense. Why would they say it was just a heart attack? Didn't that go against the deterrence theory that Governor Warren had bragged about?

"I'm so sorry, Lucas," she whispered. She thought of Governor Warren plotting to kill Lucas's father and anger swelled within her.

"I've had time to come to terms with it. It used to make me sad. Now, it just makes me angry." He took a deep breath. "My father, the group he led—they were planning to overthrow Community's government. They said that Governor Warren had been holding onto a secret."

The water from the spout sputtered. They had a minute, maybe two at most before it shut off and their voices would be heard.

"What secret?"

"Earth is safe," Lucas said. "It has been for years."

Seren frowned.

"I know, it sounds far-fetched," he said. "I didn't believe it either at first, but it didn't take much evidence to convince me that they were right. Earth healed itself after most of the human population died. It can support life again."

Seren's head spun.

Lucas sounded so genuine about everything, and Seren realized that true or not, he believed it all. He believed it—and he had kept it from her.

Lucas searched her eyes. "What're you thinking?" he asked.

Seren wasn't sure whether she wanted to laugh, cry, scream, or tell him that he was an idiot. But above all that, a feeling of betrayal emerged.

She looked at him. "Why didn't you tell me?" It was impossible to keep the hurt out of her voice.

"I wanted to keep you safe."

"And now?"

"Now, I think you can help."

"If it's true," she said, "then why has no one told us?"

Lucas looked exasperated. "They're selfish, Ren. You think they want to give up the lifestyle they have? They have people farming for them, creating electricity, taking care of their waste and their trash. They have nice homes with warm beds and showers that'll run as long as they like. Outside isn't like that. We'd have to hunt and gather and make shelters and deal with the fallout of our ancestors' mistakes. We wouldn't have a steady amount of food or clean water or heat. *You're* the one who has always been obsessed with…" He stopped himself, looked around, and lowered his voice. "You know what. If we left, you could experience it all—the rain, the stars, the ocean, all of it."

I can do that here, Seren thought. She'd seen more in the Simulator than she would ever see on Earth. She'd already experienced more than most people probably used to in a lifetime. The world Lucas was describing was not what she wanted.

Seren stopped herself. What kind of thinking was that? Who had she become? *Of course* she wanted freedom! She wanted freedom from Governor Warren's evil grasps, from his curfews and his listening ears. She wanted that for herself—but more importantly, she wanted that for Ma and the baby. She wanted that kid to have so much more than she'd ever had. She wanted it to have fresh air and a life outside these stifling gray walls.

"Let's say for a minute that you're right. How would you leave? We're trapped here. Even if we weren't, we don't even know where we are—"

"We're on a stretch of land in North Dakota, built right by the Mississippi River."

Seren blinked. "What the hell is that?"

"You're asking the wrong questions, Ren!" Lucas said, sounding annoyed.

"Then what're the right questions?"

"Well, first, how do we feed ourselves?"

"Okay. Yeah. Start with that," Seren said, crossing her arms. She was acutely aware that their time was coming to a close. The water started to slow, and Lucas had to speak even more quietly to avoid being heard.

"We could keep Community's greenhouses, while still allowing members to go outside. Just because it's safe doesn't mean we have to travel far."

"You just said you want to be nomadic."

"I didn't—why aren't you more excited about this?" His frustration was palpable.

"Because, Lucas, it seems impossible. There's no way out of this place. Even if there was, things would fall apart immediately. If you get rid of Governor Warren, who's going to run Community?"

"All of us. We'll make it a democracy, like things used to be." Lucas paused. "And you're wrong about that first part. There is one known exit."

"Where?"

"The Governor's office. We're going to break in there and then break out."

Seren tried to absorb what Lucas was saying. *Break in, break out...*

Her body turned cold.

"No. No way," she said, furiously shaking her head. "Do you have a death wish?!"

"I'm not the only one working on this, Ren. There are more than a few dozen people in Defectio. You haven't even seen how people in Tier Five live. We have it good compared to them. They're farmers, but they're starving. They're starving—and they're angry.

They're ready to fight for this. They're ready to fight for power and for freedom."

Seren rubbed her forehead and groaned. Why wasn't he listening? "Lucas, are you hearing yourself?" she asked. "This is crazy."

"Don't you want to get out of here, Ren?" Lucas asked, grabbing her chin so that she looked directly at him. "We've always had the same dream: to see Earth. To live there. Now's our chance! Come with me and your mother and the others. Be a part of something."

Seren cast her eyes down. "Lucas…"

"Why not? Answer me that. What could possibly be holding you back?"

Seren's mind flashed to the videos Governor Warren had showed her in his office last night. She thought about the starvation, the violence, the blood.

"We don't know it's safe," Seren said. "People were horrible back then; the world was terrifying. What if we help everyone escape just to have them die?"

"Isn't it better to die free than to live as a slave?" Lucas asked.

Seren wasn't going to get through to him. She wouldn't change his mind; she could see that from the way he looked at her.

Lucas's voice was gentle as he continued. "The upper Tiers are corrupt and sinister; you said it yourself. They *killed* my father. They slaughter people who get in their way." He shook his head as he looked at her. "I will not start and end my life in Community, Ren—and I don't think you want to, either."

Seren bit her lip. What if none of what this Noa girl had told Lucas was true? What if Henry *had* died of a heart attack? She thought about Governor Warren's deterrence theory. Punishments were imperative to keeping Community orderly—but what had come from *that* punishment? What was the purpose of teaching a dead man a lesson?

And what of Tier Five? Seren had never seen it; she had no idea how they lived. Of course, Seren hadn't known how the Tier Twos lived before a month ago, but now she had become accustomed to the lifestyle. It was difficult for her to imagine giving it up.

Was that what was holding Seren back: her new way of living?

Was she just as bad as the rest of them?

The water stopped abruptly, and both Seren and Lucas drew in a breath.

Lucas stood and stared down at her. "I promised I would do everything possible to keep your mother safe. Are you going to help me, or not?"

"I … I don't know."

The disappointment in his eyes was her undoing. She'd never seen him so repulsed.

"Right," he said tersely. "Let me know when you figure it out."

32

ZAIDEN

That night, Zaiden dreamed of his mother.

In his dream, the two of them were together on the Ferris wheel, riding up into the sky. Zaiden told her all about his position on the council, and how he'd ranked first in his class—and Seren. While he spoke to her, she'd been looking dreamily out across the water, but when she turned to look at him, her eyes were gone—and in their place were dark black holes.

She opened her mouth and screamed, just as Marcus had.

Zaiden jolted awake. He blinked up at a disheveled man standing over him.

"Father? What time is it?" he asked groggily.

His father's hair was a mess, and his tie hung loosely around his neck. The light in the hallway shone in and reflected off his clock: 3:15 a.m. What on Earth was his father doing in his room at this hour?

"Get up," his father said. His breath stank of moonshine.

Zaiden stared at him, unmoving.

"I said, get *up*!" he bellowed, bodily pulling Zaiden from his bed.

Zaiden stumbled, and his bare feet hit the cool floor with a slap. In the moment it took him to regain his balance, his father swung at him. Zaiden didn't even have a moment to comprehend what was happening when the punch connected with his eye. A loud crack resounded through the air. It knocked Zaiden off his feet, sending him spiraling backwards onto his bed. Pain worked its way to his forehead, and colors pulsed beneath his eyelids.

"Get up," his father snarled again.

"You're drunk," Zaiden said, his voice lacking conviction. "We need to get you to bed."

"I said, *get up.*"

Once again, he pulled Zaiden from the bed, but Zaiden was more prepared this time. He landed firmly on the ground.

His father threw a punch, which Zaiden blocked with his right arm. He didn't have time to think. His father was on the offensive, and though he was drunk, he still fought meticulously like the fighter he was trained to be. He threw another punch, aiming lower this time. Again, Zaiden blocked it. It hit his forearm in an awkward place, sending pain shooting up to his shoulder.

"If you're under threat of attack," his father said, "it's vital that you are always prepared. You cannot get complacent, and you cannot get lazy."

The next punch surprised Zaiden. He didn't move quick enough, and his father's fist glanced over his chin. Zaiden put his hands up to protect himself from the next blow, but his father aimed lower, hitting him in the stomach. The impact expelled the air from his lungs, and Zaiden doubled over.

Zaiden was on full alert now, no longer debilitated from sleep. In the streaming hallway light, he finally recognized the true anger in his father's features. Governor Warren had never done anything like this before. Some would call his behavior abusive, sure, but it had never been so outright as this.

Zaiden stayed on the defensive, despite being better suited for a fight now than his father. He didn't want to hurt him—not while the man was in such a bad state. His father stumbled each time he swung, still in control, but clumsy.

Zaiden moved backwards towards his dresser, and his father followed like a predator stalking its prey. Light hit him from the side, illuminating him in a sinister glow.

"Fight *back*," his father snarled as he approached. He stumbled closer, his gait unbalanced.

Zaiden blocked another punch. "Stop," he pleaded. "You need to go to bed."

Zaiden searched his father's eyes for a sliver of humanity, but whatever benevolence had existed there before had vanished. The alcohol had seen to that.

Zaiden's eyes flickered to his bedroom door. If he could get there and run, his drunk father wouldn't be able to catch him. They could talk when he was sober, and everything would be alright.

"FIGHT BACK!" Governor Warren bellowed, shoving Zaiden backwards. Zaiden stumbled and hit the wall. He fell to the floor hard, and his clock clattered down with him, shattering on the hardwood. Zaiden gasped for air and clutched his ribs. The pain was great—greater than Zaiden had ever experienced during a fight. Judging by the difficulty he was having just breathing, he feared his ribs might be broken.

Zaiden's father took a step back and waited for him to stand again, but he was unable to move. He clutched his stomach, rolled over, and prayed his father would not kick him while he was down. He desperately wanted the violence to end.

Through his watery eyes, Zaiden saw his broken clock lying just inches away. If he could grab it, he might have a fair chance of knocking his father out with the tough wooden backing. At this point, it seemed like his only option. Zaiden had given his father a chance to stop, but the fire in his father's eyes told him that the violence would not end. He didn't have a choice.

Carefully, Zaiden grabbed the clock and pulled it to his stomach. The hard surface steadied him as he took a shaky breath and stood, keeping his back towards his father and the clock out of view.

"Turn and fight, you coward," his father snarled.

Zaiden did not turn. He heard his father inch closer.

"You are *weak,*" his father said, the words sharp and dangerous as a knife. "Your mother was right. She said you'd never be a good leader. She said you were too soft."

Zaiden dug his nails into his palms. He reminded himself that his father was drunk. He didn't mean the things he was saying; he couldn't. It was just his way of antagonizing Zaiden, but Zaiden wouldn't let him win. He wouldn't fight—not in the way his father wanted.

Governor Warren took another step, now so close that Zaiden could feel his breath on his neck. "You're pathetic," he whispered into Zaiden's ear. Zaiden flinched.

Finally, he turned, and in one swift motion, he brought the thick wooden base of the clock down on his father's head. It hit with a nauseating crack, and Governor Warren slumped to the ground, motionless.

Zaiden looked down at his father. His chest heaved. "I'm sorry," he whispered.

But he wasn't.

Zaiden tossed the clock onto his bed and dropped down beside his father to check for a pulse. It took him a moment to find it, but there it was, *thump thump thump...* Its pace quickened by alcohol.

Zaiden used his last bit of strength to roll his father onto his side, away from the broken glass. He placed his hand beneath his father's chin so that, on the off chance he got sick, he wouldn't choke. When he pulled his hands away, he saw that his father's shirt was blood red. He checked his father's body for injuries, but there were none.

Shocked, Zaiden looked down at his own hands. The clock's shattered glass had pierced his skin, and now blood trickled down his arms. He examined the blood as it dripped from his arms onto the floor. He tried to comprehend what had just happened. His eyes flickered to his father, and he felt ill.

Zaiden stumbled from his bedroom, shutting his door firmly behind him. His father would wake up in a room surrounded by shattered glass and blood-stained walls, but Zaiden hoped he would be sober by then.

Zaiden stumbled from his penthouse into the hallway, clutching his arms to his chest. He shivered as the air hit his skin. His head hurt where his skull had hit the wall. He touched it gingerly. Did he have a concussion? Maybe... He felt tired and confused. He should go to the infirmary to get checked out; he knew that. But he also knew that going there like this at three in the morning would raise too many questions. They couldn't afford to have people questioning his father during such a volatile time in Community's history. He could go to Rocco's or Atlas's place, sure—but their fathers were on the council, and that would only lead to the same issue.

He'd have to take care of it himself.

33

SEREN

Seren sat at her kitchen table and stared blankly at the wall. There were only four hours left until the Awakening, and she still hadn't been able to coax herself to sleep. There was too much going on in her head. Lucas's disappointment felt like a crushing blow, but what was she supposed to do? Join him in a suicide mission? Governor Warren might be evil, but Zaiden wasn't. And when Zaiden came into power, everything would change. They just had to wait until then. Couldn't Lucas *wait*?

Can Ma? a voice in Seren's head said. *Can the other women who are unlucky enough to get pregnant in the lower Tiers?*

"Shut up," she said to the voice.

Exhausted, but still unable to shut down, Seren stayed in a quasi-sleep state, seated, and staring into the abyss. When she heard a banging on the door, she thought she was imagining it.

But then the banging came again, more desperate this time.

Seren sprang up from her seat and opened the door to find Zaiden hunched over, his shirt covered in blood.

"Oh my God!" she said. "What happened?"

Zaiden's eye was swollen shut, and he had a bloody cut on his lip. His hair was a mess, and he was half dressed. He blinked at her, as if he, too, was surprised to find himself standing there.

"I'm sorry," he said, looking around. "I didn't... It's late. I should go."

"No!" Seren said, far too quickly. "No. What... Are you alright?"

Are you alright? What a stupid question. Of course he wasn't alright. His skin had lost all color, as if it had drained right out of him.

"Can I come in?" he asked.

"Of course." Seren ushered him in and sat him down in the chair by her table. He fell backwards into it, nearly knocking it sideways. Seren caught it in time and steadied it as Zaiden closed his eyes. His breaths were shallow.

"I'm sorry to wake you," he said.

"You didn't wake me," Seren replied. Her eyes traveled over his bloodied arms. Innumerable questions came to her mind, but she held back. "We should get you cleaned up."

She went to the sink and wet a towel before also grabbing a bottle of rubbing alcohol and a pair of tweezers she had stashed away in her bathroom drawer. Zaiden remained still, his eyes fixated on the wall as Seren knelt at his side. She examined his arms. Bits of glass stuck out of his skin, like the quills of a porcupine. Nausea rose up, but she shoved it down as she opened the bottle of alcohol.

"This may hurt," she said, pouring it over his wounds.

Zaiden flinched, but did not cry out.

She took the tweezers and began to painstakingly remove the glass. The pieces were mostly just piercing the first few layers of skin, but some were deeper. Zaiden cringed each time she removed a piece, but he did not complain once. Seren tried hard to keep her hand steady.

They did not speak, which was fine by her. Seren wasn't sure what she'd say if they did. She did not want to assume the worst; he could have gotten in a bar fight, or a spat with one of his classmates. This didn't have to be what she thought it was.

But from the look on his face, she feared the worst.

Zaiden still wouldn't meet her gaze. Seren pulled the last bit of glass from his arm and examined it gently.

"There," she said. "All done."

He mumbled a thank you.

"I'm going to get you something cold for your eye," she said. He didn't answer, so Seren stood and went to her freezer. She pulled out a bag of vegetables she'd frozen to make broth with and handed it to him.

Zaiden took the bag and brought it to his skin while Seren sat on her cold hands and tried to warm them. Neither spoke.

"Are you okay?" Seren asked finally. Again, it was a stupid question; of course he wasn't. Still, Zaiden nodded. Seren bit her lip. "Does he do this a lot?"

When Zaiden didn't deny it, Seren knew for sure: Governor Warren had done this.

She felt sick.

"Not like this," Zaiden said, shifting the baggie on his face. He paused. "Please don't tell anyone."

Seren knew she shouldn't trust him, but seeing him sitting there, looking so defeated, made her want to more than anything. "I won't tell a soul."

"Thank you."

Seren stayed by his side. The gentle hum of the radiator filled the silence. It was the first time anyone had been to her Tier Two place, and Seren realized she liked the company. With another person there, it felt more like home. Zaiden felt like home. She searched for the right thing to say to him, but nothing came to mind.

"I try to tell myself that he's not a bad man," Zaiden said. Seren looked up at him. "I try to tell myself that everything he does, he does for the people of Community. He tries to protect us; I know that. But sometimes, it feels like he's making the wrong choices—choices I would never make."

He went quiet. Seren looked at him, urging him to go on.

He sighed. "Like these birth control shots. I know the aging population is a problem. I know placebos are the only solution. But tricking women into getting pregnant, just to lose their lives... It feels like he's playing God. It feels wrong. So much of what goes on in that Council Room feels *wrong*."

Seren froze. Placebo shots? Tricking women into getting pregnant? Playing God...?

Oh my Warren... Ma's unlikely pregnancy finally made sense. It wasn't that she'd had forgotten to get the shot; the shot just hadn't worked. And that wasn't by accident—it was by *design*. Women got pregnant, had the kid, and were subsequently killed. One in, one out—the perfect solution to an aging population.

Seren felt like she was going to be sick.

"I'm sorry I'm unloading all this on you," Zaiden said, finally looking up at her.

"It's okay," she choked out. But it wasn't okay. It would *never* be okay. How long had Zaiden known about this? How long had he sat on this information and done nothing about it? Suddenly, she saw him in a different light. No longer did he have this beautiful, mysterious glow. He had become one of *them*.

Instinctively, Seren backed away.

Zaiden didn't notice. "I'm also sorry for waking you up," he said.

Seren shook her head absentmindedly. "I wasn't asleep," she managed to say.

"No?"

"Sleep hasn't been coming easily recently."

"For me either," Zaiden said. He crossed his arms, like he was giving himself a hug, and looked at the floor, suddenly shy. "Hey, I hate to ask any more of you, but ... do you think I could sleep here tonight?"

"Sure," Seren said, forcing her voice to remain steady. "Of course."

Zaiden looked relieved. "Great. Thanks," he said. "For everything."

. . .

He was gone before the Awakening. The only evidence that he'd been there at all were the pieces of blood-stained glass on Seren's side table and her blanket, folded neatly on the arm of the couch.

Sighing, Seren tossed the blanket back onto her bed. The way Zaiden had looked standing in her doorway the night before was seared into her mind. He'd looked so fragile, so broken—much like Seren felt now, knowing the truth.

Governor Warren had blackmailed her, all the while knowing that he was the reason Ma was pregnant. He had led her to believe that he would spare Ma's life, when he was the reason her life hung in the balance at all. The man was a sociopath, sick—and Seren would stop at nothing to bring him down.

Seren wondered if Zaiden had any idea what he'd done by coming to her door last night. He had provided her with the clarity that she needed. She had made her decision.

Now she just had to work up the courage to act.

34

SEREN

Lucas was administering an injection when Seren walked into the Tier Four medical center. He looked tired. Still, he was smiling and chatting animatedly with the woman sitting on the table in front of him.

"Lucas," Seren called.

He looked up, surprised.

"Would you excuse me for a moment?" he said. His patient nodded, sat back, and put her hands on her belly. She had a stomach even larger than Ma's. Seren wondered if it was her first child, or if she, too, had been wronged by Governor Warren. Her anger returned in full force.

"Twice in one week?" Lucas asked, approaching her with a smile. His voice was light, but Seren knew him well enough to recognize that underneath his bright exterior lurked disappointment from yesterday's conversation. He had expected more from her. Now, she was ready to give it.

"I'm in," Seren said quietly.

Lucas's eyes widened. "Are you sure?"

"I'm sure."

Without warning, Lucas yanked Seren into a hug and held on tight. "You're making the right decision," he whispered.

Seren thought back to Zaiden's wearied face and battered body. She remembered the way he had stared off into space as she removed the glass from his arms. He looked so young, so innocent—and so hopeless. She thought about the placebo shots being administered and the women that Governor Warren was allowing to die. She thought about the horrific images Governor Warren had shown her and the pleasure he'd gotten from watching the violence.

He was evil, and he had to be stopped.

Seren pulled away. "How can I help?"

. . .

In the privacy of the surgery room, Lucas described to Seren in detail where to meet him after his shift that afternoon. It was risky to go during the day, he said, but riskier at night after curfew. He knew a secret way into Tier Five—one that wouldn't require Seren using her identity card. In turn, she told him briefly about the real reason she'd been brought up to Tier Two to work. He pursed his lips as she spoke, explaining the blackmail and Governor Warren's cruelty and his promise to help her mother. Lucas took a while to respond, and Seren feared this may be the straw that broke the camel's back in their relationship, but once she'd finished speaking, he nodded.

"This is perfect," he'd said. "You're in the perfect position to help us. I can't talk about this more now. We'll talk later."

Lucas returned to work, and Seren promised to meet him after his shift.

That afternoon, Seren met Lucas where he indicated: an old abandoned public bathroom on the far edge of Tier Four. Most public bathrooms had gone out of use after the leaders of Community discovered they had the potential to spread germs. Consequently, many restrooms had been torn down and repurposed, but this one remained, blockaded only by an Out of Order sign and bright yellow caution tape.

"This is it?"

When Lucas had described a secret way into Tier Five, she'd expected something more exciting. This was not that. Even from outside the door, Seren could tell that the bathroom was totally dilapidated. Strips of white paint hung from the walls, and bits of broken mirror lay in the sinks.

"This is it," Lucas replied.

"How has no one figured this out?" Seren asked. She couldn't imagine that Community had many secrets left. Two hundred thirty years was enough to discover most if not all of them. This entrance to Tier Five had to be one of the only remaining secrets.

"There are no cameras in this area," Lucas said. "No bugs, either."

"No bugs?"

"The resistance isn't just a bunch of bourgeois, Seren," Lucas said, giving her a pointed stare. "We have friends in high places."

Who? Seren wanted to ask, but Lucas had already moved on. He lifted the caution tape and ushered Seren beneath it before following her inside.

The bathroom was even worse beyond the caution tape. It looked as though someone had changed their mind halfway through its destruction. Half the sinks were smashed, their porceline remains littering the floor. Most of the stalls were missing their doors, and the toilets held no water. Seren watched her step, careful not to bring her foot down on any of the broken pieces of sink.

"I can see why no one would want to come in here," Seren said, her eyes trailing the chipped walls.

She caught a glimpse of her reflection in the cracked mirror and flinched. The girl staring back at her looked exhausted. Her auburn hair and rosy cheeks lacked luster, and the sterile light in the bathroom did nothing to help.

"Yeah, it's not the most glamorous of locations," Lucas said. He removed a key from his pocket. "Are you ready?"

Seren tore her eyes away from her reflection and nodded. "As ready as I'll ever be."

She followed Lucas to a thin wooden door at the end of the bathroom, beyond all the stalls. He fumbled with the key, wiggling it in the lock a few times before something clicked, and the door unlocked. He pulled it open to reveal a dark, damp tunnel, its ceiling nearly as low as Seren was short. The tunnel tilted downwards, halting the flow of light and making it impossible to see the end.

Seren's pulse quickened. She'd never liked the dark. "You should have told me to bring the flashlight," she whispered.

Lucas laughed. "You'll be fine. I've done this plenty of times. It's not as scary as it looks. Come on."

He hunched over to fit beneath the low-hanging ceiling and walked a few paces before turning back to Seren. "Are you coming?" he asked.

Though she really didn't want to, Seren nodded and followed Lucas into the dark tunnel, closing the door behind her.

The air in the tunnel was cold and stale. It smelled putrid, like rotting fruit. Seren followed Lucas closely, holding onto the back of his shirt for support. She blindly moved along, stepping carefully, and tried to avoid touching the walls. She was on edge, nervous about both the tunnel itself and what was on the other side of it.

"How long is this thing, anyway?" she asked.

"Why? Are you scared?"

"No," she responded a bit too quickly.

Lucas chuckled, and his laugh echoed, momentarily creating the illusion that they were being followed. Seren stiffened.

"It's just a bit further," he said.

They walked for a few minutes more before Lucas stopped.

"I want to warn you before we go in," he said, his tone becoming suddenly serious. "Things are different in Tier Five. I wasn't expecting it the first time I came, and I want you to be prepared."

"Different how?"

"I think it makes more sense for you to see it. Hold your breath," Lucas suggested.

"What?"

He opened the door. For a moment, Seren was blinded by the light. Before her eyes had adjusted, a horrible scent struck her nose harder than a fist. She stopped breathing.

What the hell have I gotten myself into?

35

ZAIDEN

Zaiden's body ached with each step he took, but no pain quite matched the humiliation he felt about last night. He didn't regret going to Seren's apartment, just everything that happened afterwards. Not only had he broken an important council rule (*Thou shalt not share anything that happens in the Council Room*), he had betrayed his father's trust—and all in a matter of minutes.

And the way Seren had looked at him, with such pity... It made his skin squirm. He wasn't weak or pathetic, but now that's exactly what she thought of him. And how could she not, when he wasn't even strong enough to fight off his own father?

When Zaiden got home, he found Alaster seated at his kitchen table, sipping coffee and reading a pile of notes. He glanced up as Zaiden walked in.

"What the hell happened to you?"

Zaiden caught a glimpse of himself in the kitchen mirror. His eye was nearly swollen shut and surrounded by deep purple bruising. He looked horrific.

"Bar fight," he mumbled, walking past without meeting Alaster's gaze.

Zaiden's bedroom resembled a crime scene. It was an absolute mess, everything scattered and out of place. The glass from the shattered clock littered the floor, and there was a large hole in the wall where Zaiden's body had slammed into it after he was pushed.

All that, but no sign of his father.

Zaiden threw on a T-shirt and walked back out to the kitchen, where Alaster sat watching the Awakening with mild interest.

"Bad weather today," Alaster commented, motioning to the weather report projecting rain for the whole day.

Zaiden crossed his arms. He didn't feel like doing the small talk thing today, especially not with his father's best friend. "What're you doing here?" he asked.

Alaster set the coffee cup down. "Your father didn't mention it? We're doing target practice today—on the off chance that you need it."

Zaiden stifled a groan. The last thing that he wanted to do was spend a day with Alaster or learn how to use a gun, especially after killing Marcus the other day. Taking a life was something Zaiden never wanted to experience again.

But if his father ordered it, Zaiden didn't have a choice.

"I didn't know we had a place to do target practice," he said.

"There are many secrets of Community that you have yet to learn." Alaster stood, leaving the steaming mug of coffee on the table. "Shall we?"

...

Alaster led Zaiden to an armory in Tier One, nuzzled deep within a maze of hallways Zaiden hadn't explored before. It amazed Zaiden that he'd managed to miss such huge parts of Community. How many other secrets did these walls hold, and when would his father finally think he was old enough to be privy to them?

Alaster looked over his shoulder before unlocking the armory with his IC. He motioned Zaiden into the room and swiftly closed the door behind them.

The armory was small, but crowded with dozens of guns lining the walls, varying in size and shape. They hung equidistant from each other, creating a mural of black and gray. Zaiden observed them tentatively, running his hands along the space beneath them. He knew that guns had been a part of Earth's downfall, but they seemed so harmless on the wall—almost like toys.

"Your father wishes me to impart my knowledge to you," Alaster said, breaking Zaiden's trance. "He thinks it's important that you start to carry for your own safety, but first, you have to learn how to shoot."

"Where did you learn to shoot?" Zaiden asked as Alaster removed a gun from the rack.

He opened its chamber and inserted a bullet. "Your grandfather taught me," he said, closing it.

Zaiden perked up at the mention of his grandfather, Arch. Zaiden didn't really remember him—Arch had died when Zaiden was six—but Zaiden knew he'd been a powerful man. That was the extent of what Zaiden knew of his grandfather; Arch's name was now as taboo in their home as Ivory's was.

"I didn't realize you and my grandfather were close," Zaiden said.

"I was closer to him than your father was. My father, Elijah, and your grandfather were best friends. After my father died at a young age, your grandfather treated me like another son. He's the one who appointed me to the council, not Pluto."

"My father never told me any of that," Zaiden said.

"I wouldn't think so," Alaster said, slinging a gun over his shoulder. "It's a sore subject."

Zaiden pictured Alaster and Pluto sitting side by side at the dining room table, fighting for Arch Warren's attention. Pluto was a competitive man; he must have despised Alaster's relationship with his father.

None of this was deceptive now, though. Pluto treated Alaster like his most trusted ally. Zaiden wondered if their relationship had always been this way, or if it had changed once Arch died.

"Speaking of," Zaiden said, trying to keep his tone casual, "where is my father this morning?"

Alaster raised an eyebrow. "I was hoping you could tell me."

"You haven't seen him?"

"Not since last night—and I'm afraid that I delivered some rather miserable news."

Zaiden touched his bruised collarbone gingerly. *That explains the drunken anger.* "What news was that?" he asked.

Alaster waved a dismissive hand. "It'll only bore you."

Zaiden frowned. He thought that he and Alaster had turned over a new leaf after the man had shared with him about the placebo shots, but maybe Alaster didn't trust him after all.

Zaiden's fists tightened. When would they stop treating him like a child?

"Ah, yes. Here we are," Alaster said, oblivious to Zaiden's shift in mood. "Most of these are handguns, semiautomatic. I've personally always been a fan of the Strum nine millimeter."

He removed one of the smaller guns from the wall and placed it into Zaiden's hands. "Let me know how that feels."

Zaiden flipped the metal device over in his hands. It was heavier than he'd expected, and cold to the touch.

"It feels fine," he mumbled.

The gun seemed to hold so much weight—not just physical, but otherwise, too. With just a tug on the trigger, he could take a life. No needles or screaming, like with Marcus, just aim and fire. A rush of adrenaline zipped through his veins.

"Why did the founders of Community allow these? Aren't they dangerous?"

"Guns are the ultimate bulwark against citizen misbehavior," Alaster responded as he removed the gun from his shoulder and began to load it. He handed a box of bullets to Zaiden and described how to load them. Zaiden followed along, trying to imagine what would happen if the rebels knew that this room existed. There'd be anarchy. Was it really worth it to have a room that held so much potential for danger?

But then Zaiden thought of his mother being slaughtered by the rebels. Would she still be here today if she'd been armed? He ached thinking about it.

Once his gun was loaded, Zaiden followed Alaster into a dark, lengthy room with little in it apart from five targets hanging on the fall wall, lined up next to each other in a neat row.

Alaster handed Zaiden a pair of earmuffs. "Put these on."

Zaiden obliged and watched as Alaster held his gun at arm's length.

"It's important to have a strong hold," Alaster shouted. "Otherwise, the kickback is dangerous."

Alaster steadied himself, planting his feet shoulder width apart. He demonstrated how to hold the gun, how to turn the safety off, and how to pull the trigger. Once he felt confident that Zaiden understood, he fired four shots. Zaiden flinched each time the gun went off. After he'd finished, Alaster went to retrieve the target. There was only one hole in the center, though Zaiden knew he'd hit it every time. Alaster had managed to hit the bullseye with every shot.

"Now you try," Alaster said, taking a step back and motioning for Zaiden to go ahead.

Zaiden took a deep breath. He tightened his grip around the handgun and clicked the safety off. Slowly, he raised it so that it was chest-high and pointed it as best he could at the target ahead. He tried to mirror Alaster, with his feet shoulder width apart and his chin up high. He squinted and shut his left eye, certain the right was stronger and more accurate, and fired three times in quick succession. The kickback of the gun surprised him, but he kept his arms strong as Alaster had told him to.

Once Zaiden put the gun down, Alaster retrieved the target and held it out to Zaiden, smiling. The first two shots had missed, but the third hit the outer edge, just an inch from the large circle.

"Not bad for your first time," Alaster said.

Zaiden felt power surging through his veins as he took the paper. *No wonder people love guns,* he thought. He'd done that just by pulling a trigger.

He and Alaster spent half the day doing target practice. By the end, Zaiden hit the target with each shot. He even landed a bullseye once.

Alaster clapped him on the back. "Nice work," he said. "You certainly did better than your father did his first time."

Zaiden grinned. "Really?"

"Absolutely. It took him weeks to hit the target."

Zaiden liked the idea that he was better at something than his father.

"What do you say we call it a day?" Alaster asked, pulling his earmuffs off. "Maybe go get something to eat?"

"Alright," Zaiden said, grinning. Maybe he and Alaster had turned over a new leaf after all.

36

SEREN

Seren hadn't known what to expect. She had been taught about the jobs of Tier Fives in her classes—taught the things she needed to know. Tier Fives grew food. They created electricity. They worked with sewage. She was told they were happy to work down there and never leave. In school, they never described what life was like for Tier Fives. For most of her life, Seren had been shielded from it

Now she knew why.

Immediately, she was struck by the odor. It was a pungent, overwhelming smell of trash and waste. Tier Five was in charge of waste and water management, something Seren had assumed was segregated to a small part of the Tier, but clearly she'd been wrong. The scent was everywhere. She breathed through her mouth so she wouldn't be physically ill.

"I warned you," Lucas murmured.

Seren had no response.

She followed Lucas deeper into the Tier Five compound, through the first floor of greenhouses. There were hundreds of people at work, some old, but many young—younger than Seren and Lucas, even. They were hunched over rows of vegetation, either planting or harvesting. Some carried large baskets of produce on their shoulders or heads. Seren saw apples, corn, watermelon, carrots, and some produce that she now knew was only accessible in the upper Tiers. The greenhouses smelled like a mixture of sweat and dirt.

Tier Five spanned multiple floors, Lucas explained as they walked between rows of plants. The bottom floor held the waste management facilities, the middle held the trash incinerator, and the top two held the greenhouses, illuminated by bright lights meant to imitate the sun. Seren made the mistake of looking up into one and nearly blinded herself.

In her history of Community class, Seren had learned the population breakdown of the Tiers. Tier One had the smallest population, only one percent, as it was made up of the council members and Warren Family alone. Tier Two had eight percent, Tier Three had ten percent, Tier Four had thirty-five percent, and the remaining forty-six percent lived in Tier Five. It was packed, to say the least. Seren had to squeeze through crowds to keep up with Lucas.

"What did I tell you?" he asked.

"Not enough."

Seren's eyes fell on a particularly old woman pulling root vegetables from the soil. She was hunched over, her shoulder blades protruding from her back. Cuts and bruises covered her thin, fragile skin. It was not as horrific as the images Governor Warren had shared with her of Earth, but it was not much better, either. With great difficulty, Seren tore her eyes away.

"They don't even get to eat most of this," Lucas said quietly. "They eat what they're given, which is less than us. Inventory is kept by Tier Threes. If anyone tries to hoard food, their children are punished."

In the distance, Seren heard a child's cry pierce the air. Though the greenhouse was warm, she shivered. Did Zaiden know all of this? She couldn't imagine him being okay with it.

Suddenly, Lucas's anti-Warren, anti-government rants made sense. If she'd known about this before today—if she'd had any idea—she would have been just as angry as he was. She felt herself becoming angry now, her cheeks turning red from a mixture of her frustration and the greenhouse heat.

Lucas led her down a few floors to the water treatment facility. Seren was happy to be out of the greenhouses, but her relief didn't last long. The water treatment plant was just as crammed with men and women, their skin covered in layers of dirt and sweat. A few turned to watch Seren and Lucas as they passed, their eyes passing over their bodies, their skin, their clothes. Seren tried to shrink herself, moving closer to Lucas as he navigated the maze of titanium water tanks towards the center of the facility.

There, in the center of it all, a young woman was waiting for them. Seren's eyes went to her immediately. She was beautiful in an unusual way: long and limber with large, doughy brown eyes and thick, unwavering curls. Her skin was a light brown, like freshly brewed black tea. Whereas everyone else Seren had seen in Tier Five seemed overworked, this girl seemed refreshed.

Seren and the girl made eye contact for a brief, breathtaking moment, and then the girl's attention flowed to Lucas. Her features burst into a radiant smile, and she ran to him, wrapping him in a tight hug. He grinned and lifted her from the ground, and her legs swung, nearly hitting Seren.

Lucas put the girl down, and Seren caught a glimpse of his face. He was grinning from ear to ear. She couldn't remember the last time she'd seen Lucas smile like that. A pang of sadness went through her. She couldn't remember the last time *she'd* made Lucas smile like that.

Finally, the girl turned her attention to Seren.

"Seren Quinn. At last, we meet," she said. "Lucas has told me so much about you."

Really? He's told me nothing about you, Seren thought. Jealousy prickled her skin. It seemed unfair that this girl had been privy to information about Seren, and Seren had not even known of her existence until mere hours ago.

"Seren, this is Noa," Lucas said.

"Hi," Seren said, trying to keep the negative feelings out of her voice.

"Our fathers were friends," Lucas said by way of introduction.

Noa grinned. "They were more than friends; they were practically brothers! Henry used to come down all the time and read me his books. I was heartbroken when he was murdered."

Another surge of jealousy flew through Seren. *Henry.* Her Henry. Her books. Her Lucas… All this time, she'd been sharing them.

How had she not known about any of this?

"This is probably a lot to take in, huh?" Noa said.

Seren frowned. There was nothing wrong with Noa. She was beautiful, charming, and obviously emotionally intelligent. Maybe in another circumstance, Seren would've even *liked* her. But here? Seren felt nothing but animosity for this girl. She felt like a wife who'd just learned her husband had been cheating on her for years.

So, no, Noa. It's more *than a lot.*

"It's nothing Seren can't handle," Lucas said, slapping her on the back. Seren tugged uncomfortably at her shirt sleeves.

"Well, Defectio isn't meeting for another hour," Noa said. "In the meantime, how about a little tour?"

Lucas grinned. "That's a great idea."

. . .

As the three of them moved further into the depths of Tier Five, Seren followed a few paces behind. Noa and Lucas seemed to communicate without speaking. They jested, making faces and gestures that Seren couldn't read. Their exclusion of her didn't feel malicious, but Seren still ached each time they looked at each other and laughed. It was as if they had their own secret language—a language that Seren could never hope to learn.

Noa led them through the water treatment facility, pointing out different machinery and babbling off facts. The facility felt like a Tier in its own right, populated by people dressed in wetsuits and long purple gloves. A few men and women with clipboards that were examining each tank and tube closely.

As Noa spoke, a radiant smile covered her face. Seren couldn't stop staring. *She's beautiful,* Seren thought. And the way Lucas looked at Noa made it clear that he thought so, too. Seren chomped down on her lip.

Noa gestured to the massive tanks. "Here's where the dirty water is purified, tested, and pumped back into Community. We maintain a laboratory that tests samples three times a day for chlorine residual, settleable solids, pH, temperature, total coliform, and more. These results are reported to the Tier Three scientists daily. I recently joined the lab team," she added.

Lucas grinned. "Genius," he said.

Noa gave him a playful shove, and Seren looked away. Her eyes fell instead on the men currently working at the facility. They worked quickly, climbing the ladders to the giant tanks, taking samples, adding chemicals, and inspecting the equipment. Seren watched as one tall man in strange gear scrubbed the inside of a tank. She caught a glimpse of the interior; it was filthy.

After the water treatment center, Noa led them into the incinerator. It smelled of burning trash and rotting food. The air was heavy with ash.

"This is where Community's trash comes," Noa said. "Here, it's thermal-treated and converted into ash, gas, and heat. Some of the heat is used to generate electricity, but most of our energy comes from the solar panels on the outside of Community."

Seren stared at the piles of trash being shoveled into the fire. The heat burned her eyes.

"Cool, right?"

Seren nodded, though she had been thinking more along the lines of *gross.* "Is it safe to be breathing this in?" she asked.

"Honest answer? No. There are vents, but they don't do much. A lot of the people who work in this trade die early," Noa said. She said it so casually, Seren wondered if she'd misheard her. "But our incinerators do reduce the solid mass of the original waste by ninety to ninety-five percent, which is huge. At the beginning of Community, it was only eighty percent."

"Where does it go?" Seren asked, watching a man push a wheelbarrow of ash past.

Noa gestured towards square stainless-steel doors in the wall about three feet from the ground. "We dump it out through those chutes."

"Where do *they* go?"

"Earth."

Seren choked on her own breath as the word sent chills down her spine. *Earth.* She was reminded that Earth was so close— just a wall away.

Seren looked at the chute. "Has anyone ever tried to ... escape that way?"

Using the word "escape" felt strange. Community had always been home for her. But for the people in Tier Five, who'd spent their whole lives burning trash and breathing in poison, escape was a perfect word.

Noa shook her head. "They're too small. Only a toddler could fit, and Warren knows no one is going to send their kid through that thing alone."

There was a limit, then, to their desperation.

Seren pictured a child alone in the scorched landscape of Earth. Could it survive out there? Could any of them?

No, Seren thought. Earth was uninhabitable. That's why they were all still within Community's walls.

"We should head back up and prepare for the meeting," Noa said.

Lucas agreed, and Seren followed them away from the incinerator and back to the highest floor of Tier Five.

As they plunged back into the busy halls, Seren's discomfort heightened. She felt overwhelmed by the noise and the crowds, certain that everyone here could sense she did not belong. Seren always preferred to travel on the outskirts, out of sight, free from the shuffle of bodies. Now, the three of them charged through the crowds, passing back through the greenhouses before coming to a small room sandwiched in a residential area. They received few stares, but still, Seren did not breathe easily until Noa directed them into the meeting room and shut the door behind them.

The meeting room wasn't much—just bare white walls and a few chairs scattered throughout. Seren perched on the edge of one, pulling her knees tightly into her chest. Noa and Lucas remained standing.

"Why don't we talk about the plan before we go into the meeting," Noa suggested.

Seren watched the line of Lucas's jaw tighten as he nodded.

"Lucas explained to me your situation," Noa said, breaking Seren's stare. "I'm so sorry about your mother's condition."

Seren frowned. She didn't like the way Noa said "condition". It felt robotic and dehumanizing.

You're being unfair, Seren thought. *Give her a chance. Lucas trusts her. You should, too.* She wrapped her arms tighter around her knees. "Thanks," she mumbled.

"I need you to help me understand better, though," Noa said. "Why would Governor Warren ask for *your* help to find the rebels?"

It wasn't until that moment that Seren realized Noa didn't believe her. She didn't come out and say it, but she didn't have to. The way she asked the question said it all.

She doesn't trust me.

"I don't know," Seren said.

Noa leaned back, her gaze dismantling Seren slowly. "It's just odd," she said. "A girl from Tier Four, with no prior connection to the Governor or anyone in Tier Two, being chosen to spy. What value does that bring?"

"Look, if there's something you want to say, just say it," Seren snapped.

Lucas didn't look at her.

"There's nothing I want to say," Noa said. "Lucas trusts you, and that's enough for me. I just don't understand the Governor's motives—and frankly, I don't know if I understand yours."

Seren felt a defensive wall beginning to build. "I'm spying for him to help my mother. It was that or death."

"Right, that's what Lucas said. But how do you know that Governor Warren will actually allow your mother to live after all this? Or *you,* for that matter."

Seren's blood turned cold. She'd considered that possibility herself. "I don't. But I have to try."

Noa shrugged. "Fine. I guess it doesn't matter, does it? This is a huge breakthrough for us. We've been planning our attack for years with no concrete outcome, but with your help, we can finally take some action."

Seren frowned. Lucas and Noa had never met Governor Warren; they didn't understand how much power he held. Here, he was hated, but in the upper Tiers, he was idolized. He had an entire army of Harmonizers backing him, ready to lay down their lives, and what the upper Tiers lacked in size, they made up for in power. They were stronger than the rebels, better trained, better fed. Did Noa and Lucas understand that? Did they see the risks, or were they too blinded by their hatred for the Warren family?

"The most important piece of all of this is convincing Governor Warren that Defectio has no plan to attack. He's suspicious of us now, more so than before, and we have to assume you're not the only spy he's sent out. You have to be convincing enough that he believes you above all else. We've been inactive for this long; they have no reason to guess that we'll strike soon."

"When are you really planning to attack?" Seren asked.

Noa leaned back against the wall. "That's privileged information."

Seren felt heat rising to her cheeks. "I'm risking my life for you."

"And we appreciate that," Noa said. She spoke to Seren gently, as if speaking to a child mid tantrum, which really pissed Seren off.

"Then what's the problem?" Seren snapped.

"I don't know you. I know that Lucas trusts you, but you're way too close to the Warrens for me to feel comfortable giving you that information. You could slip up and accidentally give the date, or you could be secretly working for him—"

"Are you serious?!"

Noa simply shrugged. "I'm just trying to keep my people safe."

Seren huffed. "Fine. What do you want me to say?"

"We want you to inform him that we have no weapons and a very small army, but that we are determined and bloodthirsty. Tell him that we want to take over his position as Governor. Under no circumstances should you mention that we know anything about Earth. Does all this make sense?"

"Where am I supposed to say that I got this information?" Seren asked, crossing her arms.

Noa and Lucas exchanged one of their deliberate glances. Neither spoke.

"What?" Seren asked.

"You'll say *I* told you," Lucas said, finally meeting her eyes.

The color drained from Seren's face. "No. Absolutely not."

"Seren—"

"Are you *insane?* I'm not going to do that! I'm not going to put you in danger, Lucas."

"It's our only option. How else would you know so many details?" Noa asked.

Seren glowered at her. "I could have overheard something or, or seen something, or—"

"Where would you hear it?" Noa interrupted. "What would the person look like? Who would they be talking to?"

Seren frowned. "I… I don't… Okay, fine. Maybe I don't see them; maybe I just hear them from around a corner—"

"What do the voices sound like?" Noa asked. "Young, old, male, female? Do they speak like Tier Fives with maladroit drawls, or do they speak with the musical cadence of the upper Tiers?"

"I … I don't know…" Seren faltered. How could Noa *do* this? Didn't she care about Lucas? Didn't she want to keep him safe?

"This is our only option, Ren," Lucas said quietly. "It makes sense that you heard it from me. People know we're friends. And they know my father was a part of the rebellion. They're already looking at me. You're just shoving them in the right direction."

Seren was overcome with emotion. She hadn't agreed to this.

"Then what?" she asked, her throat tight. "They come for you in the middle of the night? They execute you and Jean?"

Lucas shook his head. "I'll go into hiding until the attack. They won't be able to locate me during that time, but they'll be so busy trying that their manpower will be tired and dissipated, and they won't be prepared for an attack."

Seren's throat tightened. "Lucas, I can't let you do this. What if you fail?"

"We won't," Lucas said firmly.

"But what if you do?"

"We *won't*."

Seren sat back in the chair and dug her palms into her forehead.

This hadn't been part of the plan. When she'd agreed to help, this was not how she thought it would go. Lucas was taking a big enough risk just by being a part of the attack, but this took it to a whole other level. He'd have a target on his back. How long before he died of a "heart attack," just like his father?

"What happens to me and Ma when they find out that the information I fed them was all lies?" Seren asked, her voice soft. "They'll kill her. They'll kill me."

Noa shrugged. "Plans change. You aren't in control of that."

Seren shook her head, refusing to look at Noa. If she looked at her, she thought she might snap. Instead, she focused on Lucas.

"Governor Warren won't believe that I turned you in," she said. "He knows how much I care about you. He knows *everything*."

"He'll believe you," Lucas said. "Because your mother's life is on the line, and sometimes, family is more important than friendship."

"Lucas," Seren said. How could he expect her to do this? How was she supposed to turn in her best friend? "I can't—"

"You have to," Lucas said firmly.

So that was it then. There was no arguing with him. Seren closed her eyes. She felt exhausted. She wanted to be alone, to think about her decisions in seclusion. She wanted to lie in the darkness and sleep and forget all of this.

"Seren?" Lucas asked.

Seren opened her eyes and saw Lucas's father in his furrowed brow and concerned eyes. Henry had fought for this and now Lucas had to, too. Seren took a deep breath. Just because Henry had died didn't mean that Lucas would. He was better prepared. He knew the risks.

"I'll do it," Seren said, garnering big smiles from both Lucas and Noa. "But I get to ask one question."

Noa opened her mouth to argue, but Lucas touched her wrist and stopped her. "It's only fair," he said. Seren nodded at him.

"Thanks. I just can't wrap my head around—" She took a deep breath. "How do you know for *certain* that Earth is safe?" It was the question that had been bothering her ever since Lucas told her about it. It was the one piece of the equation that still didn't make sense.

"I don't see how that's relevant—"

"Noa," Lucas said.

Noa let out an exasperated sigh. "Fine," she said.

She hesitated for a moment before reaching into her bag and pulling out a small book that looked to be as old as Community itself.

"We have this."

Seren stared at it. It looked plain. No significant markings, no designs of any kind. The only thing special about the notebook was the way in which Noa held it— as if it may burst into flames at any second. "What is it?" Seren asked.

"My father got this from Ivory Warren," Lucas said. "He gave it to Noa's dad a few days before his death."

"What was Henry doing with Ivory?" Seren asked.

Lucas shook his head. "I don't know."

"Henry told my dad that Ivory got this from a Tier Three scientist who died of a 'heart attack' a few days after the last entry," Noa said, putting air quotes around *"heart attack."* "Ivory died a month later."

Seren took the book from Noa gingerly and flipped through it, careful not to tear the yellowing paper. Its pages were filled with words, each page in in different handwriting. It began in scrawls.

January 22, 2120. Year 15 of Community. Pollution levels outside 450. Still extremely hazardous. Temperatures above normal. Will continue to monitor.

She flipped further.

April 9, 2137. Year 32 of Community. Pollution levels 400. Temperatures closer to normal.

December 12, 2205. Year 100 of Community. Pollution levels 200. Temperatures are normal.

Seren shook her head. "How do you know that this is legitimate?"

"Because the official Warren seal is pressed into the binding," Lucas said, showing Seren the side of the book. Sure enough, there it was: the official Warren seal: the familiar gold-and-blue shield flanked by a ferocious-looking tiger and dragon. *Such strong animals for such a week family,* Seren thought.

"Anyone could have forged that," Seren said, though she wasn't sure that was true.

"I know. But..." Lucas took a deep breath. "My father was killed because that book went missing."

Seren didn't bother asking how he knew that; the glint in Lucas's eyes told her it was true. For a moment, it felt like she'd lost Henry all over again, the reminder of him pressed into the pages of the book in her hand. She flipped to the end, where one final entry was written, dated twenty-two years prior.

February 16, 2303. Year 198 of Community. Pollution levels below 150. Temperatures normal. Earth is safe.

So, it was true: Earth was safe—and they'd known. They'd known for longer than Seren had been alive, but they'd kept everyone inside Community's walls. They'd kept this information from them.

Trapped.

The feeling when she learned that the world was ready for the taking, and they were still imprisoned within these same walls under the rule of a tyrant... Seren had felt trapped before, but never like this. It was suffocating, invasive.

Seren closed the notebook and gasped for breath. Her breathing felt restricted all the sudden.

"Any further questions?" Noa asked, her gaze pointed.

"No," Seren said between gasps. She passed the notebook back, and Noa stored it deep within her bag. Seren felt sick again, but it wasn't from the smell this time. She could've had a life beyond Community. She could've grown up with fresh air and grass and stars and endless possibilities—but it had been stolen from her, stolen from all of Community. And for what? So the Warren family could stay in power? So the upper Tiers could be comfortable...?

"Now do you see why we have to attack?" Noa asked. "Why we have to escape? Governor Warren knew and he kept us trapped here. He kept us poor, hungry. He killed people who got in his way."

"I do."

Seren's stomach tightened. She thought of Zaiden, with his kind eyes, his bruised skin. She thought of the incredible things he'd shown her, all the pieces of Earth he'd exposed her to in the Simulator. Just because Governor Warren was evil didn't mean that his son was. There was no way that Zaiden could've known about this. He shouldn't be punished for his father's actions.

"I have a condition," Seren said, the words leaving her before she could take control of them.

Noa raised an eyebrow. "I didn't realize this was a negotiation."

Seren bit her lip. Briefly, she considered what she planned on asking for. Was this really worth it? Was it a good idea?

Yes, she answered herself.

"I'm willing to risk my life, Lucas's life, and my Ma and Pa's lives," Seren said firmly. "All I ask is for one thing."

"Fine," Noa said, crossing her arms. "What is it?"

"Zaiden Warren is left alone."

The room stiffened under the weight of her words.

When Noa spoke, her voice was sharp as a razor. "No."

"Zaiden is not his father," Seren said, doubling down. "He cares about the people of Community. He won't get in your way."

"You don't know that."

"I do." Seren knew that she was losing Noa's trust (whatever shred of trust she had started with, anyway), but she also knew that Zaiden was good.

"My people are angry. The Warrens have murdered their family members. They've killed our children. I can't control every one of them."

"Then I can't help you."

There was silence. Seren could hear her own heartbeat pulsating in steady, quickening thumps.

Noa stood abruptly. "I need to talk to you," she said to Lucas.

Seren tried to meet his gaze, but he refused to look at her. The two of them stepped into the hall, closing the door behind them. Seren heard their low, intense whispers through the door, but couldn't make out what they were saying.

Their absence stretched on for what seemed like an eternity. Finally, Noa and Lucas returned, both aggravated. Neither of them would look at Seren.

"I have to go get everything set up for the meeting," Noa said. "I'll have someone come retrieve you when we're ready."

"Noa, wait," Lucas called, but Noa left without so much as another glance at him. The tension between them was palpable.

Lucas turned on Seren. "What the hell was that?" he growled.

"What was what?"

"Zaiden? Zaiden *Warren?* You want to save a guy who is just as monstrous as his father?"

Seren stood, but Lucas still towered over her. She could see the tiny veins bulging from his neck.

"Are you seriously upset with me?" she demanded. "You tricked me! You didn't tell me that I'd be putting your life in danger just so your rebellion can have the element of surprise!"

Lucas scoffed. "It's funny how you're suddenly so concerned about my life, when your little crush on Zaiden could ruin this entire thing."

Seren didn't bother acknowledging the crush comment, though it made her cheeks flush. "Sparing Zaiden's life won't ruin anything."

"No? What happens when he decides to seek revenge for his father's death? Or decides that he wants to take power and becomes just as much of a tyrant? What happens when we're right back where we started?"

"He's different, Lucas."

Lucas laughed, but there was no humor behind it. The sound turned Seren's blood cold. "Are you in love with him?"

Seren nearly choked on her own saliva. *"What?"*

"Are you in love with him?"

"No!" Her voice came out sounding foreign.

She wasn't in love with Zaiden Warren; she hardly knew him. That's not what this was about. Zaiden wasn't the same as his father. Seren hadn't believed it at first, either, but she'd seen it time and time again—in the Simulator, in her room, at the gala. She wanted to save him because he was a good person, not because of her feelings towards him.

Lucas seemed able to read Seren's thoughts. He shook his head, disgusted. "What did I tell you about trusting them?"

"I don't!"

"Then why is it so damn important to you that we spare his life? Don't you think that as soon as his father dies, he's going to take his place?"

"He wouldn't do that. He's—"

"Different. Yeah, so you said." Lucas ran his hands through his hair, pulling as he reached the ends. His eyebrows furrowed in deep concentration.

"Lucas, if you knew him, you'd understand. We shouldn't kill innocent people."

Lucas recoiled. "Innocent people? The Warrens killed my father, Ren! They were just as willing to let your mother die to control the population. They don't care about you or me. They only care about themselves!"

"Lucas..." Seren reached for his arm, but he pulled away.

"Noa agreed, by the way. I hope you're happy."

Seren felt frail, like she might break.

Lucas shook his head slowly. "I don't think I know you anymore," he mumbled. He slammed the door behind him when he left.

It took all she had not to cry.

37

ZAIDEN

"Zaiden."

Governor Warren stood at his son's door, his hands stuffed deep in his pockets. Zaiden looked up from his book. Though his father's clothes were pressed, his hair perfectly in place, he looked weary. Zaiden wondered if he, too, had not slept a wink last night.

"Hello."

He tried to keep the anger out of his voice, but it was difficult. He could still hear his father's words as clearly as if he were saying them now: *"You are weak. Your mother was right about you. You are not fit to lead..."*

Governor Warren's eyes skimmed over the broken clock and scattered furniture. Zaiden tried to read his expression, but his father's face remained stoic. Then his gaze fell on Zaiden's black eye.

He looked away.

"Alaster tells me your shooting practice this morning went well," he said.

"Yes."

"That's good." He cleared his throat. "Are you carrying now?"

Zaiden nodded, imagining what it would be like to take the gun out and place a bullet right between his father's eyes. The lack of emotion he felt at the thought frightened him.

"Good."

Governor Warren hovered in the doorway, shifting his body weight from foot to foot. Zaiden had never seen him like this: timid and subdued. It was as if a stranger stood in his father's place.

"Is that all?" Zaiden asked.

Governor Warren struggled for a moment before speaking. "No."

Zaiden closed his book, placed it beside him, and waited. His father looked up at the ceiling, as if the words he needed were written there. Zaiden, meanwhile, kept his gaze fiercely on his father.

Governor Warren cleared his throat. "No, I wanted to come say that, uh, my behavior last night was… Well, it was…" he faltered.

Zaiden's eyebrows shot up. Was his father trying to apologize? He did not move, fearful that one finger out of place would scare his father off.

Governor Warren scratched his chin, where a five o'clock shadow had grown. Sprinkled in with his brown hair was some gray.

He looks old, Zaiden thought.

"You're a good son, Zaiden," Governor Warren said. "I don't tell you enough, but I'm proud of you. I'm proud of the man you're becoming." It may have been a trick of the light, but Zaiden thought he saw a glimmer of tears in his father's eyes. "I'd like for you to shadow me tomorrow, learn the ropes of the job. How does that sound?"

As hard as he tried, Zaiden could not prevent the smile from growing on his face. "That sounds good," he said.

His father looked relieved. "Good," he said. He looked around. "I'll have someone clean up this mess while we're gone. Wear something sharp. We have a lot of people to talk to."

He tapped the doorway three times before he left. Zaiden watched him walk away. There was a lightness in his step that hadn't been there before. Zaiden knew the feeling; it was as if a huge weight had been lifted from his shoulders. Maybe he was imagining it, but it seemed that the pain in his abdomen had already begun to subside.

Today might be a good day.

38

SEREN

Seren tore through the halls of Tier Five, determined not to let anyone see her break down. She was meant to attend the rebels' meeting, but she knew Lucas didn't want her there. He'd looked at her like he never wanted to see her again.

Seren left the way Lucas had taken her in. The small tunnels felt even smaller now and somehow darker. She held her arms close to her body and fought through the suffocating fear. When she finally reemerged into the hallways of Tier Four, she took a long, deep breath. She welcomed the antiseptic scent.

It was then that she finally allowed herself to cry.

She didn't understand how Lucas could expect her to do this. How could he allow himself to be put into the line of fire? She was angry at him, and at Noa for encouraging it, but most of all, she was angry at herself.

Zaiden's family had killed Henry. Though Zaiden had been a child at the time—he'd played no part—it was an inarguable fact. Lucas had every right to hate the Warrens. In sparing Zaiden's life, Seren was taking away Lucas's right to justice.

She imagined Lucas now, face grave as he sat beside Noa at the head of the table, speaking to the rebels, telling them the stipulations of his friend's help. She felt ill.

Seren wasn't sure what to do. Her head hurt badly from thinking, and her eyes were now swollen from crying. She resolved not to make any decisions tonight. Instead, she went to the place she thought would have the best chance of giving her clarity.

. . .

Pa looked ten years older when he opened the door. Seren immediately catapulted herself into his arms. He grunted in surprise before wrapping his arms around her. His warmth enclosed her like a blanket.

Seren hadn't realized how much she needed a hug from Pa until she was in it. After a day of tormenting guilt, she needed the comfort and reassurance.

Finally, Pa pulled away. "You look good," he said.

"Thank you," Seren said. She could not return the sentiment; Pa looked awful. Stress had taken its toll. Half of his eyebrows had grayed, and the bags beneath his eyes were so dark, it looked as though he'd gotten punched. Her heart ached looking at him.

"Are they treating you well in Tier Two?" Pa asked. Beneath the innocent question was something more sinister: *"Are they hurting you?"*

She sidestepped the question. "Is Ma home?"

"She's in bed. I can go get her."

"No, that's okay. We can talk there." Seren started on her way to Ma and Pa's bedroom.

Pa didn't follow. "Your mother told me about the stunt you pulled with the medicine," he called after her.

Seren stopped in her tracks. *Shit.* She turned to see Pa's arms crossed tightly over his chest, his eyes narrowed.

"Your behavior was reckless," he said, more firmly than he'd said anything in Seren's life. "You not only put yourself at risk, but our entire family could have been killed, including your mother's unborn child."

That was kind of the point, Seren thought bitterly. She didn't reply.

Pa held her gaze. "What did we tell you about always adhering to Community laws? You're blessed to have gotten a chance at life; many of your ancestors were not so lucky. And for your mother to tell me that you would throw it all away—"

Seren winced and waited for the punchline.

Pa's face softened. "You showed extraordinary bravery," he said quietly.

That was not what she was expecting. "I did?"

Pa rubbed his eyes, his expression pained. "I only wish your mother weren't so damn stubborn."

Seren almost laughed in relief. She knew the feeling. Ma's decision had created a snowball effect. Seren couldn't help but wonder what would have happened if Ma had just taken the pill. Seren wouldn't have gotten angry, so she wouldn't have run to the Simulator. She would have never gotten caught by Zaiden; she wouldn't have even met him. Defectio would still be doing what they'd done the last few years: just sitting and waiting. Everything that had happened and that was to come was due to Ma's stubbornness.

Seren placed a hand on Pa's arm. "It's going to be okay, Pa. I promise."

His eyes welled up with tears. "I don't know how I'm going to take care of a child alone."

Seren shook her head. "You won't have to."

Ma will be there, too.

It was then that Seren decided. She would tell Governor Warren about Defectio and their plans. She would turn Lucas in. Then, with Governor Warren gone, they could finally escape. She, Ma, and Pa—they could live with the new baby on Earth. They could finally be free.

Pa sighed and pulled Seren into a hug, kissing the top of her head.

"I love you."

"I love you too, Pa."

"Now, what do you say we go visit your Ma, huh?"

Pa led the way to the master bedroom. As they passed Seren's room, she noticed that it looked the exact same as she'd left it, kept perfectly intact. Her bedding was still crumpled as if she'd just gotten up. It was almost shrine-like. Guilt gnawed at her again. She pushed it away.

Ma was sleeping on her back when they arrived. Her chest rose and fell slowly, the tiny baby bump lifting the covers with each breath.

Seren climbed onto the edge of the bed and ran her fingers gently through Ma's hair, feeling the soft, thin curls.

Ma opened her eyes slowly. "Seren?" she mumbled.

"Hi, Ma."

Ma sat up with a tiny grunt, resting her hand on her belly. "It's so good to see you, chickpea," she said.

"It's good to see you, too."

Seren's eyes fell to Ma's belly, the bottom of which protruded from her shirt. Underneath the stretched skin lay Seren's brother or sister, its heart beating, ready to come out and see the world. And Seren was doing all she could to make sure that her sibling would get to see the *real world,* not the enclosed walls that she had grown up in.

A tear streamed down Seren's cheek.

Ma wiped it away. "Why are you crying?"

Seren felt the tears starting to come harder now. "I just missed you."

"We've missed you, too," Pa said. He remained in the doorway, his body resting against the frame. Seren could see in Pa's shrunken belly that he had been sharing his rations with Ma. She felt another surge of love for them both.

She was crying before she knew what was happening. The tears came on hard, and Seren couldn't seem to stop them. She wasn't even sure *why* she was crying. Maybe it was because she couldn't be certain of what would come from the rebellion's attack. She couldn't be certain that her parents would be safe.

Ma and Pa looked at her, surprised.

"Is everything okay?" Pa asked.

At the same time, Ma said, "Seren, what did you do?"

"Nothing stupid," she said, noticing the fear in Ma's eyes.

Pa ran his hands over his face. "If you're in danger—"

"I'm not, Pa." He looked at her skeptically. *"Really."*

Seren wished she could tell Pa how she was going to save Ma and the baby. She wished she could explain that everything was about to change for them—but even if she could, she wouldn't know how to.

"It feels good to have you home," Ma said, running her thumb up and down Seren's cheek, wiping away another falling tear.

"It feels good to be home."

The three of them stayed that way for a while, Ma under the covers, Seren on the edge of the bed, Pa in the doorway. Even in the silence, Seren felt safer than she had in weeks. She laid her head on Ma's shoulder, closed her eyes, and breathed in the smell of Ma's shampoo.

She didn't even notice as she drifted off to sleep.

· · ·

"Seren?"

Seren's eyes flew open.

"What time is it?" she mumbled. She was lying in her parents' bed, fully tucked in, and her shoes lay untied on the floor beside the bed.

Pa peeked into the room, a soft grin on his burly face. "It's nearly seven o'clock. Do you want to stay for dinner? Maybe join us for the Evening Broadcast?"

"I'd love to, but I should get home."

"Well, you're welcome any time."

"Thanks, Pa."

Seren climbed out of the bed and kissed her parents goodbye, promising to be back. She paused at the door before leaving and took Pa's hand in hers.

"One last thing," she said, quietly. "Promise me that you will not leave the apartment after curfew for the next few weeks. No matter what you hear."

Pa looked at her with a mixture of amusement and concern. "Seren, I've never, not once in my forty-three years, gone out after curfew. *Some* of us follow the rules."

He was making a joke, but his eyes had narrowed. Pa was a wise man. Always had been.

"I know," Seren said. "But please. Just … please. Be safe, okay?"

His expression clouded as he nodded once, firmly. "Okay."

Seren shut the door behind her, heart beating wildly.

She had one final stop to make before she headed to Tier Two.

. . .

Lucas's mom, Jean—or Edu Snyder, as Seren better knew her— smiled as she opened her door.

"Seren! What a surprise," she said. "Lucas tells me you're a Tier Two Thinker now What're you doing back in our parts?"

"Is Lucas here?" Seren asked.

"No, he's working late tonight. That boy has been working non-stop lately. Did you hear he's a nurse? Never thought I'd see him go into medicine. He used to avoid me like the plague when I had even a runny nose."

It was a joke, but Seren couldn't even bring herself to fake a laugh. She glanced anxiously over her shoulder. A couple of men on their way home from work walked past. They largely ignored her, but she still felt too exposed.

"May I come in?" she asked.

"Of course," Jean said brightly. She opened the door further, and Seren stepped inside. "I was just preparing dinner. Lucas usually gets fed at work when he works this late, so I'll have extra if you want anything."

"I'm okay, thanks." Seren bit her lip as Jean returned to busying herself in the kitchen. "Is there somewhere more private we could go?"

She tried to keep her tone light, but Jean's shoulders tensed. She turned to Seren and forced a smile. "Of course, dear. Follow me."

She led Seren to the bathroom, shut the door behind them, and turned on the shower, just as Seren had weeks ago. The running water created a steady stream of white noise. An invisible five-minute countdown began.

"Is everything okay? Did something happen to Lucas?" Jean asked. Seren could barely hear her over the water.

"Lucas is okay," Seren said, her voice just as low. She knew it probably wouldn't matter if *they* heard her. Once Seren told Governor Warren about Lucas, her visit to Jean would make sense. After all, Seren was the concerned friend—the loyal, ethical, but careless young girl. Governor Warren might have been suspicious had she *not* visited. Still, she didn't want him to know the ins and outs of their conversation. Her goal was to ensure Jean's safety. "But I don't think you're safe here. You should make yourself difficult to find. If you go to my parents' place, you can hide there until things die down."

Jean grabbed Seren's hands and held on hard. Her sharp nails dug into Seren's palms, but Seren ignored the pain. She didn't pull away.

"He's joined them, hasn't he?" Jean asked, her voice so desperate that it pained Seren to hear.

"Joined who?" Seren asked innocently.

Jean narrowed her eyes. "I'm not naive, Seren."

Seren's throat tightened. She nodded.

Jean sighed and dropped Seren's hands, leaving small crescent indents in her palms. "I should have known Defectio would come for him, when his father died," she said. Her eyes searched Seren's face, silently asking what role Seren played in all of this. Seren wondered the same of Jean. She must have known her husband had illegal books; she must have heard the stories he told Lucas and Seren. If Seren tried hard, she could conjure up memories of Jean and Henry in heated arguments about his choice to share so much with Lucas. She could still recall Jean's angry whispers.

"You're going to get us all killed," she would say.

"I'm won't allow my son to grow up ignorant," he'd respond.

These disagreements had seemed unimportant back then, but somewhere along the line, Henry had slipped up and had gotten himself killed.

So, Jean had been right after all.

"He won't succeed," Jean said quietly.

Seren didn't know how to respond.

Jean squared her shoulders and looked Seren dead in the eyes. "You need to promise me you'll be careful," she said. "This will not end well for anybody."

"I—"

"Promise."

"I promise."

She nodded and stepped away. "Do your parents know anything?"

"No, nothing."

"Good. I'll head over there this afternoon. I'll watch out for them. Maybe we could hide out in Tier Five for a bit."

"Thank you," Seren whispered, tears in her eyes.

Jean pulled her into a hug, and Seren relaxed in her arms.

"Be careful, Seren," Jean whispered.

39

ZAIDEN

Government work, it turned out, was not as dull as Zaiden thought it would be. His experiences in council meetings thus far had been bone dry, but today, his father moved so quickly that there wasn't time to get bored.

They began the day in his father's office, speaking to his head Harmonizer, a man by the name of Jarren Kris. Jarren briefed Zaiden's father on the sensitive intelligence that had been collected throughout the last twenty-four hours. He played video recordings of strange conversations happening in the halls, in apartments, and in offices. Most seemed inconsequential, but his father seemed interested in a few of the conversations.

"Subject 13824 took another trip below," Jarren said in a low voice.

Zaiden turned to his father for clarification, but none was given.

"How long?" Governor Warren asked.

"Four hours," Jarren said. "And he brought someone along. A girl. She was—"

Governor Warren lifted a hand to silence him. "We can discuss later. Keep up the good work."

"Thank you, sir," Jarren said, then he left.

Zaiden watched him go, aware once again that things were being kept from him. He said nothing, though. His father had trusted Zaiden enough to let him accompany him today. For now, that was enough.

After Jarren's briefing, Zaiden followed his father to a meeting with Tier Three scientists. Two of them stood in a lab, wearing white coats, goggles, and gloves. Zaiden and his father put on white coats and entered the lab.

The scientists explained that there had been a rise in a strange chest cold through Tier Four.

"We're monitoring it closely," said the first scientist, a woman with dark eyes and dark skin.

"What are the symptoms?" Governor Warren asked.

The other scientist, a tall, lanky, pale guy, jumped in. "Sore throat, tight chest, rattling cough, and fever are the few we're seeing frequently," he said, pushing his glasses up to the bridge of his nose. They slipped again immediately, sliding down his sweat-soaked face.

Both scientists' voices quivered, and Zaiden looked at his father. *They're terrified,* he realized. Would he, too, make people this nervous someday?

"And how are you doing with containment?" Governor Warren asked. He seemed oblivious to the power he had over them.

"As of now, the disease is contained," the woman said.

"Is it reacting to any herbs?"

She nodded. "Peppermint and honey tea seems to calm symptoms, and bromelain has also shown good results."

Zaiden's father took the packet of information they'd provided and handed it to Zaiden.

"Thank you. Keep me updated," his father said, and then they were off to another meeting, this time with the Thinkers.

"When do you know whether a disease is cause for concern?" Zaiden asked as they returned to Tier Two.

"When they tell me it is," his father said. "If I worried about every single issue brought to me, I'd have died of stress long ago." They rounded a corner. "Are you ready to meet the Thinkers? These guys are absolute idiots."

His father laughed, and Zaiden grinned. It had been a long time since he'd heard his father laugh. He couldn't even remember the last time. It had to have been before Ivory's death.

Both his father and Seren were right about the Thinkers. They were certainly interesting. Of the groups of thirty Thinkers that Tier Two had, only two seemed to do any real work. They were the two representing the greater group today, and they spoke quickly and passionately about potential ways to fix the population issues (none which would be as effective as his father's plan, Zaiden realized uncomfortably), as well as ways Community could contribute to Earth's healing from within its walls (Governor Warren shot these ideas down), and different ways to alter the electricity usage to make it more equitable throughout the Tiers (again, his father didn't seem particularly interested).

Zaiden half expected to see Seren amongst them, head bent over a book, but she was nowhere to be found. He tried not to let his disappointment show.

"This is all very interesting," Zaiden's father said to the Thinkers once they'd finished. "Keep up the great work."

The two men beamed and gave thanks before scampering back to their chairs to continue their thinking.

Later in the day, Alaster came by to talk about Governor Warren's legislative strategy. Most members of Community didn't have time to concern themselves with how Community was being governed. As long as their needs were met, they were happy.

But a select few upper Tiers *did* take a particular interest in government. They called themselves "grassroots advocates"—apparently a term from the old world—and Alaster's responsibility was to help Governor Warren appeal to them. "To keep them from bugging me all the damn time," was how Zaiden's father put it.

This meeting was, in fact, boring. Zaiden found himself zoning out as Governor Warren and Alaster spoke about mobilizing, legislative agendas, and how to keep the grassroots advocates out of the government while simultaneously making them believe they had a say. After a grueling ninety minutes, their meeting came to an end, and Alaster left. Zaiden checked the clock and realized with a start that it was five o'clock, and he hadn't eaten anything since breakfast. His stomach rumbled urgently.

"What did you think?" Governor Warren asked, leaning back in his chair.

"I can't believe you do this every day," Zaiden said. He was exhausted, and all he'd done was listen.

His father nodded. "It's difficult at first, but once you get used to it, I think you'll find that it's rewarding to make decisions that benefit the members of Community."

"I think so, too." Zaiden paused. "Can I ask you something?"

"Sure."

"Why don't we have more procedures in place to deal with rebellions?" Zaiden asked. The rebellions hadn't come up yet that day, but Zaiden could tell they were always on his father's mind. They'd been on his mind, too.

"We do," Governor Warren said. "We use the Awakening to deliver uplifting rhetoric and to convince people that they're happy, we maintain strict barriers between Tiers to ensure continued ignorance, and our educational system is well monitored. As you know, lower Tiers don't have access to the same books or knowledge that you do."

This struck Zaiden as somewhat wrong, but he didn't say so. He thought about his drunken conversation with Seren, about how hurt she'd looked about the book.

"With all of those defenses, how could there be a rebellion?"

Governor Warren shrugged. "Someone showed them what they're missing."

Zaiden remembered that his father had said one of their own might be a part of the rebellion. He shivered.

"Our goal, Zaiden, is to squash this rebellion and create enough negative rhetoric around it to ensure that it never happens again." Zaiden's father placed a hand on his shoulder. "Thank you for joining me today."

"Thank you for letting me come," Zaiden said. "I'd like to do it again, if you'll let me."

Zaiden's father gave his shoulder a squeeze. "I'd like that too. We'll start you off at once a week, alright? How about that?"

Zaiden grinned. "That sounds perfect."

40

SEREN

Seren stood outside Governor Warren's office, her hand inches away from the door. As with a veteran returning to the battlefield, her body had a visceral reaction to this place. Her fight-or-flight response told her to run. Her hand shook. She was not sure she could handle another one of his lessons, could not witness any more of Earth's horrors. But she had to talk to him—*had* to tell him about Lucas and Noa.

The Harmonizers standing guard outside the office eyed her with morbid curiosity, as though they could not wait to the entertainment about to unfold. She avoided their gaze, took a deep breath, and opened the door.

Seren was disturbed to find that Governor Warren was not alone. Zaiden stood by the edge of his desk, facing his father. The bruises around his eye had been covered up, and if she hadn't seen him just a few nights before, Seren would not have been able to tell that anything had happened.

Both Governor Warren and his son turned to look at her as she entered. Their expressions were eerily similar. Seren felt as though she were looking through a portal at two versions of the same man, separated by years and cruelty. Unwittingly, she took a step backwards.

"Seren Quinn," Governor Warren said, a smile growing on his face. "What a nice surprise."

A flash of confusion crossed Zaiden's features. Seren tried to avoid looking at him. She avoided the Governor's gaze as well. All she could think of when she looked at him was the placebo birth control shots and Zaiden's bruises. Anger pulsed through her veins, stronger than her blood. She focused her attention on the ground instead.

"I need to speak to you," Seren said. She struggled to keep the hatred out of her voice.

Governor Warren's smile widened, as if he knew this and took pleasure in her anger. He gestured towards the chair in front of his desk.

"Of course. Have a seat."

Seren's eyes darted from the chair up to Zaiden. They had not spoken since *that night,* just two short nights ago. She couldn't believe that he was here now, with his father, as though nothing had happened. She couldn't believe Governor Warren had the nerve to look his son in the face after what he'd done.

"Could I speak to you alone?" Seren asked. She did not want Zaiden present for this. She did not want him aware of the nature of her relationship with his father.

"He has been shadowing me all day," Governor Warren said. "He will be a part of this conversation."

His tone left no room for argument. Seren knew what he was trying to do. He'd seen her building a relationship with his son, and he despised it. Now, he was going to tear it apart by forcing Seren to reveal to Zaiden that she had been lying to him all along.

"I could come back tomorrow—"

"That would be unnecessary," Governor Warren interrupted. "It would be best if you would tell us now."

Best for who?

It would be best for the rebels. The sooner Governor Warren knew their "plan," the better. It would be best for her mother, too, to be rid of this psychopath before she got too deep into her pregnancy. But would it be best for Zaiden?

She felt Zaiden's eyes on her as she fixed her own on Governor Warren. What she was about to do would leave Zaiden fatherless, no better than what Governor Warren had done to Lucas. She couldn't believe she was taking part in this, allowing it to happen.

He'd never forgive her.

Seren tried to push the thought away. She didn't want to think about Zaiden.

"Well?" Governor Warren pressed, his mouth still in a horrible smug grin. He was enjoying this—every second of it.

Seren knew she should say something, but she couldn't find the words. Her tongue felt heavy.

Come on, Seren.

She remembered her conversation earlier with Lucas: *"The Warrens killed my father. They were just as willing to let your mother die."*

What he'd said was true. There were too many injustices in Community that needed to be solved. Seren couldn't let Zaiden get in the way of that.

She took a deep breath and centered herself. "I was visiting my mother the other day, and I ran into an old friend. Lucas Snyder," she said. Governor Warren raised an eyebrow; he recognized the name. "He and I got to talking, and he mentioned that he might have a way to save my mom."

From the corner of her eye, Seren could see the cogs turning in Zaiden's head. She looked down at her hands, willing them to stop shaking.

"He said that he's part of a small organization," she continued. "It's called Defectio. He said there's two dozen of them that want to take over your place. I told him that it was stupid and that you have more people, more weapons, more agility, but he wouldn't listen. It's..." Seren's voice faltered. "I don't want to see him get hurt."

She could feel her eyes welling up with tears. *At least my emotions are finally coming in handy,* she thought, blinking them from her eyes. She was crying not because she was worried about Lucas's safety, though that was true; she was crying because she couldn't shake the feeling that no matter how this turned out, someone would be dead—and she'd be to blame.

"That's perfectly understandable," Governor Warren said, moving from his desk and placing a strong hand on Seren's shoulder. She flinched. "You're doing the right thing by telling us. The safety of the people in Community—your friend especially—is our main concern."

Yeah, right, Seren thought spitefully.

"Did he mention when this would occur?"

"No," Seren said as convincingly as she could. "They're too small right now. They have no weapons. Lucas said they're trying to get more people to join, but that could take months..." She trailed off. "I just... I need to make sure he doesn't get too involved. I can't see him get hurt."

Governor Warren stroked his chin thoughtfully. "Thank you for bringing this to my attention, Seren. We'll be sure that Lucas is kept safe."

"Thank you," Seren said. It was the first honest thing she'd said to him tonight.

Zaiden studied her expression, his mouth pressed in a tight frown. Seren still couldn't bring herself to look at him; she feared that meeting his eyes would break her.

"Is there anything else?" Governor Warren asked.

"No. That's all."

"Very well, Miss Quinn. As we previously discussed, in exchange for this information and your continued loyalty to our cause, your mother's life will be spared. Her pregnancy will not end in her termination."

If Zaiden didn't understand before, he did now. His mouth opened into an O as he looked between Seren and his father.

"Thank you," Seren whispered.

"You may go," Governor Warren said, his smile seemingly ten times wider than when she'd first come in. The man was absolutely giddy.

Seren nodded and walked towards the door, feeling both of the Warrens' eyes boring into her back as she went.

"Excuse me for a moment," she heard Zaiden say as the door shut behind her.

Seren's heartbeat increased, and she picked up the pace, moving quicker through the Governor's hallway.

"Seren, wait!" Zaiden yelled after her. Seren pretended not to hear. "I command you to STOP!"

Seren turned, face burning. "You *command* me?"

Seren was angry at Zaiden for standing next to his father tonight, for acting like the other night had never happened. She was angry that he'd been complicit in the placebo shots. Most of all, she was angry at him for ruining whatever shred of friendship she and Lucas had left.

Zaiden breathed heavily and stared down at her with narrowed eyes. "What the hell was that?"

"What was *what?*" Seren snapped.

"Do you want to explain to me what you've been doing for my father?"

"Why don't you ask him?"

"I'm asking *you*," he said. "You've been … what? Collecting intel? What the hell does that even mean?"

"I don't need to talk to you about this." Seren turned to go, but Zaiden grabbed her arm.

"Let go of me," she growled.

To her surprise, he did. When he released her arm, he took a step back.

"Your bruises look good, by the way. Covering them up must have made you forget about them, right?" Her tone was cruel, but effective; Zaiden looked as though he'd been slapped.

"You don't understand," he said quietly.

"You're right. I don't."

Maybe he wanted to say more, but Seren didn't give him a chance. She took off down the hall, leaving Zaiden standing there, more bewildered than she'd ever seen him.

41

ZAIDEN

"You've been quiet," Governor Warren observed.

He and Zaiden sat at a table in their foyer, sipping their coffee. This brew was especially bitter, and Zaiden made a mental note to ask their maid to make the next batch less strong.

Zaiden's breakfast sat untouched in front of him, its contents growing cold. He stabbed the soy scramble mindlessly with his fork. "I've just been thinking," he said.

"About the rebellion?"

He nodded, though that had hardly crossed his mind. The truth was that he couldn't stop thinking about Seren. She'd been working for his father all this time, as what? An informant? Why would she hide that from him? Did she not trust him?

Or did she not tell him because she was spying on him, too?

At least Zaiden finally had the answer as to how she was still alive. He'd never thought to ask why; the reason hadn't mattered. Now he couldn't help but wonder: if she hadn't spied for his father, would she have screamed like Marcus as poison was injected into her veins?

The thought brought another wave of nausea. He pushed his plate away.

"I have a meeting this afternoon to discuss our plan for the attack," Governor Warren said, wiping his mouth with a napkin. He crumpled it up and threw it on top of his empty plate.

"With whom?" Zaiden asked.

"The Chief Harmonizer and some of his men. While I'm gone, I want you to continue your target practice. Understood?"

Zaiden nodded. "But Seren said they aren't planning on attacking yet."

"She did. Do you trust her?"

The question took him back because, in truth, Zaiden had spent the last thirty-six hours wondering the exact same thing.

His father didn't wait for a response. "Starting tomorrow morning, you'll have a contingent of Harmonizers following you everywhere you go. You must follow their orders, regardless of how ludicrous they may seem." His father rubbed his eyes with his palms and sighed. "This job is not easy, Zaiden. You never know who you can trust."

Zaiden's mind went to his friends, Atlas and Rocco. He liked them, sure—but did he trust them? And now Seren. Was she trustworthy?

"Is there anyone *you* trust?" Zaiden asked finally.

Governor Warren sighed. "I trusted your mother."

The words hung in the air. They sat for a moment in painful silence.

"Do you miss her?" Zaiden asked quietly.

Zaide's father looked up and focused his watery eyes on Zaiden. "Every day. It isn't easy when I have a mirror image of her right in front of me."

Zaiden didn't have pictures of his mother. Somewhere out there was a painting of her that had been done when Governor Warren was painted for the Council Room wall, but Zaiden hadn't seen it since she passed. He suspected that his father had locked it away, hoping that concealing the only relic of Ivory Warren would help to erase her from his mind. Still, Zaiden had been told that they looked similar, and even more so as he aged. *"You have the same smile,"* people would tell him, or *"You have her kind eyes."* This was the first confirmation he'd received from his father that any of that was true.

His father cleared his throat, and Zaiden knew that this part of the conversation was over.

"Did you arrest Seren's friend yet?" he asked, thinking about the other thing that had been bothering him. *Lucas.* Seren had called him Lucas. How long had she been friends with this guy? He would be too young to have been a part of the concrete group that had killed Zaiden's mother, but that didn't absolve him from guilt. Had Lucas put any of his ideas into Seren's mind? Zaiden couldn't bear the idea of Seren thinking of him and his family the way Defectio did.

His father observed him. "No. Not yet. We haven't been able to locate him."

A few months ago, this would have shocked Zaiden. He used to believe his father knew where people were at all times. But he'd learned more since he'd graduated. Now he knew the intricacies of Tier Five. Lucas was likely hiding down there, and they couldn't just go kill a bunch of people to figure it out.

"What will happen to him, when you do?" Zaiden asked.

"The same thing that happens to all traitors," Governor Warren said. A chill ran down Zaiden's spine as his father stood. "I'll be out late tonight. Is there anything you need from me before I go?"

"No."

"Good." Governor Warren walked behind Zaiden and placed a firm hand on his shoulder. "I love you, Zaiden."

Three simple words, yet the effect was immediate. It was the first time his father had said that to him in years. In that moment, Zaiden forgot all his father's wrongdoings. He forgot the violence and cruelty and neglect. In that moment, Governor Warren became the father Zaiden had always wanted. It was instantaneous and overwhelming. Zaiden choked back tears.

"I love you, too."

42

SEREN

Seren stood in the darkness of the Simulator, staring out into the nothingness ahead. She felt useless, like a clock with no hands. Ten floors down, the rebels were likely preparing for a battle, but up here, things were serene. There were more Harmonizers roaming the hallways now, but apart from that, she hadn't noticed any change since she'd informed Governor Warren of Defectio's plan, or lack thereof. She wasn't sure if he'd believed her or if he suspected she was lying. The increase in Harmonizers suggested that it was the latter. If that were true, what would it mean for Ma? For Lucas?

Seren worried about Lucas. She wished she could go to him, to tell him to be careful, to give him one last hug. But even if she could have, she was probably the last person he'd want to see. In all their years of friendship, they'd never had a fight like this. It made Seren feel so alone. She wondered if Lucas felt the same, or if Noa was enough to keep him company as they prepared to bring down the Governor together.

When had life become so hard? Back when they were little, things were so easy. Seren remembered how she and Lucas would play make believe and create worlds in their minds. The worlds they invented had felt just as real to her as the world in the Simulator.

Her favorite game had been "warriors." She and Lucas used to pretend they were soldiers, battling an evil army of men who'd come to kill their emperor. They'd run through the imaginary snow-covered mountains, their swords drawn, and fight any bad man or woman who came along. Lucas's father helped them construct costumes from fabric he claimed to have found in the trash. They were red. *"Like your hair,"* Lucas's father said, placing the cloth around Seren's shoulders. She wore it with pride.

Seren wondered how their lives would be different had they been allowed to live on Earth. They could've played make believe in the fresh air. They could've run down real mountains, played in real snow.

But that had been stolen from them. Now, all Seren had was the Simulator. Today, the dark room felt like a blank canvas, waiting for her to form it into a work of art.

"Simulate snow-covered mountains," Seren called into the blank space.

"Simulating snowy mountains," the Simulator answered.

The temperature dropped long before the mountains formed. Seren could see her breath in each exhale, as distinct as steam wafting from scalding water. She hugged her arms tightly around herself and watched as the black room shifted.

This is what children have to look forward to. This is what we're fighting for, Seren thought as the mountains grew in the distance. She could not believe that anything had the ability to be that beautiful.

"Hi."

Seren jumped. Zaiden stood in the doorway. Light poured in from behind him, eerily illuminating him in a sea of brightness. His expression was indiscernible, but he didn't seem surprised to see her there.

"What're you doing here?"

"I came to talk to you," Zaiden said. He glanced at the mountains. "Is now a good time?"

"Sure. End simulation," Seren said. Warm air filled the room, pushing the temperature back to a comfortable level. "How did you know I was here?"

"Lucky guess."

They stood in silence, a palpable tension surrounding them.

"You lied to me," he said. His tone wasn't so much accusatory as matter-of-fact.

"I know."

"You've been spying on me."

Seren looked at him, her eyes widening. "No! Not on you. Just… in general."

Zaiden looked across the Simulator at the dark wall, his expression impossible to read. "You could have told me."

"You father asked me not to," Seren mumbled. Zaiden did not look surprised by this information. "I'm sorry for what I said the other night. That wasn't fair."

"No, it wasn't," Zaiden said. His eyes found hers. "Why didn't you tell me about your mother?"

"I was afraid," Seren said. She shifted as the weight of her words rested on Zaiden.

He frowned. "Of me?"

Seren didn't know how to respond. The answer was yes. Yes, she had thought that by telling him, she would be breaking the rules of her agreement. Yes, because if Zaiden brought the issue up to his father, she would have ended up lifeless in an incinerator, lying next to Ma and Pa as the fire turned them to ash.

Yes, Zaiden, I'm scared of you. But not because of you. I'm scared of the man who raised you, and the man that you may become.

Add that to the list of things she would never say out loud.

"Do you trust me?" Zaiden asked. He held her gaze, his eyes searching hers. In the fluorescent light, the deep purples of his bruises seemed saturated, their color even more pronounced.

"I never wanted to hurt you," Seren mumbled. She reached out and touched his cheek. Zaiden flinched as her cool fingers came into contact with his warm skin.

"I tried to cover them," he said.

"It isn't that noticeable," she lied. Her fingers traveled down his face to his chin.

Zaiden stood, statuesque, his eyes boring deeply into hers.

Why did he have to make things so complicated? It should have been simple. She should've wanted nothing more than to help liberate Community from the Warren Government's suffocating rule. But it wasn't simple. Zaiden was a part of the Warren government. Hell, he was a Warren himself. That made him different. It made him dangerous.

"You're an anomaly, Seren Quinn." *Anomaly.* The word was foreign to her, but the way Zaiden said it made her shiver. "I understand why you did it—why you spied for my father. I would have done the same in your position."

Seren breathed deeply. With Lucas still mad at her, Zaiden's forgiveness meant the world.

"I want to give you something," Zaiden said. He reached into his pocket and pulled out a small, rectangular piece of glass.

Seren stared. "What is it?"

He placed it in her palm, and Seren looked down at it, turning it over gently in her hand. Pressed within the glass were three delicate lavender flowers with yellow-freckled centers and light green foliage. The flowers were arranged so that they overlapped, and a metal casing surrounded them like the frame of a window.

"It's beautiful," she whispered.

"It was my mother's," Zaiden said. "And her mother's before that. The founders had a law about bringing in items from outside Community when people first took refuge here. They feared they could ruin our fragile ecosystem with toxins or germs. But my great-great-great-grandmother found a way to sneak it in. I want you to have it."

Seren held it out to him. "Zaiden, I can't."

"You said you wanted something real," Zaiden said. He stuffed his hands in his pockets and cocked his chin towards the glass. "*That* is real. It's the realest thing here."

The spotlight reflected off the glass, and Seren could almost make believe that she was seeing the sun reflecting off real flowers. She yearned for the place where she could see real wildflowers growing.

What would Zaiden say if he knew that Earth was ready for them? Would he be willing to give up everything he had? Or would he want to keep his luxuries, choosing filtered air over fresh, simulated windows over real rain, snow, and sleet, security over freedom?

"Thank you." Seren clutched the gift to her chest. "This means the world to me."

"I'm glad you like it."

Zaiden brushed back a stray piece of her hair. Seren could feel his breath on her as he leaned in closer. Her own breath caught in her throat.

And then his lips were on hers, and he was pulling her close, closer, closer... Seren had never been kissed; she'd had no idea what to expect. This exceeded all her expectations. The kiss began gently, but quickly intensified. Seren's trepidation melted away as Zaiden ran his strong hands through her hair and pulled her in closer. They could not be close enough.

As soon as it began, it ended, and Zaiden pulled back. Seren finally opened her eyes, fearful that she would see regret in his, but instead, he was smiling.

"I've wanted to do that for a while," he said.

Chills flooded down her spine. "Me too," she said. It was only after she said the words that she realized they were true.

They stood there for a moment, Zaiden's hands resting on her waist, until he finally dropped them. She felt their absence immediately.

"You didn't answer my question," he said quietly. His breath was warm on her forehead. "Do you trust me?"

"Do you trust *me*?" Seren asked.

"I don't know," he paused. "Your friend, what's his name ... Lucas?"

The mention of Lucas momentarily shocked Seren. She took a small step backwards, her palms tightening, and nodded.

"They haven't found him yet," Zaiden said.

Seren's heart clenched. "Oh," she said, trying desperately to hide her relief.

"I'm not sure I'll be able to protect him when they do."

Her tongue went numb. "Oh."

Zaiden bit his lip. "I've seen what they do to traitors, Seren. My father... He's vengeful. Defectio killed my mother. He hates them with all his being. I don't know whether he'll keep his promise to you, but I'll do my best to ensure he does."

Seren shook her head slowly. "Why? If they killed your mother, why would you protect them?"

"I don't know. I guess I don't think killing them will fix anything. I want to be better than that."

Seren felt a rush of respect for Zaiden. She'd been right: he *was* a good guy. And someday, if Lucas and Noa and all of Defectio saw it, too, he'd be a good leader.

"I should get going," Zaiden said finally. "But … can I see you again soon?"

"Yes."

She watched as Zaiden left the Simulator, leaving the lingering scent of him behind. She breathed it in deeply, placed the pressed flowers down gently next to the control panel, and once again stared out into the darkness.

There was a reason this decision was so difficult. This was a zero-sum game.

Lucas, or Zaiden.

Either way, someone had to lose.

43

SEREN

Late that night, after tossing and turning for hours, Seren accepted that she would not be able to sleep. Her mind kept bouncing from Zaiden to Lucas. What would happen to Lucas when he tried to kill Governor Warren? What would happen to Zaiden once his father was dead? Could she be certain that the rebels wouldn't turn on him, thirsty for more blood?

And no matter how many times she shoved it down, one question kept slipping to the forefront of her mind: what if Earth was horrible? What if it drove people to do all the things Governor Warren had shown her? Would people die of starvation? Would they slaughter each other for power…?

Seren rolled over onto her side and stared at her bedroom wall. Community's walls were all she'd ever known. Would she even like Earth once she was there?

She wished she could talk to someone about this—Lucas or Zaiden or Ma or Pa, or even Edu Snyder. Everyone had answers except her. Everyone had opinions.

She held on tightly to the flowers Zaiden had given her, rolling the glass piece over and over in her palm. She smelled the glass, as if the flowers' scent would break through. Zaiden had forgiven her for keeping a secret from him, but he'd never forgive her for allowing his father to be killed. Her stomach lurched at the thought. She did not like the man, but she did not know whether he should die.

"I don't know what to do," she whispered to her empty bedroom. The dimmed lights flickered back in reply. Seren turned over, scrunched her eyes shut, and tried again to sleep.

Suddenly, a scream pierced the air, stopping Seren mid-toss. She sat up quickly and listened for a moment, thinking perhaps she'd imagined it. There was a long, heavy silence.

But then another scream sounded through the hallway, followed by a loud, ear-shattering bang, and Seren knew.

They're here.

Her response was automatic. She leapt out of bed and threw on a pair of shoes, nearly toppling over in the process. No way in hell was she staying in her room while the battle raged on outside.

Seren ran into her kitchen and yanked open her silverware drawer. She searched through it desperately for a weapon of sorts, settling on the only thing available: a butter knife. The knife had a dull blade and a thin handle, but it was the best she had.

Heart pounding, she dashed to her front door and tugged at the handle.

The door didn't budge.

"No," she whispered.

Of course they had locked the doors. It was smart, really, to keep everyone inside and make sure no innocent civilians got hurt (though "innocent" was a stretch.) Still, even though Lucas and the rebels hated the Tier Twos, they wouldn't want them to die.

Or they didn't want them to interfere.

Seren hoped it was the former.

There was another scream.

"Come on," she urged, trying the handle again to no avail.

Desperate, Seren took a running start. Using a sloppy front kick, she drove her heel into the door just below the lock. Pain shot up her leg, and she hopped backwards, swearing silently. Amazingly, though, it worked. The door swung open.

Seren stepped into the hallway. It was dark, cold, silent. The door to her apartment swung shut, hitting her. She stumbled forward.

Darkness encompassed her. She blinked a few times until her eyes adjusted. The only thing Seren could hear was her own labored breathing. Her neighbors must have still been asleep; no light shone from beneath their doors.

Seren could just barely make out the outlines of familiar things: the convenience store, the medical center, a bar. Still, the darkness made it difficult to see. More than once, Seren stumbled over her own feet. Fear pulsed through her.

Slowly, Seren moved down the hall, keeping one hand on the wall and the other holding the knife out ahead. She would have been better off bringing a cutting board, she realized too late. At least she could have knocked someone out with that. The butter knife would probably do no more than create a bad bruise.

Oh, well. Too late now.

Seren moved down the long hallway, doing her best to keep her steps quiet. The lights above flickered once, startling her. She pressed her back against the wall and breathed deeply. She was still alone.

Seren continued, determined to find Lucas. She wanted to be at his side, whether he wanted her there or not.

She turned the corner—and gasped.

The hall was a war zone. A few men and women were scattered across the floor like fallen soldiers, their bodies limp and lifeless. They had all been shot in one place or another, and their blood pooled on the floor. The metallic scent of it all overwhelmed Seren's senses. They were not dressed in Harmonizer uniforms, so Seren had to assume they were members of Defectio. Her stomach churned. How were so many of them already dead? She scanned their faces, terrified that she'd find Lucas among them. To her relief, he was not amongst the fallen.

She took a moment to mourn the losses before continuing, creeping along the wall. She had no plan, no weapon, nothing. If she encountered a Harmonizer, she'd have no idea what to do. Her only hope was that she could surprise anyone she ran into and take them down before they had the chance to shoot her.

Not a great plan.

Another gunshot fired off in the silence, and Seren jumped— just as a hand clamped over her mouth. She tried to scream, but the noise was muffled. The attacker pulled her backwards into the shadows.

"Don't move," a voice whispered.

Noa?

Seren stayed still, her back pressed against Noa in the doorway of a convenience store. Three Harmonizers ran by. Seren's heart was beating so hard that she feared it might be audible, but they continued without so much as a pause. When they were out of sight, Noa removed her hand from over Seren's mouth.

"What the hell are you doing?" she hissed, shoving Seren away from her.

Seren hid the butter knife behind her back, embarrassed. "I want to help," she said.

Noa looked at her incredulously. "You can help by going back to your room," Noa whispered angrily. "You're going to get yourself killed. If Lucas knew you were out here—"

"But he doesn't," she said. Noa narrowed her eyes, and Seren bit her lip. "Please, Noa. I feel awful about … everything. Let me do something."

"You've done enough."

"I can't just sit around while you put yourselves in danger!"

Noa huffed. "Fine—but only because this is going poorly for us. There are more of them than we thought, and we knew some of them would be armed, but we didn't think they'd *all* have guns. And it seems like they keep coming out of nowhere." For a split second, Noa's characteristic strength disappeared, and Seren could see a scared, lost girl behind her hard exterior. She felt connected to her for a moment. They were fighting for the same thing.

"What can I do?" Seren asked.

Noa bit her lower lip. Her eyes darted as she spoke. "Take this…" She handed over a strange-looking canister. "… and spray any Harmonizer you meet. We need them debilitated, and this is all we've got."

"What is it?"

"It's an anesthetic that they use in the health centers. Lucas has been slowly stealing it over the last few months. It's strong stuff, but use it sparingly; there isn't much left. Oh, and you have to be in three feet of someone for it to work, so … good luck." She turned to leave.

"Noa?" Seren whispered after her.

The two girls locked eyes, and for the briefest of moments, an understanding passed between them. They wanted the same thing: freedom and safety for their families and the ones they loved.

"Be safe," Seren said.

Noa nodded. "You too."

And then she ran off in the direction of the Harmonizers who'd passed. Seren watched her go, awed by her bravery and strength.

She understood Noa's appeal. Like Lucas, Noa was headstrong, determined, brave.

Seren crept from the doorway and went the other way, the anesthetic clutched in one hand, butter knife in the other. She kept her footsteps light, moving quickly.

Take down the enemy. That was her goal. Lower their numbers. That's all she had to do. Seren was grateful that Noa had not given her a gun. She didn't think she would have been able to use it.

Seren pressed her back further against the wall, breathing hard, and looked over the hallway. The lights above flickered again—a rarity for Tier Two. The Tier Fives probably weren't generating electricity tonight.

What was happening down in Tier Five now, Seren wondered. Had the Harmonizers gone there or were they too busy protecting themselves up here?

Suddenly, a scream pierced the silent air.

Automatically, Seren tore down the hallway towards the source. As she rounded the corner, she found a Harmonizer holding a gun to a young girl, not more than ten years old.

Seren's heart stopped. What was a *child* doing here? Did Lucas know? The sound of the Harmonizer clicking off the safety echoed down the hallway.

Seren sprinted forward. "STOP!" she yelled, throwing her entire body towards them.

The Harmonizer looked up in shock. Seren recognized him; he was one of the tall, broad men that kept watch over Governor Warren's door. Recognition flashed in his eyes, too, as he took his attention off the child for a split second, allowing the girl to dive out of his line of fire and scamper away. The girl disappeared around the corner, and the Harmonizer rounded on Seren.

"That was a *child*," Seren said, as if the man hadn't known—as if he hadn't been prepared to shoot that little girl anyways.

The Harmonizer took a step towards her. Seren's body trembled. Her eyes fell on the space between them. He was about four feet away. He just needed to get a little closer…

"That was a *child!*" she repeated.

In one swift move, Seren stepped forward and pulled the canister from behind her back, pressing down on the trigger. The can made a swishing noise, and the Harmonizer grinned, but his amusement quickly disappeared as gas began to flow. The Harmonizer raised his weapon, poised to shoot—but before he could, he collapsed at Seren's feet. She stared down at his body and kicked it gently. He did not stir. Seren bent down and lifted the gun, holding it far from her body. She pointed it at a wall, and released the bullets (which wasn't all that hard to do) before stuffing it in her waist band.

One down…

Seren sucked in a deep, shuddering breath and continued. Once again, she found herself alone in a silent hall. *Where are they?*

Why hadn't Defectio known what to expect? Why were they overwhelmed with people? Lucas had told her that they had friends in high places. Had those "friends" failed them in their moment of need?

Seren worried about Lucas. Just because he hadn't been in the first pile of bodies didn't mean that he wasn't lying somewhere else in Tier Two, dead.

He's not dead, she tried to tell herself. *If he were dead, you'd know.*

Seren wasn't sure why, but she really believed that. *You have to keep going,* she told herself. *Disarm Harmonizers. That's your job. That's what you can do.*

Having a clear purpose helped. She took a deep breath and pushed off the wall.

Before she had the chance to go anywhere, another Harmonizer rounded the corner. Reflexively, Seren lifted her canister and held it at an arm's length in front of her. It felt clumsy in her grasp.

The Harmonizer didn't lift his own weapon, but he didn't show any signs of fear, either. His eyes flickered behind Seren, and she barely had time to wonder what he was looking at when she felt something cold and metallic on the back of her neck. She froze.

"I wouldn't do that, if I were you," a familiar voice said.

Seren's breath caught in her throat. *Alaster.*

In place of a response, Alaster dug the gun deeper into her skin. With his other hand, he grabbed Seren's wrist and shook. The canister of anesthesia clattered from her grasp and rolled down the hallway.

"Interesting choice of a weapon," Alaster said. "You didn't want to use the gun from the man you knocked out?"

"I'm not a killer," Seren said. She meant it to sound sturdy, but the quiver in her voice gave her away; she was terrified.

Alaster pulled the unloaded gun from her waistband and threw that onto the floor as well. He nodded at the Harmonizer in front of them. "I can take it from here, Chris," he said.

Alaster led her silently down the empty hallways. He kept a firm hand on Seren's wrist, but he removed the gun from her neck. Seren thought for sure that they would run into Lucas or Noa or another member of Defectio, but they saw no one else. It was as if they were the only two in Community.

"Where are we going?" she asked.

Alaster didn't answer. He went left, shoving her ahead of him. Seren tried to keep track of the landmarks, but she quickly lost count of the number of corners they turned, and the familiar hallways faded. Until...

A realization sparked in Seren. She knew exactly where Alaster was taking her.

But why?

The Simulator's massive double doors came into view, and Alaster's grip on Seren's arm loosened.

"What're we doing here?" Seren asked, terrified. Memories of her time nearly drowning flashed in her mind. What was he planning.

Again, Alaster did not answer. He led Seren to the end of the hall, opened the Simulator doors, and gestured inside.

"After you," Seren said with as much bravery as she could muster.

Alaster grinned. "Nice try," he said, giving her a gentle push through. She stumbled in, and Alaster followed, shutting the door behind them.

"Turn off the spotlight," he called.

Then there was darkness.

44

ZAIDEN

A loud noise woke Zaiden from a night of dreamless sleep. He sat up groggily and clutched the gun beneath his pillow. Even though he and his father had mended things, he still feared a repeat of last week. He kept his new weapon beneath his pillow at his father's request, but ironically it was just as much protection against his father as it was against a stranger.

Zaiden's eyes focused on a patch of light in the darkness. It slipped through the crack in his doorway, casting a thin beam onto his wall. Zaiden tried to turn on his lamp. Nothing happened. He tried once more. Still, nothing.

That's strange, he thought. Never in his life had the power not worked. Something was wrong. Zaiden retightened his grip on the gun and swung his legs over the side of his bed. He listened for a moment, but the air was silent. Quietly, he stood and stepped from his room into the foyer.

His apartment was eerily quiet, and the air was cold—colder than he'd ever felt outside the Simulator. The windows in his kitchen depicted a dark, starless sky, emitting no light themselves.

Zaiden did a double take. That wasn't a starless sky; the windows were black. For the first time in his life, the simulations were turned off.

"What the hell?" he murmured.

Zaiden crept towards his father's room, expecting to find him asleep, but the bed was empty. Zaiden checked the time: 2:00 a.m. Where was he?

Zaiden's heart leapt into his throat. *What if the rebels got him?*

No. no, his father was too smart, too guarded, and beside – the rebels weren't meant to attack for another few weeks at least. Zaiden pushed back the thought and crept towards the apartment exit. He still didn't know what was going on, but he was going to get to the bottom of it.

As he stepped into the long hallway, he found it was empty. Zaiden kept his gun drawn ahead of him as he crept down the darkened hall. His mind played tricks on him. Three times, he thought he was being followed, but when he looked over his shoulder, there was nobody there.

Zaiden headed towards his father's office. If anyone could explain the cold and power outages, it would be him.

You're over thinking this, Zaiden told himself. There was nothing for him to be afraid of. At least, that's what he tried to think as, heart beating wildly, he rounded the corner. Suddenly, his legs went out from under him. Zaiden flew forward, landing hard on his hands and knees. Pain shot through his wrists, and he cursed, rolling over onto his back. Dots danced across his vision.

The ground felt wet. With a sinking feeling of dread, Zaiden sat up and looked down.

He was in a pool of blood. But as he examined himself for injuries, he realized that it was not his blood at all. Slowly, he turned to look behind him. A loud gasp escaped him.

Even in the darkness he could see them. Two bodies lay just a foot away, their limbs bent under them at horrifying angles. Blood pooled around their heads, drenching their light hair in a deep red. They were dead, but their eyes were wide open, their faces frozen in a look of horror.

It took all he had not to scream. Zaiden scampered away, the scent of blood overwhelming him.

How had this happened? Seren had said that Defectio did not plan to attack yet. Was this the work of another terrorist group? Or had she been wrong? Fear clouded his mind.

It didn't matter who it was; they were in danger. He had to find his father.

Shouts came from around the corner, and Zaiden jumped, his instincts kicking in. Leaving the gun tucked in the back of his pants, he ran at top speed through the corridors. Deafening gun-shots surrounded him, their echoes bouncing off every wall, making it impossible to tell where they were coming from. Ear-piercing screams followed.

Zaiden ran faster. He rounded a corner and collided with three young men, their faces bony and thin.

They were on him in an instant. A blow from one of their fists knocked Zaiden off his feet. He skidded across the floor, his head banging into a wall. The pain left him temporarily blind, and before he knew it, a rebel was on top of him, his knee digging into Zaiden's chest. The pressure of it knocked the wind from Zaiden's lungs. He struggled to breathe as the man held a gun to his forehead.

Zaiden's first instinct was to fight back. It was what his father had taught him, to punch the attacker with everything he had, to knock him unconscious and take his chances with the other two. But with a gun pointed at his head, Zaiden wouldn't win. He'd be dead before he'd even taken a swing.

Where did the rebel get a gun?

It didn't matter; he had one. Zaiden held in an angry grunt. He shouldn't have put his gun away. Now it was out of reach. The cold metal dug into his back mockingly.

"Zaiden Warren," the man on his chest said. "What a lovely surprise this is."

Zaiden struggled to roll out from under him, but the man dug his knee deeper into Zaiden's chest and laughed, his dark brown eyes bloodthirsty.

"Your father killed my mother, you know," the rebel said as he dug the gun into the place right between Zaiden's eyes. He licked his lips. "I wonder how he'd feel if I did the same thing to his son."

The knee on his chest made it difficult to breathe. Zaiden thought he might die of suffocation before the man even had the chance to shoot him. "Please," he gasped. He couldn't believe it had come to this—to lying on the ground, begging for his life.

The man let out another cold laugh and clicked the safety off.

Zaiden closed his eyes.

"Enough!" a voice called.

Another rebel, an older man, stepped forward and placed his hand on Zaiden's attacker.

"You've had your fun, but Noa was clear. The kid lives."

The attacker pressed the gun deeper into Zaiden's forehead. "Noa doesn't care. He ruined her life, too."

"He lives," the older man said firmly.

With an angry sigh, the man on top of Zaiden jumped off, but not before striking his face with the butt of the gun. Blood gushed from Zaiden's nose and found its way into his mouth, saturating his taste buds with a metallic flavor.

In a moment of clarity, Zaiden shut his eyes. Fight-or-flight took over, and he chose flight. He pretended to be unconscious.

"What did you do?" he heard the older man ask.

"He's fine. He's breathing, isn't he?" the younger one said.

The older man let out a loud, exasperated sigh. "We can't leave him here. He could get trampled."

"What do you suggest we do, then?"

"There. The classroom."

Zaiden remained immobile as the two men dragged him by his feet into an open, empty room. They knocked his head against the corner as they pulled him in, and Zaiden bit his tongue to keep from crying out.

"Better?" the young man asked, dropping his feet roughly.

"Shut up," the older guy said.

Then the men left, shutting the door behind them. Zaiden stayed down until the sound of footsteps was long gone. When he was certain he was alone, he sat up and spat blood from his mouth. He pressed his shirt to his nose, trying to stop the flow. He felt woozy. He was almost positive that his nose was broken, and he might've been concussed from how hard they'd hit his head on the wall, but apart from that, he was fine.

He let out a long breath and shut his eyes for a moment, trying to slow his beating heart. He had thought for sure he was dead. They'd had him down and unarmed, but they didn't kill him.

Why didn't they kill me?

With an excruciating push, Zaiden scrambled to his feet and ran as fast as he could from the scene, drawing his gun as he did so. He wouldn't be caught unarmed again.

It took all of his might for his legs not to give out from under him. Stabs of pain ricocheted through his ribs. If they hadn't been broken by his father, they certainly felt broken now. But Zaiden didn't let the pain slow him. He moved quickly, trying to breathe through his mouth to avoid the putrid smell of blood.

Who are these people? Zaiden wondered as he ran. *What do they want?* Who was Noa? He had so many questions, but his woozy mind couldn't focus on any of them for longer than a moment.

Zaiden made it to his father's office without running into anyone else, but the second he touched the mahogany door, his blood turned cold.

Something prickled at the back of his neck. He paused, his hand frozen on the door, and listened.

A male voice radiated through the doorway. Zaiden's heart pounded. The voice did not belong to his father, or to Alaster. A trickle of fear ran down his spine.

Zaiden risked pushing the door open a centimeter and peered in. He could see only part of two bodies, standing against his father's bookcase. He held his breath.

"I don't understand. Where could he be?"

"They must've known we were coming." This time it was a woman speaking. She gestured with her hand. In it was a gun. Zaiden's grip tightened around his own.

"That's not possible," the guy said.

"Maybe Seren tipped them off."

Zaiden froze. *Did they say Seren?*

"She wouldn't do that."

"How else would they have been so well prepared for our attack?"

"It wasn't her," the male voice snapped.

Zaiden didn't need to hear any more. With his gun readied in his right hand, he mustered up the courage to push open the doors.

A boy and a girl stood with their backs to him, flashlights drawn as they searched his father's bookcase. Zaiden quickly cast a look around, checking to see if there was anyone else in the room. There wasn't. They were alone.

Good, Zaiden thought. Two to one wasn't bad odds, especially since he was armed.

He took a silent step through the door.

Books were scattered across the room, clumsily thrown and lying open. The large screen behind his father's desk was black. Zaiden took another step. A page crunched under his foot. He froze.

The girl's eyes flickered to him.

"We have company," she mumbled. The boy turned.

"Drop your weapons," Zaiden said.

"Zaiden Warren," the boy said, a sly grin growing on his face.

Zaiden turned the safety off. It deactivated with a click. The boy didn't so much as flinch.

"I said, drop your weapon."

"Why? So you can shoot me while I'm unarmed?"

"Lucas, don't be stupid," the girl hissed.

So, this was Lucas, Seren Quinn's lifelong friend. He was different from what Zaiden had imagined. He looked harder than Zaiden had thought he would be. He had pictured him kind and gentle, like Seren, but this man had eyes that looked like he'd seen too many things.

"Listen to your girlfriend, Lucas," Zaiden snarled, surprised at the cruelty in his own voice.

Lucas held steadfast to his gun. "Funny you should mention girlfriends, since yours is the only reason I haven't killed you yet."

Zaiden's finger went to the trigger, but he stilled, his finger hovering a centimeter away. "What did you say?"

"Lucas—"

Lucas laughed. "I don't know what you did to manipulate her, but whatever it was, it worked. She really cares about you, you know. She thinks you're *different.*" He spat the word, his eyes glowing madly. "But you aren't any different than your father."

An inhuman sound came up from Zaiden's throat. He could shoot Lucas. It wasn't a matter of aim; he was a good shot now. He could put a bullet right between Lucas's eyes.

But if he did that—if he killed Seren's best friend—she'd never forgive him. And if he killed someone else, he would never forgive himself. The gun shook in Zaiden's hands. He fingered the trigger.

"At least I'm not so power-hungry that I'm willing to kill innocent people," Zaiden said.

The girl flat out laughed. "Oh, that's rich. What do you call what you and your father do every day?"

Zaiden's anger heightened. "Say what you want; I saw the bodies out there. Looks like a lot more of yours than mine. Give it up. You lost."

The girl shook her head. "Not yet."

In one swift motion, she lifted her gun and pointed it at Zaiden.

A gunshot went off.

A body fell.

Someone screamed.

45

SEREN

Seren wondered if she should try to run.

If she could just get to the door, maybe she'd stand a chance. The darkness would hide her movements. She'd be a difficult target.

But the gun in Alaster's hand stopped her. Once, she would have had no reason to fear it—she'd never seen a gun before—but Governor Warren had shown her what those weapons could do. And now, she was too scared to take her chances.

"Lights on," Alaster said. His voice echoed through the empty space.

The light turned on, and Alaster became illuminated. His eyes were red and weary with a lack of sleep. He looked like a different man now than he had a minute ago in the hallway. He looked like the man Seren had first met at the ball—the one who'd warned her against ignorance.

She stared at him. There was a moment of silence.

"I'm sorry for scaring you," he said finally, lowering the gun.

Seren eyed the weapon uneasily. *What is he doing?*

His face remained unreadable, but there was a gentleness in his tone that hadn't been there before. "I want to show you something."

He left her in the center of the Simulator and went to the control booth. Seren watched, still uneasy, as he navigated the panel with a certainty that suggested he had done this plenty of times before. She still felt too scared to move, though now she was more confused than frightened. She wasn't sure what to expect.

"Come," Alaster said.

He gestured for her, leaving his gun on the table beside him. Seren hesitated a moment before joining him.

The screen of the control booth was illuminated to display a memory of a past simulation. It was dated from years ago.

"What is this?" Seren asked.

Alaster pressed a button, and the memory began. It was odd, watching an old simulation play back on the screen. Seren imagined this was what it had been like to watch movies or television back in the old days. She felt like a distant part of the simulation.

The Governor appeared. Curiosity rippled through her as she watched the screen.

In the images, Governor Warren was not alone. Next to him stood his late wife, Ivory. They were bickering, their faces animated and their voices low. Seren strained to make out what they were saying, but they were inaudible beneath the crashing waves.

Seren recognized the simulation. They stood on the boardwalk that Zaiden had taken her to, right at the edge, where the beach met the ocean. But this simulation was different. The weather was not as forgiving. Clouds covered the sky in a dull gray haze, and the water crashed threateningly against the shore.

Ivory said something to her husband and started to walk away, but Governor Warren stopped her, wrapping her tiny arm in his strong grasp. She shook her head and yanked it away.

Something about the scene felt wrong. A feeling of discomfort filled Seren as the simulated boardwalk faded away until Governor Warren and Ivory were left standing under just a spotlight. Their voices rose. Without the ocean, Seren could finally make out what they were saying.

"Ivory, let me explain," Governor Warren said, reaching for her once more. In his voice was emotion Seren hadn't believed him capable of.

Ivory shook her head. "I'm sorry, Pluto. I can't. Not after all this."

The Governor stepped back and clutched his chest as if physically wounded. He looked broken. For a bizarre moment, Seren felt sorry for him.

Until he hit Ivory.

Seren gasped. Alaster averted his gaze from the screen, but Seren couldn't tear her eyes away.

Ivory looked stunned. Her hand went up to her cheek reflexively as fear and anger filled her eyes. She turned to walk away again, but Pluto Warren followed.

"Don't walk away from me."

He grabbed her arm and yanked her back, sending her flying in the other direction. She struggled to maintain her balance, all the while trying to pull her arm from his grasp.

"Let go," she growled. Her voice was strong, but Seren could see she was trembling. Governor Warren held on relentlessly, so tight that Ivory's arm seemed to shrink to half its size.

"You slept with him, didn't you?" He grabbed her chin and forced her eyes to meet his. "You owe me an answer."

"I don't owe you anything," she spat.

A tear rolled down Governor Warren's face. "I thought you were different. I thought I could trust you."

Ivory shook her head. "I thought I could trust you, too."

The two Warrens stared at each other. Seren waited.

Nothing happened.

Then a sharp crack rang out as Governor Warren's fist collided with Ivory's jaw.

Seren gasped, reeling from the scene. "Stop it!" she cried out, as if her voice could carry through the time and space.

But Governor Warren didn't stop. He hit Ivory again and again in a series of devastating blows, until she fell into a heap on the floor. She lay so still, Seren wondered if she was dead.

Governor Warren stared at Ivory, his chest heaving. "I loved you!" he shouted at her limp body. "I cared about you! And you betrayed me!" His voice cracked. "You betrayed me," he said again, quietly.

Blood trickled from a cut in her forehead and dripped down her face and onto the floor.

Seren waited, her jaw clenched. She thought Governor Warren might realize the horror of what he'd done, that he would help Ivory up from the ground and cry out apologies until his voice was raw.

But Governor Warren did not show any remorse. All the hurt that had been in him moments before was replaced by pure, unrelenting rage.

"I loved you!" He shouted again. His face was hard and unforgiving. "I trusted you! I raised a son with you! And *this* is how you repay me?" Governor Warren choked on his words. "You ungrateful bitch!" he spat. He took four steps back. He looked ravenous, monstrous, unhinged. "Simulate fire!"

Seren was unable to tear her gaze away from the screen as a flame formed on the Simulator floor. Smoke billowed from it, floating up to the ceiling and spreading, filling the entire room. Governor Warren took more steps back as the fire slowly grew, making its way towards Ivory's crumpled body.

Get up! Seren thought desperately. The thought echoed in her head. *Get up, get up,* get up*!*

This was not how Ivory died. She was killed by rebels, not by her husband. This was not how her life ended.

But if it wasn't, then why was she still lying there?

The fire licked at Ivory's skin.

"Get up!" Seren yelled.

But Ivory didn't rise. She stayed lying down, her body a bit of calm amongst the chaos. The flames swarmed her like an infestation.

Seren knew she was imagining it, but it was almost as if she could smell the smoke and ash, suffocating her as Ivory burned.

Governor Warren watched as the flames disfigured his wife.

An unyielding rage filled Seren, billowing through her like a flame. Every last ounce of sympathy and humanity that she'd held for Governor Warren burned away, leaving ashes of hatred in their wake.

The playback ended, and the images disappeared from the screen, but they remained etched in Seren's brain. She just stood there, staring, her body unable to move.

Alaster shifted. For a second, the spotlight illuminated his face in its dull glow, and maybe it was a trick of the light, but Seren thought she saw a wet stream of tears flowing from his eyes.

"Why?" Seren whispered finally. "Why would you show that to me?"

"You and I are more connected than you may think," Alaster answered, voice tight. "We both have done stupid things for love. You risked your life to save your mother's. I have dedicated mine to seeing that Ivory's death is avenged."

"Why?" she whispered again, though from the look in his eyes, she knew. She'd seen the same look in her parents' eyes.

Alaster looked off into the distance as he spoke. "Ivory always wanted more than Community had to offer. Pluto knew that. She made it her entire life's work to figure out a way to get us back to Earth. She worked with the Tier Three scientists and the Thinkers and the policy makers... She did everything she could. And then, one year after Zaiden was born, she found out the truth."

Seren let out a long breath. She couldn't imagine having someone she trusted keep a secret like that from her, betraying her trust in that way.

"When she found out that Pluto had allowed everyone to stay here, stuck, for so many years, when he'd known all along Earth is now safe ... that betrayal was unforgivable in her eyes. She came to me that night in tears and begged me to help her take him down." Alaster met Seren's eyes. "How could I say no?"

"I don't understand. Why didn't she just go on the Awakening and tell everyone the truth?"

"It isn't that easy. Governor Warren controls the media. He controls the people who run it. And even if by some stretch of the imagination, she found a way on, no one would've believed her."

That was probably true. Seren hadn't believed Lucas—not until she saw proof.

"She knew she couldn't do it alone, so she brought in the two people she trusted most: me, and Henry Snyder."

Seren's head snapped up. "Henry Snyder? Lucas's father, Henry?"

Alaster nodded.

"But, how ... how did Ivory know Henry?" There was no reason their paths should have ever crossed.

"Henry wasn't always a Tier Four. He was born in Tier One."

Seren's eyebrows crinkled in confusion. "No," she said slowly, unsure why she was arguing. "His father was a miller, and his mother worked in infrastructure." At least, that's what he'd always told her, and what Lucas and Jean had always confirmed.

Alaster shook his head, and a small smile grew on his lips. "Henry always did make up the best stories. But no. He grew up a Tier One, just like me and Ivory. He was in our year, and the three of us were inseparable. We spent every minute of every day together. Pluto was always jealous of Henry's friendship with Ivory. When the two of them got married, he sent Henry down to Tier Four, threatening his family if he didn't go quietly."

Suddenly, it felt as if she'd never known Henry at all.

"I don't understand," Seren forced out, her voice strained. "Why would Ivory let that happen?"

"She didn't know. She thought that Henry had made the decision on his own. It wasn't unbelievable; he always did talk about going to live in the lower Tiers. He said he wanted a simpler life." Alaster chuckled softly.

"They didn't see each other much after that. He married Jean and had Lucas, and Ivory gave birth to Zaiden shortly after. But then Ivory found out about Earth and brought the three of us back together. Things were going well for a while. We were meeting weekly in secret, and we had a strong plan. But Pluto began to get suspicious. He had Ivory followed. When he saw her meeting up with Henry, he believed they were having an affair. He didn't know that I was the one who … who loved her."

Who loved her. Seren's suspicions had been right, then. He'd loved her.

Alaster sighed. "When Lucas's father died, Ivory knew the truth. She knew who killed Henry. Before then, I think there was a piece of her that couldn't have hurt Pluto. I think she still loved him. But when he killed one of her best friends…" Alaster shook his head.

A lump rose in Seren's throat. Henry's death had been hard enough before, but now, knowing the reason behind it … it hurt even worse.

"Governor Warren went to confront Ivory. You saw what happened next."

Seren stood in rigid silence, trying to digest everything Alaster had said.

"Does Zaiden know?"

"No. I've thought about telling him, but … I couldn't." Alaster paused. "When Henry and Ivory died, I continued working to bring Pluto down. Months ago, when you went to steal that pill for your mother, you received my identity card from Lucas. Did you ever stop to wonder where he got it?"

No, she hadn't. Seren had believed that Lucas stole the card, but now she realized that was foolish. How would he have gotten access to it?

"Lucas had my card because I gave it to him." Alaster looked at her. "I am the leader of Defectio."

Seren had thought nothing else could surprise her. She was wrong.

For her entire life, she'd understood Community and everything it was, but now, she felt as though her entire life had been flipped upside down.

Seren closed her eyes and tried to think, but her mind was clouded by concerns for Lucas, for Zaiden—even for Alaster, who stood before her looking more destroyed than she'd ever seen a grown man look.

He avoided her eyes now, staring out again into the blackness of the Simulator. "Your mishap almost ruined our plan," he said. "Pluto came to me and asked where a Tier Four girl could have gotten my identity card. I claimed to have dropped it. For some reason, he chose to believe me. I don't think Pluto wanted to believe that another person he trusted had betrayed him. He planned on executing you, but I suggested that he spare your life. I told him you'd be more helpful to him alive—and again, he believed me. That was a bit of a harder sell, but we managed."

"Why would you do that?" Seren asked. It must've put Alaster under such suspicion for him to have argued for her safety. By doing so, he was risking himself and everything they'd worked for.

Alaster shook his head. "I was the reason Lucas lost his father; I couldn't be the reason he lost someone else he cared about."

Seren's heart ached as she thought about how Lucas had looked at her the last time she'd seen him. Maybe he had cared for her before, but he didn't now; Seren had made sure of that. And now he was fighting for his life, and he could die at any moment, and he hated her.

Which brought up another question. "If you're the leader of Defectio," she said slowly, "then why is the attack going so poorly? Why are we losing?"

Alaster's face hardened. "Pluto knew they were going to attack tonight."

"But I told him that they weren't planning an attack yet! I said—"

"It was my fault," Alaster interrupted. "I left a notebook with our plans in the drawer of a desk in my apartment. I thought it would be safe there. I returned late tonight to find that drawer empty." He looked just as numb as Seren felt.

There was a long silence.

In the dull flicker of the light, Seren saw a man who'd given up. He had not brought her here to send a new wave of defiance through her, nor did he have some larger plan in all this. He was here merely to absolve himself from the guilt that had been plaguing him since Ivory's death.

Seren wouldn't let him get off that easily.

"You have to finish the job," she said firmly. "This isn't over. We still have a chance."

Alaster looked at her the way adult men had been looking at her for as long as she could remember. In his eyes, she was no more than a silly girl—a girl who, Seren remembered guiltily, had almost wrecked sixteen years of efforts to take down Governor Warren.

"You must have some kind of backup plan," Seren said. "Some way to bring down Governor Warren."

Alaster shook his head. "It isn't that easy. Pluto Warren isn't the only one who wants to hang onto power. Even if he goes, there's a long line of people after him waiting to continue his legacy. Why would anyone want to dismantle a system that benefits them?"

Seren looked up at Alaster. "Why do you?"

He didn't answer.

46

ZAIDEN

Zaiden blinked and looked down at the gun. Had he missed? He'd meant to miss.

Lucas and the girl lay on the ground. The screen behind them had shattered, leaving a web of cracks weaving through the glass. Zaiden lowered his gun, his legs trembling so hard that he struggled to remain standing.

"Lucas?" he called, unable to stop himself.

There was no response.

Zaiden's heart pounded. Had he hurt them?

He hadn't meant to hurt them. He didn't want to hurt anyone. He felt sick.

As Zaiden doubled over, certain he was going to be ill, a group of Harmonizers crashed through the door. Without acknowledging him, they ran towards the fallen rebels, their boots crunching on the broken glass. Zaiden's father followed close behind.

Zaiden stood there, helpless, as the Harmonizers surrounded Lucas and the girl, the barrels of their guns digging into Lucas's skull.

"Get up," one snapped.

Zaiden waited with bated breath. There was an excruciating moment when he was sure that Lucas would not rise—that he had killed him.

But then Lucas did get up. He stood slowly with his arms raised above his head. Bits of broken glass fell from his clothes and hit the floor. One of the Harmonizer's jerked him up, and Lucas stumbled, catching himself at the last moment.

Zaiden surveyed him. Apart from a few cuts from the broken glass, Lucas looked unharmed. His eyes connected with Zaiden's.

Zaiden looked away.

Lucas kept one arm raised above his head and reached down with the other. In unison, the Harmonizer's cocked their guns; some clicked their safeties off. The air in the room seemed to stiffen. Lucas froze.

"I'm just going to help her up," he said dryly. He motioned to the gun on the floor. It had skidded a few feet and now lay underneath Governor Warren's desk. "It isn't loaded, by the way."

One of the Harmonizers checked the chamber. He gave a nod to Governor Warren.

Zaiden stared at Lucas in disbelief. He'd been carrying around an empty gun? What kind of an *idiot* would do something like that? Zaiden could've shot him. He almost *had* shot him! Was that what Lucas had wanted? Was this all just some weird game to him?

They allowed Lucas to help the girl up. She, too, looked unharmed, which sent a renewed wave of relief through Zaiden. No one was hurt. He hadn't realized how terrified he'd been until he knew for sure.

"Lucas Snyder." Governor Warren's voice cut through the silence.

... *Yet,* Zaiden corrected himself as his father took a step forward.

Governor Warren walked over to Lucas, a gun of his own in tow. He twirled it around in his hands as he made his way through the mess his office had become. "You're a hard man to find."

Lucas's eyes flickered once more to Zaiden, and Zaiden wondered what, if anything, Lucas wanted from him.

If Governor Warren noticed this exchange, he did not acknowledge it. "Did you have a nice time exploring my office?"

"Up until about a minute ago, I was having the time of my life," Lucas said.

Governor Warren laughed humorlessly, a terrifying gleam in his eye. "You're just as witty as your friend Seren."

At the mention of Seren, both Zaiden and Lucas tensed up. Zaiden had nearly forgotten Seren. Where was she now? Was she safe?

"Screw you," Lucas spat.

Governor Warren held his gaze for a moment before turning his attention to the nearest Harmonizer. "Bring them to a holding cell. I have some questions I'd like to ask ... *separately.*"

The Harmonizers dragged Lucas and the girl out of Governor Warren's office. Neither of them fought back. As Lucas passed, Zaiden felt his eyes trailing him. The feeling continued until Lucas was well out of sight.

Once they'd gone, Zaiden's father surveyed the scene. His gaze landed pointedly on the shattered glass window.

"I have to ask," his father said finally, "did you spare Lucas's life because of Miss Quinn, or has Alaster exaggerated your shooting abilities?"

Zaiden shrugged. The truth was that neither of those was true. It had been Marcus on his mind, not Seren, when he had purposefully aimed away from Lucas. Of course, he could not say this to his father—that he had been too weak to kill Lucas, despite thinking his own life was in danger.

Governor Warren sighed and placed a hand on Zaiden's shoulder. "There's something I think you should see," he said.

There was no more discussion about Zaiden's intentions as his father led him out of the office and into the security control room, a tiny space tucked away just a few doors down. It was Zaiden's understanding that this served as the center of Community security, with twenty-four-seven surveillance of every hallway, room, and stairway in Community.

The room was an overwhelming scene of video feeds, with dozens of screens stacked on top of each other, displaying grizzly recordings from the attack in vivid color. In front of the screens sat three Harmonizers, all intensely focused. They spoke in hushed voices as the scenes flickered from one to the next.

"We need more people in the east wing," one mumbled into a headset. "The rebels there are higher in numbers."

"Three men injured in 5N," another said. "On my signal, deploy a group of healers."

Zaiden's father cleared his throat, and the three men turned, saw him, and jumped to their feet.

"Governor Warren, sir," one said, bowing his head. "Our mechanics were able to fix the video issue. The interference the rebels used only hits a few radio waves. We've changed the wavelengths the cameras are on, and they're back up and running, sir."

Zaiden scanned the screens for a familiar flicker of red hair, but he found none.

"Thank you, gentlemen. You may go."

"But sir—"

"Just momentarily," Governor Warren assured them. "You may return to your duties in five minutes' time."

Reluctantly, the men shed their headsets and exited, nodding at Zaiden and his father as they left.

Once the door had shut behind them, Governor Warren walked over to a nearby control panel. He tinkered with it for a moment until all the screens turned off, and the room was plunged into darkness.

"You'll want to be seated for this," Zaiden's father said into the emptiness.

Zaiden settled nervously in a chair as the screen directly in front of him lit up. His father's face became illuminated by the recording, which displayed the interior of an old broken-down bathroom Zaiden had never seen before.

A girl with deep red hair appeared. Though the video did not show her face, Zaiden could tell immediately that it was Seren. If the hair weren't confirmation enough, her quick, gentle movements gave her away.

In the video, Seren wasn't alone. Zaiden squinted at the blurry image. Either someone had attempted to distort the image purposefully, or the camera was an older model. Still, Zaiden thought he could identify the other person: Lucas Snyder.

Lucas walked a few steps behind Seren, his hand in hers, guiding her through the minefield of broken glass. Though the image was blurry, the sound was clear as crystal.

"This is it?" Seren asked.

"This is it."

Zaiden could even hear the glass crunching beneath their feet as Seren asked, "How has no one figured this out?" Seren asked.

The video froze for a moment, buffering. Zaiden waited on the edge of his seat until it resumed.

Lucas spoke. "There are no cameras in this area. No bugs, either."

"No bugs?"

"The resistance isn't just a bunch of bourgeois, Seren. We have friends in high places."

The video went on to show Seren and Lucas climbing into the wall through what Zaiden could only assume was a secret tunnel. He didn't need to see any more; the video was simple enough to interpret. Seren had been a traitor this whole time.

"Turn it off," he demanded, shoving away from the desk.

How could she?

Zaiden had given her so much of himself, and she had been lying to him all along. How could she lie *repeatedly*? How could she, after all he'd shared, be a part of the plot to take down his father—a man who had so generously spared her and her mother's lives? Zaiden wasn't an idiot. He knew what the rebellion planned to do. They didn't just want his father overturned; they wanted him dead.

Seren had tried to rid Zaiden of the only parent he had left.

It pained him deeply, but his father was right: you couldn't trust anyone.

The video began again, a repeat of what they'd just seen.

"This is it?" "This is it."

Zaiden slammed his palm on the table. "Turn it off, God dammit," he growled.

His father finally did as he asked, and once again, the room went dark.

"I'm sorry to show you this," Governor Warren said. He didn't sound sorry at all.

Zaiden wanted to scream. He wanted to drive his fist through every screen until his knuckles were bloody. He wanted to cry and yell and throw over every table, chair, and object he could find.

Zaiden wanted nothing more than to hate Seren for lying to him, for making him care for her. If he could hate her, it would make the idea of arresting her—of having her killed—easier. But he didn't hate her; he didn't hate her one bit.

Stop. You can't think that way. You don't feel sympathy for criminals.

But there was no truth behind the thoughts. Zaiden felt nothing but sympathy for Seren. And now, he had no idea what to do.

"I need a minute," he said.

His father didn't miss a beat. "Take all the time you need."

47

SEREN

Alaster didn't have to say much to convince Seren that it was important for her to find Zaiden before Governor Warren did.

"Now that he knows your allegiance, he'll do whatever it takes to turn Zaiden against you."

Seren hesitated. She knew she had to tell Zaiden what his father had done, but just the idea of breaking the news to him tore her heart in two. He'd be devastated.

"What will you do?" she asked.

Alaster looked so weary, so vulnerable, that Seren hesitated to leave him alone. He had a target on his back now that Governor Warren knew about his betrayal. It wouldn't be long before the Harmonizers found him. What then?

"I don't know," Alaster said. "I don't know."

He removed his gun from the band of his pants.

"Take this. They're after you."

Seren stared at it. "I can't," she mumbled. "I don't know how to—"

"You aim and shoot. That's it." Alaster shoved it into her hand. "Now, you should go. There isn't much time."

There were a lot of things Seren wanted to say. Though she'd played no role in Ivory's death, she wanted to apologize. She wanted to tell Alaster how sorry she was that the woman he loved had died. She could only imagine the pain that would cause.

But she also wanted to berate him, to ask how he could have been so *stupid.* Why had he felt a need to put the plan in writing? Why would he just leave something like that in his drawer? Had he not grown up with the knowledge that in Community, someone was always listening or watching? For someone who had worked so hard to fix things, he sure had a way of screwing everything up. And his carelessness had caused tons of innocent people to die.

But she didn't need to say any of that. He already knew.

"Thank you," she said quietly. "For saving my life."

Alaster gave her a sad smile and one solitary nod.

"I guess I'll be going, then," Seren said. She went to leave.

When she turned to look over her shoulder, Alaster had vanished.

. . .

The halls were empty now.

Somehow, in the time Seren had been in the Simulator, someone had come and collected all the fallen bodies. Now all that remained were the blood stains. *Does this mean it's over?* Seren wondered. Had the rebels lost?

Alaster had warned her that their only chance now would be Zaiden. Seren had to find him, *now,* but she wasn't sure where to start.

She walked with urgency through the empty halls, feeling the watchful eyes of the cameras on her. Their red lights flickered on and off sporadically, and Seren hoped this meant they weren't fully restored. She prayed that whatever the rebels had done to interfere with them had not yet worn off.

She wasn't sure where to begin. Her apartment seemed as good a place as any. Maybe it was naive of her to think and hope, but if Zaiden cared for her the way she hoped he did, maybe he'd stop by and check to make sure she was okay. And if not, at least she could grab the glass-enclosed flowers Zaiden had given her. Maybe they would remind him of what was at stake—what his father had so desperately tried to hide from them all.

It was dangerous, though, to go to her apartment when they were looking for her. She kept her hands tightly wrapped around the gun, her heart beating. She wasn't sure she could use it, even if it came to that.

Seren finally arrived at her apartment, finding the door hanging from its hinges from when she'd kicked it open. Tentatively, she pushed it open.

Familiar eyes stared back at her through the darkened room.

"Zaiden! Thank Warren," she gasped. He was here. He'd come to check on her after all. A wave of relief rushed through her as she threw her gun down, ran to him, and pulled him into a tight hug. "Are you alright?"

Zaiden was stiff as she wrapped her arms around him. For a moment, Seren feared she was hurting him. She pulled away, examining him.

"Did they hurt you? Is everything—"

"Sit down," Zaiden said calmly.

"There's something I have to tell you—"

"Sit down!" he bellowed.

Seren recoiled. "What's going on?" Her eyes flickered to the gun enclosed tightly in his hand. She hadn't noticed it before. But now, she couldn't take her eyes off it; it was pointed directly at her.

A wave of chills went down her spine.

"You lied to me," Zaiden said.

"What are you talking about?" she asked, her voice cracking.

"Don't play games with me, Seren. I know you've been working with them."

Seren's blood went cold. *Governor Warren got to him first.*

"I can explain everything…"

"Did you lie about the timing of the attack?" Zaiden asked, his nostrils flared.

"Yes, but—"

"And you helped Defectio?"

"Yes, but Zaiden—"

"Stop talking!" he yelled, pointing the gun at Seren's chest.

She froze. In his eyes was a side of Zaiden that Seren had never seen, angry and full of fire. In that moment, Seren didn't see Zaiden anymore.

She saw Governor Warren. And it terrified her.

This was what she'd been afraid of. This was her worst nightmare.

"You plotted to kill my father, to kill the only family I have left, and for what? To get the power for yourself?"

"No. I would never! That isn't…" Seren choked on the words. She wanted to say something more, to explain her actions, but she couldn't find the words. Even if she could, would he believe her?

"Zaiden, your father isn't a good man," Seren said, as calmly and sincerely as she could manage. "He's been lying this whole time—to everyone. He did something awful, Zaiden. You have to believe me—"

Zaiden clicked his gun's safety off. "Seren, stop."

Seren stared at the barrel and her heart sank. This wasn't how this was supposed to go. Zaiden was supposed to listen to her. He was supposed to *believe* her.

"You've got it all wrong," she whispered—just as the apartment door swung open, smacking into the wall with a loud bang. The hinges gave in, and the door fell atop the couch, covering the gun Alaster had given Seren, and with it, any semblance of safety. A group of nearly a dozen Harmonizers stormed in. Two of them rushed Seren, grabbing both of her arms. Only once she was apprehended did Zaiden lower his own gun. He looked so tired.

Seren closed her eyes and took a deep, shuddering breath. There was nothing she could do now.

"Zaiden," she whispered once more.

Zaiden looked away. He nodded to the Harmonizers, and they pulled Seren away with their guns at the ready. It was as if they expected Seren to put up a fight.

But they needn't have worried; she had no fight left.

With a final look at Zaiden, she surrendered.

48

SEREN

They threw Seren in a dark cell somewhere deep in the sub-terranean basement of Community. It was cold and wet, and Seren shivered as they descended deeper into depths she hadn't even known existed.

No one spoke to her until she was behind bars. As the largest of the Harmonizers shut the cell door behind her, he gave her a cruel smile. "I'll see you at your execution."

They closed the door to the outside world when they left, submerging her in darkness. She slowly lowered herself onto to the floor and hugged her legs to her chest. The chilly air was thick with moisture and smelled stale, like month-old bread. Seren put her head between her legs and closed her eyes.

What would happen now? Ma would be executed, most likely. Lucas, too. And Pa and Jean. And her—they'd kill her too.

A tear trickled down Seren's cheek. She wiped it away hastily. On the off chance there were cameras in this prison, she would not allow them to see her cry. She resolved to not break. They'd have to kill her before she let that happen.

Seren leaned her head back against the hard metal bars of the cell, finding a sliver of comfort in their solidity amidst the darkness. She focused her attention on the mechanics of the periodic drip of water somewhere in the cell. To distract herself, she counted the beats between each drip.

Drip.

One.

Two.

Three.

Drip.

One.

Two.

Three…

For a while, it almost distracted her from reality.

Almost.

She wasn't sure how long she sat like that, legs drawn in close, body quivering from the cold, counting the seconds. After an immeasurable amount of time, the door to the prison opened, and light flooded in. Seren squinted up at it. Her eyes hardly had time to adjust before a plate was thrown in sideways through the thinly spaced bars. The plate clamored through and shattered, leaving fruit and bread scattered over the cell floor. Then the door was once again closed.

By now, her eyes had grown accustomed to the darkness, and she could make out the outlines of the food. She crawled to it. Seren was hungry—too hungry to leave the food on the floor. She had to use her back teeth to break through the bread, but even stale, it tasted fine. Seren recognized the flavor. It was the same bread—the sweet one with the dried fruit—that she'd had at Zaiden's inauguration gala. She picked up a piece of fruit from the floor next, a green one with seeds.

She was halfway through eating it when it occurred to her that she'd eaten this all before. With a sinking feeling in her stomach, Seren examined the rest. It was the exact same stuff as what she'd eaten at the gala, no more, no less. It was as if Governor Warren had watched each and every bite she'd taken that night and recreated it for her today—as her last meal.

Seren's stomach clinched as she scooted away from it, somehow more terrified of this than she had been of the barrel of a gun. This was a message, a reminder that Governor Warren had eyes everywhere, that he was always paying attention, even to inconsequential choices.

Just when she'd thought he couldn't get any more disturbing...

It was then, staring down at the remnants of the scattered food, that Seren realized Governor Warren would see to it that she suffered in the last hours of her life. He'd want to see her broken before he killed her. He would kill Ma and Pa and Lucas in front of her, slowly and painfully, until she broke. Above all else, the man was a sadist.

Overcome by a sudden wave of nausea, Seren pushed the food away and focused instead on the shattered plate. She tried to piece it back together, like the puzzles she used to do with Ma and Pa. She sat bent over with her legs beneath her for a while until it was whole again.

At least she'd fixed something that day.

The sound of dripping water continued every three seconds, like the ticking of a clock. With nothing else to do, she leaned back and listened, closing her eyes and counting the seconds between them again.

In the craziness of the last few hours, Seren had failed to realize how tired she was. Now, exhaustion rammed into her like a flying brick. It was difficult for her to clear her mind, but after a while, sleep came.

. . .

Seren wasn't sure what time it was when she woke up.

Her sleep had been restless, her dreams full of fire, blood, and fear. The nightmare continued when she woke up on the cold, damp floor of the cell and remembered the last few hours.

Seren sat up, ignoring the stiff creaks of her muscles. An onslaught of approaching voices made her tense. Was it already time for her execution? Had she slept that long? Fear clawed at her, and she choked on it.

She wasn't ready to die—not when she'd barely lived.

The cell door opened. Seren pressed herself against the cold stone wall and awaited a Harmonizer's cruel grip. To her surprise, they paid her no mind as they shoved someone into the cell with her. He stumbled, tripping over his own feet.

Not just someone.

Lucas.

Lucas, limp and tired. Lucas with blood covering his face and his hands and his shoes.

"Lucas!" Seren exclaimed. She ran to his side after the cell door closed. When it became apparent that he couldn't walk on his own, she wrapped his arm around her neck and helped him stand. His skin was hot and clammy to the touch.

She led him over to the cell wall, which he slid down clumsily. He slipped from her grip, and his body hit the floor with a dull thud. If it hurt, he did not vocalize it.

In the background, the dripping continued.

Drip.

Drip.

Drip...

Seren knelt beside him, her eyes scanning through the darkness for injuries. His breathing was faint and labored, but steady.

"Are you going to ask if I'm okay?" he asked, his eyes shut.

Seren nearly cried with relief at the sound of his voice. "No," she said. She didn't have to; it was clear that he wasn't. Her eyes flickered from his bloody nose to his hands. He clutched his side like he was trying to hold himself together.

"Who did this?" Seren asked.

Lucas shifted, a small moan escaping his lips. He met her eyes. "Who do you think?"

The words weren't angry; they were a surrender. There was no fierceness in Lucas's gaze. His dark eyes were empty, like a starless night sky.

Hatred rose in Seren.

"Where's Noa?" she asked. "Is she..."

Dead? The word stopped before it reached her lips.

"They have her upstairs," Lucas said. He shifted slightly, but even that seemed to pain him, and he moaned.

Seren wanted to comfort him, but she knew what he needed now more than anything was strength. She grabbed the leftover bread and fruit from the floor and gave it to him. He took it, but he didn't eat.

There was silence.

"This is all my fault," Lucas said.

He pulled the bread apart without eating it, like a nervous tic. Seren watched as crumbs fell to the floor. Her hand went to the giraffe spots on his arm. "It's not," Seren said.

"Yes, it is." Lucas looked up, his eyes brimming with tears. "We got cocky and careless. We went in thinking that we wouldn't see a single Harmonizer, but they were ready for us—*all* of them. Governor Warren had to have known..." He trailed off.

"I did what you asked me to," Seren said quietly. "I told him you weren't going to attack."

"I know," Lucas said. 'I know. Alaster told me. It wasn't you. It was... We should have been more careful."

The mention of Alaster spurred a memory.

"It wasn't your fault, either," she said suddenly. "Governor Warren found a notebook in Alaster's room with your plans. If Governor Warren seemed prepared, it's because he was. He knew when you'd be coming, and he knew where you'd be coming from. He was ready for you. There was nothing you could've done."

There was a slight pause before Lucas looked at her. "How do you know that?"

"It's a long story," Seren said sheepishly.

Lucas rested his head on the stone. "I guess it doesn't matter now." He closed his eyes.

Again, Seren saw the young boy she'd known as a child—the young boy she sat next to in Year One on her first day of school, the one who'd shared his snacks and copied her drawings and played make believe with her all those years.

When had they gotten so old? When had life become so complicated?

The moment the Governor killed Henry, Seren thought. *That's when.*

"We messed up, Ren," Lucas said with his eyes still closed. "We shouldn't have been so naive. I thought if we had the element of surprise... But even then, even if he hadn't found Alaster's notebook, we'd still be..." He trailed off. "I thought our plan was perfect, but Governor Warren won. He always does."

Seren reached over and grabbed his hand. "We're going to figure this out."

"It's too late."

She lifted his chin, and their eyes met. In Lucas's deep brown gaze, all Seren could see was Henry.

"Your father didn't lose his life for you to just give up yours."

Lucas looked away. "No. My father lost his life for no reason at all."

And then it was silent again, apart from the *drip, drip, drip.*

Seren scooted closer to Lucas and rested her head on his shoulder. "Do you remember that time you copied my essay on *The Final Photograph?*" she asked. She wasn't sure why that memory came to mind, but it felt like the right moment to think of something positive, the right moment to reminisce. They say before you die, your life flashes before your eyes. Maybe this was Seren's version of that.

Lucas chuckled and then cringed before saying, "Yeah, that book was horrible."

Seren sat up. "How would you know? You didn't read it!"

"I didn't have to read it to know it was upper Tier rhetoric designed to keep us in our place."

Seren shook her head and smiled. "No one else thinks like you, Lucas. Everyone in our class loved that book."

"Everyone in our class was brainwashed." Lucas shrugged. "My father put too many anti-Warren thoughts in my mind for me to fall for that bullshit."

Seren wondered what Lucas would say if he knew his father had been born a Tier One, or that Henry had been friends with Governor Warren and Ivory. Would he feel the way she felt? Would he, too, feel like he hadn't known his father at all?

It wasn't important to mention, she decided. Not now.

"He never said anything anti-Warren to me," Seren said.

Well, he had, once. He accidentally let the word "propaganda" slip when Seren was talking about one of their schoolbooks, yet another novel negatively depicting Earth. When he said the word, Jean shot him a look that could have killed. Seren never asked anyone about it—she was old enough by then to understand that there were some things you shouldn't talk about—and she never heard the word *propaganda* again.

Seren wished Henry would have told her about the rebellion. Then Lucas wouldn't have been alone through this whole mess. She could've helped him from the beginning. If she'd known, she would've never used Alaster's identity card. She would've snuck into Tier Five with Lucas and helped with the rebellion.

She would've never met Zaiden.

Lucas sighed and leaned back. "I remember that I copied that essay word for word."

"I had to sit in a dark closet for the entire school day and write, 'I will not cheat' five hundred times."

"It isn't my fault that you took the blame." Seren heard the grin in his voice.

"It *is* your fault for cheating," she said, gently poking his leg. "I gave that essay to you for inspiration, not to copy."

"It was a life lesson. I was much better at hiding my dishonesty after that."

There was a layer of seriousness behind his joking tone, and Seren knew that he meant it.

They looked out into the darkness.

"They've been brainwashing us this entire time, haven't they?" Seren asked.

She felt Lucas shift beside her.

"Thoughts are dangerous," he said. "Thoughts create revolutions."

Failed revolutions, Seren thought, kicking her heel against the cement floor.

"You never told me how you like being a nurse," she said.

Lucas received this subject change with a groan. "I hate it," he said, and Seren chuckled. It was a forced laugh, but something about the act made her feel lighter. "But at least I wasn't forced to be a spy for a tyrant."

"It wasn't so bad. They fed me well."

She half expected Lucas to laugh, but he seemed distracted, staring at the wall with his brows furrowed. Seren knew him well enough to know what he was thinking.

"Noa is going to be okay," she said quietly. "She's strong."

Even as Seren said the words, though, she wasn't sure they were true.

There was silence again. *Drip, drip, dr—*

"In happier news, I met Zaiden," Lucas said with a small grin. "He sure is dreamy."

Seren poked Lucas's leg, harder this time. "Shut up."

"I'm sorry things didn't work out between the two of you."

Seren groaned. "Please stop talking."

She felt a wave of gratitude towards Lucas. Even tortured, tired, and terrified, he still found a way to make jokes. Seren leaned her head back onto his shoulder, and Lucas draped his arm around her.

"I love you, Lucas," she said.

He kissed her forehead. "Love you too, Ren."

49

ZAIDEN

"Are you ready, Governor Warren?"

Marcie McIntosh sat poised at her anchor news desk, her legs crossed gracefully beneath it. She'd traded in her usual brightly colored wardrobe for a subdued black dress with a low neckline that showed off her most recent surgery: a pair of boobs the size of small babies' heads. Zaiden had to pull his eyes away more than once. Beside Marcie, there were two additional chairs: one for Governor Warren, the other for Zaiden.

It was 7:15 a.m., the morning following the attack. Many people had already awoken to find their apartment doors locking them in. All Tiers were still on lockdown, though that was to be lifted in a few short hours. By then, the hallways of Tier Two and Tier One would be cleaned of the bodies and the blood, and all physical evidence of the rebellion would be gone.

After getting no sleep in the last thirty hours, Zaiden was running solely on adrenaline. His heavy eyes drooped, and his head felt foggy. He ached with desire at the thought of his warm bed and comforting sheets. At least asleep, he could forget that any of this had happened. Asleep, he could forget about Seren.

After Seren's arrest, an emergency council meeting had been called. The members of the council, most of whom had slept through the attack, were informed of the night's events. Alaster Holland's betrayal was greeted with shock. The council members couldn't believe that Governor Warren's most trusted ally would betray them. Searches were employed immediately, but so far, they'd proven fruitless. Alaster was nowhere to be found. Still, Zaiden wasn't worried. Community was big, but not big enough to hold a fugitive. Alaster wouldn't be able to hide for long.

The council decided that Governor Warren should make an immediate appearance on the Awakening to announce the attacks and get ahead of the story before rumors spread too far.

"You know how rumors fly," Sawyer said, his deep brown eyes drooping with exhaustion (and the effects of the moonshine he'd likely consumed the night before).

The council agreed that Zaiden was to join his father, to demonstrate loyalty and the continued generations of Warrens dedicated to Community's safety. Zaiden wished they'd just let him sleep instead.

"We are live in twenty seconds," the man behind the camera announced, pulling Zaiden back to reality. All Zaiden could make out beyond the blaring light was the man's rolled-up sleeves and hairy wrists.

Governor Warren straightened his tie for the umpteenth time and motioned for Zaiden to sit up straight. Zaiden obeyed, squaring his shoulders. "Just introduce me, Marcie, and I'll take it from there," he said.

Zaiden felt his pulse quicken as the cameraman counted down.

"Three ... two ... one..." The man pointed a hairy finger at Marcie, and the camera light turned on.

"Good morning, Community," Marcie said in a far more somber tone than usual. Zaiden realized that they hadn't even played the anthem. "This morning, we have an important announcement from our Governor, Pluto Warren."

The camera spun to face his father, and Zaiden sat up even straighter. He focused his eyes on the camera and attempted to appear as commanding as he could, following the years of lessons his father had provided.

Even through the thick walls of the newsroom, Zaiden could hear enthusiastic applause from the members of Tier Two. Governor Warren gave a small nod of acknowledgement, but he did not provide his customary smile.

"Beloved members of Community," he said, his tone matching the seriousness of Marcie's. "Last night, at one fifteen a.m., Tier One was deliberately attacked by anarchists from the lower Tiers."

Zaiden kept his face straight. *Do not incite alarm,* he thought as he raised his chin.

Governor Warren continued. "Community has always been a place of peace and posterity. Myself and my council members have been open to conversations and communication with all our twenty-thousand-plus members, and we have prided ourselves on our handling of all disputes that come our way.

"This attack had been in the works for many months. Their aim was to assassinate me and implement a dictatorship. In their ideal government, your freedom would have been stripped from your hard-working hands. In their ideal government, you would have starved, your homes would have been taken from you, and the population of Community would have increased to fatally unsustainable levels."

Governor Warren paused to allow this news to settle in.

"As you can see, their plan was unsuccessful. I am still very much alive. Myself, my son, and the members of our council understand the implications of these attempts on the life and safety of our Community. I have directed that all measures be taken for our defense, and I vow that we will not only continue to defend ourselves, but we will make certain that such treachery will never endanger the members of Community again."

More applause.

"The leaders of the attacks have been brought in for questioning. Tonight, live on the Evening Broadcast, they will be executed. We do not wish to upset anyone; we merely wish to give justice to those whose mothers, fathers, and children were taken from them in last night's attacks."

As he spoke, his head tilted, and his eyebrows lifted in sympathy. Zaiden understood why the people of Community liked and respected his father. He was a strong, empathetic, reliable leader.

Zaiden hoped that one day, he would be just as great.

"To the families of the anarchists who were killed, I'm sorry for your loss. The actions of your family members are not reflections of who they were as people, but reminders of the dangers that these anarchist groups hold. They will brainwash you and tell you lies until you cannot trust your own thoughts. My sympathies are with you as you recover from your losses as well."

A final bout of applause sounded through the studio. The camera panned back to Marcie. "Let's take a moment of silence to honor the brave men and women that fought last night and lost their lives."

Zaiden joined Governor Warren and Marcie in bowing their heads.

When an appropriate amount of time had passed, she looked up. "Thank you, Governor Warren, for keeping us informed and keeping us safe."

And just like that, it was over.

The cameras switched off, and Zaiden and his father stood and unclipped their mics. Governor Warren made a beeline for the back of the room. The bright studio lights dimmed, and Zaiden saw where his father had gone. Governor Warren now stood in the far back corner of the studio, speaking with Jerren Kris, the Chief Harmonizer. Jerren's burly arms were crossed over his wide chest as he and Governor Warren spoke, their voices low.

Curious, Zaiden walked a few steps closer, attempting to remain nonchalant as he returned his mic to the sound guy. He heard his father speaking first.

"I want you to send a few men to the Quinn and Snyder households to apprehend Mr. and Mrs. Quinn and Miss Snyder," Governor Warren said quietly. "They'll be executed tonight alongside their children. Take care not to make a scene. Bring tranquilizers just in case."

Zaiden felt sick. *Executed.* He should've expected as much, but the news still shook him to his core. He knew he should stay quiet, but he couldn't bring himself to.

"What about forgiving the families?" he interjected.

Governor Warren did not seem surprised that Zaiden had been listening. Nothing ever surprised him. He gave Zaiden a warning look—the kind that said, *"Do not question me."*

"Killing their families is the only way to ensure that we exterminate the anarchist ideals," he said firmly.

"So, what you just said was all a lie?" Zaiden asked. He understood his father's anger and fear, but … this wasn't punishment; it was revenge.

"Henry Snyder killed your mother," Governor Warren snapped back. "Lucas Snyder attempted to kill *you* earlier tonight. Why do you believe the mother will be any different?"

Henry Snyder. Zaiden blinked. It was the first time his father had named Ivory's murderer. It was a name Zaiden had never heard before, but suddenly he was the most important man in Zaiden's life. So, Lucas's father had killed his mother. A newfound hatred for Lucas clawed at Zaiden—but his empathy for Seren remained, no matter how hard he tried to make it go away.

"You can't kill Seren's mother," Zaiden said. "She's pregnant."

If Jerren was surprised by this news, he didn't show it. He stayed standing at attention as Governor Warren's eyes narrowed. The look he gave Zaiden was one of pure contempt.

"Two birds, one stone," he said coolly. "Now, if you'll excuse me."

Governor Warren pushed past Zaiden roughly, followed closely by Jerren, who gave Zaiden a sharp nod as he left. Zaiden watched them go, confused and bewildered. He never claimed to know his father, or even to understand him, but this man… this man was a stranger.

"Great job up there," Marcie said, pulling his gaze to her. She sashayed over and placed a warm, manicured hand on his shoulder. Zaiden felt the urge to shove her off. Miraculously, he refrained.

"Thanks," he grumbled with as much kindness as he could manage.

She smiled. "You remind me so much of him," she said. "Your father is a wonderful man." Then she winked and patted him on the back as she walked away.

The words rolled around in Zaiden's head for long after she'd gone: *wonderful man, wonderful man, wonderful man...*

Zaiden left the studio with the intention of returning to his apartment. A heavy, metallic smell lingered in the halls, serving as a reminder of last night's atrocities. He breathed through his mouth.

He missed his mother. He would've given anything to talk to her one last time. Every day, his memory of her faded more and more, and he worried that someday the memories would disappear altogether. Then all he'd be left with was their boardwalk.

Though he'd been intent on getting some much-needed sleep, Zaiden found himself walking the familiar path to the Simulator. He was desperate for a sliver of clarity, and he hoped the Simulator could provide that.

Unsurprisingly, it was empty this morning.

"Would you like your usual simulation, Mr. Warren?" the Simulator asked on his arrival.

Zaiden hesitated.

There was something he had always wanted to do, a risk he'd never taken. After the night he'd had, it felt like there was nothing left to fear.

"Show me Ivory Warren," he said in a shaky voice.

He wasn't supposed to simulate actual people; it was one of the rules. Simulating a specific person was unethical. It robbed the person of their individuality and their autonomy. It also had the potential to be emotionally taxing on the person running the simulation; you could build an emotional connection with someone who wasn't real. That kind of thing could drive a person mad.

But Zaiden didn't care about rules or ethics or emotional stability right now. He needed to see his mother one more time.

The Simulator whirred in response, a loud, painful noise that it had never made before. For one heart-stopping moment, Zaiden was certain he'd broken it. But then the whirring slowed, and the Simulator spoke.

"Simulating Ivory Warren."

Zaiden's heart lurched as he waited for her to materialize.

And then there she was, standing beside him in full form, exactly as he remembered her. Not a thing had changed, not a hair on her head had shifted—but everything was different now. Zaiden himself had changed so much. As a child, he'd barely reached her waist, but now he was a head taller than her. He looked down at her dark brown hair and cried.

"Mom," he choked out.

Losing her years ago had been devastating. He'd felt as if life could never go on. Standing so close to her now, smelling her familiar perfume, only made him realize all the things she had missed, all the things she continued to miss. There was so much he wished he could tell her, so much he wished he could say.

But instead, he cried.

Zaiden didn't have the energy to be angry at Lucas's father for killing her. He didn't have the energy to be angry with any of the rebels. He just felt heavy. He'd been robbed of a mother, a friend, a confidante. It ripped him apart from the inside.

"Mom," he said again.

Ivory looked past him in a daze, and Zaiden realized that this was not as comforting as he'd initially hoped. He needed more—an interaction. Perhaps a memory they'd shared. Zaiden thought back.

On the day before his mother's death, Ivory had taken Zaiden to the Simulator. They'd ridden the Ferris wheel together and walked along the pier, just as they had so many times before. It was completely ordinary in every way. Zaiden had thought about reliving that memory before, but he'd never been brave enough.

He felt brave now.

"Show me Ivory Warren's last simulation," he said.

The overhead light switched off as the simulator whirred again, and a new scene came to life. Ivory stood on the beach at dawn, alone. Her hair whipped around her violently in the wind, and her skin glowed in the orange light of the rising sun.

Zaiden squinted. He thought that she'd brought him to the pier at midday. Unless he was mistaken, this was not the simulation they'd run together.

"Show me Ivory Warren's final simulation," he said again, impatient this time.

The scene didn't change.

Zaiden sighed in exasperation. He was about to end the simulation when he heard a voice.

"Ivory."

He and his mother turned to see a much younger Governor Warren walking towards them. His skin was wrinkle-free, and the bits of white had yet to make an appearance in his dark hair. He looked eerily like Zaiden: dark eyes, dark hair, kind smile. Zaiden finally saw the resemblance everyone else claimed to see.

"Father?"

Governor Warren didn't hear him. His attention was fixed on his wife. Zaiden took a step back as the scene continued to unfold, undeterred.

"I knew I'd find you here," Governor Warren said to Ivory. "Why'd you run away?"

Ivory returned her focus to the ocean. "I needed some space."

"You can't avoid me forever."

She kicked her toes, sending lumps of sand into the ocean.

Governor Warren stepped closer to her until he stood by her side, his eyes pleading. "Ivory, we need to talk."

"It can wait," Ivory replied, her tone unlike anything Zaiden had ever heard from her before.

"Ivory, please," Governor Warren said, reaching out to her.

She turned on him, her eyes brimming with tears. "I know you've been lying to me."

Zaiden watched as his father's expression shifted from upset to … to what? Was it anger? He couldn't tell.

"What are you talking about?" he asked, almost emotionless.

Ivory glowered. "Do not play dumb with me, Pluto. Community is a prison, and you and your family have kept us locked up here for years. And for what? So you could continue to play the hero?"

Zaiden didn't understand what she was saying, but the words clearly had an effect on his father.

Governor Warren's eyes narrowed. "Who told you that? Was it Henry?" He spit out the name as if it were vile.

Ivory threw up her hands in frustration. "This isn't about Henry, Pluto. This is about *you*. This is about you lying to the world to fuel your ego! This is about you being a cruel, callous, power-hungry man." She kicked the sand once more, and it flew at Governor Warren. He recoiled as it hit his face.

"End simulation," Governor Warren said. The simulated pier began to fade, but Ivory and Governor Warren's figures remained. "Ivory, let me explain…"

She shook her head once more, pain etched across her delicate features. "I'm sorry, Pluto. I can't. Not after all this."

Zaiden took a sharp breath in, his heart tearing apart at the words.

His father recoiled. For a moment, there was nothing but painful silence. Zaiden's parents looked at each other, both unwavering in their strength.

And then it all went wrong.

Zaiden watched, horror-struck, as his father whacked her across the face. She stumbled back, just as shocked as Zaiden. And he hit her again and again.

"Stop!" Zaiden screamed, running at the scene. He tried to tear them apart, but his hands went right through them. "Stop!" he cried again.

It was useless.

Ivory tried to leave, but Governor Warren yanked her back. The scene continued to escalate, and Zaiden stumbled backwards and watched it all unfold.

He did not tear his eyes away until his mother had been fully consumed by flames.

"End simulation!" he cried. "END SIMULATION!"

He collapsed onto the floor, tears streaming down his face. His sobs echoed through the room and bounced off the walls, surrounding him like reflections in a fun house mirror. This had to be a mistake. Rebels had killed his mother. *Henry Snyder* killed his mother. The Simulator had to be playing tricks on him. It had to be messing with his mind.

It wasn't real. It *couldn't* be real. Zaiden gasped through his sobs, just enough to take in a mouthful of air.

What did she mean when she said Governor Warren kept people "locked up" in Community? Earth wasn't safe. It *couldn't* be safe. Yet his father hadn't denied it. He'd just said, *"Let me explain."*

The Simulator made all kinds of things up, though. It created scenarios from what it knew. Surely, that's what had happened here. Zaiden's mother and father had been in the Simulator many times. It must've taken an argument they had—something—and transformed it. That *must* be it.

He breathed in deeply through his nose and twisted his hands together, pinching his skin. Try as he might, he could not make himself believe it.

There must be an explanation.

Someone had to have an explanation.

Zaiden stood. He needed answers.

And he knew who could give them.

50

SEREN

"Seren?"

When Seren first heard the voice, she thought she was imagining it. Exhaustion, dehydration, and fear were a terrifying cocktail, and she wouldn't be surprised if it was driving her to madness. But soon, the voice came again, louder this time.

"Seren?"

Seren lifted her head from Lucas's shoulders. She squinted out into the darkness.

Zaiden stepped out from the shadows, and Seren's heart skipped a beat.

"Zaiden," she whispered. Lucas stiffened beside her. "What're you doing here?"

"I need to speak to you," Zaiden said. "*Both* of you."

"Have you come to collect us?" Lucas asked coolly. "Or is it just to clear your conscience before they do?"

Zaiden shot Lucas a look before shifting his focus back to Seren. "I need to know what you were going to tell me earlier," he said. Seren hesitated. Was this a trap? Zaiden seemed to sense her uncertainty. "I saw something today. In the Simulator. I need to know if it was real."

"She's not going to tell you anything," Lucas snapped.

Zaiden's concerned expression turned quickly to frustration, and he slammed a hand on the bars. "Shut up."

"Lucas, please, it's fine," Seren mumbled.

Lucas huffed and sat back down, but he didn't look thrilled about it. Zaiden didn't look too happy either, and Seren found herself grateful for the barrier between them. Otherwise, they probably would've torn each other's heads off.

She walked over to the bars. As she got closer to Zaiden, she saw that his eyes were red and puffy, as if he'd been crying. She paused, unsure. It didn't *feel* like a trap.

"There are cameras here," she said.

"I shut them off," Zaiden replied. "They won't notice for at least a few minutes. It's usually pitch black in here anyway."

Seren wasn't sure why, but something in his tone made her believe him. About that, at least. Seren took a deep breath. "Okay. What did you see?"

He wavered and closed his eyes. "My father and mother were on a beach. They were arguing. She … she said something about Earth. And then…"

He laid his head against the bars. Seren knew he couldn't bring himself to finish, and she didn't let him. She laid a hand on Zaiden's arm.

He grabbed it and held tight. "So, it was real?"

Seren nodded.

Zaiden looked like he was trying so hard to control himself, but he couldn't. The tears came on fast. "He *killed* her," he wept, and Seren was overcome by grief.

Behind her, Lucas drew a startled breath.

"I know," Seren whispered. "And I'm so sorry."

They held each other's eyes for a moment before Zaiden looked away. "I don't understand any of this. I don't understand why he would kill her. Why he would do this?"

He turned his attention to Lucas. "He mentioned your father," Zaiden said. "Right before he killed her."

At the mention of Henry, Lucas looked up. "He did?"

Zaiden nodded. Lucas joined the two of them at the cell bars.

"Hey," Zaiden said uncomfortably. Lucas gave him a curt nod.

They stood there in excruciating silence for a moment.

"What did he say?" Lucas asked. "Your dad. Before he killed your mother."

"He asked if Henry was the one who'd told her Earth was safe."

Lucas looked at Seren, and she gave him a reassuring nod. Zaiden looked between the two of them.

"What?" Zaiden asked. "What do you know?"

"Why should I tell you?" Lucas asked. He no longer sounded angry and guarded. Now, his tone was gentle. Even with his hatred for Zaiden, Seren knew Lucas felt for him. She was sure that seeing Zaiden break down over his mother's murder reminded Lucas of the time he found out Henry's real cause of death. It didn't matter how many differences the two men had – this one thing brought them together.

Zaiden, too, seemed to have changed as he said, "I'll help you out of here."

Lucas laughed, not kindly, but not unkindly either. "You didn't seem so inclined to help a few hours ago, when you were trying to kill me."

Seren's mouth dropped open. *"What?!"*

Neither man seemed to hear.

"I missed the shot on purpose," Zaiden said.

"I hope you did," Lucas retorted. "Otherwise, you're an awful shot."

A smile tugged at the corner of Zaiden's lips. This was not an apology from either man, but it was as close as it was going to get.

"Alright," Lucas said. "You may wanna sit down for this."

Zaiden obeyed, taking a seat on the floor about an arm's length from the cell bars, as if a tiny part of him still worried Lucas might try to strangle him. Lucas joined, and Seren, not wanting to be the only one standing, followed.

"How much do you know?" Lucas asked.

"You should start from the beginning," Zaiden said.

Lucas dove into the story without warning, which was probably for the best. His words were rushed as he spoke, but cohesive. He told the story with a surprising amount of clarity, starting at the beginning with his father's obsession with Earth and moving into Henry's death, the Tier Fives, the rebellion.

As he told the story, Seren found herself transported back in time to all those afternoons playing Earth with Henry. When Lucas talked about Tier Five, Seren could almost smell the thick, ashy air from the incinerators. If Lucas had been a Tier Three, he would've been a good Writer, Seren thought.

Zaiden listened intently, his entire focus on Lucas, while Seren kept one eye on the stairwell.

To Zaiden's credit, he did surprisingly well with everything Lucas told him. When Lucas got to the bit about Earth, though, Zaiden looked overwhelmed. When the time came, Seren interjected with what Alaster had told her about his role in the whole thing. She left out the part about Alaster's love for Ivory. That felt like something Alaster should share himself if the time came.

By the time they finished, Zaiden looked like he might pass out. He rubbed his hand over his eyes, and a small, exhausted sigh escaped his lips.

"Are you okay?" Seren asked.

"It's a lot to take in."

"I know."

Zaiden shook his head. "My father's not a good man, but I never thought him capable of all this."

"Sorry to be the bearer of bad news," Lucas said. And Seren could tell he really meant it.

"I just can't wrap my head around why," Zaiden murmured.

"Apart from him being a psychopath?" Lucas asked. Seren punched his arm. "Ow!"

Zaiden ignored the comment, and Lucas rubbed his shoulder.

"It's human nature," Lucas said. "He wants power, control. If he told us all that Earth was habitable again, he'd run the risk of everyone leaving Community. The lower Tiers would be the most likely to go, and they're the ones we rely on most. Without them, there'd be no food, water, or electricity. Governor Warren—and the rest of the upper Tiers—would be screwed. His lifestyle would change completely, and he could say goodbye to his influence." Lucas shrugged. "He's scared."

Scared. What a generous way for Lucas to describe him, Seren thought. She was sure Lucas had more than a few other choice words to say on the matter, but he didn't, and for that, she was grateful.

Seren glanced at Zaiden. Who was to say he didn't feel the exact same as his father? After all, it wasn't just Governor Warren who stood to lose all that. Zaiden had everything: a bright future, a promising job, the potential for power as the next Governor of Community. Not to mention all his material possessions.

Zaiden didn't have to give any of that up. He could let Lucas and Seren be executed tonight. With their deaths, he could erase the proof of Earth's habitability. He could rule Community just as his father had.

All he had to do was walk away.

Seren waited for him to say something. Her eyes sought his, persistent, until he finally met her gaze.

His blue eyes were unmoving. She held her breath as he opened his lips to speak.

"What do I do?" he asked.

A wave of relief washed over her like a tsunami.

"You can start by letting us out of here," Lucas said, clutching the metal bars.

Zaiden hesitated. "I'm not sure that's a good idea. Half of Community knows your names and faces. If they see me walking through the halls with you, someone will alert my father. Not to mention the cameras—"

"What do you suggest?" Lucas asked.

"It's risky, but … we have to wait. I'll request to escort you to your execution tonight. You can escape then."

"They won't let you take us alone," Lucas said.

Zaiden nodded. "You're right. They won't. There'll likely be four or five Harmonizers who come with me."

Lucas snapped his fingers. "If you bring an anesthetic spray and slip it to Seren, we can knock them unconscious."

"Good idea," Zaiden said. "And I'll make sure they don't lock the door, so you and Seren can get out."

"And then what?" Seren asked.

"Then I guess you and Lucas go to the Simulator, and I'll meet you there. With my father."

Lucas eyed Seren. She could tell what he was thinking, because she was thinking the same thing. Did Zaiden realize how this had to end—that his father had to die?

Try as Seren might, she could not come up with another conclusion. As long as Governor Warren was alive, Community would not be safe. They couldn't lock him up or change his mind. They couldn't talk sense into him... Surely, Zaiden knew this. But Seren couldn't fathom him wanting to play a role in his own father's death.

Then there was the actual act. Seren wasn't sure she or Lucas had what it took to do the final deed. Seren couldn't live with herself if she took someone's life, even if the man was evil.

"One condition," Lucas said finally. "The girl I was with … Noa. She's upstairs. They took her for questioning."

"I can get her out," Zaiden said.

Lucas nodded gratefully. "If you take her to the Tier Four infirmary and tell them she's my friend, they'll take care of her."

"Fine." Zaiden turned to Seren. "What about you? Any requests?"

"Be safe," she said.

Out of the corner of her eye, she saw Lucas roll his eyes.

Zaiden held her gaze for a second, and Seren had the fleeting feeling that he might kiss her. Instead, he reached through the bars of the cell and took her hand, giving it a short, strong squeeze. "I'll see you in a few hours," he said.

And then he was gone.

"Are you sure he's going to be able to do this?" Lucas asked once the door closed. Seren stared at the empty stairwell.

"No. No, I'm not."

"We're screwed."

Seren didn't answer. Maybe they *were* screwed, but enough of her believed Zaiden would go through with their plan, and somehow, that troubled her more.

Lucas stared at her. It was the same expression he used to wear when they were younger, and he was trying to read her thoughts.

"What now?" he asked.

"We wait."

51

SEREN

Six o'clock came slowly. Seren and Lucas took turns trying to rest, but neither was successful. At one point, Seren got close, but then Lucas sneezed, viciously ripping sleep from her grasp. She wished she could sleep. Asleep, the hours wouldn't have felt so long.

Lucas occupied his time by pacing back and forth. His tempo was steady, and his eyes remained glued to the cement floor, as if at any moment, an answer would appear there in bright red letters, beckoning him.

"Lucas, sit down. You need to preserve your strength."

He continued to pace. "I just can't stop thinking about Noa."

Seren understood; she couldn't stop thinking about Zaiden. She feared that he might unravel. She recalled how she'd reacted when she learned about Ma's pregnancy. She'd felt like the world was going to end. And a surprise pregnancy was hardly comparable to the finding out your dad had killed your mom.

Seren hoped Zaiden could hold himself together for a few more hours. Their lives depended on it.

"Can you please just sit down?" Seren asked. "You're making me nervous."

Lucas sighed and leaned his back against the wall.

"Thank you."

Seren closed her eyes, leaned back, and tried to focus on slowing her heartbeat. She could hear the pounding in her ears, could feel it from her fingers down to her toes. She took deep breaths, doing as her mother had taught her to do when she was little: breathe in for four, out for eight. She did this exercise a few times until the nerves began to subside.

The peace didn't last long. Lucas channeled his nervous energy from pacing into tapping his heels on the ground. They hit with small clicks. Seren let out an exasperated sigh and clamped her hand around Lucas's knee.

"Sorry," he mumbled.

Seren held onto his knee for a moment longer before letting go. Lucas looked like he might tap his heels again, but upon seeing her deadly glare, he didn't.

"I'm sorry for what I said about Zaiden," Lucas said. "He seems like an okay guy."

"Really?" Seren asked.

"Really." Lucas wrapped his arm around Seren's shoulder and pulled her in close. "I'm not sure I trust him, but I think I finally understand him."

"Thanks," she said. "I could tell how hard you were trying."

Seren pulled her knees close to her chest. In the last hour alone, the temperature seemed to have dropped ten degrees. *What do they care if we get hypothermia? We'll be dead soon anyway.* She shivered.

Wordlessly, Lucas pulled off his sweatshirt and handed it to her.

"No, Lucas, I can't—"

"You need it more than me," he said firmly.

Seren accepted the sweatshirt reluctantly and pulled it over her head. It was extra warm from Lucas's hot skin. She nuzzled into it and closed her eyes.

Just moments later, the door to the cellar opened, and Zaiden walked in, flanked by three large men dressed in blood-red Harmonizer uniforms. Seren sat up, her heart racing. She hadn't been sure Zaiden was going to come. She'd thought seeing him would ease her nerves, but it didn't. His presence wasn't any kind of guarantee; there was still a lot that could go wrong.

Seren and Lucas stood as Zaiden and the Harmonizers approached the cell. Nervous chills pulsed through her in waves. She grabbed Lucas's hand for support. He squeezed.

"Stand back," one of the Harmonizers said. His voice was low and severe. Seren pressed her back against the icy wall as the man unlocked the cell door. Her eyes flickered to Zaiden, hoping for a little reassurance, but his face remained stoic.

"Hold out your wrists." The Harmonizer held out a pair of handcuffs.

Seren eyed them wearily. "Is that necessary?"

"Wrists. Now."

Seren held her hands out, and in one swift motion, the Harmonizer cuffed them, rendering her arms practically useless.

How was Zaiden supposed to get her the antiseptic spray now?

The cold metal from the cuffs dug cruelly into her dry skin. She tried to mask her discomfort, reluctant to give the Harmonizers the satisfaction of seeing her pain.

The four of them flanked Seren and Lucas, two on either side. Zaiden took hold of Lucas's upper arm, and the Harmonizers and Zaiden led them from the cell. She tried to slow their pace down, hoping to give Zaiden opportunities to get closer to her, but the two Harmonizers walked briskly, pulling her along. Seren watched

Zaiden from the corner of her eye, waiting for some indication that the plan was still on, but he just walked in silence.

The Harmonizers led Seren up the dark, damp flight of stairs. Zaiden, Lucas, and a third Harmonizer followed closely behind. The further Seren got up the stairs, the more worried she became. Had Zaiden changed his mind? Had he been lying to them after all...? The thought terrified her.

They were almost to the top of the staircase when a small thump echoed through the stairwell. Seren's heart rate sped up, and she resisted the overwhelming urge to look behind her. Neither of the Harmonizers seemed to notice.

"Hey." Lucas's voice came from close behind, and the Harmonizers turned. They barely had time to register the man lying at the bottom of the stairs, unconscious, when Lucas sprayed the anesthetic directly into their faces. It exited the bottle with a small hiss. Seren held her breath and clamped her eyes shut.

"What the hell?" one of them said. The other shifted, maybe reaching for a weapon, but before he could do any damage, she felt both bodies go limp beside her. Neither man loosened their grip on her arm, though, and Lucas had to lean his entire body into hers to prevent her from tumbling down the stairs with them.

Seren cracked open an eye as the men fell, jostling down the stairwell and landing at the bottom in a heap. One of their heads hit the wall with a loud *crack!*

Lucas waved away any remaining gas and pulled Seren up a few steps, where she finally took a deep breath.

"That had to hurt," Lucas said, looking down at the three men.

Zaiden lay next to the Harmonizers, his legs twisted beneath one of them.

"You knocked Zaiden out, too?" Seren asked.

"He told me to," Lucas said defensively. Seren raised an eyebrow. "Well, maybe not in so many words. But we had to make it believable."

It was believable, alright. Zaiden looked just as debilitated as the other men.

"I almost thought he had decided against our plan," Lucas said.

Seren let out a sharp sigh. "Yeah. Me too."

Seren glanced at the men uneasily. They looked pretty out of it, but it was only a matter of time before they were back up, and she wanted to be long gone by the time that happened.

"Are you ready?" Lucas asked, pulling her gaze away.

Seren nodded. "I'm ready."

Lucas tore up the stairs with Seren close behind and went to open the door. Seren stopped him and held up her handcuffed wrists. "Can we get these off first?" she asked.

Lucas looked at her blankly. "Why are you asking me? I don't have a key."

"Did Zaiden not give you one?"

Realization flashed across his face. "Check my back pocket," he said. He turned, and Seren reached down and fished in both of his pockets with her clasped hands. They closed around something.

"Got it," she whispered, pulling out a small silver key.

"And I thought he was just getting handsy."

Seren rolled her eyes but grinned as Lucas undid her restraints. She undid his next, and they tossed their cuffs down, rubbing their sore, chafed wrists.

"Okay, now I'm ready," Seren said.

Lucas pushed open the door, and a flood of light spilled in, momentarily blinding Seren. After hours in the dark, it felt like she was looking directly into the simulated sun.

"Coast is clear," Lucas said in a hushed voice.

"We should head to the Simulator and figure out what we're going to do when Governor Warren gets there." She turned to go, but Lucas didn't follow. "Are you coming?"

He hesitated. It took a moment for Seren to understand.

"Oh. Right. You should go," she said. "Make sure Noa is alright."

Relief spread across Lucas's face. "Are you sure?" he asked anxiously. "I can come if you need me."

I do need you, she thought. *I can't do this alone.*

But she nodded anyway, because that's what a good friend does, and after all she'd put him through, it was the least she could do.

Lucas pulled her into a lung-crushing hug, and Seren reciprocated. She smelled his soap, smelled the notes of vanilla and pine. It conjured up memories of creeping into his kitchen before dinner and sneaking slices of the warm bread Henry baked. It always tasted better warm, she remembered. When she closed her eyes, she could almost taste that bread, hearty and homey. She leaned into the memories and allowed herself to be transported somewhere else for a moment. It felt so good to forget.

When she pulled away, the images disappeared, and she returned to reality.

"I'll meet you there as soon as I can," Lucas said, holding her by the shoulders. "Are you sure you'll be okay?"

Seren gave a brave smile and nodded.

Lucas placed the anesthetic spray in her palm and closed her fingers around it. "Good luck," he said quietly.

Seren watched him go, an ache in her chest. *You told him to go to her,* Seren reminded herself. But it still didn't ease the pain that he'd chosen Noa over her.

Seren shook her head. There wasn't the time for selfishness or self-pity. She had a job to do.

Seren allowed herself three seconds of panic, just three seconds of utter dread, as a new thought made its way into her head: without Lucas there, she would have to be the one to kill Governor Warren.

Seren straightened and took a deep breath, trying to slow her racing heart. Her three seconds were up.

Quickly, she moved herself away from the cellar and walked through Community's hallways. She thought she could remember the path they'd taken her to get there, and soon, Seren had made it back to the residential part of Community.

The halls bustled with the evening commute, and Seren froze, momentarily petrified. She should have anticipated this, but she hadn't. Of course, no one expected to see her, with her execution coming up and all, but she couldn't be too sure. And her bright auburn hair was a dead giveaway. Hastily, Seren stepped back into the side hallway and wrapped it up into a high bun. She pulled Lucas's sweatshirt hood over her hair and pulled the strings, protecting her appearance as much as she could. She wasn't sure whether she looked even more suspicious now, but she stepped back into the main hallway and began her trek.

Seren kept her head down as she moved, the anesthetic spray clutched tightly in her hand. For the first few minutes, she felt safe amidst everyone's preoccupation and absentmindedness. No one paid her much attention, and she fell into step behind a group of Doctors, following their pace and mirroring their strides.

She was a mere three-minute walk from the Simulator when she spotted a familiar face coming towards her. *Geoff.* He was carrying an armful of dark fabrics, likely materials for Governor Warren's funeral pieces.

Before she had time to hide herself, their eyes locked. Recognition flashed across his features, and he stopped dead in the middle of the hall. Moments passed, slow as molasses, as Seren waited for what would come. She could not bring herself to run or hide. She stood absolutely still, as if not moving would make her invisible.

After the longest moment of her life, she watched Geoff regained control. He gave Seren a slight nod, and an understanding passed between the two. Geoff was not going to say a word to anyone. Seren did not have the time or energy to consider why he would not turn her in; she merely thanked her lucky stars and finished the remaining walk to the Simulator.

Seren slipped unbothered through the crowds until she came to a stop outside the familiar doors.

Here goes nothing, she thought.

She opened the door and stepped inside.

52

ZAIDEN

Zaiden came to on the floor, piled in a heap with his father's men. At first, he did not understand how he'd gotten there, but then realization struck him. *Lucas knocked me out!* Zaiden found himself torn between anger and amusement. Lucas had balls, he had to give him that.

He sat up slowly, his movements slow and pained. He felt disoriented, tired. Looking at the others, he realized that he was the last to wake. One of the bigger guys had already sat up and was looking around, bewildered. Two of the men were still down, a thin guy named Sergio and a shorter, stout man named Jasper.

Sergio moaned. "What happened?"

A noise came from Zaiden's right, startling him. His eyes flicked over to see Jasper sitting up, his eyes red and blotchy. It took him a moment to get his bearings—Zaiden could practically see the wheels in his head spinning—but once he did, his face turned a bright, angry red.

"Those kids knocked us out!" he shouted, eyes bulging.

There was a resounding bout of yelling as the anger set in. Zaiden did not join in. *How should I react in this situation?* he wondered. Should he be calm and controlled, or angry like the others?

"We've got to call Governor Warren," the biggest of the men, Andrew, said, jumping to his feet. Zaiden settled on calm and controlled. He stood and held up a hand to silence the three men.

"I'll break the news to my father," he said.

"But—"

"Unless, of course, you want to tell him that you let his prisoners go," Zaiden retorted with a raised eyebrow.

Andrew looked furious. "They ambushed us!" he yelled.

"Two unarmed teenagers ambushed you?" Zaiden repeated. "That's not how my father will see it."

Andrew, Sergio, and Jasper exchanged glances. It was clear that none of them wanted to take the blame in this situation. Zaiden had counted on that.

"That's what I thought," he said coolly. "I'll go speak with him. You three focus on finding the prisoners."

He left before they could argue further.

. . .

Zaiden went straight to his father's office. In the last few hours, it had been returned to near perfect condition. The window had been replaced—it was back to simulating its usual city skyline—and the broken glass cleared up. Even the papers on Governor Warren's desk had been returned to their meticulous stacks. If Zaiden hadn't been there the night before, he wouldn't have thought anything out of the ordinary had happened.

Zaiden's father was there as expected, sitting behind his desk, preparing for his appearance on the Evening Broadcast. Geoff was applying concealer beneath his eyes to mask the dark circles beneath

Governor Warren's eyes. He wore his best black suit, paired with a bright red tie, which was partially concealed by a small white smock, presumably there to protect the fabric from makeup.

An angry urge overcame Zaiden. Momentarily, he fantasized about storming into the room, tackling his father to the ground, and strangling the life from of his body. He wanted his father to suffer, the way the man had made Zaiden's mother suffer.

Zaiden's stomach lurched as his father's eyes opened and met his own.

"Zaiden," Governor Warren said with a thin smile. He motioned for Geoff to stop applying make up.

"Hi," Zaiden said in a voice that didn't sound like his own.

"Jerren tells me you requested to help pick up our prisoners," his father said. "How did the transportation go?" His smile was sickly sweet and condescending. Zaiden had to grab the wall to keep himself in place.

"It didn't," he said. "Seren and Lucas escaped."

"Did they?" his father asked calmly. "That's too bad."

Zaiden couldn't believe his father. How *dare* he look at Zaiden, knowing what he'd done to his mother? How dare he wake up every morning and live as though nothing had happened?

"Why aren't you surprised?" Zaiden managed to ask.

Governor Warren leaned back in his chair and motioned for Geoff to continue. The short man did so, and Zaiden noticed that his hands were trembling.

"Jerren already showed me the footage," Governor Warren said. "Nasty little knockout you had there."

Zaiden knew his father well enough not to expect him to ask whether he was okay.

"I already have all of my men on the lookout for them," Governor Warren continued. "If they run, I have ordered my men to shoot to kill."

Zaiden's blood went cold.

Governor Warren lifted a hand to stop Geoff again, and he stood, tossing the makeup smock down onto the floor. Geoff rushed to pick it up.

"You're taking this well," Zaiden said.

Governor Warren smiled. "I'm confident that things will work out in our favor," he said. "They can't hide for long. If we don't find them by the Evening Broadcast, we will publicly execute their parents, one at a time, until they turn themselves in."

His eyes sparkled with ... what was that? Excitement? Zaiden felt sick.

His father took a few steps towards him, and Zaiden flinched.

"You look upset," Governor Warren said with a tone of insincere concern.

"I'm not," Zaiden replied stiffly. His father was just a few feet away now. Zaiden could take him down easily, with the element of surprise on his side. He could slam his father's head against the ground over and over until his skull became unrecognizable. Zaiden clenched and unclenched his fists.

Calm down, Zaiden. You need to calm down.

He dug his fingernails into his palms and took a breath. "You know how I feel about killing Seren's parents."

"You always were soft." His father smirked as Zaiden flinched at the thinly veiled insult. "You should get dressed now. We've got a show soon."

Zaiden nodded. His throat felt tight. He wasn't sure how to get his father to the Simulator without raising suspicion. Governor

Warren was a smart man. Zaiden doubted he bought that Lucas and Seren just *happened* to escape.

He took a step closer to Zaiden, his eyes gleaming. "Was there something else you wished to say to me?" he asked, his voice icy cold.

"Jerren has already showed me the footage," his father had said. Zaiden's body seized in fear. Surely he didn't mean... He *couldn't* know that Zaiden had—

"Sir!"

Zaiden and Governor Warren both looked up in shock as Jerren stormed into the room, his large chest heaving.

"We've just gotten word from one of our men. Someone claims to have seen Seren in the halls. We think we know where she may be."

53

SEREN

Waiting was hard—painfully so.

Seren stood in the Simulator, enveloped in darkness and silence. She tried to occupy her mind. She tried to recount all the terrible things Governor Warren and his predecessors had done. If she could remember that, maybe she could convince herself that what they were about to do was right—just, even. Seren made a mental list.

1. He had Tier Fives working like slaves. They lived in terrible conditions and worked extremely hard, getting next to nothing in return. They could hardly feed themselves, let alone live fulfilling lives.
2. He controlled the members of Community's thoughts, words, and actions. He had people watch their every movement. He inserted ideas into their minds.
3. He had kept them trapped for at least thirty years. They had no autonomy in the matter.
4. He tortured and killed people who plotted against him.

5. He used unthinkable tools for population control. He allowed women to be slaughtered, just to ensure Community could continue, even when it didn't have to.

Seren repeated the atrocities in a loop round and round in her head until only five words remained: slaves, controlled, trapped, tortured, killed.

The man was evil, no doubt. But even with all he'd done, Seren was conflicted. If the time came, could she really be the one to take his life? Would Zaiden ever forgive her?

More importantly, would she ever forgive herself?

Seren kept her breathing quiet as she listened for footsteps.

Today, her fear tasted different, like copper. She choked on it. It was unlike anything she'd experienced before. Her legs wobbled beneath her, and it took all she had to stay standing. The waiting was the worst part.

Slaves, controlled, trapped, tortured, killed, she thought. *Slaves, controlled, trapped, tortured, killed...*

Finally, Seren's ears picked up on the light click of shoes. It sounded like there was more than one man outside the doors. She clenched her fists and dug her nails into the palms of her hands until it hurt. The pain soothed her, but her fear intensified. The footsteps grew louder and louder until they stopped. Seren drew in a shaky breath and straightened as the Simulator door opened.

Governor Warren stood in the doorway, alone and unmoving. He looked handsome, but it was a terrible, bone-chilling beauty.

She shivered as his eyes fell on her.

"I thought I might find you here," he said. His voice echoed, filling the Simulator with his deep, seductive tone. The light from the hallway swept over his face as the door closed. Seren saw that his expression was relaxed, but she could tell he was angry. The terseness in his voice gave it away.

"And I thought that I was so mysterious," Seren responded with feigned disappointment. Her skin crawled as Governor Warren looked at her, as if he were an animal examining its prey before attack.

"I'm surprised to find you alone. Where is your dear friend, Lucas?"

Seren clenched her fists at the mention of Lucas's name. How *dare* Governor Warren mention him after what he'd done to Lucas?

"He had other matters to take care of," Seren said.

"I was surprised to hear of your escape."

"I didn't like the cellar. It was too cold."

The contrast between the fear Seren felt and the confidence she portrayed was jarring. She knew that Governor Warren did not believe the act—all he had to do was take one look at her trembling hands to know she was faking it—but still, he chuckled. He respected her and her act, Seren could tell. If she weren't trying to destroy him, maybe he would have even liked her.

"Tell me, what did you expect to come from your escape?" Governor Warren asked. "Did you really think you'd be able to hide?"

"I just wanted to talk. Set the record straight."

Governor Warren grinned. "Is that right? Well, you have approximately..." He checked his watch. "... fifty minutes until your execution, so talk away, my dear."

My dear. The pet name prickled her like a thorn.

"I think you're a horrible man," Seren said. "You created placebo birth control shots so that women would get pregnant. You don't give them a choice to end the pregnancy, but you kill them for breaking a law they had no intention of breaking."

Governor Warren shrugged. "Those women chose to engage in risky behavior. I cannot be held responsible for the outcome."

"They didn't realize it was a risk!" Seren tensed up with anger. Governor Warren was antagonizing her on purpose; she had to calm down. If she could stay calm, she could maintain control.

"What else do you want to talk about?" Governor Warren asked. His tone was condescending, like he was talking to a child.

"You brainwashed the members of Community. You control our thoughts, our education, our words. You kill people who don't like you."

"Information and knowledge are a privilege. You should know that better than anyone. I and the Governors before me merely ensured that knowledge would only be awarded to the right people." Governor Warren grinned, but the smile did not touch his eyes; they remained narrowed and cold. "If you can control information, you can control people. That, Miss Quinn, is perhaps the most important part of Community. In a world as small as ours, it is imperative that everyone be on the same page. Otherwise, we may risk free thinkers, like yourself, messing with our homeostasis."

Seren frowned. "That isn't how the world works."

"How would you know how the world works?" Governor Warren snapped. Seren could see his patience slipping away.

She took a deep breath. "I know that Earth is safe now."

Governor Warren did not react, nor did he turn as the Simulator door opened. Zaiden entered, and briefly, Seren met his gaze. He gave her a small nod of acknowledgement, and Seren got up the nerve to continue.

"I know that it's been safe for years, and you haven't told anyone. You've allowed us all to stay trapped, just so you could keep your power and your lifestyle."

Governor Warren looked at her, disappointed. "Is that what you think?" he asked quietly. "After all I showed you, is that truly what you believe?"

The hairs on the back of Seren's neck bristled. He was asking her the questions she'd asked herself, and the answer remained the same: *no.* No, she wasn't sure.

Governor Warren clapped his hands together, and the Simulator awakened.

"Hello, Governor Pluto Warren and guests," it said. "What would you like to see?"

Governor Warren looked at Seren, his gaze unwavering. "I'd like to see a field."

The Simulator whirred. "Generating field simulation."

Governor Warren remained unmoving as the floor around them morphed from blackness into a deep yellow. Long whisps of grass sprouted up and tickled Seren's ankles. They continued to grow in height until Seren was knee-deep in the golden grass. The sky turned a deep blue, and the sun formed into a dull bulb on the horizon. A light wind whooshed through, causing the grass to dance in the breeze. Seren shivered.

"Do you know where we are, Miss Quinn?" Governor Warren asked.

"A field," Seren said.

He chuckled. "Very astute. I see why you were at the top of your class. But do you know *when* we are, Miss Quinn?"

She shook her head.

"We are in the year 1950." He paused. "Simulate the same field in 2022."

The simulation changed. Seren watched as the bright blue sky became clouded with a grayish fog. The air grew heavy. The dense fog was suffocating and left a burning pain in her chest that she could not quell. The yellow grass receded into the floor, only to be replaced by layers of garbage: plastic bags, water bottles, food containers, napkins. It crunched under her feet as she took a step backwards.

"Welcome to the city of Dhaka, Bangladesh," Governor Warren said.

In the distance, people slowly formed. Their skin was dark, their bodies frail. They waded through the trash, some carrying younger children on their backs, others holding their shirts over their noses and mouths.

"In 1950, this city had a population of three hundred and thirty-five thousand. By 2020, the population had reached twenty-one million. The high levels of toxicity caused severe respiratory and skin diseases. Two hundred and sixty-one thousand people in Bangladesh died from pollution-related diseases every year." Governor Warren picked up a drinking straw from the trash pile and rolled it around between his fingers. "You're a smart girl, Seren. You must see the correlation. It only took seventy years for humans to ruin something beautiful. They found ways to kill themselves, even without weapons. What makes you believe things will be any different now?"

Seren hesitated. Governor Warren was a master manipulator; she had to remember that. Things wouldn't be the same this time around. The members of Community could learn from the old world's mistakes. They could work together. They could create a better world.

Seren repeated the words in her head: *slaves, controlled, trapped, tortured, killed. Slaves, controlled, trapped, tortured, killed...*

"That's not your choice to make," she said. "People have a right to know. They have a right to choose. You're holding them hostage."

"I'm saving lives," Governor Warren sneered. "When are you going to get it through your thick skull that life in here is one thousand times better than it would be out there?"

"Not for everyone."

He scoffed. "You're naive."

"Is that what you said to your wife, before you killed her?"

Seren did not have time to register Governor Warren's reaction before he charged at her. He grasped her neck and slammed her against the control panel. The antiseptic clattered from her pocket and rolled beneath the control panel and out of view.

The impact somehow ended the simulation, and the black walls returned. Governor Warren stood very still, staring at Seren with his hands around her throat. Spots danced in her vision as his grip tightened, and she struggled to breathe.

Seren forced air into her lungs, but her breaths came out like strangulated gasps. She looked to Zaiden desperately for help, but he stood motionless with widened eyes.

He can't do it. He can't hurt his father.

Governor Warren lowered his voice. "I am going to take great pleasure in killing you, Miss Quinn."

He released his grasp on her neck, and she collapsed to the floor, gasping for breath. The ghosts of his hands remained, and it felt like she was still being choked.

"You're going to come with me," Governor Warren said calmly. "And you're going to behave yourself at your execution—or I'm going to kill your parents in the most painful way I can think of. Is that understood?"

Seren clenched her teeth as he grabbed her arm and yanked her to her feet. She tried to tear her arm away, but his grip was too strong. Governor Warren pulled her towards the door. Desperately, she looked to Zaiden again, who still stood frozen in the doorway.

"Out of the way, Zaiden," Governor Warren snapped.

The mention of his name seemed to have an effect on him. Zaiden blinked and looked from Seren to his father. Then, slowly, he shook his head.

"No."

"*What?*"

"I said no."

Governor Warren's eyes narrowed. "Don't be stupid."

The two of them stared each other down.

"Why'd you do it?" Zaiden finally asked. "Why did you... Why would you kill her?" His voice cracked.

Governor Warren's nostrils flared. "I don't know what you're talking about."

"You're lying," Zaiden said.

The grip on Seren's arm tightened as Governor Warren rolled his eyes. "You can't seriously believe anything this girl has to say. She's a traitor, an anarchist! She's a part of the group that murdered your mother, and—"

"Stop lying!" Zaiden bellowed. He pulled a gun from his waistband and pointed it directly at his father. Seren flinched.

"Put the gun down, Zaiden," Governor Warren said calmly. Slowly, almost unperceivably, he moved Seren into the line of fire. She found herself once again staring into the barrel of a gun.

Zaiden shook his head, his chest heaving with each breath. "You killed her."

Governor Warren raised an eyebrow. "You wouldn't shoot me."

Zaiden clicked the safety off. "I wouldn't be so sure," he said. But there was uncertainty in his quaking hands, and Seren knew that Governor Warren was right: Zaiden would never shoot him.

"Put the gun down, Zaiden," Governor Warren said again.

Zaiden hesitated and for a moment, it really looked like he might.

"That's what I thought," Governor Warren said, his lips curling into a cruel smile.

That was the breaking point. Zaiden charged at his father, slamming him against the nearest wall. In the scuffle, Seren broke free from Governor Warren's grip and stumbled backwards.

Zaiden held the barrel of the gun to his father's forehead. His chest heaved. Through it all, Governor Warren's face remained stoic. He wasn't afraid of his son, but Zaiden was plenty afraid of him. Zaiden's hands continued trembling as he pressed the barrel deeper into his father's skull.

"Have I taught you nothing?" Governor Warren murmured.

Seren and Zaiden both realized a second too late what he meant.

Governor Warren threw his elbow up in the air and brought it down violently over Zaiden's arms. Zaiden's grasp on his father broke, and he stumbled backward. His father came for him quickly, throwing punch after punch, his fists connecting with Zaiden's stomach, his nose, his eyes. In a sudden tactical shift, Governor Warren brought his foot back and kicked Zaiden. The gun slipped from Zaiden's hand and clattered to the floor.

"STOP IT!" Seren cried, rushing forward.

In one swift movement, Governor Warren grabbed the gun and pointed it at her, stopping her dead in her tracks.

"You brainwashed my son," he snarled.

Zaiden lay on the ground a foot behind him, clutching his stomach and moaning. Seren looked from Zaiden back into the barrel.

"I only told him the truth," she said.

"I could kill you right now," Governor Warren hissed, his finger stroking the trigger. "I could shoot you right between the eyes and end your life."

Seren's stomach lurched. *He won't do it,* she tried to tell herself. He didn't want to kill her in the darkness of the Simulator; he wanted her execution to be public. Otherwise, what was the point?

"You could," she said, unsuccessfully trying to hide the quiver in her voice. "But where's the fun in that?"

Governor Warren grinned. "My thoughts exactly."

He clapped his hands. Once again, the Simulator whirred to life.

"Simulate fire," he said.

"Simulating fire."

The humming of the Simulator turned into a raging buzz as a small fire formed. Though it was a few feet away, Seren could feel its heat from where she stood. Her eyes jerked to the flames, watching them with trepidation.

What is he doing?

"It would be ironic, wouldn't it," Governor Warren asked quietly, "if you died just as my wife did?"

Her blood went cold.

"End simulation," Seren said. Nothing happened. "End simulation!"

The fire spread, its flames licking towards the sky, casting a sinister glow. Governor Warren stood in front of the door, positioning himself as a barricade. His eyes were empty, just dark black holes, emotionless.

Zaiden stirred on the ground nearby, a small moan escaping his lips. Both Seren and Governor Warren looked at him.

The heat came next. It started like a warm blanket and began to grow hotter and hotter until it was scalding. Beads of sweat formed at Seren's hairline.

An overwhelming stench of smoke filled the air, and Zaiden stirred again, sitting up this time. Seren was motionless as he blinked and took in the scene unfolding around them. His eyes darted from his father to the fire and back.

"What are you doing?" he demanded. Governor Warren said nothing. Panic appeared in Zaiden's eyes. *"What are you doing?!"*

He stood and took a clumsy step towards the door. The gun in Governor Warren's hand stopped him—and the Governor did not lower it.

"I'm sorry," he said. "I didn't want it to end like this."

Seren's heart slammed against her chest. Smoke surrounded them; it burned the back of her throat. The fire had taken on a life of its own now, and it climbed as high as it had all those years ago, when Ivory had met the same fate.

Governor Warren watched the leaping flames with an expression of true sorrow, as if he did not want things to end this way, but believed that he had no other choice.

"Father," Zaiden choked out.

Seren looked back at him and recognized the terror in his eyes. If Zaiden believed his father to be capable of this, if he thought that Governor Warren was willing to kill them both...

He's going to do it, Seren realized with a start. *He's going to kill us!*

The fire grew larger, as if fanned by an invisible flame, and Governor Warren's expression turned from regret into joy. His eyes seemed to dance in the light of the fire.

"Are you scared now, Miss Quinn?" he called to her.

Yes.

Bullet or fire; those were her two options. And with the way she was gasping for air, Seren knew she didn't have much time left.

"You're going to kill your own *son* just to see me dead?!" Seren yelled as spots danced in front of her eyes. Fog clouded her thoughts, and she had to actively work to stay focused. She swayed and clutched the wall to keep from falling over. The room danced in and out of focus.

Think, Seren!

Zaiden stumbled towards her and placed a hand on her arm. His touch reinvigorated her, but it didn't matter. It was over. Governor Warren had won.

That was the last thing Seren thought before she completely lost her mind. In the haze of the smoke and fog, she saw a figure step from the shadows. She blinked, and the man danced.

Seren knew little about fire—there was no reason for her to know anything about it, safe within Community's walls—but she was certain that the smoke was driving her to madness, because her eyes had to be deceiving her.

Alaster?

She was imagining him, illuminated in the fire's harsh glow like an angel sent from heaven to save them all. He was so calm as he approached, a beacon of light amidst the darkness.

Governor Warren remained oblivious to the effects the fire was having on Seren. She smiled and swayed as Alaster held up a finger to silence her. In the dizzying effects of the smoke, she found that she did not even fear death anymore.

"Do you want to know what's funny?" Seren called over the roar of the fire. The flames were close enough that she could reach out and touch them now. The heat radiating off them burned her skin, but the pain felt like nothing more than a distant thought. She thought about the real Alaster as the imaginary one got closer and closer to Governor Warren. "You were so scared of betrayal—but the man betraying you was right in front of you all along."

Alaster continued to move forward, his movements slow and calculated. He gave Seren a small nod of recognition, and she laughed.

"This whole time, you've thought you had all the power, when you've just been a pawn in a bigger game."

Governor Warren growled and clicked off the gun's safety.

"Father, no!" Zaiden shouted.

Governor Warren looked at him. "You are no son of mine," he snarled. He aimed the gun at Seren's head. "Goodbye, Miss Quinn."

Seren laughed, closed her eyes, and braced for death.

When it did not immediately come, Seren opened her eyes.

Governor Warren barely had time to conceive what was happening. He fired the gun just as Alaster tackled him from the side. Seren stared, open-mouthed, as the bullet flew past her and disappeared amongst the flames.

Governor Warren lifted his gun once more, preparing to put a bullet in Alaster's head, but Alaster was too fast. Seren watched as Alaster wrapped his arms tightly around Governor Warren. The Governor thrashed, pressing the gun's trigger over and over and sending a sea of bullets zipping around the room. Zaiden threw himself on top of Seren and covered her until the click of an empty barrel rang out over the roar of the flames.

In the end, the gun wasn't much use to Governor Warren. It stayed tightly wrapped in his hand as Alaster launched himself into the fire—pulling Governor Warren along with him.

Zaiden and Seren watched, horrified, as the flames began to devour them both. For a moment, Governor Warren fought to escape the fire, but it was no use. His screams were silenced as he choked on the smoke. Only a moment later, he and Alaster disappeared behind a wall of flames, and the air grew heavy with the scent of burning flesh. Seren gagged and covered her mouth with her shirt, just as the boys in the simulation had done.

Zaiden's gaze remained fixated on the spot his father had been. Even with Governor Warren gone, the fire raged on.

"END SIMULATION!" Seren tried once more, but the Simulator did not listen. It had taken on a mind of its own. The fire crept steadily towards the exit. In only a few moments, their path would be blocked, and Seren and Zaiden would be trapped.

"We need to get out of here!" Seren yelled to Zaiden over the sound of the roaring fire. A spark flew and landed on her arm, scorching her skin. She flinched. "Zaiden? We need to go!"

Zaiden remained motionless.

Seren tugged at his shoulder desperately. "Zaiden, come *on!*" The smoke dizzied her. She swayed once more, catching herself on him and pulling at him again. "We need to go *now!*"

Zaiden came to and cooperated as Seren pulled him towards the exit, just narrowly missing the growing flames. There was no sign of Governor Warren's or Alaster's bodies. Seren wondered how the Simulator would rid itself of their ashes. It was a terrifying thought.

With all her remaining strength, Seren opened the Simulator door and lifted Zaiden over the frame. Cool air hit her like a cement wall. She slammed the doors shut behind them and prayed it would be enough to keep the fire out.

She and Zaiden collapsed to the floor, and Seren gasped. Her lungs desperately drank in the smoke-free air. Beside her, Zaiden was frozen, eyes wide and unmoving. His hair hung in lose, thin strands around his face. Seren was certain she'd never seen someone look so broken in her whole life.

She turned towards him, slowly, so as not to scare him, and took his face in her hands. Desperately, she searched his eyes. They were empty.

"I'm so sorry, Zaiden," Seren whispered. "I'm so sorry." Zaiden's cheeks were damp with tears. Seren wiped the moisture away with her thumb, stroking his face gently, just as her mother had done for her when she was a child.

Zaiden closed his eyes, his muscles tensing, and Seren wrapped him in a tight hug as the tears continued to fall. Her own throat choked up from Zaiden's silent cries.

She should've been glad to see Governor Warren dead. That was how things were supposed to end. Governor Warren's death had been the goal.

So, why did it feel so wrong?

Zaiden pulled away, wiped his tears, and looked at her.

"You're bleeding," he said.

Seren was so surprised to hear him speak that it took her a second to process his words. She looked down in astonishment. She *was* bleeding—quite profusely. She examined the wound curiously, placing her fingers gently where the bullet had grazed her.

"It doesn't hurt." In fact, it was so painless that Seren could hardly believe that the injured arm was attached to her body. The adrenaline must have been masking the pain.

"Seren!"

Seren looked up to see Lucas running towards her with Noa close behind. He abruptly stopped upon seeing the two of them. "You two look like you've been through hell!"

Lucas and Noa didn't look much better. In the light of the hallway, Lucas's injuries were more visible. His right eye had swollen shut, and his lip was cut in the center and already turning a deep purple. Noa didn't look much better. Her shirt was covered in blood, presumably her own, and she looked about as close to death as a person could get. Still, she stood strong. Seren had to admire her for that.

"You're bleeding!" Lucas exclaimed, gently taking Seren's arm.

"So I've been told," she said.

Lucas examined her wound from each angle. His touch was gentle. Lucas was a good nurse. She could tell.

"It looks like a bullet just grazed you, but we should disinfect it," he said, gently rolling her sleeve back down.

"Thanks, Lucas, but that can wait."

Lucas helped her to her feet, and Noa came over to help Zaiden. She held out a hand for him, but he just looked past it like he didn't even see it. Noa took one look at his expression and mumbled, "So, Warren's dead?"

Seren nodded.

"Zaiden?" she said.

He blinked and looked at her, like he had just realized they were there. Noa held out her hand again, and Zaiden allowed her to pull him to his feet.

"Are you two alone?" Lucas asked.

"Yes."

"Good. We narrowly missed a few Harmonizers on the way over here."

At this, Zaiden raised his head. "My father and I... We came with a group of ten of them. They could be close."

His voice cracked when he said, *"my father,"* and the energy in the room shifted. Lucas looked down at his feet.

"Then we shouldn't stay here," Noa said. Seren agreed, but she didn't want to push Zaiden. Any extraneous move, and she feared he would break.

Noa turned to him. "Zaiden, I know you're going through a lot, but we don't have time for you to grieve right now. The Evening Broadcast is in thirty minutes, and the members of Community are expecting an execution. Not to mention, Marcie McIntosh is going to lose her mind if someone doesn't tell her what's going on. She was expecting us twenty minutes ago, handcuffed and ready to die."

Zaiden nodded. In a swift moment, his body language completely changed. He appeared strong again, determined.

"You're right," he said. "People are going to have questions."

"So, what do we do?" Seren asked.

To her surprise, Noa and Lucas both turned to Zaiden for an answer.

"Zaiden? You're our Governor now," Lucas said. "What do you think?"

"I don't... I don't know. Don't you two have a plan?"

"We did," Noa said. "But this wasn't exactly how we pictured everything going."

"My father wasn't the only power-hungry man in Community," Zaiden said. "The threat isn't over just because he's dead."

Seren nodded. Alaster had said the same thing. There was a long line of people behind Governor Warren, waiting to take his power. They had to play this carefully.

"I don't think we should announce anything yet," Zaiden said.

Noa shot him a look. "Why shouldn't we tell everyone Earth is safe? Why shouldn't we let everyone decide whether they want to leave?"

"If we tell everyone now, there will be chaos. Anarchy." He paused. "We need to prepare."

"We've been preparing for the last thirty years," Noa said.

Seren understood Noa's passion; this was what she'd been working towards her whole life. She loved Noa's strength, but she found herself annoyed. Seren looked to Lucas for a response.

Lucas took a deep breath. "I think you're both right. We need to go about this slowly." He checked his watch. "Twenty-seven minutes."

"I'll accept a slow start, for now," Noa said. "The most important thing tonight is that Zaiden goes on the Evening Broadcast and denounces his father's response to the so-called 'rebellions'. We're walking targets. If we don't act quick, all of this will have been for nothing."

"He can't go on the Broadcast. He just watched his father *die!*" Seren hissed. Strong or not, that was too big a task.

"Oh, right," Noa said. She glanced in Zaiden's direction. "He should announce his father's death, too."

Seren rolled her eyes. Did *no one* have any sensitivity?

"I can do it," Zaiden said firmly. "I'll announce my father's death. But I don't want to mention anything else tonight. Not before we've thought it over."

Noa opened her mouth to argue, but Lucas held his hand up gently to stop her. She pressed her lips together and frowned.

"We need to start with education and positive rhetoric," Zaiden said. "Tomorrow, we'll create a new council, made up of members from all the Tiers. We will gather a team of our best scientists to do tests on the air, water, and soil on Earth. Then we'll plan to start exploration."

To Seren's surprise, Noa nodded. "Fine," she said.

"Noa, I'd like you to be on the council," Zaiden continued. "I can't think of anyone better to represent the Tier Fives than you, and I think your insight will be invaluable when we start making these decisions."

Noa's lips pulled up in an almost grin. "I'll accept," she said. "With minor stipulations … but we can discuss those later."

"Perfect." Zaiden looked at Lucas. "The same goes for you. I think you are the right man to represent Tier Fours."

Lucas's eyebrows shot up in surprise. "Really?"

Zaiden nodded. "Really. You've been a huge part of this for years, and I think that the knowledge of Earth you seem to have, along with your experience in creating and implementing plans, will be invaluable."

Lucas nodded. "I'm in."

Zaiden did not ask her to join the council. In fact, he seemed to have forgotten about her entirely. Her cheeks felt warm.

"We should head to the studio if we're going to make it on time," Noa said.

"We should," Zaiden said. "But there are about a hundred Harmonizers out looking for the three of you."

Lucas nodded. "You're right. It's probably best if we hang back, find somewhere to hide."

Seren shook her head. "I want to go with you."

Zaiden gave her a barely-there smile and nodded. "Okay."

"We can hang back," Lucas said, grabbing Noa's hand. "Noa should rest, anyway."

"I'm fine," Noa said. "I'm not the one who got shot."

They all looked at Seren, and she blinked.

"Oh, right!" Seren glanced at her shoulder. How had she forgotten? The bleeding seemed to have slowed. She felt a deep throbbing coming on as the adrenaline subsided, but otherwise, she was fine. "We can worry about that later."

"You two should get going," Lucas said, checking his watch one final time.

"Be safe," Zaiden said.

Lucas nodded. "You too."

54

ZAIDEN

Zaiden must have been walking. He could feel himself moving, but his mind was elsewhere. The image of his father's burning body was etched into his memory. Like a tape on loop, the scene played over and over in his head. His father … the gun … Alaster sneaking up behind him … the fire … the screams. Every time he blinked, the image of his father's blackening body returned.

Seren kept her hand tightly clasped in his on the walk, steadying him. They didn't speak to each other, and he was grateful. Zaiden didn't have anything to say.

Somehow, he and Seren made it to the studio without her being recognized. He supposed that was the nature of people, though: to be distracted.

He certainly was.

Zaiden stared at the studio door for a moment. He'd been here just twelve hours prior, with his father. In just twelve hours, his life had turned completely on its head. How was it possible for so much to happen in so little time?

"Are you okay?" Seren asked gently.

"No," Zaiden said. "But I will be."

She squeezed his hand. The gesture gave Zaiden the courage he needed to go in. With a deep breath, he opened the studio door. Silently, Seren let go of his hand and indicated that she was going to stand in the back. She gave him a final squeeze, and then she disappeared in the darkness.

Zaiden turned his attention to Marcie, who stood in front of her anchor news desk. She was deep in conversation with one of her cameramen—the one with the hairy wrists.

Zaiden froze. Could he really do this?

You have to do this, he thought.

"Marcie," he croaked.

Her eyes snapped up, and Zaiden forced a diplomatic smile onto his face. She ran to him and engulfed him in a hug that squeezed the air from his lungs.

"Zaiden! Oh, thank Warren. You look terrible. Where's your father?" Her rushed words mashed together. She paused and looked him over once, her face contorting in mild disgust.

Zaiden knew he looked like a mess. His hair stood on end, his nose was bloodied, and his clothes were covered in soot. He would need some serious cleaning up in the next fifteen minutes if he planned to go on camera.

"My father isn't coming," Zaiden said. His voice cracked on the words, but he cleared his throat to hide it. He pushed past her and took the seat at the anchor table. Marcie followed close behind, her heels clicking obnoxiously on the hardwood floor.

"What do you mean, he's not coming? We had a plan. He has to—" Her nose crinkled as she neared Zaiden. "What's that smell?"

My father's burning flesh.

"I mean, he isn't coming," Zaiden said firmly. "I will be speaking in his place."

"So, the executions—"

"Are off."

"I don't understand. I thought your father said—"

"My father is dead," Zaiden snapped.

Marcie recoiled.

"What?" She choked the word out, disbelief distorting her beautiful features. Marcie placed a hand on the table to steady herself. "I ... I don't understand," she stammered. "We were... He was—"

"Pull yourself together," Zaiden snapped. He flinched at the harshness of his own voice.

Zaiden remembered that when his mother passed, someone—Sawyer, maybe—had told him about the five stages of grief: denial, anger, bargaining, depression, acceptance. Looking at Marcie, he was certain he'd entered the anger stage. He tried to steady himself.

It isn't her fault.

Zaiden knew he was being insensitive. Marcie and his father had been close. The two of them had spent many evenings together, talking business—and likely engaging in romantic behavior, too. In any case, she was clearly upset.

"I'm sorry," he said, touching her shoulder gently.

She shook with sobs beneath his touch. Uncomfortable, he removed his hand.

Even in the dark studio, he could feel the curious gazes on him. Zaiden tried to ignore them. They'd hear the story soon enough—or at least, the story Zaiden planned to tell.

He took a deep breath and composed himself.

"Can I get some makeup over here?" Zaiden called into the darkness.

A team of makeup artists rushed to Zaiden and began to fix him up, wiping the blood from his skin and covering the bruises. They had questions in their eyes, but none dared to ask them. Zaiden stopped them after just a few minutes of work. There wasn't enough time for perfection.

"How many minutes until we're on air?" Zaiden called to the hairy-wristed cameraman.

The guy checked his watch. "About five," he said gruffly.

"Great." Zaiden swiveled to Marcie. She was still staring out into the distance in a state of shock. He touched her gently again. "Marcie?"

Marcie looked up, surprised that she was being spoken to.

"I'm going to announce my father's death. You will sit beside me. None of your usual pep lines or evening announcements. I will also denounce my father's response to the rebellions and call off the executions. I want no comments from you. Understood?" She nodded, wordless. "Yes, like that."

He caught Seren looking at him. Their eyes met, and she gave him a reassuring nod. Zaiden gave her a small smile in return.

Following Zaiden's gaze, Marcie spotted Seren.

"Intruder!" she shouted, pointing at Seren. *"Rebel!"*

Seren's eyes widened.

Zaiden held his hand up before anyone could overreact.

"Don't. She's with me," he said.

To his surprise, that was all he had to say. Everyone returned to their post, leaving Marcie baffled.

"But, but … but she's a *rebel.* She's a murderer! She—"

Zaiden rubbed his eyes. "For once in your life, Marcie, please just shut up."

Marcie's mouth dropped open.

"Two minutes," the cameraman said.

Seren, now presumably safe from harm, stepped out of the shadows and moved closer—close enough that she was just out of the camera's shot. "You look great," she said to him.

Zaiden looked down at himself and his singed clothing. His father would have never been caught dead looking like this on the Evening Broadcast.

"Really?" he asked.

"Really. Like a true leader."

The cameraman gave a signal that they had one minute until they were on the air, and Zaiden's nerves intensified. Twenty thousand people would be watching. *Twenty thousand people*—and he had no idea what he was going to say, unsure whether he'd be emotionless and empty, or if he'd fall apart and cry.

"Are you ready?" Seren asked.

Zaiden took a deep, ragged breath. "As ready as I'll ever be."

The cameraman held up three fingers … two … one…

The clock struck 7:30 p.m.

The camera flickered on.

The Evening Broadcast began.

55

Acknowledgements

Writing a book is harder than I thought and more rewarding than I could have ever imagined. None of this would have been possible without my mother, Ginny, who read this book more times than I did, and supported me every step along the way.

I'm eternally grateful to the Wolfe family for giving me the creative space to start this novel during a wildly uncertain time in all our lives.

To Robin Fuller, who spent hours helping me edit these pages – thank you. To Julia Bender, for making Seren come to life on the cover– you are my hero.

To Aaron Rizzo, Zoe Waltman, and Nectarios Papadopoulos – for encouraging me to write the damn book over drinks in my parent's kitchen. Thank you.

A very special thanks to Kali Greenwood, for being my first and most enthusiastic reader.

To all my friends who have supported me in getting there by reading early drafts: Chris Hellmer, Erin Breen, Chris Davis, Joanne Meredith, and Becky Holmes-Farley. You guys rock.

Finally, to those who took a chance on an unknown author and made it this far in your reading journey: thank you. Thank you, thank you, thank you. I hope you enjoyed the journey, and I cannot wait to share the next one with you.

Nicole Meredith is a Denver based writer, hiker, and coffee enthusiast. Nicole was born in Rochester, NY and graduated from Villanova University with degrees in Analytics, Finance, and Peace & Justice. Her work has appeared on theBolde.com, a website for women dating in their 20s, as well as various travel websites. Nicole's passion for storytelling began at six, when she used to write plays and force her sister to perform in them. She has since learned that book writing is a better way to preserve friendships. This is her first novel.